DARKER
ANGELS

S. P. SOMTOW

DARKER ANGELS

TOR®

A TOM DOHERTY ASSOCIATES BOOK

NEW YORK

A Tor Book
Published by Tom Doherty Associates, Inc.
175 Fifth Avenue
New York, NY 10010

Tor Books on the World Wide Web:
http://www.tor.com

Tor® is a registered trademark of Tom Doherty Associates, Inc.

Library of Congress Cataloging-in-Publication Data

Somtow, S. P.
    Darker angels / S. P. Somtow. — 1st ed.
        p.   cm.
    "A Tom Doherty Associates Book."
    ISBN 0-312-85931-7 (acid-free paper)
    I. Title.
    PS3569.U23D37   1998
    813'.54—dc21   97-29848
                                                 CIP

First Edition: February 1998

Printed in the United States of America

0 9 8 7 6 5 4 3 2 1

This book is fondly dedicated to
Edward Bryant,
friend, critic, and mentor.

ACKNOWLEDGMENTS AND DISCLAIMERS

The action of this story takes place in approximately the same universe as *Moon Dance* and the *Vampire Junction* series—a world almost identical to, but subtly different from our own. Numerous historical personages appear in this book, but they are used fictitiously. Nothing in this book is true, none of these things really happened, and no one really uttered any of the dialogue herein, except for the quotes from Messrs. Lincoln and Whitman used as epigraphs to the various sections, and the odd line here and there of Walt Whitman's, and Lord Byron's, poetry. Any other resemblance to any persons, places, or events is pure coincidence.

Despite all this, much research went into investing the novel with the veneer of verisimilitude. I must express special thanks to Denise Angela Shawl, a practicing priestess, for some insights into the workings of African religion and magic; Dr. Ellison Sanders for teaching me the subtle differences in the various plantation creoles and other African American dialects of the nineteenth century; a number of *houngans* who do not wish to be identified; Carline, the Haitian exchange student; and the late Richard Evans, who was always fascinated with the history of Hispaniola and who encouraged me, years ago, to start penning this novel. Since there seem to be at least three official or semiofficial ways to spell Haitian creole, consistency has not always been followed. Mistakes, as always, are mine alone.

I also want to thank my parents, Dr. Sompong and Thaithow Sucharitkul, and my extremely patient editors, Greg Cox and Jo Fletcher, as well as my agents, Eleanor Wood and Leslie Gardner, and my publicist, Valerie Lee, for giving me the support to work on this novel during a period of searing personal crisis, and my adoptive son, William John Raitt, for being patient and helping to run the household during the time that it took to disgorge this monster from the womb.

There is a physical difference between the white and black races which will forever forbid the two races living together on terms of social and political equality.

—Abraham Lincoln

You dim-descended, black, divine-souled African, large, fine-headed, nobly-form'd, superbly destin'd, on equal terms with me!

—Walt Whitman

The real war will never get in the books.

—Walt Whitman

A Dead Man
in New York

1865

1

WHEREIN MRS. GRAINGER HAS AN UNEXPECTED ENCOUNTER WITH THE ALMIGHTY

1

A dead man in a darkened room . . .

I had never seen a dead monarch before. It occurs to me now that viewing a dead president of these grandly named United States of America might be the closest I will ever come to such an experience. Lincoln might not have been a king, but in this topsy-turvy country where I have made my home these past two decades, he had been at the very zenith of that which passed for civilization.

In time I was to learn that passing for civilization is all one can ever truly expect. I was to learn that society's most Apollonian achievements are but a kind of sleight of hand, a mass mesmerism that conceals a seething barbarity few ever dare to confront. That morning, in the darkened room with the dead man, I was to begin a journey that would end in such a confrontation. And that was a strange thing, for that morning I had sought only some fleeting frisson, some brief epiphany concerning my own, and man's, mortality. Not that I did not admire the president of this borrowed country of mine; but I was born in a more ancient land, where men are far more cynical about the slogans of idealism.

My late husband, not I, had been the dreamer, contributor to a thousand noble causes of which abolitionism was the only one that proved not to be lost. He was the one who would truly have been in mourning. It was he who had espoused so fervently the liberal positions of Mr. Lincoln's newfangled Republican Party, and he who had printed handbill after handbill at his own expense—or rather, to be precise, at mine.

I wanted to gaze on the face of the man my husband had admired so much. But I did not expect to see much more than another face of death. I hardly expected to spend the morning having a conversation with God; still less did I imagine that, that selfsame afternoon, I would be inviting the Almighty to tea.

2

"**I'm going to see Mr.** Lincoln this morning," I told my servant, Phoebe, as she laid out a selection of widow's weeds on the bed. "Mr. Lincoln has been at the Capitol in Washington for some days; yesterday he passed through Philadelphia, today he rests in Manhattan, and tomorrow he will travel by train to Illinois."

"Don't know a Mr. Lincoln," said Phoebe, "but it high time. A year too long to be wearing black. Too long to be lonely, Mrs. Paula."

"Well," I said, "I will only be visiting him the once; and he shan't come calling, never you fear. He's a dead man, Phoebe, a dead president."

"Dead man better than no man at all," she said, and chuckled as she laid the tea tray down by the bay window that overlooked Washington Square and drew the curtains for me.

Gaslight played over the brownstones; from the coach house across the way came the whinnying of impatient horses. I don't know why I still insist on rising before dawn. It's not as though we need to hurry down to the printing presses to get our broadsides posted before sunrise. I could be an idle woman if I wanted to be, now that my grandfather's legacy of thirteen hundred pounds per annum does not need to be expended on my husband's charitable lunacies.

I selected the plainest of all my mourning clothes, an unfashionable hoop skirt with an incongruous sacque. No jewelry, and the most concealing of all my veils. Phoebe gathered the other garments in her capacious arms and disappeared into my closet. She, too, had been one of Aloysius's lunacies; having trounced some impecunious Virginian colonel at poker on one of his visits to Arlington, he had taken her, a scrawny dark whelp of a slave girl, in lieu of a fifty-dollar bet.

He had had this grand vision of teaching the child to read and write and to become some ultimate symbol of the Negro's capacity for self-improvement; for years he had kept a meticulous journal of the girl's attempts at literacy; she had proved something of a disappointment to him. I did not really mind his taking her to his bed after her thirteenth birthday; I have never been a particularly jealous woman, and had always found his amorous attentions to be something of a bother in any case.

When Phoebe returned, her demeanor was more solemn. "Me want to go too, Mrs. Paula," she said. "Me want to see this dead man that won't come calling."

"I," I said. "I want."

"Yes," she said, "me want, me want." Thirteen years among New Yorkers had never liberated her tongue from the singsong patois of the plantation.

"It seems that they won't let you, Phoebe; according to yesterday's *Times*, Negroes will not be permitted to participate in the funeral parade."

"Then what they fight that war for?" Phoebe cried out in a sudden flash of passion. She checked herself; embarrassed, she shrank back.

"My dear girl," I said, "you have betrayed yourself. You knew who Mr. Lincoln was all along. You've been with me and Mr. Grainger for thirteen years; surely you've learnt by now that you don't have to feign stupidity in my presence. This is not Virginia, and you are as free as I am, and have been since you crossed the Potomac thirteen years ago."

"Then why me not go with Mrs. Paula?"

I could not answer that. Instead, I sipped my tea and stared out over the square. Perhaps I should let men come courting, I thought. I am no beauty, but I do have a reliable income. And I am not *that* old. I'm not even utterly past childbearing. Or perhaps I'm fooling myself. Being a widow does have privileges of a sort. I can walk into a bar without a chaperone and not be deemed a whore.

In a sense, I told myself, we are all slaves.

I drained my cup. Phoebe poured me another. Her hand was shaking. The clatter of the tea strainer against my fine bone china disrupted my reverie. "Sorry, Mrs. Paula," she said. "Me thinking bout Mr. Lincoln."

"He was a kind of king," I said.

"King, yes," she said. "In Africa they plenty king."

"The freedom of your people became his death," I said, half to myself, really; one did not converse with Phoebe; one talked, she talked, neither listened.

"In Africa, olden time, a grand king he name Shangó; he done hung his self from off a great big tree. Many day, many night. My mammy tell me this. Three night, three day he come down from the tree. Now he a god. He alive again. He bring us out of the dead country. You lie in the ground long time, mayhap he call you. And you live again. My mammy allus be saying, *oba kosó, oba kosó*. Me don't know what it mean. Shangó powerful. A god of gods. White folks they call him Jesus."

Today, for a change, I did listen. What was the woman prattling on about now? Half blasphemy, half sophisticated religious syncretism? My husband, doubtless, could have constructed some outlandish hypothesis out of such tantalizing palimpsests. St. Mark evangelizing to the Ethiopians, perhaps, and the gospel spreading southward up to the Nile's source, leapfrogging through the jungle to some savage kingdom, and thence by word of mouth to Phoebe's ancestors? "Are you saying," I asked her, "that there is some kind of native African version of the story of the sacrifice and redemption of our Lord Jesus Christ?"

"Just nigger talk," she said. "Don't pay it no mind."

But I knew her better than that. My husband had possessed a simple perception of this girl as some half-formed innocent, closer than our cultured selves to the clay of creation. It was his duty to drag her from the mire of barbarity with the magic of the printed word and the great tongue of Shakespeare and Milton and the King James Bible. But for all his altruism and idealism, he had never entertained the notion that the world Phoebe had sprung from might have had its own Shakespeares, its own Miltons, gibberish to us. Men, you know, have a tendency to see everything in primary colors. That is why they will always end up going to war.

Phoebe was a woman. I knew that she had subtlety. I had always sensed that while my husband was ranting on at her about the pluperfect subjunctive, or the difference between simile and metaphor, she was viewing him with a bemused tolerance, knowing that his perfervid passion for educating her was a mask that concealed another species of ardor altogether.

"I'll tell you what Mr. Lincoln looked like," I said to her, as she helped me into my whalebone corset, "when I come back. You can tell me if he is anything like your Shangó. They say he was a tall man, almost superhuman in stature."

"Maybe he live again. Maybe he come back from the dead country. Maybe he come back as a god."

I smiled. "Here in America," I said, as Phoebe laced up the hoop skirt and I held my arms out so she could put on my sacque, "we only have one god, dear Phoebe, and that, as you well know, is the Lord God of Hosts."

It is always best to pay lip service to monotheism, and when one has been married to a minister (albeit a freethinking, radical minister) it is very easy to pretend that one has no doubts.

3

Before dawn, the street in front of the city hall was already full of people, white and colored, and all ominously silent. The well-to-do stood right at the edge of the pavement. The Negroes stood farthest off. Some carried banners in praise of the president or expressing funereal sentiments. I walked briskly, but as I approached the front steps, a raggedy boy tugged at my sleeve.

"Ma'am," he said, "if you want to stand up front, you'll need a ticket. I can get you one for four dollars."

"That is a great deal of money," I said. "A week's salary for a boy like you." As I brushed him off, though, another ragamuffin offered me a ticket for a mere three. I ignored them all. I knew that I would eventually be recognized and permitted to enter the building itself.

It was one of the petty clerks, in fact, who hailed me with a solemn "Mrs. Grainger, I presume," and allowed me to pass into the vestibule. None of the dignitaries had as yet arrived. One or two soldiers bustled about. Men in frock coats stood gravely at attention. One or two nodded curtly to me; I did not know them, but to be a middle-aged woman of aristocratic comportment does have a few advantages. It was simply assumed that I was there as the ornament to some august official. I was seen, yet ever invisible. I wandered through the hall, down a corridor, following a trail of muted conversation. At length I reached the hallway outside the chamber where, presumably, the president lay in state.

There is less pomp and ceremony in this young country than back home; only two guards manned the entrance to the chamber, one of them—a token of the spirit of the age, no doubt—a Negro. They were youths, really. Most of the grown men in this country were already dead, after all; in a sense, Mr. Lincoln was only one casualty amongst the nameless thousands. The foyer was dimly lit, but I could see that they had taken great pains to look sharp. But their coats were mended in places, and the black youth's sleeve had a bullet hole in it. Perhaps it was the flickering of the shadows, or the lofty contours of the arches and the upward sweep of the Corinthian columns, but the men somehow seemed dwarfed and vulnerable. And that was strange; were they not within days of winning the war? Of course, we had heard that many times before. The eyes of the boys seemed haunted. I did not want to ask what action they had seen.

One of the guards—not, of course, the Negro—I knew vaguely; he had once been my butcher's apprentice.

"Mrs. Grainger," he said, with an awkward salute. " 'Tis good to see a familiar face, ma'am." A hint of a brogue; as a child, I remembered, he had been shipped over from Ireland, his indenture papers bought sight unseen by that dour-faced butcher in Alexandria.

"Good to see you, too . . . Christopher, isn't it?"

He beamed. "Yes'm," he said. The Negro boy stared sullenly at the floor.

"I was wondering . . ." I said. "I mean, might I . . . mayn't I . . ."

"Go on in," said the butcher's boy softly. "Before the crowd gets let inside. I know that's what you come for, Mrs. Grainger. To have a moment alone with the president."

"I'll be quiet as a mouse," I said.

And crept inside, hardly daring to breathe.

The hush, the closeness of the air, the sooted texture of the light, the luxuriant thickness of velvet and brocade, all lent the room a numinous quality; one missed only the fragrance of incense to imagine oneself in some popish chapel.

And there was Mr. Lincoln at last.

He was as tall as they said. His complexion had become waxen over the days; I dared not touch his face; in death, he seemed already to have assumed a monumental quality, as though he were not flesh at all, but were recast in bronze, or sculpted from a block of granite. His very ugliness partook of the nature of myth. The light played only over his face; gloom blanketed the rest of the chamber. I fell to my knees, I know not why; I was not here to worship, only to gaze, scrutinize, retain.

I did not love Mr. Lincoln. He had, after all, cost my husband his life. And I cared not a fig for noble causes, except that the late Mr. Grainger had been so devoted to them; I knew, furthermore, that Mr. Lincoln's own allegiance to some of those sentiments had shifted, by political expediency, from pragmatism to altruism these last four years, though history, I was certain, would view things differently. And yet, as he lay there on the dais like an ancient pharaoh beneath dark draperies and golden tassels, overlooked by marble busts, I knew that the world had changed irrevocably with his passing.

I also knew that my husband was truly dead.

I did not expect to weep, nor was I entirely sure whom I was weeping for: this ruler of a foreign land, my husband, vanquished by his own dreams, or myself, widowed at last after a year of widowhood. Or was it all those nameless soldiers slain in the name of unity? The tears came suddenly, and then came swiftly. I pride myself on being a woman not easily seized by paroxysms. Neither am I subject to hysterical imprecations, as are many of my sex. Yet now, in the grip of a grief beyond my very imagining, I called out to the Almighty. "God," I cried, "Oh, God, God, God, if only you would turn back the tide, bring them all back from that farthest shore."

There came a voice: "Be careful, madam, what you ask for."

It was a mellifluous, soft voice, deep, authoritative. It was the kind of voice one would expect from the Almighty—the still small voice within the raging flame. One might imagine the possessor of that voice to be a kindly old man with a white beard.

"Why?" I said. "Because I might get it?"

"Nothing," said the voice, "is utterly beyond possibility."

I looked up. The shadows wavered. I turned; in the doorway I could see the backs of the two young men who guarded the chamber. I turned again. Was it one of the busts that stared down from marmoreal pediments? My husband had longed for a sign from the Almighty all his life; what an irony it would be if I, the agnostic, were to be the one to receive such a visitation.

Stillness. Surely it was an echo, a trick of the building's reverberant acoustics, a conversation from some other room. No. Nothing now. Only a dead man in a darkened room, the shuffle of distant footsteps.

I laughed a little, from fear and from nervousness. "You're a figment of my imagination after all."

"Hardly that," the voice said softly, "my dear Mrs. Grainger."

"You know me?" I said. "Then you must indeed be who I think you are. Can you really raise the dead?"

"I have seen it done," said the voice, "but never in New York."

"But it could be done."

"Sometimes I think of time as a two-way train. Sometimes I think of death as a double-hinged door."

Growing more accustomed to the dark, I thought I saw something in the shadows. Looming above the casket, perhaps. White whiskers catching the light for the merest moment. Eyes. Piercing. Clear. Youthful eyes set in an ancient face. The white beard, certainly. The classical image of God the Father.

"Can we bring him back? And my husband? Could there really be a chance to correct the past?"

"I don't know, Mrs. Grainger."

"But you know everything!"

"Some would not say so. Were it not for the extremity of the moment, I think you too would have a few doubts."

"I know now, sir, that I am caught in some vision or dream. I must suspend all disbelief."

"I would not have ventured to address you at all, madam, except that your passion seemed to demand succor."

"Oh, sir," I said, "I have searched my heart for the first time since my husband's passing, and have found therein a profound and pitiless void; I am like a dead woman who has lived a simulacrum of life these past twelve months, and has only this moment learned that she is dead."

"Interesting," he said. "So you believe yourself to be a *zombi*."

"What, may I ask, is that?"

"I believe the word derives from Kikongo, a language of Africa; it refers to an animated corpse, the living dead, as it were."

"Is that what I am? The living dead?"

"Merely a metaphor, my dear Mrs. Grainger, natural to a poet."

My husband had always said to me, stumbling across some particularly felicitous passage in the Psalms or Lamentations, that God is nothing if not a poet; it did not surprise me that the old man would make of my entire existence a living metaphor.

"This is no dream, Mrs. Grainger. We have all become as the living dead. This monstrous crime has robbed us of our souls."

"Oh, God," I wept. "God, heal me, heal me."

It was then that I felt the old man's hand against my cheek; a gnarled hand, an all-too-human hand, callused, grimy; I smelled the sweat of a man. I looked up. If God were indeed a spirit, he had made himself flesh of a sudden, and become a disheveled man clad in a tattered serge coat, his demeanor and countenance considerably less than divine.

"You're not God at all, are you?" I said.

"Hardly, Mrs. Grainger!" said the man. "I'm from Brooklyn."

"Then how did you know my name?"

"Young Flanagan told me," he said, laughing.

"This is a breach of propriety," I said, hiding my discomfiture with the indignation appropriate for a woman who fears being compromised. "I am a widow, a respectable woman, and we have not been properly introduced."

"Then I shall introduce myself, ma'am," he said, shaking his white mane out of his eyes. "I am Walt Whitman."

2

WHEREIN MRS. GRAINGER DREAMS OF DEATH

1

"I've heard of you, Mr. Whitman," I said. "You're some kind of poet; a bad one, if truth were told. Very modern, if you please; no rhyme and little reason. My late husband spoke of you at times." I did not really know much about Mr. Whitman's so-called verse, but one hears things at luncheon parties and soirées.

"I don't mind," he said. "There is a time for rhyme and reason, but we don't live in such a time. This is a century of madness and of chaos."

I did not feel like talking about poetry now. I had poured out my heart in this dark room, imagining myself in the presence only of the dead and the divine. I really did not want any intercourse with this man, though he presumptuously continued to dab at my tears with a dirty handkerchief.

"If you don't unhand me, Mr. Whitman, I shall scream," I said. I wouldn't have, of course, but I know how to threaten like a lady.

Mr. Whitman knelt beside me. He made no move to take away his hand. "My dear Mrs. Grainger," he said, "it's too late to retract yourself from this entanglement, for we have by accident revealed to each other too much of our secret selves."

At that, I began to weep anew. And I did not mind so much Mr. Whitman's consolation, for he had a kindly gaze, and I gradually understood that he was still the same person now as he had been when I had thought him an incarnation of the Almighty. Yes, he was unkempt and unwashed; but those eyes still held that quality of wonder; they were a child's eyes, and I had lost three sons in childbirth, and the only creature I ever called child was Phoebe, my servant, my dependent, my rival.

"You surprised me as much as I you," he said, when I had calmed down a little. "I came here to write a poem, you know. I was sure I was alone, and then I heard you crying to the heavens. Please, Mrs. Grainger, do not be alarmed at my strange appearance. We have both suffered a terrible loss. Let us grieve together, Mrs. Grainger."

I could not begrudge him that. Especially since Mr. Whitman, too, began earnestly to weep. The spectacle of a grown man shedding tears is not common in our modern society, where overt emotion is deemed unmanly. I might not think much of his verses, but it was clear that the well from which they sprang was as profound as any poet's.

It was with some alarm that I found myself not only warming to his touch, but actually sinking into his arms. In fact, Mr. Whitman was embracing me most tenderly, and I had to admit that the fact that this was occurring beneath the gaze of a dead president was lending a certain piquancy to the proceedings. In fact, a thing happened which had never happened during my entire life with the late Mr. Grainger. I became desirous of more intimate touching. I was a harp in need of strumming. This was not at all the turn of events I had envisaged when I set out from Washington Square.

The oddest thing was, the passion was in me alone. I felt no corresponding ardor from Mr. Whitman; his was an utterly chaste embrasure, full of comfort and compassion, far more *agape* than *eros*.

"Don't misunderstand my intentions, Mrs. Grainger," he said softly. "You seemed so much in need of caring. I am a nurse, you know. I've held many a dying boy in these old arms, kissed many a lip, stolen away many a man's last breath. I'm not the sort of man who would compel a hapless woman . . . or indeed any woman. . . ."

The sentiments were honorable, but a heavy sadness emanated from him when he said those words, as though there lay, behind his gentlemanly abstinence, some dark secret which he dared not speak aloud.

Perhaps that was what impelled me to invite him to tea that afternoon.

Or perhaps it was that strange, intriguing talk of death and resurrection—that little hint of blasphemy in my conversation with the imagined God—the touch of sin that somehow clung to my every moment spent with this rough-and-ready poet.

When we left the chamber, a few moments later, I saw that the Negro guard had been replaced by a white boy who could almost have been Christopher's twin. Someone's sense of propriety had doubtless been offended. Or perhaps it was simply a precautionary measure, since the public was about to be admitted, and I remembered that Negroes had been forbidden to march in the funeral parade down Broadway.

It was when we parted at the front entrance to the city hall that, pressing his hand, I whispered, "Tea, perhaps, Mr. Whitman, this afternoon?"

"How English of you, Mrs. Grainger. I'd be just delighted."

The voices of morning were strangely absent: the news butches did not call out the headlines in their shrill boyish voices, nor did the pavement rattle with constant traffic, nor the hawkers press their wares on passersby. The Babel that is New York was muted.

I was afraid to speak more; in my mind, the city's unwonted silence amplified even a whisper to a shout.

"I'll see you at teatime, then," I said. "My servant will bake some scones." Speaking of tea and scones was a way of avoiding speaking about all that had transpired in front of Mr. Lincoln's casket.

"I shall not fear you, Mrs. Grainger, in spite of what men say about widows. I shall be chaperoned," he said, chuckling softly. I was curious as to what he meant, but did not presume to question him.

I turned from him and set off slowly down Broadway; no need to hail a hackney; the sky was gray, but there was as yet no drizzle; though the street was crowded, no one accosted me. Grief builds an invisible wall around one's person. I saw no one and no one saw me. The sky and the throng were all one gray.

Because the news butches were not shrieking it out, I almost missed an interesting tidbit. But as I walked, eyes downcast, trying desperately not to think at all, I almost collided with a portly gentleman who was perusing the *Times* with a pince-nez, and thus noticed, in an inconspicuous corner of the first page, the following legend:

MAYOR HAS CHANGE OF HEART;
NEGROES TO BE ALLOWED TO MARCH AT THE BACK
OF THE FUNERAL PROCESSION.

I would have to remember to tell Phoebe that she would, after all, be able to set eyes on poor Mr. Lincoln, savior and martyr.

2

When I told Phoebe we would have company, she had the smuggest I-told-you-so expression on her face. In vain I tried to protest that this was by no means a courtship. She didn't believe me at all, but merely muttered something under her breath that sounded like, "It working, it working now." Whatever *it* might be.

We had not used the sitting room since Mr. Grainger's death; the overstuffed fauteuils were covered up, and the covers were caked with dust. I set Phoebe to work making the room presentable, and retired to my bedroom for a brief nap. They say that when you approach middle age, a nap does wonders for the complexion. But why did I care? Suddenly I had become as giddy as a debutante. I even searched through my drawers for the old powders and rouges I had once used to bestow upon myself a modicum of attractiveness. I found very little. On the other hand, I reflected, Mr. Whitman had already seen me at my worst, and he had not seemed to care. And then again, I had no indication whatsoever that he would have found me attractive in any case, even were I was painted as the proverbial whore of Babylon.

I removed my mourning clothes and put on a silken dressing gown, feeling a twinge of sinfulness, I know not why. I lay down. I knew I was tired, but I tossed and turned for some time until I remembered a trick that one of my late husband's acquaintances, a carnival mesmerist, had once taught me: I closed my eyes, relaxed my whole being, tried to imagine myself sinking, sinking, sinking . . . down toward a warm dark place deep inside me.

Laudanum would have been a lot simpler, but I do not like to use artificial aids unless I absolutely must.

I sank indeed, but I did not lose consciousness. I found myself inside the territory of dream, even though I was still awake. It is a condition that mesmerists often induce, the better to impose their will on some volunteer from the audience.

I found myself in a forest of sorts. I tried to open my eyes, but could not. I stood there, enrobed in the sheer silk, and it was as though I were waiting for someone . . . a lover, perhaps? But it would not do to think of such things. I am past forty now. I am a widow. Love should be something of the past.

The forest . . . not a memory of a past experience, but a perpetual present, buried beneath my consciousness. I knew this place, though I was sure I had never been there before. I knew the smell of it. The dead leaves liquefying into the humid earth, the air misty and dense with the breath of wild animals. I lay in this forest clearing and watched the stars wheel over me. There was for a time a timelessness. A breeze played over the clearing, moist and warm.

Then—in a moment that is not of the same texture as other moments, in a moment neither past nor present, a tall man looms above me. He smells of embalming fluids. He is dressed in black. In the moonlight, his face is as pitted as the moon itself. He has no eyes; rather, his eyes are always in shadow, and to look into them is to gaze into some other place, a place of fear.

"Mr. President," I whisper.

He leans over me. Grazes the back of my hand with a finger, chill as marble; then, straightening himself, puts the finger to his lips.

"It is almost time," he says.

"For what?" I ask him.

"Listen, listen, listen," he says, and the breeze whips up into a howling wind, and within that wind is the call of a distant bugle.

"Who are you? Some kind of demon lover?" For I know the Greek myths, and have heard of creatures that prey on women in the dead of night.

There is a half smile on Mr. Lincoln's lips. He pulls me to my feet. He is strong, as strong as history.

My dressing gown flutters behind me. My feet hover a few inches above the ground. A fresh new odor assails my nostrils. The perfume of decay.

"Come," says Mr. Lincoln. "Come." The bugle call is louder now. It is an angular, melancholy distortion of reveille.

We float.

Presently I see that we have left the clearing and entered the wood itself. The smell of putrefaction is stronger now. It comes from deeper in the forest. The wind is more aggressive, slicing the leaves from the branches, stripping the bark from the tree trunks. Dry leaves are whipping my face. Mr. Lincoln holds my hand fast. His grasp sucks all the warmth in my body and leaves behind an arctic void. I am beyond terror now. I am in a state of emptiness and cold. Even my heartbeat seems to have been stilled. We drift. Deeper. Deeper. To a place where the moonlight is reduced to a few small mottlings of silver in a tapestry of black. Always the stench of death. Choking me now.

And then there's that other feeling. Down below. The feeling of being woman, all woman, all wise. That is the strangest thing of all. The wind against the fabric of my robe, rubbing up and down against the most private area of my person, as though nature herself were conspiring to rob me of my virtue. I am excited and afraid. But I cannot wriggle free of Mr. Lincoln's grasp. Perhaps I do not want to.

The darkness has become almost palpable. Even the dots and dashes of moonlight have disappeared. At the very moment that it has become all but unbearable, however—

There is a break . . . a shaft of light that rives the dark, a cold blue light clouded by swirling dust motes. I sigh. We are free of that terrifying forest at last. But that's when I see the bodies.

The faces emerge from the gloom in ghoulish chiaroscuro. The eyes bulge from their sockets. A pussy rheum oozes from pocks and pores. Here and there the maggots have already eaten all the way to the bone. Arms and legs are intertwined. Enemy embraces enemy. As we move slowly over the dead, our feet barely skimming over the sea of putrefaction, the swath of light widens to encompass what seems to be an unending meadow, and the dead lie everywhere, all the way to the horizon, two, three, four corpses deep; here and there a scrawny dog scavenges; here and there a buzzard perches. Oh, but this vision is a nightmare beyond all nightmares; yet the terror I felt earlier has retreated to some innermost part of myself, so that I feel only this dull, pounding emptiness somewhere far away, and my conscious thoughts are void of emotion.

In the distance, a woman is dancing.

A naked woman, in the moonlight, glistening. Black. The night itself. She dances.

"Why," I say, "it's Phoebe, isn't it? Phoebe in the moonlight. How very queer. Phoebe means moonlight, does it not? She is the moon goddess."

"Delve deeper," says Mr. Lincoln, "and you may find other meanings."

"And now," I say, "I know for certain it is a dream. I know, after all, that Phoebe is my maidservant, not some goddess dancing over the dead."

"She is doing more than that," Mr. Lincoln says softly.

We move. Silently, swiftly, across the field of twisted torsos, severed limbs, faces without eyes and eyes without faces. We move toward the horizon, where my servant is dancing.

We are close to her now.

"Phoebe," I whisper, "Phoebe, come back soon, for Mr. Whitman is expected to tea."

She does not seem to hear. She leaps. Her arms flail about. Her neck hangs at an unnatural angle, as though it were broken. She seems possessed. Perhaps it is her god. The one who, hanging from a tree, became the resurrection and the life. Shangó. Perhaps.

"Phoebe!" I cry out. The blast of a trumpet drowns me out. But she has heard me. She turns to me. She has no eyes—rather, her eyes have rolled up in their sockets.

"Me bring Mr. Grainger back to you, Mrs. Paula," she says, "so you don't be lonely no more."

The corpses are beginning to twitch. And Phoebe dances.

Dances. Flings out her arms. Jerks back her head. Her skin is slick with sweat. She dances. Now and then she shrieks out an infernal gibberish. Some African tongue, no doubt. She hops from body to body. Spins around. Somersaults. The perspiration glistens like quicksilver.

"No marching in no back of no parade," she screams. "Me a missus of this here dark country, me dance the dead back out of the cold cold ground, me do a sacred holy thing here, me a goddess, me earth, me wind, me fire."

The corpses are twitching. Limbs are grappling with the air. Dead eyes are opening, dead mouths gaping, spewing forth a wormy vomitus. Hands grasp other hands, bodies clamber up over other bodies, the fetor makes me retch, Mr. Lincoln never lets go my hand. They are so young, these dead, mere children some of them; dead little hands pound on cracked drums, the skin as torn as the children's own skin, the sound not the smart rat-tat-tat of impending battle but a hollow patter, like the skittering of cockroaches in a haunted house.

The moon goddess dances.

And then, out of the quivering ocean of the dead, a man crawls up to the surface, rises, stands before me. His face has been torn away. Where his tongue was, a serpent slithers. He beckons to me with his one arm, and I see that he is wearing the collar of a military chaplain. It is my husband.

"Mr. Grainger," I say softly. I have always been formal toward my husband, even in our most intimate moments. It is, I realize now, because I have never truly had an intimate moment, not even that infamous fate-worse-than-death moment, because though I have opened my body, I have never opened my soul to any man.

"I go now," Mr. Lincoln said. "I have brought you face-to-face with your destiny."

He releases my hand. I turn. "Don't go!" I cry out, but he is already striding across the field of corpses, back to the forest of ultimate darkness, his frock coat billowing behind him. I realize I am standing on a dead man's face.

At the limit of my vision, Mr. Lincoln turns briefly. His face is now a skull, and over his shoulder he carries the scythe of the grim reaper.

The corpse of my late husband comes to me across the lake of putrefying flesh, and in the moonlight the moon goddess dances. . . .

"Paula, Paula," my husband says. The wind whistles through a windpipe severed by the slice of a bayonet. "Paula, Paula, there is so much to regret."

He moves ever closer. And I stand rooted there, my person half exposed through the sheer fabric of my dressing gown, and he comes to me, he caresses my cheek with his cold, gray, desiccated hand. . . .

And Phoebe cries out: *"Egungun, egungun, egungun . . ."*

"Oh why, Paula," he says, "oh why did you never love me?"

And I scream and scream, but—

3

Now, at least, I was awake.

Now, at least, the sunlight was visible through the draperies, though Phoebe must have drawn them shut while I slept. I hoped I had not wakened half the city with my screaming. I lay for a moment, trying to still the palpitation of my chest.

I breathed deeply several times, in and out, in and out, trying to think pleasant thoughts . . . until I realized that the stench of putrefaction lingered in the air . . . that it clung to the very bedsheets. Something was amiss.

I'm still dreaming, I told myself.

Yes. That's what it is. This is one of those times when, in your dream, you wake up to a familiar room, a familiar place . . . not realizing that your nightmare was a dream within a dream. All right then. I'll just ride it out. It can't be that bad. It's a dream. A dream.

I sat up. The odor was overwhelming. I pulled up the sheet so as to cover my nose, and I saw that there was a growing bloodstain on one edge. I looked over the side of the bed and saw the blood now. It was siphoning up from underneath. Just a dream, I told myself. A dream, a dream. I yanked away the sheet, leaned over the side of the bed, and peered down there.

There was a dead rooster on a silver platter. Its throat had been slit. That was where all the blood was coming from. And there was a strange brown egg-shaped idol with crudely painted eyes and a cowrie-shell nose and mouth.

Time to wake up, I told myself. I pinched myself in the arm. Hard. Harder. The pain was intense. But I didn't wake up. I screamed. I didn't wake up. I screamed louder now. Loud enough, I'm sure, to wake the very dead.

Then Phoebe was there, not naked, but attired in her black maid's uniform, brandishing a feather duster. I went on screaming.

"Just look at all that blood," Phoebe said. She pulled out the platter and glared at the dead bird in dismay. "What a waste."

"I'm not dreaming?"

"Me know the magic not work here in the white man country." She was scrubbing furiously at the blood with an old washrag now, on her hands and knees, muttering to herself.

"I'm not dreaming? But Mr. Lincoln—and my husband—and the field of corpses—"

"Mrs. Paula, you done seen Mr. Grainger?"

"What do you know about what I've seen? What is the meaning of this—superstitious tomfoolery? Damn you to hell, Phoebe, but you are an ignorant savage after all—" I screamed, and many other curses besides, becoming quite unladylike in my confusion.

"*Egungun!*" Phoebe said softly, then crossed herself. Paganism and popery all in one. For all my liberal thinking, I was appalled. And she had said that word. The word she had been chanting in the dream.

"What is *egungun*?" I said.

She looked up at me. "Mrs. Paula hear that word before."

"No! I am merely curious," I said, trying desperately to stay calm.

"Yes," she said. "Mrs. Paula hear that word before. Maybe in dream country."

"How would you know about my dreams?"

"Dream," she said, "not-dream, all one place. God, he reach everywhere."

"But what does that word mean?"

"So," she said, "she working after all."

"What?" I cried out. "What's working after all?"

"Me sorry," she said. "Not want you see. Blood she run too far, too fast. But the spell she working. Mr. Grainger come back to you out of the dark country. Hallelujah! Praise-the-Lord-bless-His-holy-name-bless-Him-and-sanctify-Him-forever." This last was one polysyllabic utterance, learnt, no doubt, by rote from one of my late husband's preachings.

"Mr. Grainger," I said, attempting to conceal my skepticism by raising my voice, "is in heaven, Phoebe, and will not return in the flesh until the last trump, when we will all be called to judgment."

"You not believe that!" she said. "There. Clean now. Blood gone."

We heard the doorbell ring, and Phoebe hastened downstairs to admit my guest.

I was alone, and still uncertain of how much of the afternoon had transpired in the realm of dream.

3

WHEREIN MR. WHITMAN HINTS AT AN UN-CHRISTIAN AFTERLIFE

1

When Phoebe returned to my bedchamber, she was cackling like a witch.

"What kind of man you call that?" she shrieked. "A man? A man?"

Well, Mr. Whitman was not the most savory of gentlemen in appearance, to be sure; but I did not see why my maid would find him so risible. "That is Mr. Whitman," I said coldly, "some sort of poet, as he styles himself. I would require that you show him the same respect that a darkie would have for any white man," I added. "You've been very impertinent of late, answering me back, casting your superstitious spells in my very bedroom. I ought to—"

"What you gone do, whup me?" Phoebe said.

And looked me right in the eye. There was nothing of the slave in this creature, no obsequy, no cringing. Had the emancipation of her kind changed her that much, she who had had her freedom since long before the war even began? What was it about her that made me so angry now, when I had tolerated her well enough during Mr. Grainger's lifetime, had not even minded her occupancy of my very own bed?

"You know very well, Phoebe," I said, "that I will not whip you. I can never tell when you're going to be servile, and when you're going to be an impertinent little demon."

"That Mr. Whitman a devil!"

"Now fetch me some clothes. Plain, I think. For Mr. Whitman, there is no need to be elaborate."

Phoebe went to the closet and found me something suitably severe. As she helped me dress, she alternated between decorum and fits of hysterical giggling. Perhaps Mr. Lincoln's death was driving us all mad.

"What is the matter with you?" I said at last. "Just because a man is coming to tea—"

"That man, man outside," she said, "woman inside! Two of them downstairs, missus—two man-woman things. Devils!"

"What the devil—" I said, astonished that such profanity had escaped my lips.

"Me tell you, time to bring home man. You bring this!" She spat. "Devil! Magician!"

I am normally a very self-controlled woman, but her jabbering was the last straw. I slapped her face. I regretted it immediately—Mr. Grainger *never* believed that a well-brought-up person should stoop to violence—for I had never done such a thing to her before. Still, to apologize would have been insufferable. And I was furious, simply furious. Her many rudenesses of the day, and then that ghastly nightmare, and her taking the credit for it, and the bloody fowl beneath my bed—I threw myself on her and slapped her again and again, until her nose bled and she bashed her head against a mahogany armoire.

"You—you detestable creature!" I screamed. "You dirty little nigger whore!"

She gazed at me. Hatred smoldered in her eyes. "I knew," said my servant, drawing herself up to her full five feet, "that your abolitionism was only skin-deep."

It took me a moment to realize that she had not spoken to me in that barbarous creole of the plantation, but in proper English, her accents indistinguishable from that of a white woman.

"Phoebe," I said in astonishment, "what else have you been hiding from me?"

She would not answer me. But I suddenly knew that in all the years she had resided with me and my husband, I had not known her at all; she had woven about herself an illusion that was only now, with the tumultuous happenings in the world and in our lives, beginning to fray.

She wiped the blood off her face with a sleeve.

"I don't know what came over me," I said. "It won't happen again, I promise."

She did not answer me. Her silence was even more unnerving than her defiance had been.

I went on, "Can you tell me, in good plain English, why there is a rooster with its throat cut lying beneath my bed, and what that idol with cowrie-shell eyes is?"

No response. With eyes downcast, she turned from me and, with an exaggerated shuffling, made her way to the door.

I finished dressing myself. Never had I felt more a stranger in this land. I hadn't minded coming to America, hadn't missed the fog or the hypocrisy, but now I wished I had never left England. Everything was wrong here—the buildings too angular, the servants too surly, the war too bloody. Today's events had removed every vestige of the familiar from my universe. I had to remain calm. Tea, as always, would soothe my spirits a little. Perhaps Mr. Whitman and I could speak of such pleasantries as the weather. Banality can be very comforting at times.

I had to admit that what unnerved me the most was the fact that Phoebe, whom I had deemed an ignorant barbarian, had seen right through my façade, had penetrated my veneer of decorum to glimpse the woman within, passionate, frustrated, and perversely fascinated by that which a respectable widow should shy away from—I mean the sins of the flesh, the allure of the powers of darkness. I could not escape the realization that in my dream, embraced by a rotting corpse whose caresses must elicit opprobrium in any woman of virtue, I had felt, stirring beneath my fear, something other than horror . . . something akin to attraction.

There was a thing of darkness in me. I desperately wanted it to be something alien to my sensibilities; I knew that to acknowledge its existence would be to acknowledge it my own, no invading demon, no incubus, but a dark part of my very own self.

That terrified me more than anything else that had happened that day.

2

Mr. Whitman had a friend with him, a young man. The disparity in their ages was quite striking. The youth was flaxen-haired, his naturally pale complexion bronzed, doubtless from much exposure to sunlight; he was the type of boy one imagines in a field of grain, his eyes rivaling the sky and the cornflowers; he had a natural comeliness, but had an awkwardness that could have come from youth, or from being unfamiliar with our urban, and urbane, environment. His clothing was poor—he had not even bothered to beat the creases out of his store-boughten Levi's—yet he wore them with a certain unconscious grace. He could not have been older than seventeen.

Mr. Whitman, standing next to the boy, seemed age

personified. Except for his eyes, that is. A child looked at me through those eyes. Not that I know much about children; I am, and have always been incapable of bringing forth a child that was not stillborn. We buried many children, Mr. Grainger and I. They are all buried in an apple orchard in Connecticut, where there is a plot of land we purchased once, near Branford, my husband dreaming of some kind of tenure at Yale after the war. The land has graves and apples, but, alas, no house; we never had the money for that; my husband's lost causes saw to that.

But I was speaking of Mr. Whitman's eyes. Oh, he could dazzle you with those eyes, he could surely steal the heart of a widow who had never loved, who dreamed betimes about what might have been if her children had only lived.

"Mrs. Grainger," said Mr. Whitman, "I'd like to introduce you to Zachary Brown; he heard your husband preach once. Zachary, this Mrs. Grainger."

"How do you do?" I said. I shook the boy's hand.

"I'm right proud, Widow Grainger," he said, "right proud. Your husband, ma'am, he sure fired me up. I was thinking about deserting when I heard him preach over a field of dead bodies . . . he made me change my mind. Of course, if I hadn't changed my mind, I wouldn't have got myself shot in the leg, but then they wouldn't have shipped me to that hospital in Washington, neither, and old Walt wouldn't have nourished my soul, and nurtured me back to life from the land of the dead."

"Oh," I said. "Mr. Whitman, one of your resurrectees, I suppose."

"If only I had the power, Mrs. Grainger," said Mr. Whitman. "You don't know how many times I've wished for such a power. When I was a nurse in the hospitals of Washington, young boys turned to stone as I held them in my arms. If only I could have breathed the life back into their lips! But, as you've already discovered, Mrs. Grainger, I am not God."

I invited the two men into the salon, where a bay window

overlooked the square. Though there were several armchairs, they both elected to squeeze onto the divan beside that window; perhaps it was the view that enticed them so.

Phoebe had now come into the room. She had cleaned up her face—I still found it difficult to realize that I had raised a hand to her, for I have never been predisposed to violence—and she moved about the room, setting out the teacups, scones, butter, and jam, not saying a word, not even looking anyone in the eye.

The two men looked out at the square, and now and then Mr. Whitman made jottings in a tattered notebook.

I sat on an overstuffed damask fauteuil, and I poured three cups of tea. I have heard that the Japaners make an almost religious ritual of this tea pouring. I understand why. I tried to still my trembling hand.

Phoebe walked back and forth past the guests. I caught her stealing a glance at them. Then she strode towards me, and whispered, "You see, Mrs. Paula, what me tell you. Outside man, inside woman. Beast-who-transform."

"What are you babbling about?" I said.

"In the beginning Mawu-Lissa created the heaven and the earth," she intoned, in a strange parody of my late husband's voice. "God is a man-woman. Man be a man-woman, abomination. Mr. Grainger done teach me."

The two men now turned to stare at her.

"Abomination!" cried Phoebe. "Repent, O children of Sodom!"

"That's enough!" I said. "Or do you want me to—" And for the second time that day—the second time in my entire life—I found myself raising up my hand to strike her. I was maddened—*maddened!* I wanted to crush that little darkie into the dirt. What was it about her? I knew that it was wrong, that it betrayed all that my late husband believed in, and yet—I rushed at her.

She dodged away. She did a little wiggling sort of dance,

taunting me. "Oh, oh, Mrs. Paula," she giggled, "me 'fraid, me 'fraid."

"I know you can speak proper English," I said. "Stop that barbaric chatter."

She sprinted to the far corner, the only part of the room that the light from the square did not reach. She folded herself up into a little rag doll of a girl, and all I could see were the whites of her eyes, and she continued to whimper, "Me 'fraid, me 'fraid."

"What am I to do with her?" I said aloud. "Oh, Mr. Whitman, I apologize profoundly for this extraordinary disturbance! We are all so profoundly aggrieved over Mr. Lincoln's death, and I fear that we are none of us quite our normal selves."

Mr. Whitman rose from the divan and, in a shocking breach of civility, took me in his arms. Yet I was not as appalled as I should have been, even though this liberty was being taken in the presence of both a total stranger and a domestic servant. For his embrace had no hint of licentiousness about it. He hugged me as children hug, innocent of the implication of sin; there was in his embrace a kind of love. I was grateful for it.

Mr. Brown led me back to my chair and sat me down. The three of us sipped tea, looked at one another, and I tried not to notice the little black creature still crouched in the corner.

"It's a dreary day," I said at last, for if one cannot discuss the weather, then there's an end to all civilized discourse. "I do hope it won't start drizzling for the funeral parade."

There was a long silence in which I buttered my scone.

Then, at last, Mr. Brown said, "Walt, we should tell her."

Mr. Whitman said, "I don't know, Zack."

I waited.

Mr. Whitman sipped his tea, and said, "Mrs. Grainger, you have heard your servant's amazing utterances. What is your reaction?"

"That she is an impertinent Negress, Mr. Whitman, and not entirely appreciative of the liberty we have always allowed her, nor of the favor shown her by my late husband, who undertook to remove her from her servitude as payment for a gambling debt."

"Well, that is but one interpretation of what we have just witnessed. I know that you only have a poor opinion of my poetry, Mrs. Grainger—"

"Well, I spoke hastily. I've heard others talk of it. Personally, I haven't read much poetry."

"But I assure you, as a poet, that your servant, too, has a poet's visionary powers."

"Oh, nonsense," I said nervously. "Why, she cannot even distinguish the nominative from the accusative in a personal pronoun."

Mr. Whitman smiled. "I take it, Mrs. Grainger, that her ancestors are of the Yoruba tribe?"

"What do you mean? Her mother was from Africa, I've heard." I glanced across to the corner, and I could now discern that Phoebe was listening intently to him, half-fearful, half-fascinated.

"I've been told, ma'am," Mr. Whitman continued earnestly, "that in the language of the Southern Yoruba the word for 'I,' under certain circumstances, is *mi*. Perhaps, then, she is not speaking barbarous English at all, but perfectly grammatical African!"

"Is this true, Phoebe?" I said to the servant.

"This magic," she said. "Me done told you, he devil."

"Oh," said Mr. Whitman, "and I see that her name is Phoebe . . . an African name, or so I've heard."

"Hardly, Mr. Whitman," I said. "As a poet, you must surely know your classical allusions; Phoebe was the moon goddess of the ancient Greeks, was she not?"

He smiled again. Broader now. The cat had a mouse by the tail. "I haven't had the benefit of a classical training," he said, "so there are times when I might be a little less blinkered than the average pedant. I've heard, for example, that in certain parts of

Africa, children are named according to the day of the week they were born on; and amongst such children, the name *Fibi*, or Girl Friday, is not uncommon."

Phoebe pricked up her ears at this. Then she mumbled something and cackled.

"What did you say?" I asked her.

" 'A little learning is a dangerous thing,' " she said, once more in unmistakable mimicry of my dead husband's voice. " 'Drink deep, or taste not the Pierian Spring.' Man-woman cunning. First he say me Yoruba. But *Fibi* not Yoruba word for Friday. *Fibi* whole other African language. You thinking, Africa, Africa, Africa, all big place all full same same nigger. You see, white folks not so superior."

"Alexander Pope," said Mr. Whitman, astonished.

" 'Thou shalt not suffer a witch to live,' " said Phoebe, quoting yet another distinguished source, and then she relapsed into a bizarre, childlike state, hugging herself and rocking slowly back and forth.

"Is she plumb out of her mind?" asked Mr. Whitman's friend.

"No," said Mr. Whitman. "She's a kind of dark Hamlet, you see, she is dissembling, always dissembling. She's feigning her condition, Zack, the better to deceive us. But she has glimpsed something of the nature of our friendship. . . ."

"Are you trying to tell me, Mr. Whitman, that there is something to my servant's accusations of abomination?"

"That is not what *I* call it, Mrs. Grainger. I prefer to think of it as the love of comrades. A love forged out of the harshness of this war, born in the battlefields, kindled in the dying. A love spoken of in passionate terms by Plato, Michelangelo, Shakespeare—"

"You impute such shameful lusts even to the Bard himself?" I said, shocked beyond all measure.

" 'Shall I compare thee to a summer's day', Mrs. Grainger," said Mr. Whitman, "was not written about a woman; surely you knew that."

I did not want to admit the utter paucity of my acquaintance with Shakespeare's work. I did not want to admit that I had sheltered a pagan sorceress in my home for over a decade, all the while thinking her some simpleton. I certainly did not want to consider the fact that there were, sitting in my very own salon, two practitioners of unspeakable vice, who could not have appeared more normal, wholesome, even.

I did not want to confess to myself that everything I had ever held to be inviolate truth was fast becoming falsehood. I do not love adventure; I love to curl up in front of the fire with the latest installment of some penny-dreadful. Yet adventure of a sort was coming to me unsought. Not darkest Africa, but the mundane world about me was to be my undiscovered country.

Like the shepherds at the Nativity, I was sore afraid.

And yet there was this burning curiosity. . . .

And so I asked Mr. Whitman: "You seem to know so much about them. Where do you glean such information? Do you know the meaning of a dead rooster under a bed? Do you know what kind of sorcery my servant is up to?"

"Nothing of note," he said. "She probably despairs of your ever finding a husband, and so has placed fetishes and sacrifices under your bed to, as it were, stoke the fires within your person."

"That's ludicrous," I said.

"Not to her," said Mr. Whitman. "I imagine she thinks her spell is already working. Perhaps she thinks she has called your late husband to you out of the land of the dead—"

"*Egungun!* She kept repeating that word," I said. "Is that a sort of revenant?"

"I don't know. I'm not omniscient when it comes to Africa," said Mr. Whitman, "although I keep my ears open sometimes, where others wouldn't bother. Lately, however, Mrs. Grainger, I've been hearing a great deal about revenants. . . ."

"Well, I do believe in the resurrection of the body, I'm sure,"

I said, though I was sure of nothing of the kind. "But that the bloody carcass of a chicken could somehow bring back my husband—"

And I remembered the dream again, remembered Mr. Grainger's blistered hands, grasping at my shoulders through the sheer silk, remembered the emptiness that was his eyes, remembered gazing into that emptiness, past the dirt, past the wormy depths, through to a fiery darkness which surely must have been inferno itself, although my husband, my real husband, was surely amid the heavenly multitudes, enthroned amongst the angels, for he was a good man, a man who labored mightily for the liberation of the slave . . . oh, and I remembered those searing words, "Oh why did you never love me," and knew that they were both painful and true.

Mr. Whitman, seeing that I was in a transport of terror and torment, placed his arm around my shoulder and let me weep. And he said to me, in a grave and melancholy voice, "I have heard Africa call out, and I have seen the dead dance upon her shoulders. There is another resurrection, not the one promised in ancient testaments, but one that has happened—is happening, somewhere, today. But the angels of this resurrection are not golden-haired and clothed in raiments of light. I know, Mrs. Grainger, I've seen them. Their song is not the keening of sweet choirboys, but the drum taps of desolation. I know, Mrs. Grainger, I've heard them. They are the darker angels. They are the angels that come with the descent of night. Oh, Mrs. Grainger, I've seen them, and I'm afraid they've stolen the poetry clean out of me. I don't know that I'll ever sing another song. Mayhap I'll become a prose hack now, and churn out journals and memoirs of the ghastly war. Without poetry, what am I but a pathetic old man trawling for youth in a sea of the dying?"

"Oh, Walt," the young man said. "Old, old, but never pathetic. I swear to God, you pulled me back from the brink."

I waited, and quietly drained my cup of tea.

"Tell her, Zack," said Mr. Whitman. "Tell her about how you came back from the other side."

And the boy, who had said so little during the course of the afternoon, became suddenly loquacious, and began pouring out his whole life story.

You came, taciturn, with nothing to give—
we but look'd on each other. When lo! more
than all the gifts of the world you gave me.

—Walt Whitman

A WOUNDED MAN
IN WASHINGTON

1864

4

WHEREIN ZACHARY BROWN LOSES HIS FAITH

1

I ain't much for telling tall tales (Mr. Brown began) so I'll just tell it plain and simple as can be. Never traveled more'n ten miles from home before that war, never even laid eyes on a nigger, never thought I'd be a soldier, let alone lay bleeding to death on a pallet in Washington, D.C., let alone have a whole poem wrote about me. Me! Imagine that! Me, a tan-faced prairie boy, grown up with cows for company, my hands rough as corn husks, my lips all chapped from the summer sun.

I didn't join the war to kill secesh, and I sure as hell didn't enlist to liberate no darkies. I guess it was just the adventure of it. A brevet general with long blond hair come riding into town one day, and he was so handsome that the girls all swooned, and so brave that the boys all clamored to be sent forth to war. The general made a great to-do as how he wasn't no better than us once, and he'd made it all the way up the ranks on account of his bravery, and because in war you can be in the right place at the right time. Yessiree, he told us, standing on the boardwalk in front of the general store, the war will be over real soon now, and when it's done there'll be Indians to fight right here in the Territories, and who knows how far a military career might lead? Hell, he told us, I intend to be president one of these days! And that was the first and onliest time I ever laid eyes on George Armstrong Custer, who was one of the youngest heroes of the war, but I enlisted the next day, so I guess he was the one which made me do it.

I knew I was doing God's work. The preacher told me so when I went to say good-bye. "The Union," he told me, "is like a marriage. What God has joined, let no man put asunder. Look at Europe—godless, divided, a clear exemplary manifestation of a modern Tower of Babel. We are different. God intends for us to show the sinful multitudes of those decadent old countries that there can be a new Eden, with nations all speaking one tongue, in one voice; that these rich and diverse states can all rise to the status of becoming one indivisible nation. You understand that, boy?"

I nodded, trying to look solemn. I wondered why he was so anxious to preserve them thirty-four states, seeing as Nebraska wasn't even one of them yet.

"Didn't hear you," said the preacher.

"Yes, sir," I said.

I guess he was practicing for his Sunday sermon, for I didn't understand a word of what he said, which was common for them sermons, but since we left town on a Friday, I never got to find out. Didn't much matter what he said. I believed in God then, and I believed in heaven and hell, and I believed that my life was a trial run for the great hereafter. Never questioned, never doubted. Why should I have? Didn't nobody else. Me and my best friend Drew Hammet prayed in that church a long time, well, all right, we didn't just pray, we played, too, you know, horseplay; in the closet where the reverend kept his hymnals, we talked about how we were going to waylay fresh young Mary Moore on her way to milking the cows, and stick it up her and all. Begging your pardon, ma'am, but we also played a little with each other; boys will be boys and all, and none of us could ever save up the seventy-five cents to hire Miss Evelyn down at the saloon; and our mothers didn't hold with trafficking with ladies of ill repute. I wouldn't tell you this part at all, ma'am, except that it sheds light on a later part of my story.

The Reverend Jones gave each of us a shiny half-dollar that he'd saved out of the church collection, so we'd have something in our pockets against payday, which only come once a month, and came to thirteen dollars. I never had thirteen dollars all at once before, and even four bits felt mighty hefty in my pocket; at the guest house by the Union Station in Omaha you could get a steak dinner for four, five courses, and all the beer you could drink for that kind of money. It didn't stay in my pocket for long, if truth be told.

My cousin Rodney came with us as a drummer boy. Because he was only ten, the Reverend Jones only gave him a quarter. He spent it on gin, and wandered around the camp in a daze and knocked over Captain Rawlins's stew; got a sound whupping for that, and deserved it too; he had always been a wild one. But after that, he shaped up. He never sassed his elders, and every word that come out of him was "Yes, sir, no, sir, right away, sir." So it done him good.

We was all of us young. For a day or two we marched and we sang loud songs and stood smartly to attention and watched the officers ride by, all buttoned up bright and brassy. I sure as hell didn't know what the fighting was all about. I knew we were going to kill a lot of rebs. I knew some of us might die, too, but I didn't think on that too much, because I was too young. We marched, and evenings we told stories, about our mothers' cooking and our fathers' drinking, and we told lies about the girls we'd kissed, and fights we'd won, and the horses we'd stole. By the third day we already run out of stories, and we sat by the fire just drinking and fretting, not wanting to say out loud how scared we was. The only one who ever said so was my best friend Drew, who blubbered and carried on about his ma's fine sugar cookies; he was only fourteen, though he was big for his age, almost as big as me. The third night he cried himself to sleep, but I told everyone it was a wild coyote I'd shot in the leg.

Rodney never cried at all.

When Drew got real scared, he calmed himself down by polishing his pa's Enfield rifle, which was the only thing he had to remember his pa by. Number 353 in that Schuyler, Hartley and Graham's *Illustrated Catalogue of Military Goods* it was, as Drew never tired of telling me. Thirty-nine-inch barrel, ten pounds in weight, elevated sights. He polished that bayonet until it glowed.

By the seventh day our uniforms was getting tore up, and, ma'am, forgive my language, some of us was getting the shits real bad, and our heads weren't held up nearly so high, and the fifes were hurting our ears, and the drummer boys couldn't hold their rhythm no more. Nebraska was a world away now, and Preacher Jones's words didn't mean nothing to me; Nebraska was my country, not some shapeless giant terrain that was ruled from Washington.

We met up with another regiment on the eighth day, and for a while the singing got boisterous again, and we tried to look good so they wouldn't outdo us; they was veterans, they'd already seen one battle somewheres; can't remember the name of that place now, some dry creek I think. We lay encamped, and brought out the same old stories for a new audience to listen to; and then we listened to their stories, which were a little different: they told us about blood, dismemberment, and death. But we didn't think too much on them stories yet; the world they told of was beyond our ken.

Rodney loved them stories of bloodshed; they was like fairy tales to him, only more believable. He sat right next to the fire

and crunched them stale biscuits with the best of them, and listened to the tall tales till his eyes closed all by themselves and
he'd start snoring right there, still sitting cross-legged, till I carried him back to the tent we shared, me and him and Drew and
Kaczmarczyk, who didn't speak no English; he was some kind of
bohunk, I think, and kept to himself, and now and then he drew
sketches of me and Drew and Rodney with a stick of charcoal in
a little notebook, mighty lifelike we thought them, too, but I'm
getting mixed up now in the order of telling how it happened,
all I meant to say is that we shared this tent, the four of us, that's
all.

They didn't give us no training beyond marching up and
down and a little bit of target practice. I didn't care to ask where
we were; I just wanted to get to the action. Nobody told us
where we were going; nobody told us nothing.

They needed us fast, needed our warm bodies anyways, to fill
up the spaces on their strategy boards. So, all of a sudden, we
found ourselves in battle.

2

It's hard to even think about it now.

You've seen the pictures. It's different when you're there.
The gray of the photography can cover up a hell of a lot of ugliness. The cannon smoke hangs in the air in them pictures, and
the bodies lie all motionless. You can't hear the screaming. You
don't feel the mud clinging to your shoes. You're not drenched
in the drizzle or spattered with gore, sticky as molasses. You're
not slipping and sliding on vomit and ordure. You're not clench-
ing your bladder tight against the terror of pissing right into
your trousers.

There was a lot of screaming. The rebs screamed worse than
injuns when they come charging at us, and the dying screamed
worser yet. There was so much smoke that you couldn't tell if

you were shooting at a man or a horse or nothing at all. When the cannon fired, the ground shook, and arms and legs come flying through the air and it rained blood. We did as we were trained to do at first, massing in short lines, kneeling, firing, reloading, as long as we could.

Almost the first thing that happened was, Drew's beautiful shiny Enfield blew up on his shoulder, and it took his head clear off. One minute I saw him, smiling like he wasn't afraid no more; the next I saw his neck bones wiggling in the wind. The blood just come spewing. His head lay in front of us, staring back, and he looked, well, you could say, surprised. The eyes wide open. The neck stuck in the mud, like we'd buried him there for a laugh and we were going to come dig him back out in an hour or two and we'd all go on home, cackling and clapping each other on the back. Drew kept on staring as we fired and reloaded and fired and reloaded. None of us looked back at him, tried not to anyway, we all tried to look up and over him, at the enemy, which was charging and hollering and shrieking and running right up against our line of fire. And we just fired and reloaded and fired and reloaded and took their fire and around me people kept slipping into the mud. The strange thing was, Drew never slipped, even though he didn't have no head. He stood behind me, jiggling back and forth and gushing blood.

And off somewhere ahead—sometimes you saw him when the mist parted—was Rodney, scruffy-faced and tousle-haired, banging away. His eyes were fierce and clear. He stood like an angel of death, not flinching when the soldiers circled him, wielding their bayonets, stabbing, flailing, slicing into throats, limbs, stomachs, reeling out strings of intestines, popping out eyes.

After the command "Fire at will," I stopped thinking. There was no pretense of military order. The whistling of miniés, the wind, the shrilling fifes, the rush of blood, it was all one. I know I stood my ground right next to my best friend's head, and I knew that I slashed and smashed and thrashed and bashed until I too fell, not wounded in my flesh but in my spirit, fell cradling my dead companion's head in my arms. I thought I was dead too. Everything went black. I felt, you know, ma'am, what the preacher used to call "the peace that passeth understanding."

It seemed that the tumult of battle softened. In the end all I could hear was the tap of a single drum. And though it was utterly dark, I knew that Rodney was at the center of the blackness, pounding out the heartbeat of the world. In the darkness there were only his eyes. An angel's eyes to be sure. And a voice that seemed to say, "Sleep now, sleep now, in the arms of mother death." The voice kept whispering, the darkness seemed to last forever, but then, slowly, I floated back to the brink of the abyss, and I opened my eyes. They told me the battle was won. I don't know how they could tell. Their dead and our dead was all twisted up together like twine.

When the smoke cleared I saw we were in a valley, and the sun was about setting, and up the hill, past all the dead bodies, was a blue-green forest. If you looked past death, if you held your nose against the stench of the dead, this was a beautiful place. A stream flowed down the side of the slope. The carrion birds were gathering, and my eyes were misted with sweat and blood, but I still knew that this land was as fair as Nebraska, and that we had made it ugly.

I didn't weep, though. I wanted to be strong, like Rodney.

They told me the battle lasted fifteen minutes. Rodney was never found. They set out after him because they couldn't find his body. If he ran, I pray that he got away. They wouldn't shoot a ten-year-old boy for desertion, would they? But they had orders, they did.

Later, Captain Rawlins called us; he wanted to say a few words, a prayer for those which had given their lives that day. I knelt beside my comrades to pray, and for the first time in my life I could not say that word, I mean *God, God.* God would not come to my lips; I choked on God like God was a chicken bone.

3

There was more battles after that. Maybe I did kill a passel of secesh, and maybe I didn't. Didn't stop to count. Didn't think about killing that much after the first battle, more about staying alive. Didn't think about praying either. Didn't want to know why I couldn't say God's holy name. Didn't want no one to know. I was more like a machine than a human being. Went where they told me, fired when they said "fire," killed when they said "kill."

You could say I had lost my faith. Only I never really had no faith to lose. I mean, in Reverend Jones's church I sang them hymns as lustily as the next man, and I said amen as fervently, but what I'm saying is, when I lay in the mud with my arms wrapped around Drew Hammet's head, and when they went looking for Rodney in the woods with orders to shoot him on sight, and I heard the world's heart beating in the yawning darkness, I knew that them hymns had been sung in vain. God had never been with me, and I had never been with God.

When I closed my eyes each night, I could see Rodney standing in the black forest, banging the drum, looking straight through me at a truth I would never see.

After a while, without my friends, without my faith, I decided it would be best to go to where Rodney was, even if it meant they'd shoot me. I planned my desertion carefully. I saved a few pieces of hardtack every day. I was all ready to run when I met a man who showed me a new way to see the world. I mean your late husband, Widow Grainger, the reverend, who came riding through camp.

It's strange how people riding through your life can change your life. First General George Armstrong Custer, then the Reverend Aloysius Grainger, the second-most unusual man of God I ever met . . . I say the second, because later on in this tale we will surely come to the first.

5

WHEREIN MRS. GRAINGER FIRST COMES TO APPRECIATE MR. WHITMAN'S POETRY

1

At the mention of my late husband's name, I knew that this visit from Mr. Whitman and his friend was more than coincidence. Some design was at work, though whether it were of God, Satan, or man was yet to be apprehended. The young man's words, rough-hewn though they were, had a heartfelt simplicity which surely partook of the nature of the poet.

The tea, alas, had grown cold, and the sun had set. Although I had been acquainted with these two men for less than twenty-four hours, it was clear that we had reached a certain intimacy. I was therefore emboldened to invite them to stay for the night, as the trek from Washington Square all the way to Brooklyn, in the rain, was not the most inviting of prospects, and I was not sure that a hansom to the ferry could be found at all, since so many mourners had swollen the city's population.

"Forgive me," I said, "for making an offer which might seem to offend propriety; but I am, as you see, a widow, and unlikely at my age to be compromised by two gentlemen such as yourselves."

I did not want to add that I was, for the first time since my late husband's death, afraid to go to sleep, afraid of dead animals under my bed and dead lovers in my dreams, afraid even of my dusky servant, who had suddenly become so much more than a woman in waiting. I wanted desperately to hear the rest of Mr. Brown's tale, appalled though I was at some of the details thereof. But I knew that I needed time to digest what had already transpired, before I could assimilate what was to come—which was, I was certain, even more unsettling than what had gone before.

While Mr. Whitman and his friend walked down to the corner for a quick supper at the Coach House, I ordered Phoebe to make up the guest room, one floor above my bedroom and one beneath the garret where she herself dwelt. The room had not been occupied for a year; in Mr. Grainger's lifetime, it had seen a steady stream of visitors, from European worthies to cavalry officers, from servants of God to servants of Mammon. I told her to heat up some bricks for the warming pan, and to pull out an extra eiderdown. She didn't speak to me during this whole business, and indeed acted like an exemplary maidservant, demure and swift to obey. It was easy to pretend that her outbursts of the afternoon had been aberrations, some kind of distemper, such as one might find in a recalcitrant canine. I wanted desperately to pretend so. To treat Phoebe as though she were as civilized as a white woman . . . that would have been most disturbing. As Shakespeare so eloquently put it:

> *Take but degree away, untune that string,*
> *And hark what discord follows. . . .*

I was afraid of what might happen if that string were to be untuned. Would Negroes be attending our dinner parties and soirées, even using our water closets and teacups? The prospect was none too comforting.

2

Well, I left Phoebe at her labors and came downstairs to straighten out the salon a little bit, and I found Mr. Whitman's notebook lying on the sill of the bay window. I looked at it, worried a little about being caught, and then, at last, was so overcome by curiosity that I began to leaf through it.

This is what I read:

> *. . . heart! heart! heart!*
> *O the bleeding drops of red,*
> *Where on the deck my Captain lies,*
> *Fallen cold and dead.*

Why, I thought to myself, he is writing about Mr. Lincoln.

My Captain does not answer, his lips are pale and still—

This was by no means the avant-garde, arhythmic nonsense that Mr. Whitman was said to have composed. This was a poetry of grave and puissant import. The images were vivid, the rhythm clear and elemental. Surely no one could call these words lacking in rhyme or meter. They brought to mind all that I myself had felt, standing in the presence of the dead president and hearing the voice of one I had mistaken for the Almighty. I freely admit that I was close to tears. This was a person of grand sentiment and deep sensibility.

I resolved to tell Mr. Whitman straight away that I had been ill-informed. The opportunity soon presented itself, for he and

Mr. Brown came knocking at the front door, and Phoebe hurried down to admit them.

"Oh, Mr. Whitman," I said, as the old man came shambling into the foyer and I came out to greet him, still clutching the notebook in my hand, "your poem is utterly, utterly brilliant."

He seized the notebook from my hand. He grew quite red in the face, in fact. I almost thought he would strike me.

"Doggerel!" he shouted. "Doggerel, plain and simple!"

"But it is a fine poem," I said, "and I was moved."

"But did you hear those silly rhymes, that childish rhythm, clattering away like a tin drum?"

"I saw nothing silly about—"

"I told you, ma'am," he said, marching into the salon and hurling himself into the first fauteuil that presented itself, "that I'm losing the gift for poetry. This nonsense proves it. Gone are the arching lines and subtle colorings and intricate syncopations. Instead I'm forced to rely on a banging beat and to end each line with a nursery rhyme. I don't think I'll get this one published; it's an affront to the style I've labored so long to impose upon my work—"

"She's right, Walt," said Mr. Brown. "I told you it was beautiful."

Mr. Whitman stopped his fuming. "Oh, Zack," he said. "How you shame me sometimes. I can chisel and chisel at the refractory stones of poetry, but there's always something more beautiful than any arrangement of vowels and consonants. Come, give me a kiss."

Without any consciousness of shame, it seemed, the two men kissed; not chastely, as a father and son might, but with a degree of lasciviousness which caused me to turn away.

The two men stopped immediately.

"Your pardon, Widow Grainger," Mr. Brown said, seeing that I was embarrassed. "But if I did something I oughtn't to have, it's because of something I learned from old man Aloysius."

And that was another jarring thing, to hear this strange boy speak of my husband in terms of greater familiarity than even I had ever allowed myself.

I too sat down, and prepared to hear more from this strange youth.

"Tell me," I said, "for Phoebe has not yet finished making your bed, and I am more than eager to hear about my husband, about whom, it now seems, I know so much less than I thought. Pray, do go on, Mr. Brown."

"Yes'm," he said. "But if you wouldn't mind . . . ma'am . . . do you think you could call me Zack, just plain Zack? Mr. Brown's just a mite too fancy for me."

6

WHEREIN THE REVEREND GRAINGER SHOWS ZACHARY BROWN THE TRUE FACE OF LIBERTY

1

As I was saying, ma'am (Zack continued), I already come to conclude that I might as well just run for it, maybe even get myself kilt if that was the way it was going to be. I just plain wanted to die, and I didn't have the guts to just go hang myself off the nearest cottonwood. I never got no sleep because Rodney haunted my dreams. That's how I figured he was dead; saw a play called *Hamlet* once, and there was a ghost in it, and a man with a skull in his hand. The ghost haunted young Hamlet, hounded him, and presently death came for everybody in that whole play; there wasn't a soul left but some Norwegian who come in at the end to carry away the bodies.

In my dreams, Rodney was still little and frail. But he had the strength that only the dead have, because they don't care about nothing no more. And he keeps calling out to me, "Time to sleep now, time to sleep."

I never did see Drew Hammet in my dreams. I was afraid too, I guess. Just Rodney, the little blond-haired angel, drumming me to everlasting sleep.

I had it all figured out. Sunday, there was going to be a committee come from out east, to talk to us about what the war was all about. Attendance wasn't compulsory or nothing, but I knew the officers would be there, trying to look good, for there was a war reporter coming with them, someone from *The New York Times,* I heard them say. I could skip out when it started, and no one would miss me until morning. If I headed north-northwest, I reckoned I could get back to the Territories in a fortnight. I'd have to make sure I was heading the right way when I started, though, because I wouldn't have the benefit of getting the direction from the sun, leastways until dawn.

So the night came that I was fixing to run. So I up and done it. It was easy. No one stood guard, no one stopped me. They was all so dispirited, even though we were winning, least that's what the captain kept telling us. Don't think they'd have stopped me anyway.

I woke from that familiar dream, made sure Kaczmarczyk was dead to the world, and just slipped away. Maybe he heard me; I think he stirred.

I walked away. Into the forest a fair piece, till I couldn't see the fires or smell the burnt coffee no more. I was still wearing my uniform, what was left of it, which just shows you what a fool of a boy I was. So there I am, in the woods, all by myself, with the moonlight streaming down like silver on the trees.

I set to walking. Uphill for a while, then what passes for a pathway winds back down again and I think, I'm going to the other side of the mountain, where rumor says some secesh might be encamped. I try to avoid that, and I take what looks like a fork, through a clearing, around to a patch of wild strawberries, and I pick 'em all and wolf them down, but I'm still hungry, maybe from all that walking.

In a while I'm so hungry that I eat every last one of them biscuits that I had put away, and I'm looking to bayonet me a squirrel or a possum or something. And I'm walking and walking and walking and pretty soon I'm sure I've seen this creek before, maybe many times before, the water chiming on the boulders and glistening in the moon.

I've been walking in circles, I told myself.

Sat myself down on a big old ragged rock, and listened to the music of the night. The insects chittering on the leaves. The owl. The varmints skittering along the branches. I sat for a long time. Didn't even know what state nor county I was in; it could as well have been the woods back home, behind the barn. All forests are alike, ma'am, in the end. Don't matter if it's oak or pine, except for the smell, which tells you the names of the trees. Walt says that the darkest forest is the human heart.

And then it seemed to me that I heard the cry of a lost child, and I thought—yep, wasn't the most logical thing to think, but I was bone tired and out of my mind—I thought it might be my cousin Rodney.

I didn't want to call out, because now that I knew I'd been walking around in circles, I thought I was probably still pretty darn near to our camp, and I didn't want to be drug back after only a few hours of freedom.

But the cry came again. Could maybe have been an animal, but it sure sounded human. Ma'am, my heart froze from that sound, for I was sure that it called my name. Injuns believe when a animal calls your name in the night, it's the animal which owns your soul. My friend and blood brother, Wamdi, told me that. He was a Santee, and he knew a lot, but he died of the measles when he was just nigh on twelve years old. The day before he died, he saw an eagle perched above his pallet, and the eagle whispered his name. Calling him home, you see. Wamdi *means* eagle in Dakota, ma'am. I speak the language tolerably, for there was a lodge of them a mile down the plain from our farm, before the government sent them on up to the next territory.

I'm talking around and about the subject, Widow Grainger, because I'm afraid to get to the heart of it. And true, I was thinking of Wamdi then, as I sat on that rock, thinking of him dying; me and Rodney and Drew'd all had the measles, and it hadn't hurt us any. Just one of them things, I guess. In some ways, the injuns is just weaker than us. I was thinking of Wamdi, and the eagle standing guard at his head, its wings outstretched, ready to snatch away the kid's soul; and I got to wondering what animal was going to come for me. Maybe a big old grizzly bear.

And then I heard a slow, regular thudding. Just my heart, I thought. My own heart pounding. But no. It was coming from somewhere in the darkness. And it sounded like a drum. A drum with broken snares. Rodney's. I knew I wasn't dreaming this time. Or maybe I was, but the dreaming had merged into the undreaming, if you catch my drift, like a waking dream. Another injun kind of a thing, a vision. I didn't know white folks could have them. The drum kept tapping and there was words to it, too, words whispered in the dry snap of the stick on the loose snares:

> *Rat-tat-tat,*
> *rat-tat-tat,*
> *time to sleep.*

I listened for a while, and then I whispered, "Rodney, is that you?"

But all I heard in answer was this *rat-tat-tat, rat-tat-tat,* and I got the feeling whatever it was was asking me to follow it further into the darkness, away from the creek and the silver-blue light, into the densest part of the wood. And now and then there was also the creature's cry. It had to be Rodney.

"I'm coming, cuz," I said softly. "Wait up, wait up."

I clomb uphill, in the direction of the sound. As I drew close, the drumming sound seemed to flatten, to broaden . . . now it was coming from the trees themselves . . . the clatter of twigs against bark . . . and the sound of the crying child was the sigh of the wind and the twitter of nocturnal insects . . . I could feel the hairs on my arms stiffen.

"Why are you playing hide-and-go-seek with me, Rodney, boy?" I whispered.

The only answer was that *rat-tat-tat*. Well, the wind sprung up all fierce and chilled me right inside of my bones. Ahead, something glowed, something warm . . . a fire. It could have been hell itself, but the chill made me run for the flames that leapt behind the wall of trees. . . .

"Rodney!" I cried out. "Rodney!"

And saw him. Just for a moment. A silhouette against the smoke and ruddy flickering. A young boy's shadow, the pointed outline of the drumsticks, the eyes that was cold as despair . . . and the boy looked me full in the eye and his lips started to move and I knowed he was about to tell me, "Zacko, Zacko, here's your journey's end, this carpet of dead leaves is your final resting place, this canopy of branches your shroud, the moon your only mourner." And I just run toward where I think his shadow's being cast, half slipping down a steep slope, and then I find that I've slid through the trees and come full circle, right back down into a place of campfires and tents, and there, on an upturned ammunition crate, stood a mutton-chopped man in a frock coat, with his hands upraised to the heavens, and his sea-green eyes gazing up at the stars.

And Rodney's voice transfigured into the voice of—

2

A darkie woman standing atop a wheelbarrow, singing her heart out. A slip of a girl she was, right pretty in her own way, and blacker than the night itself. But she wore a kind of bridal dress, which lit up the whiteness of her eyes something powerful, and she held her palms together and sung in a language I didn't know, except that I knew from the fervor in her voice that every word of it was a prayer to the God which I didn't believe in no more.

This slip of a girl, ma'am, was none other than your servant, Phoebe. I'd recognize her anywhere. 'Sides, I knew I would see her here in your home. And what was it she sang? It was Latin, I reckon.

And then I heard a familiar voice: "Dot's a prayer to the Wirgin," and saw that it was Private Kaczmarczyk, explaining the song to some companion of his who was too soused to care. *"Ave Maria,"* he said, *"gratia plena* ... Schubert, very nice, but funny it is, to hear it vith such an primitive orchestra. I remember Lankowska, at a music hall in Danzig, she sang this song ... she vas an angel! But you vouldn't understand."

Kaczmarczyk must have roused himself from slumber after all, and gone on down to the meeting. Or maybe he was awakened by the woman's singing.

A man with one leg played an accompaniment on a wheezing harmonium, and another, duded up like a gambler, scratched on a tuneless fiddle. A third player whacked a tambourine then shook it in the air, and that was what was making the dry rattling sound that had seemed to be the drummer's distant tapping.

As I listened, the wind died down completely.

The song was popish you might say, ma'am, but it was still beautiful. The preacher in my hometown didn't hold with property, but among the injuns there was Roman Catholic padres, trying to bring them to the Lord; when I thought on it, I was sure now that the mumbo jumbo was Latin. The woman was more beautiful than the song. You see her now, all cowering, but then it was different; there wasn't no trace of slavishness about her. The song breathed right through her, and made her free, not free like freeing a slave, but the way a bird is free. She was the

first nigger I ever seen; didn't have none in my little town; nearest ones was probably in Omaha, but I only passed through
there, on my way to the war. She sang like she were possessed; I
don't mean by devils, I mean like an angel was singing through
her. Well, I guess the others thought so too; I saw tears in old
Kaczmarczyk's eyes, and the men wasn't all rowdy or disorderly,
the way men usually are.

When she was done, there was a long silence; but presently,
the mutton-chopped gentleman I told you about, your husband,
that is, he stood tall on that crate, and spoke in a gentle voice
that carried through the still night air. "Men," he said, "I am the
Reverend Aloysius Grainger, and I'm a pamphleteer, and an abolitionist, and an altruist, and there's a lot more seventy-five–cent
words that can describe me; and to top it all, I'm not even an
American. So maybe, just maybe, you're wondering what I'm
doing here at all. Some of you have fought so hard that you've
probably forgotten that today is the Lord's Day; and as I
chanced to be traveling through this bitter and beautiful country, in the company of Mr. Donovan, the newspaperman, it was
suggested to me that I preach a kind of sermon, so that you will
stay mindful of the holy purpose to which you have been called,
and of God's grand design in causing this bloody and fratricidal
war to be fought. This woman here is Phoebe, who was once a
slave; she is a slave no longer, and she is become as an uncaged
nightingale, warbling her joy at freedom above the dark night of
her compatriots' bondage.

"Do you think, men, that the true face of liberty is a woman
clothed in the clouds, brandishing a flaming torch on the reverse
of a coin or a banknote? Do you imagine liberty to be a towering colossus, robed, crowned, and ever smiling? Sometimes I
do; though I have never seen such a statue, I imagine that it
might cause us to reflect upon the nature of liberty, and to be
moved to great extremities of emotion. But we should not mistake the image for the truth. Liberty has a human face. Blood
must flow into the statue, the engraving on the coin, the words

in a testament, to bring liberty to life. Who, then, is liberty? I have seen the dark angelic muse, my friends, and she lives in the features of this black diamond, this jewel of Africa. It is you who have struck off Phoebe's chains; it is you who have liberated melody from her lips. Tonight I will speak of what liberty means to me, and what I hope it will mean to you.

"Although I am an ordained minister, I have no church, no congregation, and no collection plate. Tonight, you are my congregation. You are of many denominations and some of you may not even be Christians, for this is a country that does not demand that a man adhere to one faith or another. So I'm not going to preach to you from the Good Book, but instead from my life. And I'm not going to stand up here, towering above you like the Almighty Incarnate, but I will walk among you, I will speak to you as one man to another, I will look into your eyes; and from time to time, this girl, this flower of Ethiop maidenhood, will beguile you with melodies from many lands."

So saying, he stepped down from the makeshift pulpit, and walked about, now putting his arm on a soldier's shoulder, now shaking a hand; I think, you know, that our Captain Rawlins was none too happy about that, for he was a traditional man, who believed that God was in heaven and men were on earth and ministers were somewhere in the air betwixt them. This man, the Rev. Aloysius Grainger, didn't hold himself high above common folks, even though he spoke in a lordly English manner.

I didn't hear everything he said, because sometimes he spoke to a single man in a low voice; but after a time he was standing close to where I sat, the farthest one back, me having just slid down that hill whilst fixing to escape, and he seemed to address me directly; and that was how I come to hear old Aloysius's story about the gambler, the slave girl, and the woman who died from within.

7

WHEREIN THE REVEREND GRAINGER WAGERS A LIFE FOR A LIFE

1

Slavery, said the Rev. Aloysius Grainger, looking me straight in the eye, is a terrible and brutish vice, and for the institution of slavery to be practiced within the borders of these great and glorious thirty-four states is nothing less than a crime against God, Man, and Nature. Yes, young man, I know you have heard it said that "in my house there are many mansions," and that the white must therefore be perpetually sundered from the black, being different in capacity, intellect, and wisdom. You have also, doubtless, heard that tale of Noah and his sons, and how the Negro, Ham, and all his progeny must be punished for all eternity in servitude to Shem and Japheth, for his sin of gazing upon his father's nakedness; for this is the verse most frequently used to justify the practice of Negro bondage. You have heard these things, but know also that the Bible can be used both to justify and to denigrate slavery. True, Moses led his people from bondage, but he did not condemn bondage itself, and his chosen people owned slaves and thought it no sin. And St. Paul says that slaves must obey their masters. Yet our Lord Jesus Christ frequently berates men for the cruelty they show to other men, and is not slavery the ultimate cruelty? Let me not use the Bible at all, then, but let me tell you instead a story.

There is much hypocrisy in the world. I was born in England, which decries bondage, yet in England children toil in factories, and boys are prenticed out to masters who use them in every sort of bestial manner, who flog them, starve them, and even demand monetary compensation of the parents should a child accidentally die from his ill use.

It was the siren freedom that lured me to this land; although I knew that Negroes were held in bondage in America, I thought nothing of it; I only half understood then that a Negro is a fully human person, for when one has never seen one, one imagines them as scarcely more sentient than a baboon or a Barbary ape.

I took ship for this country with new hopes and new wife (my first wife having perished of consumption) and presently took a house in New England. Thanks to my wife's small dowry, I was able to devote myself to such causes as befit my ministerial vocation: I provided a soup kitchen for the destitute, I rescued young Irish women from being sold into brothels, I collected money to find a young boy, gallows-bound for stealing to assuage his hunger, a lawyer who succeeded in having his sentence commuted to hard labor.

It was in New England that I first learnt that here, in this bastion of liberty, there was an entire subnation of those condemned to a servile existence on the basis of race alone.

This knowledge put me in grave despair, until I found others of a like mind, and began to read the publications of the abolitionists. It was then that I heard of the subversive efforts of New England luminaries to rescue the Negroes from their enslavement. I heard of runaways being chased by packs of hounds, of the chattel return laws which made even escape to the North no guarantee of lifelong freedom; I heard of the bounty hunters, and of the laws which indulged the caprices of owners and allowed no legal recourse for the owned. I resolved to visit the slave states myself, and I began a series of journeys to the South. It was on such a trip that I encountered the girl whose voice has ensorcelled you all tonight.

In Arlington, Virginia, there are no massive plantations such as are seen in the Deep South, and when I started to go there, ten years ago, I was well received by gentlemen of quality, who discussed Milton and Moses, who had read Plato and Pliny, and who were much desirous of conversation about Europe and about London.

There was one in particular who was very kind to me, a certain tobacco farmer named Ebenezer Judd. His farm was far south of the capital, near a village called Poquoson, but he had a town house in Arlington, across the river from Washington, where he entertained lavishly and frequently. His only serious vice was gambling—or so it seemed to me at the time. I knew, in the back of my mind, that he was a slave owner; but in Arlington this was not nearly so visible, for the servants there were indentured Irish. Slaves too, of a sort, but I was not yet aware of how horrific the life of an indentured servant could be, or that they were bought and sold in a manner not unlike the Negroes, and as frequently mistreated.

We had corresponded in the past, and he had contributed to my fund for the education of orphaned Connecticut girls. On my first trip to Washington, therefore, I was his guest, and on a number of subsequent occasions, and had an opportunity to observe, though not participate in, the poker marathons which inevitably capped every soirée at his Arlington townhouse. Mr. Judd was a book-learned man, and he had a collection of biographies that anyone might envy—life stories were, indeed, his passion.

It was during my fourth visit to Mr. Judd that I saw the slave woman Eleuthera. We were dining—the party was all men, since Mrs. Judd was back in Poquoson—and, it being a fine summer evening, and very much still light out, a buffet had been set up in the back garden, with wrought-iron chairs such as are found in the cafés of Paris.

It was a rococo garden, with fountains, trellises of bougainvillea, and imitations of classical statues, modeled in miniature after the great gardens of Europe, which Mr. Judd had seen in picture books, as he had never traveled out of Virginia, unless you count the nation's capital across the river.

Poker had already begun at one table, but I was reading, next to a fountain adorned with cherubs, a *Life of St. Francis* by the renowned ecclesiastical historian Joseph Cardinal Reed. In this book, His Eminence had not balked from discussing the open promiscuity practiced by the Franciscan sect before its official recognition by the Papal See. In fact, he rather dwelt on this profligate lack of celibacy, wherein the first Franciscans took to an extreme our Lord's injunction that we should "love one another." "Free love" was what Cardinal Reed termed this sinful excess, and the book had acquired a measure of notoriety for its scenes in which His Eminence, in the interests of verisimilitude, imagined in some detail certain scenes of carnal interaction between St. Francis and St. Agnes, rendering the book as close to pornography as a religious text might dare to be.

I was engrossed in this book, and paid the poker game no mind.

But presently, Mr. Judd interrupted me. "Why, Reverend," he said, "you're reading that scandalous *Life*, which everyone talks about but no one can buy for love or money."

I said, "The bookshops of New Haven are the best in this country."

"*This* country, sir, is Virginia; you English never seem to comprehend the finer points of American governance. Is the book really as smutty as they say?"

"I'm afraid so," I said, turning the page.

"Why, Aloysius," said Mr. Judd, "I've a mind to buy that book right out of your hands."

"But I haven't finished reading it," I said.

"Ten dollars," he said, and flashed a gold half-eagle in my face.

I was not surprised that he wanted to pay so much for such a rare volume; I would have, in exchange for his many hospitalities, been glad to present it to him on my departure.

I was just about to offer to do so, however, when I heard a low, bestial moan from beyond the fountain. It was then that I saw, for the first time, that, chained hand and foot behind an enormous reproduction of the famous winged Nike of Samothrace, was some kind of human being. I had not seen this before because the garden was artfully designed, with overhanging vines and concealing shrubberies, and because nobody else in this fairly populous lawn party had been paying any attention to it whatsoever.

I put the book down for a moment and craned my neck for a better view. It was, indeed, a person. A skeletal, naked Negress. Her complexion was so dusky that she almost seemed a part of the earth piled up behind her.

"Excuse me for a moment," I said. "I was wondering—"

"Oh," said my host, very affably, "that's Eleuthera. I purchased her last month, for she was attached to a consignment of bucks; I surely do regret it now. A most intractable creature, Reverend. Right now, she's refusing to eat. If I were to leave her in Poquoson, she'd have jumped into the river by now, and I'd have a hundred more dollars to have to try to win at five-card stud."

"May I see her?" I said, trying to conceal my distaste.

"Of course, Reverend," said Mr. Judd. "In fact, perhaps you can persuade her to eat."

I walked over to the buffet table, where a butler helped me to a slice of Smithfield ham, a spoonful of fried okra, another of

black-eyed peas, and some chicken gravy. I took the entire plate-
ful over to the statue of Nike, with Ebenezer Judd following behind, curious, no doubt, as to what an English man of God
would have to say to a pagan Ethiop.

Behind the Nike, inches from the luxury of the lawn party,
was a scene of medieval squalor. The inaptly named Eleuthera—
does not that word connote *freedom* in the Greek?—was chained
in a crouched position, like a child in a womb. I could not tell
her age, but I knew she was withered beyond her years, with dry
dugs hanging, with strange scarifications on her cheeks, arms,
abdomen, and thighs. She was bleeding from lacerations on her
back, and a riding quirt lay nearby; I wondered who her tor-
mentor might be.

"Why, Eleuthera," said Ebenezer, "here's a reverend come to
see you, all the way from England. His name is Master Aloysius."

"Eat, woman," I said. I bent down toward her with the plate
of food. She stared at me with an unmitigated ferocity, and
snarled. I had heard such a snarl only once before . . . in the leopard cage at the zoological gardens in London. It chilled me.

"She's out of her wits," said Ebenezer. "Thinks she's a leopard."

"Still," I said, "she should eat."

I cut up a piece of the ham and tried to present it to her.

"You will have to ram it down her throat," my host said. He
knelt down, and, much as one might treat a dog, pried apart her
lips. "There you go, Eleuthera. Some meat for the big jungle cat.
Meat, meat. Go on, Reverend, shove it on in."

"But this is outrageous," I said. "She's not an animal."

"Until she learns to behave like a human being, why," said
Ebenezer, "I just can't afford to treat her otherwise. Now
if I can just get her fattened up enough to sell her down south,
cheap—"

"All right," I said, "I'll try to make her eat."

"This she-wolf and her daughter," Ebenezer said, "why,
there's nothing normal about them. They don't seem to know

they're slaves. Why, they don't even speak like other darkies. They seem to have a language all their own, some pidgin they speak in Africa mayhap. I'll be happy to be rid of 'em, let me tell you!"

On the one hand, it was undignified to feed her in this fashion. On the other, she clearly had to eat something, or she would die. Grimacing a little, I forced the morsel in between those lips.

At that moment, I felt little hands tugging at my sleeve. I felt the plate being dashed from my hands, saw it fly against the plaster of the statue, smash, saw pieces of food scatter onto the grass. I turned around to see a pigtailed pickaninny of about nine, who proceeded to pummel me with her fists, with all the might that her frail body could muster.

Surprised, I tripped and sprawled onto the grass. When I rubbed my head and looked up, I saw Ebenezer Judd laying into the child with the quirt, and heard her shrieking: "No, massa, no, massa, Phoebe good girl, no, massa, don't be hitting me now."

And Ebenezer was shouting, in a fine passion, "How dare you attack one of my visitors! A man of God! How dare you ruin my poker evening with your lunacy! And that porcelain dish cost fifty cents!"

It was horrifying to behold, and what happened next was worse, for Ebenezer's guests, fine gentlemen attired in the dandiest of evening dress, their attention attracted by the ruckus, began to gather around, and many began to shout encouragement to their host: "Git her good, Ebenezer!" "Damned impertinence!" "Give 'em an inch and they take a mile!" "You're just too damn good to your niggers, see where it gets you."

One young man, I could have sworn, was panting with the kind of arousal that is normally only associated with the favors of the opposite sex, and he began to moan, "Oh, Ebenezer, beat her to death, I pray! I'll pay you ten dollars for the pleasure."

At this outburst, even my host was a little perturbed. He stopped whipping the little girl, shrugged, threw down the quirt, and returned to his guests; and, the spectacle over, his friends returned to their conversations and their poker game. Only I remained to observe little Phoebe, on her hands and knees, eating my leftovers off the grass like a wild animal.

"What on earth," I said, "is happening here? Why is this woman refusing sustenance, and why will you not let me feed her?"

At which point, the old woman looked up at me, and addressed me thus, in a voice like dry leaves in the autumn wind. It was true that her accent was like none I had ever heard from the lips of a Negro. Yet she spoke with a gravity, a poetry even, which belied the grammatical solecisms of her jargon; and, though her tale was fantastical beyond belief, and doubtless the ravings of a delirious creature close to death, yet they had a visionary quality, almost like the rantings of St. John, the author of the apocalypse, or the sensual hysteria of St. Theresa, who flogged herself into an ecstasy that approached a sexual congress with the Almighty.

I could not fail to be moved; for as always, the dying prophesy.

2

You a good man, Marse Alwishus. Don't be interfering with things you don't understand. You let Leuthera die peaceful. The grave she call out to Leuthera long time now. Leuthera tired. Leuthera just want go home. You know home, you far from home too . . . home acrosst the sea. The sea be death. They say no more slaves coming from Africa, all slave be born here, but Leuthera come from Africa. From the part of Africa which the white folks calls Darkes' Africa. Africa of night, of fear, of ancient passion. Africa they fear the most.

In Africa, Leuthera a magic woman. Much power. Some call me witch, some call me wise old woman. How old, how old? You smiling cause you think me foolish woman, dreaming bout nothing.

You think me old before my time. You think me wore out from no food, too much beating, too much sadness, but inside this dried-up body still a young woman. No. Me older than you, me older than whole country of America. Leuthera older than you can imagine. How old, how old? Leuthera tell you. Leuthera old when Moses come from Egypt land. Leuthera old when Adam and Eve she walk the earth.

Think bout a time before time. Leuthera there already. Leuthera at the right hand of Mawu-Lissa, man-woman mother-father she make the heaven and the earth.

In they time, the whole world only black folks, and they dwell Africa, and the world all young and warm like the breast of a nursing mother. Leuthera happy then. Blessings stream from her. The world a happy place, a paradise. But paradise must end. Leuthera depart that place and return to the bosom of Mawu-Lissa.

Second time Leuthera come to the world, she sit on the double throne of the two kingdoms. She sit with a cobra all wrap around she head. She mete out life and death. She hold the sacred feather *ma'at* in her hand, and weigh the human heart in the balance of good and evil. They call her the lioness, mother, queen.

This kingdom not so much a paradise. Great cities there, and mighty works of art, and riches. But slavery there, and misery. Leuthera sit betwixt the pyramid and the sphinx, and Leuthera shine with the face of the sun and the moon. But time she pass, and Leuthera return again to the shadow country. Me stay in the death land forever, she say. Me not want come back to the land of misery. Bosom of Mawu-Lissa, she heal me, she give me peace.

Then come a third time. A juju man, sorcerer, call me from the country of *egungun*. In Africa once more. My people cry out to me. Sand people sweeping down from the north, and from more farther north folks with the faces like snow. Come to take away they freedom. Come to take away they pride. Come to take away they souls, they hearts, they children.

Sorcerer he call me from the grave, he king of great city of Yoruba and Fon people. Leuthera born into a leopard family. By day we human, by night we prowl the forest. Leuthera grow up as princess and leopard cub. Beautiful and strong. She wear the sacred cat marks cut into her body.

Juju man say, "O incarnation of the glorious past, go forth unto the New World, find source of the bad thing that enslave this people, go forth and heal her so there don't be sickness in she soul no more."

Leuthera say, "How can me go there, me, woman, alone, weak? They a million strong, and godhood weak inside me now."

Sorcerer say, "Drink this godhood and renew your power."

In the full moon, Sorcerer lead me into the forest. Leuthera fall down on her hands and knees, sniff the ground, smell the blood of living animals. Juju man call Mawu-Lissa out of the earth and sky. Thunder and lightning come, and the river weep, and blood stream from the tree. And sorcerer cry out in a mighty voice: "Fill this woman with the eternal truth." And we like two leopard now, leaping and growling and running in the darkness, smelling the souls of the living and the dead. And me drink power from the moon and the stars, the cat power, just like in Egypt when Leuthera be Sekhmet, lioness, mother.

And me say, "Leuthera ready go forth to the white people world."

That night come raiders from the north. They slay Leuthera family, slay cattle, slay children. Take Leuthera to the sea. By the sea is great floating island made of dead trees and inside that floating island come a sound of men and women dying inside.

Me come to America at a time she call Keresimasi. Keresimasi a great celebration of a great king coming to the world, king who can raise the dead, king of great wisdom we call Shangó, and you call Jesus, both king hanging from tree to make wisdom in men.

A preacher man name Leuthera for a ancient Greek word she mean "freedom." It a big joke to him. Me work. Mammy to white baby, cook, planting woman, picking woman, me do everything. Nobody massa keep me long. Me never learn no nigger talk, no yassa massa, nosa massa. Me never bow my head. They sell Leuthera. Leuthera see this land grow green, Leuthera see the cities grow. But Leuthera never see black child getting fat, never see black man grow rich. So Leuthera pray to Mawu-Lissa: "Great god, great goddess, take me back to the cold cold earth."

In the moonlight Leuthera hear the god speak. Not the great Mawu-Lissa, but Legba, he messenger of on high, he the horned god who speak for other gods, he the guardian of the city gates.

Legba speak to me in the howling of the night wind, he say, "Do not despair, O daughter. A great work is still for you to do. The white people worship a father god but no mother god. They don't know the god-who-is-man-and-woman-all-together. That why they rejoice in the day and afraid in the night. A magic is still for you to work. A woman magic. A woman mystery. Bring forth a girl-child who will sing day into night. Bring forth a girl-child who will melt the heart of wicked man. Bring forth a girl-child who with a voice so powerful she call even the white man *egun-gun* from out their shadow country. Bring forth a girl-child who proclaim the glory of the god-who-is-man-and-woman-all-together, who sing the god name in place that never heard no god name before. Then Leuthera go home. Only then."

Me say, "But Leuthera cannot have child. Leuthera keep herself pure, never touch no man."

Legba say, "Lay yourself down naked in the dark forest, and Legba send a man to you."

Then me say, "If me give birth to this girl-child, then the black man go free?"

Legba laugh. "The universe not that simple," he say. "But you raise this girl-child. When she ready, give her into the hands of a white man stranger. Give her to the first white man who listen to your story without he make merry about it. Then, then, then, and only only then, Mawu-Lissa take you home."

And all of a sudden heaven and earth all full of he laughing, and it make my heart to soar and to sing. It remind me of the olden time when all us'ns live in the forest and all be happy. After a long time, Legba leave me alone in the forest, and me with child, and me go back to the plantation. Some say the massa make the child in me. Some say the overseer. Some say the patty-rollers which catch me alone in the forest without no pass. Nobody know that it a angel, a messenger of the man-woman she name god.

And how the angel touch Leuthera! How she tremble when the wind of Legba come down unto her secret place to plow her and plant he seed! Oh, that memory gone last Leuthera into she next life. Leuthera the earth where the storm blow, Leuthera the ocean where the fire fall. So that how Leuthera know that Leuthera child the girl-child of she vision. Not the child of some raping massa, not the pickaninny of some nigger he come to stud, but a child of god. Me hear the laughing, but me know the truth. But massa he hear the laughing, he don't know the truth, and he throw me in with a passel of bucks, and sell me at a auction.

And so Leuthera come to Marse Neezah house.

Leuthera daughter grow inside her, and she born on a Friday, so Leuthera call her Fibi. And Leuthera teach her the old ways so she be a woman of great power. And Leuthera teach her to sing the *egungun* from out of the cold earth. And Leuthera give her all the gifts that come from Mawu-Lissa. And now it time for Leuthera go home. The darkness call me. The earth call me. The bosom of Mawu-Lissa call me.

This a time of pain. This a time of grief. This a time for much weeping. No food can make me live. No whip can make me feel. The call of Mawu-Lissa like a big wind, he shake Leuthera soul. It time for Fibi to sing forth. It time for Fibi to tell the freedom song for all to hear, the black folks and the white.

You, Marse Alwishus, you the first white man to hear this story from beginning to end. You take my daughter now and let me die, cause Leuthera go back into the dark country.

3

The slave woman's narration was the most astonishing thing I had ever heard in all my born days. I knew that Negroes, like all other children of the Lord, were gifted with reason, and with free will, for such is the teaching of the church. But I had assumed that this reason was somehow clouded, buried under the burden of bondage and of Negritude itself. Certainly, Eleuthera's tale was fantastical, and couched in an unfamiliar jargon, yet it had all the cohesion of a literary creation, or of an ancient myth. Surely I had known that the Africans had gods and goddesses; yet I assumed that such were barbarous, primeval simulacra of the divine, idols of wood and stone. Why had I assumed so? It is not an assumption one makes of the Greeks and Romans. The annunciation of Legba to this crone was comprehensible to anyone who has read the Gospel of Luke, or indeed, the *Iliad*.

Insane she undoubtedly was—for I did not for a moment believe that this creature was indeed as old as creation itself, for all that she seemed to know a little something about ancient history. Perhaps one of her former masters was an amateur Egyptologist, or perhaps she had heard some savant discoursing on the subject whilst serving at table. Yet she had woven the strands of myth and history into a credible tapestry. Deluded though she might be, she was possessed in some measure of the fire of Shakespeare and Milton, and she understood me utterly, for she awakened in me a passion to free her and her daughter, and to take them with me to Connecticut, for surely, faced with such simple eloquence, none would dare deny the creed of the abolitionist.

I left that woman, still chained up, determined to win her freedom and that of her strange daughter.

The poker game was still going on, and, though I am no gambler, I ventured to sit in on it for a while. As the evening wore on, the manservants lit torches so that we could continue to play past sunset.

"You don't play, Reverend," said Ebenezer, "though I declare you've been watching the game assiduously for nigh on two hours."

"I don't really see the point of gambling, and in any case I'm not very good at it," I said. "Moreover, I'm not as wealthy as some of you; I can't afford to lose, or else I'll find myself unable to buy my passage back to Connecticut."

"Ah, but you do have something you could well afford to lose, Aloysius," said Ebenezer Judd. He indicated the book, which I had left open on a bench behind me, watched over by a scale model of the Apollo of the Belvedere. "The *Life of St. Francis*."

Suddenly, I saw what I must do. I doubted I could buy this woman's freedom—not unless I could somehow persuade my wife to give up yet another share of her much-abused dowry—but Mr. Judd was a gambling man.

"The Negress and her daughter," I said, "against that defamatory biography."

Ebenezer said, "Not the old woman. She'll be dead in a day or two anyway. And the little girl's worth less to me than the book, so you'd not be getting the best of the deal. Still, let us play."

We played. I lost. Two out of three, I suggested. I lost again. Until one of the guests—the same who had called out to Ebenezer to drive the lash harder, who had offered to pay for the spectacle of seeing a little child walloped into oblivion, took pity on me—such is the irony of these things.

Over the buffet table, helping himself to the duck terrine, my new friend, who introduced himself to me as one David Arthur Knight, said, "You best watch the old man a little more careful-like. He's got a holdout."

"A holdout?" I said, bewildered.

"A holdout!" With his foot, he indicated the space beneath the poker table. I could see Ebenezer's knees clenched tightly together. At the cuff of his trousers, belted to his shoe, there appeared to be a strip of metal.

Ebenezer wiggled his foot, and then he called out, "Three aces," and helped himself to the pot. I realized that there was some kind of contraption on his person, operated somehow by the pressure of his left foot; that hidden within his clothing there was an elaborate system of hinged metal rods which, on cue, popped extra aces out through his sleeve, which was, I now noticed, the richly ruffed variety, easily permitting concealment.

"Heavens," I said, "but he's cheating."

"They're *all* cheating," Mr. Knight said.

I looked from player to player. All had the stony demeanor that habitual poker players affect so well. Yet, if I looked closely at their attire, there were clearly things amiss. One's elbow was crooked too angularly, suggesting a metal device within the sleeve; another's kneecaps were too prominent; a third was constantly tapping his foot. Every single one of them had some kind of mechanical assistance! I must admit that in that instant I lost what little respect I had previously had for the gambling profession.

"I want to play again," I declared. "Double or nothing, or whatever it's called. I'll wager—" I desperately reached into the very bottom of my trouser pocket—"all the money I have left."

We played. I only had a pair of eights. But at the moment of truth, when all must be revealed, I delivered a sharp kick in the shin to my host, who was sitting across the table from me—the others having since folded—and he was unable to dislodge his supply of aces into his sleeve. And so it was that I not only kept possession of my scurrilous *Life*, but acquired mastery over two human souls as well.

Ebenezer took it all with a good humor. "Well," he said,

"you have certainly bested me, sir, and as always the best man has won. Do you wish to take possession at once?"

"If I may," I said.

We wandered over to where the slave woman had been chained up. But when we reached that place, the fetters were empty, and there rose from the place of her chastisement a foul odor, similar to but far more intense than the odor of an alley cat in heat; only a few smears of blood remained, soiling the plaster robes of headless Nike. In the distance, I heard a soft and menacing purr, and I wondered for a moment whether Eleuthera's claim to be a were-leopard were any more than a old woman's fanciful imagining.

"We'll find her," said Ebenezer grimly. "As for the whelp, she will await your pleasure in the morning, as she's a little young for nighttime exercises."

4

It being night, and there being only a limited number of guest apartments in Mr. Judd's Arlington townhouse, it was suggested that I share quarters with Mr. David Knight. This caused me some worry—I was not certain that I liked Mr. Knight, who had, after all, egged Ebenezer on to an ecstasy of ferocity; nevertheless, I could not refuse to bundle with a fellow guest, and I reflected that, had Mr. Knight not shown me the mechanical holdout that had enabled Ebenezer to win so handily at poker, I would not now have won the freedom of the girl. As for the old woman, it was clear that she wished only to die; I hoped that she would now understand that at least she died an emancipated woman. Where she had fled to, I dared not think. Perhaps, in their compassion, one of the other sorry bondsmen—I'm speaking of the indentured Irish—had released her from under the very noses of her tormentors.

After the poker game, there was the obligatory session of

coffee and cigars; I stayed as long as I could, but I could not feign much interest in the talk of plantation yields, of tobacco futures, of the rampant speculation in the slave trade; even when the discussion turned to secession, I did not pay much attention; for how could I know that within but a short span war would come?

Eventually the time came to retire. Mr. Knight was already in the guest room, and a maid was tending to the warming pan beneath the bed.

The maid left us, drawing the curtains around the four-poster bed, which was ostentatiously carved in a frieze of eagles, deer, and other animals characteristic of the Americas. It was a pleasant-enough guest room, with a view out into the garden; in the moonlight, I could see the Nike, the Apollo, and the water fountains that turned this little four-story town dwelling into a miniature villa of vaguely European vintage.

David Arthur Knight was already attired in his nightshirt and preparing to bundle up. He was a comely man, of firm jaw and crisp blond hair, such as any nubile young lady might fancy. Aside from the streak of cruelty he had unwittingly evinced, he seemed as much of a gentleman as existed in these southern parts.

After a few perfunctory ablutions, I disrobed and climbed in beside him, snuffing the bedside candle as I did so.

After some time, Mr. Knight said, "What an evening. I'm damned glad I showed you Ebenezer's holdout. The others daren't say anything; they're too busy cheating themselves."

"I do appreciate it," I said.

"But why, Reverend, was you so taken by that sack of dung— I mean the old mammy there—and her willful pickaninny? I could see the sport in taking the strap to them, of course, but why in heaven's name were you willing to wager a valuable book for such a baggage?"

"I . . . I really don't know," I said.

"Did you see the hateful way she looked at me?" said Mr. Knight.

"Well, considering that you were telling Mr. Judd to whip her to death—"

"Oh, that's just an expression," he said. "The darkies don't put much store by such statements. They know they are valuable chattel—by law they're both real *and* personal property—they know you ain't going to just kill 'em."

"Still," I said.

"That girl is a firebrand," he said. "Why, when she's old enough to bleed, you'll be wanting to exercise your—what is it you fancy Europeans call it?—your *droit de twat*."

"The droit de seigneur? That's been obsolete for, what, five hundred years? Besides, I'm no lord, just a humble cleric."

"I seen the lust in your eyes, Reverend. They do that to you, even the littl'uns. That's a fact. They live their lives closer to the heart of things than us. Hunger and lust are closer to the surface. You see that, don't you? You're drawn to that."

"Please, Mr. Knight—"

"Do call me David, Reverend. Considering we're trussed up in these blankets like a couple of Christmas geese. In Virginia we ain't quite as formal as you English."

"David, I'm a man of God."

"And men of God do sin, from time to time, as I hear tell," David said. "Why else would you go after a sweet little un-plucked—"

This man was making me distinctly uncomfortable. He carried on a little longer about this pickaninny's charms, but then he seemed to have put himself to sleep with his own meandering discourse. Then something even more disconcerting occurred as I lay there—David having turned in his sleep, and the weight of his body crushing my loins a little—unable to get any rest. For I found that I could not forget the sight of those empty hand- and leg-irons, that I could not erase that foul, feline odor from my memory—not the viciousness of the little girl, nor the mythic poesy of Eleuthera's story. Images from her tale kept flashing through my consciousness. The lion queen of ancient

Egypt . . . the leopard woman prowling through the jungle . . . the horned messenger of the gods making all heaven and earth ring out with savage laughter.

Then it was that I heard that purring sound once more. Close to me.

At the foot of the bed, perhaps. And the odor, faint at first, was more than a memory. It permeated the chamber. I was almost choking, yet David Knight snored unperturbed beside me.

Then I heard footsteps.

Not human. The padding tread of some wild animal. Here. On the polished oak floorplanks, which groaned and wheezed with the creature's weight. I heard breathing. Not human.

"David . . . Mr. Knight," I said softly.

He moaned; it was clear that he was dead to the world. He murmured some name; perhaps it was some beloved woman, or some comrade-in-arms. The smell was stronger now. It was exotic and bestial, and yet there was in that malodor a bizarre hint of the erotic.

I dared not draw the curtains.

Suddenly, I heard cloth rip. I turned, but as suddenly two tiny hands descended over my eyes and held me with a grip as firm as a grown man's—and a shrill childish laughter reverberated in the chamber.

"Mr. Knight—" I cried out.

The bed began to shake. An arm flailed over me. I smelled that savage musk closer now, and the bed itself was shivering with that feline purr, and then came a rhythmic thrashing. I heard Mr. Knight scream. The hands held me as I struggled, and the childish laughter crescendoed until it filled the room and drowned out the young man's cries. I could hear flesh tear now.

"Let me go!" I shouted. "I must warn someone—"

The giggling went on. And then, from right beside my ear, came the most bloodcurdling roar. Although I had tried to extricate myself, I now found that I could not move. I could not see, and the hands clasped over my eyes exuded a sweaty rheum that brought tears that stung my eyes. I was thrown against the bedpost. I hit my head, but my cry of pain died in my throat. There was, pressing down upon me, a taut and muscular presence, and though I was not the object of its wrath I could feel that it was rending through bone and tendon, shredding flesh, spattering the bedclothes and my face and arms with gore.

I am sure I would have fainted from the horror of it, but now a new sensation assailed me. The small hands still covered my eyes, but now I felt the movement of a lithe young body against my person. And now the giggling ceased, and there came an angelic singing, a thrilling, stratospheric arc of melody, wordless, that made my entire body thrum as though I were the string of a fiddle and that heavenly voice the touch of a bow. I felt—oh, God, but the remembrance of it shames me—the arousal of my flesh—felt the teasing of a little tongue over my neck, my chest, my nipples—felt an elbow dig under my nightshirt—felt little feet toying with the most private parts of my anatomy, until—despite the transport of terror I was in—I was seized with a shuddering sensual passion that shook my body and climaxed in the spilling of my seed all over myself—seed which blended with coagulating blood into a sickening, sticky ooze—oh, God, but I felt so utterly unclean, yet so simultaneously elevated to an erotic height I never dared imagine—then, all at once, the shaking, the giggling, the hands over my eyes, all of it fell still, and—

In the corner of my eye I saw a gigantic catlike shape go crashing through the window into the gardens below and—

I saw the girl Phoebe, naked, swinging from the bed curtains, ripping them down, darting to the doorway, disappearing, and—

Next to me—partly on top of me—the mutilated corpse of David Arthur Knight.

Slowly, I took in the scene. Mr. Knight's head had been completely twisted off, and lay between his legs, gazing up his torso at the severed neck stump, from which fresh blood was still welling up. One of his arms, half-chewn, lay on the floorboards.

His chest was ripped open, and his heart, which lay atop the cracked sternum, was adorned with his severed private parts. The entire body was tied up in a trail of steaming intestines. And this had all happened whilst I lay helpless in the spasms of a sexual climax. You cannot imagine what passed through my mind. Disbelief, for one thing . . . for I desperately wanted this all to be some ghastly nightmare from which I would soon awaken.

Then the angelic voice died away.

In a moment, however, there came a most fearsome banging at my door.

"Reverend Grainger!" came the cries. "Are you all right?"

The door burst open, and there came several of Ebenezer's guests, as well as some manservants with rifles. There were kerosene lamps aplenty, and I now saw that the bed was completely drenched in gore, and that I myself was covered from head to toe in the effluvia of death.

I began to panic. After all, here I was, completely unharmed, with a man's butchered body in the bed beside me, and not another soul in sight! What if somehow *I* had—

"Thank God you've been spared," said one of the servants. "Mr. David wasn't so lucky. Did you see where it went?"

He looked at the smashed window. He called several of the men over, and soon they commenced firing into the garden. I lay there, still petrified, trying to grasp the gist of what they thought was going on. Apparently some creature had been sighted. There were others dead, too . . . and our host, Ebenezer, was even now breathing his last.

I got out of bed. I threw on a dressing gown, and followed a maid down to the master bedroom. There lay Ebenezer, as soaked in blood as I was, bleeding to death. The creature had disemboweled him and left him to die in as slow and painful a manner as can be imagined; with one hand he tried to push his innards back into his abdomen, whilst with the other he gripped mine, staring into my eyes.

"Tarnation," he gasped, "that nigger *was* a were-leopard,

after all. I'll be damned! I reckon I shouldn't be saying that now, with the everlasting fire so near and all, but I'll be damned and that's the truth."

"Surely, Ebenezer, if you repent of your sins—"

"Shit, Reverend, I don't believe in deathbed conversions; I've lived a sinner and I am to die a sinner. You take care of that little girl now, if you know what's best for you; if you don't, you'll surely be ripped asunder, same as me."

There was little I could do to comfort him save hold his hand and recite the Twenty-third Psalm in a voice which I hoped would lend him some comfort.

But as I ended the psalm, I could feel the strength ebbing from him.

"Look," he said. "The angel in the doorway. Look at how dark she is. And she has a snout, like a jackal."

"But an angel nonetheless," I said, "for God does love you."

"Forgive me," he said softly. I know not whether he meant those words for God, for me, or for the ancient Negress whom he had so recently tortured, or for the dark angel that was waiting to escort him to whatever destiny awaited him in the life beyond.

Surely, as I know my Egyptian lore, he had seen no angel, but Anubis, the black, jackal-headed messenger of death; somehow it did not seem strange to me that his last vision should be, not some Christian entity, but something out of Africa.

That night, I wrote a cordial letter to my wife, explaining that I had won a little Negro girl at a game of poker, but omitting all else; I did not want to communicate to her my terror, my exaltation, or the uncontrollable lust that terror had aroused within my flesh. And in the morning, when the girl was delivered to me at the breakfast table and I found myself telling Mrs. Judd—who, you recall, had been away for the night—that a wild animal had managed to infiltrate her townhouse, I was even less disposed to remember the truth about the night's events.

I did not remain long thereafter, though I assisted with the funeral arrangements, and delivered a brief sermon at the service; and I think that the Widow Judd was glad to get rid of me, for she may have suspected that I had had, in some mysterious way, something to do with her husband's horrific demise. But she never reproached me, and even proffered me her cheek to kiss, in the continental fashion, as I departed with the girl.

5

Know then, my friends, that the truth is not always a hard-edged, shiny, and unalterable thing. I had seen many truths that night. There was the truth which must pass, in the minds of most, for the cold hard truth—that a mad old slave escaped, that men played poker, that an animal or animals invaded Mr. Judd's house and killed several people, and that I, who do not gamble, won the ownership of a recalcitrant young girl.

Then there was the Christian truth: that the woman was some kind of demon or sorceress, that she had invoked the powers of Satan to destroy her master, that she was an ungrateful chattel, a wayward daughter of Ham who had failed to understand her rightful place at the bottom of the cosmic hierarchy.

And finally there was Eleuthera's truth: that she was an ancient creature who had already lived through several incarnations, and who had given birth to some kind of Negro messiah who would redeem her people with the power of song.

She could not, of course, travel with me in the first-class carriage of the train; she was relegated to the baggage train, though I could not in all conscience keep her in irons; since I had given her her freedom as of that morning.

By Baltimore, something very peculiar was going on. I was in the dining car, enjoying a little poached salmon, when I began to hear the whispers, and one or two passengers pointed at me and looked away. At length, I made my way toward the baggage car, all the way through the squalor of the second- and third-class compartments. The nearer I got, the more hushed the passengers became, and I became aware of the same strange singing that I had heard the night of those killings. It was, in fact, little Phoebe, and she was sitting on a leather trunk, singing to herself, and the song was, oddly enough, "Amazing Grace"; the silence of the passengers was amazing, but more amazing still the fact that her song, quiet as it was, seemed to overcome the rattle of the train, the clatter of the wheels, the roar of the wind outside, seemed to draw us all into a bubble of utter stillness, in which the song was all.

And then it was that I began to understand the strange destiny that had brought this girl to me. For this song was an angel's song, for all that it issued from the lips of a darker angel. It occurred to me for the first time that though the God I worshipped was called Jehovah, and the God that the madwoman invoked had some uncouth, barbarous appellation, the two gods might not be so far apart after all. And that, I knew, was a dangerous doctrine, heretical to every possible sect of the Christian faith, anathema to those who would hold the Negro race for all eternity in thrall to the white. Yet, having been faced with it, I could not deny its veracity. God—whether he be named Mawu-Lissa or the Lord God of Hosts—was calling to me.

And so, to all of you who have shed blood in this bitter conflict, and will shed more blood, and yet more blood in the months to come—I say unto you that freedom is a cause worth dying for. I say unto you, who have come from the prairies of the west and the lakes of the north, and even from across the sea, listen to the voice of the angel of liberty. Listen, and do battle to uncage her. Listen, and know that in despair's profoundest vale, in darkness's very heart, hope abideth still.

Listen, and know that I speak truth. May the Lord bless you and keep you. In the name of the Father, and of the Son, and of the Holy Ghost. Amen.

8

WHEREIN MRS. GRAINGER BECOMES STEADILY MORE DISCOMFITED BY FRESH REVELATIONS

1

"Well, ma'am, that was just about the sum of your late husband's sermon, and right inspiring it was, for I set aside my doubts that night and resolved to fight the good fight, no longer for myself, or for poor little Rodney, but for freedom."

It was already well past midnight, and there I was, one year widowed, and learning more about my late husband from a total stranger than I had ever gleaned in my years of being wedded to him. I was not as surprised as I might have been that my husband had lied to me about some of the details of how he had acquired little Phoebe, but other inconsistencies were considerably more discomfiting. For example, I had always assumed that my husband had not been very successful in teaching Phoebe the rudiments of civilization, and that she was to him a sort of plaything, a project at which he would tinker now and then—by no means the principal vehicle by which he heard the very voice of the Almighty. How could I have thought so? I had heard Phoebe sing now and then, but snatches only, and then I thought she was merely mimicking her betters, like a superior species of chimpanzee.

I did not think I could hear more. Not tonight, at any rate. And tomorrow was the funeral parade.

"You will need your rest," I said to Zack. "I find that I have grown tired. I'm not as young as I once was, and your tale is full of confusion."

"I sure don't mean it to be, ma'am," he said.

I rang the bell for Phoebe. She did not come down; it was, on the other hand, exceptionally late, and it was her habit to arise even before me, to prepare the morning coffee. I decided to show the two men to the guest room myself. They retired, and bade me a respectful *bonne nuit.* I stood for some time on the landing, half expecting a leopard to leap down the steps, or a decapitated head to come tumbling down. But nothing of the sort occurred.

Why should it? I scolded myself. This is the year of our Lord eighteen hundred and sixty-five, and surely science has replaced superstition by now; this house is not some jungle hovel, but a solid brownstone in the heart of New York City, surely the most modern metropolis of the world; and I am no mawkish juvenile, to be deceived by ghost stories and tales of hoodoo.

And yet . . .

Had my late husband really been so much a stranger to me? Had he really had an inner life which he made known to soldiers in the field, but not to his own wife? It certainly bore reflection.

2

In the morning, I decided that I would not attend the funeral procession after all. Mr. Whitman and his friend, of course, had to go, and now that the mayor of Manhattan had relented on the Negro issue, it was clear that Phoebe, too, must be allowed to march, and I could not forbid it, nor dared I do so, considering all that I had learnt about my wayward maidservant.

While this parade was going on, curiosity overcame me. I had never before set foot in Phoebe's little garret—why would I have, indeed?—but the urge possessed me so strongly that I found myself climbing the last flight of steps and lifting the latch of my servant's private little domain.

It was dingy, and, though it was daylight, I was forced to light a lamp. Despite the gloom, there was at first nothing out of the ordinary. A slight mustiness of odor, perhaps . . . even a trace of some feline occupant . . . though I scarcely thought this meant that Phoebe was some kind of were-creature, gallivanting around Central Park on all fours in the middle of the night, attacking hobos, perhaps, or devouring street urchins. No. There was a narrow pallet next to the bed, but I had known that Phoebe disdained sheets and blankets. There was a weather-beaten Bible next to the garret window, which was so encrusted with grime that it admitted but a few speckles of daylight. Next to the window was a battered armoire that had once belonged to me, but which had suffered some damage in the journey from Connecticut.

I sat down on the bed. I looked across at the window. The dirt on the glass—was that not dried blood? Surely not.

A human skull lay at my feet.

Nonetheless, I told myself, it's only a dead thing, it cannot harm you.

I bent down and gingerly touched it. Then I lifted it up. It was more than a skull; the cranium had been sawn open, and the inside lined with some sort of glazed porcelain to render it waterproof. A foul liquid clung to the bowl, and there were little pieces floating in it, including something resembling the eye of a small creature, and the tail of a reptile. Quickly I put it back down and made to leave the room. But once again, curiosity got the better of me.

I peered beneath the bed.

There were other skulls there—not human—and bottles of garishly colored unguents. There were feathers. There were a few statuettes with bloated heads or deformed stomach, ghastly to behold. There was also a large chest or ottoman, such as one might use to keep old blankets or rarely used clothes. Unable to control myself, I dragged it out. It was unlocked.

Within were letters, nothing but letters. Many were not even written in English, but in some outlandish system of hiero-glyphics. One or two appeared to be in Mr. Grainger's hand-writing; I feared to look at them in case some other dark secret of his might be revealed. There was also a letter in a firm, bold hand that seemed to be addressed to my husband, the address, on the top left-hand corner of the page, gave me pause, for it read:

The White House
1600 Pennsylvania Avenue

and was dated the 3rd of February, 1864. My husband's death had occurred not long thereafter. How was it that a letter from the White House was hidden in my maidservant's attic room? Why had I, Mr. Grainger's lawfully wedded wife, not been privy to such an epistle? I could not but read further.

My Dear Aloysius (it began)
   Was much moved by the performance of your dusky nightingale. I think, as you do, that there has been a certain Divine Purpose in your presenting the young Negress to us, and am much inclined to believe that Emancipation will now proceed.

Had my late husband been more than an admirer of the dead president, but an actual participant in his decision making, an advisor on policy? There was a section that mentioned "your wife's delicate sensibilities" and urged secrecy; was that the reason I had been told nothing? I skimmed through the rest of the letter, which consisted mostly of pleasantries, but I was stunned by the final paragraph:

> *As to your contention that there is, behind the mumbo jumbo of African superstition, some gleaning of the wisdom of the ancients, and even some knowledge of the lost art of resurrecting the dead, I have my own advisors on the matter, and would suggest that you correspond with a certain free person of color, by name Madame Laveau, of New Orleans, who claims to have miraculously returned from the dead in a manner not unlike that of Our Lord; I would deem it blasphemy did it not issue from a source so impoverished in the blessings of Divine Providence and so deeply entrenched in the Primeval Despond of Savage Ignorance. And yet, sir, the story is perhaps deserving of investigation, and I would be most interested in what you might be able to discover.*
>
> *I remain, sir,*
> *Yours Faithfully,*
>
> *A.L.*

What in the name of God was that about? Had President Lincoln professed a secret interest in the occult, and had my husband—and my enigmatic maid—been one of many conduits to such information? Who was this Madame Laveau, and was she in fact an example of what Mr. Whitman had referred to as a *zombi*—a member of the living dead? Was A.L. indeed the president himself, or some imposter, availing himself of some proximity to that high office?

More feverishly now, I rifled through the other papers. The

notes in my late husband's writing were hard to decipher. I read isolated fragments such as: "Breakthrough attempted with P." . . . and lists of nonsensical words such as:

Babalu-ayé
Damballah
Koulèv

including some lists that appeared to search for equivalences, as in:

Legba = Eleggua (??) question Laveau

and then a note, in capital letters:

BY NO MEANS TELL PAULA

above which was inscribed a string of incomprehensible gibberish.

The strangest was yet to come, for there were, on a series of scraps of paper, including pieces torn from notebooks, the backs of cheques, and old serviettes, a series of hand-drawn sigils:

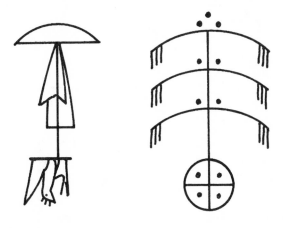

and more of the same, painstakingly written out, with tiny annotations in Mr. Grainger's handwriting, bearing such commentaries as:

> *nsibidi*—apparently a motif representing a funeral or a state of mourning
> *anaforuana*—the messenger of death

It was clear that these were notes concerning the African superstitions. That my husband, a God-fearing Christian, would be interested in such affairs was curious enough; and yet it seemed to me, from listening to Mr. Brown's narration, that my husband had undergone some epiphanic moment down in Arlington, had come face-to-face with a serious challenge to his faith, and had never seen fit to share any of it with me.

And this, to me, was strangest of all; for in all our years together I had always been the one who doubted, the one who dared not tell her spouse that she did not entirely subscribe to the cherished notions of her husband's religion. It had never occurred to me that the same things might be going through his mind.

In my whole life I had never thought myself an inquisitive woman; I had always accepted my life, and the conditions therein, with a certain equanimity. But in the last few days there had arisen in me a desire to know, as powerful as some men's need for laudanum or absinthe; and thus it was that I took the lamp and placed it by the bed, the better to discover what other ghoulish treasures lay thereunder; and the first thing I beheld, carefully drawn in the voluminous dust, was a great wheeled symbol that filled almost the entire space:

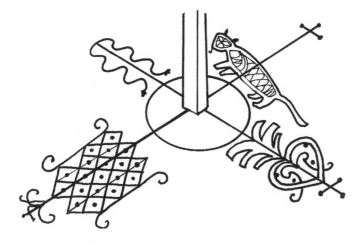

What did it represent? Some concatenation of cosmologies? Some qabbalistic symbology? I could not tell, save that the image filled me with an irrational dread, and I snatched up the kerosene lamp and sat once more upon that bed, my mind swirling with conflicts.

Presently, I heard the distant sound of a marching band, playing a solemn dirge—the funeral march of Chopin—and I wondered whether, from this high above the square, I would catch any sight at all of the procession I was missing. I did not want to remain in the room another moment; I shut the casket of my husband's letters and tried to replace it beneath the bed without disturbing the hieroglyph drawn into the dust; looked around carefully to make sure nothing was out of place; and went out onto the landing, from which a little doorway opened out onto the roof, where, on sunnier days, we hang out our laundry.

It was a barren rooftop; others have tea parties, or little vegetable gardens; I never paid much mind to ours; dusty it was, and filthy, and the few shrubberies we had kept up there in pots were all dried up.

One, in particular, attracted my notice now. It had been a rosebush once, and my husband kept it in a beautiful blue-and-white China pot that had been a gift from some Oriental worthy. The pot was cracked, and there were no roses; but there were little bottles tied to the stems with string, and here and there a curious-looking bone or feather or bundle of beads. A magpie's nest it was; and I was quick to suspect that this was Phoebe's doing, and was another exemplar of her species of magic.

I could make out Sixth Avenue in the distance; a military band was slowly making its way along the road, which was thronged with mourners. There was a slight drizzle; the damp only exacerbated my melancholy. There were, on some of the buildings, flags of the Union, flying at half mast; my brownstone, too, had a flagpole.

But what was on that flagpole gave me pause; for instead of a flag, there was, atop it, a black umbrella; and suspended beneath the umbrella a miniature frock coat, lovingly stitched out of what seemed to be the fabric from one of my late husband's garments; pointing upward at it suspended three arrows of the sort that the Indians use.

What was it? Had this humdrum brownstone townhouse in Manhattan somehow been transformed, beneath my very nose, into a hotbed of voodoo activity?

My need to know burned so fiercely within my breast that it quite extinguished all fear. If magic and witchery were afoot, surely they would not touch me. Perhaps I was not utterly pure of heart, but I did not think that the Almighty would abandon me to savagery. I resolved to question Phoebe about it all as soon as she returned from that parade. Nothing was going to stop me from getting to the bottom of all this.

I made my way down to the salon, and there I sat, looking out at the square, grimly sipping a cup of tea, waiting for the woman to return.

She did not.

3

Instead, it was Zachary Brown who came to my door. Mr. Whitman was not with him.

"Your servant, ma'am," he gasped, when I went to answer his insistent knocking. "I seem to have lost track of her."

"Where is Mr. Whitman?" Somehow I had had the feeling that the information I wanted would not be as easy to come by as questioning a recalcitrant servant.

"I don't know about him, neither, ma'am. He told me he would march with the Negroes. He didn't care what no one said about it. We agreed to meet up again at a coffee house at the corner of Broadway and Forty-seventh Street, but I waited there until closing."

"Do you think she's bolted?"

"I figure she had something to show Walt . . . Mr. Whitman, I mean. He's an easy man to distract."

"Then I suppose we shall just have to wait," I said.

"But, Widow Grainger . . ." he said, looking for all the world like a little lost child. "I could go to his place in Brooklyn to wait, but it's a mighty long walk from here, and I don't have a dime for the hackney fare."

"Don't worry," I said, and steered him toward the salon, where my tea had been getting cold. "You did, after all, know my late husband. You shall stay here whenever you like, and you shall come and go as you please. For, you know, I am a middle-aged woman and a widow, and much that would be improper were I of tender years is permissible to one who is old enough to be a young man's mother. . . ."

I sat Zack down and buttered a piece of bread for him. I did so with a certain pang of wishfulness . . . I thought of my own children, every one of them in his grave before reaching his first birthday . . . I felt a certain tenderness for this youth. How could I not? He had seen more horror in his brief time on earth than I had in my lengthier span. But it was not just tenderness that made me want to keep him. Nor was it the dread I now felt at passing the evening alone here, in a house that, after so many years, had become suddenly alien to me. It was also that demon curiosity.

"Tell me more," I said to him at last, and Zachary Brown continued his strange story, which twisted and turned like a wounded snake until I felt myself lost in a veritable labyrinth of the heart.

9

WHEREIN ZACK WANDERS IN THE WILDERNESS

1

To continue my tale (Zack said to me), well, truth to tell, ma'am, it sure does get harder and harder. I had seen one battle, suffered many nightmares on account of that one battle, and I had lost one faith and found another in the voices of a Negress and a preacher. You might say that I had lived a couple of lifetimes in them few weeks. I thought I'd seen it all, if you can understand that. Being so young and all.

Well, after Reverend Aloysius gave that stirring speech, and after I seen my first darkie, I was about ready to charge into battle one more time. The next morning I heard tell we were on our way to join with a hundred thousand other men in the Army of the Potomac. I couldn't even imagine what a hundred thousand men was like, seeing as my whole hometown had scarcely two hundred souls, if you don't count the cattle.

But on our way there, Captain Rawlins tells us, we have to do what he calls "a little grocery shopping." There's a small town, name of Hansen's Creek, and nearby a few farmhouses. Nobody left there anyway, they say, except a few niggers which we aim to liberate, emancipate, and set to work as contraband of war. Sounds good to me. Reverend Grainger's talk of the evils of slavery damn near broke my heart, and when you think about it, Rodney and Drew and all my best friends had died for something, and I was going to prove it to them, if they should chance to be looking down from heaven or limbo or wherever it was they'd gotten themselves to.

We tried to look as sharp as we could that morning. I even managed to polish my shoes with a bit of boot blacking I begged off my sergeant.

We reached Hansen's Creek in a blazing noon. It was, as promised, already deserted, and some of us was ordered to fire the town. Me and Kaczmarczyk and two others was set to foraging, and we stole us a buggy to transport whatever we could rustle up, and found us a farmhouse maybe five miles on down the road. The Johnsons, who were with us, were jaunty, and they sung all the way there, at the top of their lungs, a new song they'd learnt that day:

> *Run, ladies, run*
> *Or else we're gonna getcha,*
> *Run, ladies, run*
> *You'll never get away.*

There was a barn, but the pickings was slim: a half ham, a couple of dead rotten chickens. Not a soul in sight. There was just me and old Kaczmarczyk: the other two, Johnson and Johnson—not brothers—had gone into the house. I clomb up to the loft, and found a few more scraps: a sack of flour, and a couple three jars of molasses. I threw them down to Kaczmarczyk. Then I rooted around among the bales of straw to see what else I could dig up.

"Well, at least we liberated a few dead animals," I shouted down. "I guess the slaves have all run off."

The straw was taller than a man, and stacked real close. I poked it with the bayonet. Sometimes the secesh were clever about hiding things. Didn't find much in the first few piles, so I started stabbing more vigorous, maybe because I was all fired up from the Reverend's little sermon, maybe because I was still full of anger over Rodney and Drew and all them friends of mine.

So I stabbed and I stabbed and presently I felt the blade sliding into something soft, and I parted the straw and there was a little black girl, naked as the day she was born, and I had just tore open her throat and she sort of stared back at me, dying, with that same look of surprise I'd seen on poor old Drew, and then she fell forward into my arms and died.

I stepped back. Damn near fell off the loft. Her feet were shackled and someone else was attached to the chains. When I tugged on them, another little creature come crawling out, no more'n about nine year old. And he was chained to another kid, and so on, and so on, and there was about a dozen of them all fettered up inside of them bales, and the one on the end was an old mammy, bare-ass naked herself, with the kind of tits that hang down and swing back and forth. You see them in woodcuts of African savages.

"Don't kill me, massa," she said. And looked at me all forlorn and pitiful-like, and I thought on what the Reverend Aloysius had said, and I wanted to make her understand that I wasn't about to do her no harm, that killing that child had been nothing but an accident.

"It's fine," I said, "we ain't here to kill no one, just to collect food. And you're free. You've been emancipated . . . do you understand that? You are free to go."

"What you mean," said the old woman, "we free? Free to do what?"

The children began whining and gathering around their deceased companion, prodding and poking her like she was some kind of dead snake lying in the road.

I hollered down, "Kaczmarczyk—we need to strike off a few fetters up here."

Kaczmarczyk went looking for tools, I guess, and I found myself facing the old woman and the kids, who was all bone thin and covered with sores, and there were flies buzzing around them, but they didn't even have the strength to slap at them. They must have been hungry and thirsty, but they didn't ask for drink or victuals. They just stared into the empty air.

"Don't worry about a thing," I said, because I could feel their silence weighing down on me, and I had to fill the air with some kind of chatter, "we'll soon have you fed and get you on your way toward freedom."

"And what we gone do with this freedom?" the old woman said.

"Why, ma'am," I said, "you can do anything you wish. Open a little shop, get a respectable job as a ladies' maid, if domestic service is your calling, and leastways get paid for what you were doing for free before; learn a trade; perhaps even sing," I added, thinking about that Phoebe girl. But I had to admit that though I said those words, and meant them to comfort her, I couldn't imagine this woman doing any of them things. Learn a trade? Why, there weren't many trades a woman was good for, and what call would there be for a darkie lady of the night?

And she knew that my words were empty, because she said, "Can't teach a old dog new tricks. Don't savvy freedom, never had no freedom, don't savvy what to do with this blame freedom you yankees allus talks about. I been a mammy once, and now my teats run dry. I done picked crops before, but now these old fingers they a-aching. Slave don't need to work for finding food. Food come all by himself."

"And what were you doing chained up like this, stacked up with the straw?"

"Massa put us here. He don't want us darkies working for the yankees, don't want us become contraband of war. He say, we good as gold, as buried treasure."

Presently Kaczmarczyk come climbing up into the loft and we struck off them chains, but the slaves just sat there.

"Tell us vere de food is," Kaczmarczyk said.

The old mammy shook her head. He slapped her face.

"Kaczmarczyk!" I said.

"Just following orders," he said. "Go to farmhouses. Find food. You there, little boy, vere's food?"

He continued interrogating them for a while, but they didn't say much. Though they were alive, something had knocked the life out of them. At length, he said, "They not going to say nothing. Let's go to the main house and see how the others are doing."

We left the barn and walked over to the main house. The strangest thing was, that old mammy and her littl'uns got in line behind me, and they follered me all the way there, with them glazed eyes staring straight ahead like they were they walking dead.

Presently, we heard another strain of "Run, ladies, run" come out of inside the main house. As we reached the façade, a portly white woman in a nightgown come running out onto the porch, and those two privates who was both named Johnson come running after. She tripped and they grabbed, and they had her bent double over the porch railing and were ripping off that gown. Right frilly it was, like a lace tablecloth. I caught sight of one of her teats, which was swollen and blue; so I figured the Johnsons already roughed her up a bit. Her hair was undone, and it dangled all the way down to the mud.

"Get your hands off me, you filthy yankees!" she screamed. "I'm a respectable woman. Wait till my husband gets home!"

Well, the elder Johnson dropped his trousers to his ankles

and he began plowing her right then and there, in broad day-light, never mind that there was a mite too much meat on her. Johnson the younger, tall and lanky with pale blond mutton chops and a fancy French mustache, helped hold her down while his namesake fairly laid into that secesh factotum, grinning ear to ear, and only two teeth to show for it.

Well, at this exhibition of yankee manhood, the old mammy gets a crazed look in her eye, and for the first time she shows a little life.

"You touch the missus, you white trash scum, and old Mammy whup the living shit out of you," she cried, and then made a berserk rush for the two Johnsons, flinging herself on the elder one, and dislodging his cock from her quim with a blow of her fat fist.

"Another woman of sorts," the elder Johnson said, laughing. "Here, Sam, you dadblame fuckster, try a piece of the dark meat . . . plenty to go around."

"Ain't fucking that sack of shit," said the younger Johnson. He twirled his mustache with one hand and with the other pointed his Colt at the mistress's forehead. "I'll wait for the pricier cut of meat, if you don't mind."

"Don't interfere, Mammy," the white woman gasped. "There's nothing to be done." The elder Johnson slapped her into silence and began to have at her again, grunting.

The mammy waddled right up to him and fetched him a clout over the ear. "No yankee gone touch my missus. These teats done give her suck, these arms done hold her when she a baby." And she began to flail about, now and then landing a blow, with a fierce desperate energy.

I was still full of old Reverend Aloysius's noble sentiments. So I tried to pry her away. "Woman," I said, "we came to liberate you, not to harm you. That woman is a wicked slaveowner. She kept you in chains in the barn; if we hadn't of found you, you'd be dead. Now you're free."

"Don't want no freedom," said the woman. She began to

pummel my chest in a grand hysteria. I was taken aback and I fell back against the screen door, but before I could make her see reason, I heard a bang. The younger Johnson had shot her in the head, and her blood and brains came spattering all over the shirt I'd spent all morning pressing.

"What did you do that for?" I began.

But that one shot put the others in a shooting frenzy, and the kids, like a pack of horses, got themselves spooked, and began screaming and screaming, but pretty soon they were all dead, including the white woman, which the younger Johnson insisted on fucking anyway, for all that the life was draining out of her.

And as the blood come spewing out of the little dead darkies, the two Johnsons burst into another verse of the song, which they sung as heartily as if they was marching down the pike, or chopping wood:

> *I know a girl who lives up the hill*
> *If she don't fuck me, her sister will*
> *And if her sister can't be had*
> *She's a mother back home that ain't so bad.*

"What the hell are you doing that for?" I screamed.

"Shut up, fuckster," said the younger Johnson. "She's still warm."

I couldn't bear to look, ma'am, that's the truth, and I've seen some pretty rough doings. I've seen a hanging. I've seen a man scalped. But I couldn't stomach this no more. Slowly I turned and started to walk away from the porch. Kaczmarczyk come running after me. "For vat do you valk away?" he said. "You tink you better than us?"

"We came to free those people."

"People, schmeeple," said Kaczmarczyk. "This is war. I seen tings, much vorser tings than this. Back in the old homeland. Across the sea. Some people a hell vorse off than the Negroes."

"We come to free them, Kaz," I said, "and they didn't even

want to be freed. And then we killed them. What kind of liberators are we, you reckon? I'm mighty confused about it is all."

"They vas already dead," he said. "Dead inside. Just varm bodies, valking. No guilt in it. Hell, no guilt for you, nohow. You didn't even fire a shot."

"What about the secesh woman? Why did she have to—"

"This is var," said Kaczmarczyk, and his eyes were far away, gazing on another country.

2

The way I heard it, the campaign we were joining up with was called the Wilderness Campaign, and it was led by General Grant or General Meade—I never did get that straight, and maybe they didn't, neither, 'cause rumor had it they never agreed on anything. Though our little foraging expedition had turned up but little in the way of provender, some of our friends fared better. One even turned up with twenty cows. This was a rare thing, because—the way we heard it—the secesh was on their last legs, and many were starving.

We just kept on walking down that road—a narrow one it was, barely wide enough for our cannon—and the army just kept getting bigger and bigger as more divisions joined up with us. You can't imagine the sight, ma'am, unless you was there in person. No matter if you squinted all the way to the horizon, that line of men never stopped. No matter if you were marching uphill and looked down and the road snaking up to the north and you'd expect to see an end of the army, somewhere way out there, well, there was no end of it. The weather was sultrier than I'd ever imagined and the sweat just drenched our clothes, and the skeeters come by night and drove us damn near out of our minds, and every night more men came down with the chills, or the flux, or them spells of coughing, coughing up blood some of them. Marching, we sang the same songs till our throats were raw.

Because everyone I come down from Nebraska with was dead, I ended up sticking close to Kaczmarczyk. He didn't talk much, and I didn't care to hear no talk. In my mind, I couldn't balance up the pictures in my mind: the army the great liberator, the slave that refused to get liberated—the Reverend Grainger's Negress and the mammy in the farmhouse—the white woman jerking and shuddering as the Johnsons diddled her dying flesh—the pickaninnies dropping like a stack of ninepins—and Drew's face staring at me out of the mud—and Rodney's voice in my nightmares.

We come swooping down the Orange-Fredericksburg Pike and spread out into the forest. You think, ma'am, that men fight by day and rest by night, but in the wilderness, day *was* night. The first battle lasted two days I think, and it seemed like one perpetual night. The fog never settled and we all battled against shadows, for we couldn't see nothing until that nothing burst out of the trees or the mist and hurled itself at our face. They told us we had twice as many men as the rebs, so we probably killed many of our own. I could sit here all night and speak of the mountains of dead men, the horrible screams of the wounded and the smoke that made us to fight through our streaming tears, but I don't want to think on it too much, not if I don't need to. Hillocks of dead leaves caught fire and the forest itself was blazing for miles around us, and sometimes we just piled up a passel of dead men and used them for breastworks. Seventeen thousand of us died in that one battle, I heard tell.

How did I manage to live? In the heart of it I fell into a kind of daze. I was thinking that hell itself couldn't be no worse than this. Kaz and I were cut off and surrounded. And then, above the shrieks of the dying and the thundering and the whistling and the drumming, I heard something else . . . the beating of wings. I look up at the swirling smoke and I see something that might be a face, maybe even Rodney's face, and I hear a faint whisper in my ear, "Run to me, Zacko, and don't look back."

"What the hell do you want from me?" I shouted, but no one heard me.

Rodney said, "I want you to stay alive a couple more moments."

And all of a sudden I start running with my bayonet held out in a thrusting position, and at that moment an explosion rips through the ground right where I was standing and I keep running right on into the thick of the rebs, and I guess I shocked them so much I breached the whole line of them, and my comrades come pouring through that breach and soon we're up to our elbows in blood. Seventeen thousand dead. Lord. And not a scratch on me. All that blood other men's.

In my dreams, the battle went on. With Rodney drumming still, and calling my name, and telling me that beyond the next hill, behind the next tree, another country was waiting for me.

Came another battle, and another. Thirteen thousand Union dead at one, ten thousand at another. I saw Grant once. He wore a plain soldier's blouse and his buttons was all undone, and his stripes just pinned on to his sleeve, and he rode among the wounded, counting them up like a miser counting his pennies. Some of the men complained that he should shine himself up a little brighter, set a good example or something, but it never bothered me none. I mean, he was the general. He could dress any way he damn pleased to.

Well, the wilderness was like that old story of the labyrinth. We just wandered and wandered, and even though we lost thousands and thousands of boys, more boys come in fresh from the north to reinforce us, and nobody come to reinforce General Lee—least that's how the story went, though I doubt it was that simple—by now, I knowed that half the stories we heard was put there to make us feel more comfortable-like, so that we wouldn't mind getting ourselves kilt so much, though by now it wasn't so much the being dead we didn't like, it was the dying.

It was in the fourth battle, I guess. I took a bullet in the gut somewhere. Don't remember it much. One moment I was standing there, reloading, the next I was lying in a wagon, and most of the people in the wagon looked dead, or not long for this earth at least. I was about three corpses under, and I didn't feel no pain when I come to; I thought that but a minute had passed.

Then I heard Captain Rawlins and someone else talking . . . taking stock of the wounded I think.

"That one's moving," he said. "Pull him off."

"Pull that one off the vagon!" I heard. So Kaczmarczyk was part of this grisly detail.

I felt something wiggling way up there. Somebody's hand was over my mouth, and oozing gore into my nose. I couldn't scream. If I did, I was going to have to suck in a mouthful of another man's blood.

"Underneath . . . over to the side." The captain again, I guess. I felt more movement. Somewhere around my feet. The bodies shifted and I felt myself getting closer to the surface. I could see a little piece of air now, maybe an inch around. "Is that all?" said the captain.

"Looks like it, sir," said Kaczmarczyk.

"Bury the rest, private."

If I didn't do nothing, I was going to end up in a shallow grave. I summoned all the strength I had left—and I was feeling might poorly—and I guess you could say I rocked back and forth a little, enough to dislodge someone from off my chest and to come up to the surface like a dolphin breaching a tide of blood.

"Hold on!" Kaczmarczyk shouted. "There's vun more!"

I felt hands grabbing ahold of my ankles and tugging. Then the pain hit me once again, and everything went black. But not before I saw Kaczmarczyk's face . . . what was left of it.

3

The next thing I saw was that selfsame face, so I knew it wasn't no dream. But this time it was a little more pretty, 'cause they wrapped a bandage around most of it, and the good side of his face looked more or less normal.

We were on a train, and winding up to Washington, where many of the wounded was like to end up. And every time them wheels went around came a stab of pain in my side. I was trussed up in bandages and I couldn't move. I couldn't even shit. The compartment was third class I think, and crammed with sick men, and a few pigs and chickens besides. The only hale man there was someone in handcuffs that they sent up to be court-martialed. They could have just shot him, I suppose, but maybe it was too heinous a crime to warrant getting shot on the spot.

"I didn't know we held the railroad up from Fredericksburg," I said.

Kaczmarczyk laughed. "You been dead to the world a long time," he said. "Ve take a zigzag route . . . rail, cart, whatever . . . sometimes ve steal a train."

"It hurts," I said.

"Don't vorry, lad," said Kaz, who aside from only having half a face was as whole a man as you could find on board that train. "They gonna take care of you by that hospital, and I'll be vith you for a vile longer. They say I'm useless now. Stupid. I can fight as well as any two-eyed man."

I took a few sips of water and passed into the darkness again. The wilderness of my dreams . . .

My mother gave me a kiss and a loaf of bread, and she said to me, "Try to come back in one piece, son . . . and watch over Rodney, he don't have no one."

In all the time since General Custer come to our town, I never thought on my parents, but now, in my dreams, they are there. In the forest. Spirits. Speaking to me from rock and tree and stream. My friend Wamdi told me that rock and tree and stream can speak to you. He died. I told you that, didn't I, ma'am? The grippe. Or was it the measles? I forget now. Some white man's sickness though, I think.

A kiss and a loaf of bread . . .

. . . Rodney coming to me out of the clouds, and . . .

Rock and tree and stream.

And in my dreams I'm thinking . . . it's mighty queer, but rock and tree and stream seem bursting with life, and real people, living, breathing, seem like to the dead. . . .

General Grant riding past, unkempt and uncleaned . . . a dead man on horseback.

"Shall I tell you a bedtime story?" Kaczmarczyk said to me, so softly I thought his voice was the sighing of the ungreased couplers between the cars. "Once, you know, in another country, I too had a child, I too told stories, I too knew right from wrong. But that vas long ago, and far avay."

"Are you my mother?" I whispered, and tasted the fresh-baked loaf between my teeth, and the hard crust crunching into sweetness. When would there be another loaf of bread like that? I tasted salt on my lips. I guess the memory brung me to tears.

Somewhere, a boy whistled. The tune was "Run, ladies, run." So in my mind I seen that fat lady from the farm again, more clearly now than ever I seen her in real life; her lower body jerking up and down like a hopping bunny, and the brains caking around the hole in her head.

"Your mother's far from here," said Kaczmarczyk. An eerie wheeze come out of his mouth whenever he spoke. I think the blast that wounded him must have done something to his windpipe. "Do you vant that story?"

"Sure."

The whistle blew. The ratchet-ratchet-ratchet of the trains lulled me. The stale air stank of pus. It was night. The wind through the window was moist. It clung to the shreds of my blouse and plastered my trousers to my ass. There was a passel of linen wrapped round my belly. I thought, I'm going to die, and along, excepting for this strange man from across the ocean. And so I listened to what he had to tell me, and the tale was discomfiting to be sure, but the manner he told it, the soothing voice he told it in, like a kindly uncle to a frightened child, it comforted me some, and in times to come I thought of his tale again and again, for it had more meaning to me than he knew.

4

Once upon a time (Kaczmarczyk told me, the best I recollect it because his story wove in and out of my dreams of dying, and sometimes it wasn't even his voice that telled it, but my mother's or Rodney's, or some strange person entirely, some winged, long-haired person lit up with the kind of light that falls on you from a church window), once upon a time, there vas a beautiful queen and a just and handsome king, back in the country vere I vas borned, a beautiful fair country that vas never sullied by var or violence.

The time vas come for the queen to bear a child. A daughter she vas, her skin as white as the clouds and the snow, and her lips as red as blood and roses, and her eyes as blue as the sky and sea, and her hair as black as the bitterness of love and death. And this was the country vere I grew up, far far avay, beyond the lakes, between the mountains, vere the dead still valk by night and the living can barely live. This princess gave light and life to all of her people. When she valk through the square, the crowds parted like the sea.

There came to the palace twelve sorcerers, and gifts each vun of them presented her: vealth and beauty, fortune and pride. But the thirteenth sorcerer, Nathaniel, no invitation received he, for he vas a dveller in dark places, and they said that he spoke to Satan every Thursday night, in a cave at the foot of the mountain that guarded the entranceway to hell.

In truth Nathaniel was no follower of the darkness, but a man with a terrible pain in his heart. The pain could men see in his face, in his eyes, in the scars about his cheeks. He did not hate the light, but he hated the happiness that the light brought. And his bitterness drove him to come to the palace of the beautiful queen and the just king.

"You did not invite me to your feasting," he screamed. "I could have given you the greatest from all gifts . . . not beauty, not vealth, not health, but knowledge . . . knowledge to use all these gifts you have received . . . which are become tinsel in your hands."

And the king said, "Take avay the man and behead him, for such a man brings blight into our land."

And that was the only time the king failed to be just; and he failed because he loved his daughter; for justice is a slave always to affection.

The guards came to take Nathaniel to the dungeon. But Nathaniel screamed, "Since you vould not take knowledge, I give you death in the place of knowledge. When the princess comes of age and the first blood of woman comes, her blood vill gush until it gush no more, and she vill be drowned in her first menses, and her death vill blight the kingdom."

And they took Nathaniel to the dungeon, and they smote off his head, and they buried his head in the west, and his body in the east.

And the princess grew to the edge of being a voman.

"She cannot be allowed to come of age," said the queen.

And they sought out the most learned doctors in the land, and the best magicians, but there vas nothink could they do, though they gave her potions to keep her young, and they locked her in a tower of gold for seven years, and fed her the juice of pomegranates crushed with snow, and bathed her in virgins' blood.

On the morning that her first blood come, when she was

bathing in the spring, the blood exploded from her like a fountain. It flooded her throat, her lungs, and she suffocated and died.

They bore her body to the highest tower. On an altar of glass they put it. Under the holy relics of the gods they placed it. They brought in the cross of the Christians. The Torah did they place against her lips, thinking to vake her vith the kiss of life.

And when she died, the light and the life left the faces of the king and queen, and the people in the cities grew sad, and no more did they sing in the square by moonlight, or go courting in the gardens in spring; slowly, slowly, slowly, the country died, for it had lost its soul.

In the end vas the whole country withered away, and only remained the princess, sleeping in the topmost tower.

Buried vas Nathaniel, but he vas not dead. In time, came the vint and the rain, and the two halves of Nathaniel vas brought together, closer and closer, little by little, vhen the vint blow and the vater flow. Nathaniel knit himself back together, for he vas a powerful sorcerer, and the life flowed in him, for he had the knowledge to walk the pathway betveen life and death. The anger and the hatred had kept him yet livink.

The kingdom vas become as a vilderness, as a valley of tears. And Nathaniel vandered, vandered, vandered, till he reached that dead city and that dead castle, and saw the townsfolk and the courtiers and the king and queen; that vas become but bones, bleached bones in the desert sun. And the castle vas rubble. Only a single staircase remained, in a stairvell vidout walls, a stairvay to the sky, and there on that topmost landing lay the princess, on her altar of glass, her arms folded, her eyes closed, her flesh completely drained of blood.

In death, she yet dreamed. And in her dreams she was on a rock, girt by impenetrable fire, waiting for a mighty hero with a sword, the hero who knows not fear.

And in another dream she was a princess among the thorn

bushes, and her prince was varrink with a dragon and slashink the briars to get to her.

And in a third dream she was the spring, whom the king of the undervold had stolen, doomed for eating the seeds of the pomegranate to remain six months of the year among the shades of the dead.

Nathaniel climbed, and climbed, and climbed. The sunlight seared him. He vas full of despair. He hated vat he had done, vat he had become. His anger against the princess and the kingdom had turned over the centuries to a kind of love. Vhen he reached at last the top of the stairs and saw the princess bleached by bloodlessness, he knew that only love could bring her back.

He thrust himself upon her and knew her vith carnal passion, and his passion vas become a river of life, and he voke her from the dead vith kisses three.

And she come to life in his arms.

But as to vether they lived happy ever after, that I shall not tell you. And as to vether the kingdom prospered once again, and vether the townspeople formed themselves out of the dry bones, that is also another story.

I vill not tell you all (Kaczmarczyk told me) because you are hovering at the edge of the river yourself, and I vill not that you be pushed over. So bear vith me. Sleep now, and dream, and dream, like the princess in the tower, vaiting for the prince who is also the sorcerer of darkness.

5

And I too slept. I think I like to died. But the dreaming kept me alive. I saw everyone in my dream—I mean, everyone who was already dead: Rodney and Drew, of course, and Wamdi, and countless dead comrades—and also the figures from Kaczmarczyk's story, which was a strange, distorted telling of a fairy tale my mother done tell me when I was just a littl'un.

I don't know how long I slept for, but this is how I woke up. I was still in the dream country, and maybe lying on that altar of glass, because my bed was hard and cold. Then something touched me. Someone. Gentle. Smoothing my brow. An old hand, crusted, firm, alive.

The fingertips moved down to my cheek, rubbed away a tear that was fast drying. Faintly, faintly I heard moans and cries from all around me, and I knew they came from the land outside my dream, but I didn't want to wake yet. I wanted to feel the touch of that hand. Nathaniel the sorcerer, the prince of darkness. I guess I shuddered. The chills come on me sudden. And just as sudden, two strong arms encircled me and lifted me off of that cold, glassy bier. And something wet and warm flecked over my lips and I knew that the sorcerer was weeping for me.

Then came the kiss, slow, lingering, with the wisps of the sorcerer's beard tickling my chin a little. Such love in such a kiss. There were three kisses. The first was chaste and formal, like a father sending his son to his first day of school; the second was like a mother, comforting, a kiss to drive away pain; but the third was like a lover, and I found myself kissing back, pulling myself up out of the land of the dead.

And then there was the weight of a man over me, and I remembered me and Drew and our horseplay in the back of the church, and my manhood stirred a little, which was how I begun to come back from the place of dreaming. My eyes still wouldn't open. They were crusted over. My wounds ached. But my lips roved on, and my tongue tasted salt and gall. Oh, I knowed it was a sin, but hell couldn't be that bad; I had seen worse than fire and brimstone already; I was as damned now as I would ever be in the future, for, ma'am, as you know, I had lost my faith, and the new faith I had found from the speaking of your late husband was a faith that seemed to come more from barbaric Africa than from the teachings of a Nebraska preacher. So my tongue dove lower, seeking some place of warmth, and at length I drank of a buttery liquid, and all of a sudden I brung to mind

Kaczmarczyk's tale, and I saw that this carnal passion was become as a river of life, and that what I drunk was not some filthy man's seed, but an elixir. Oh, I cried out then, and at the moment when I too spent into my tattered, soiled undergarments, I opened my eyes and saw, by lamplight, an ancient, weather-beaten face look down upon me, with eyes as deep and placid as the infinite sea.

It was such a face, ma'am, as God might have. The white beard, the severe yet kindly gaze, and the look he had of always reinventing the world. And then he smiled.

"Oh, God," I said softly, "I have sinned."

"Don't call me God," he said, as if it were a name he was something accustomed to. "My name is Walt."

10

IN WHICH ZACK, TOO, IN HIS OWN WAY, ENCOUNTERS THE ALMIGHTY

1

It was night when I awoke, and the place I found myself in, I learned later, was a hospital, though it had once been a popish church. The man who woke me was not God, but a poet. But he gave me such proof of love, ma'am, as God never did. And so, I may say that the Almighty spoke to me through him.

"Don't speak to me of sin," Walt said. "There are thousands ready enough to cast the first stone; you don't need to do it to yourself."

"But—" I said.

"This is another time," said the old man. "Don't be afraid. You've been in hell already."

"How did you know?" I said.

"I know," said Walt Whitman. "I just know, camerado."

How? I wondered. He hadn't been there when I saw Drew's head fly off. He wasn't there when Rodney disappeared into the forest. But I knew that somehow he had seen those things through my eyes. He was a sorcerer.

I also wondered—

"Your friend, Private Kaczmarczyk," said Walt, "is lying on the next pallet. He's doing poorly, they say. But you, you they say will recover."

And so I did. I mended. I came back to the world. And in time I wrote to my mother, and I told her I was well. But I didn't talk about the horror none. She deserved better than to know. If the truth's gonna hurt too much, I say don't tell it, that's what I say.

Not two feet from my bed lay Kaz, and he was dying, for all that he claimed he was fit to fight and only traveled to Washington to bring me to the hospital. If I sat up on my bed, I could see him, never moving, barely breathing. They lifted his head once or twice a day and poured some kind of broth down his throat, and it seemed to stay down. Sometimes I called out to him, but he didn't answer.

One time I said, "Kaz, you can't die . . . or else you'll never finish telling me that story you started. . . ."

I think his eyes fluttered a little. Or his breathing quickened. But I ain't sure. Sometimes he just stared up at the ceiling, blinking once in a while, every five or six minutes.

Walt Whitman come around to my bedside every day. He told me he come on the trolley, and he boarded at a rooming house, and that he was really from Brooklyn. He washed me and he emptied my shit-pan. I was like a little child and sometimes he was a mother to me, and sometimes a father, and sometimes, truth to say, a partner in what some call sin.

When I was well enough to walk a little, he helped me up and he showed me the street outside the church, which ran alongside the river so you could see Virginia on the farther side. Virginia, the enemy; but from where we stood nothing but green, with now and then a steeple peering from the foliage, or a boathouse by the river's edge. No smoke, no piles of corpses, no cannon pointed in our faces.

I grew stronger, but Kaczmarczyk was fast fading away. It was sad, 'cause I grown to love that crusty man, and he had suffered more than he ever told any of us. The doctors didn't give him long for this world, but I always sat by his bedside and whispered in his ear, "Fight, fight, Kaz . . . you can do it, you can come back, there's still people here what's waiting on you."

But one day, Walt said something that chilled me: he said, "Maybe it's fate, Zack, that the better you get, the worse he gets."

"What makes you think that?" I said.

"It's in a sound," Walt said. "Listen. Say Zack, Zack, Zack." I did. "Now say it backwards. . . ."

"Kaz," I said. "Oh . . . sweet Jesus."

"There was nothing to what I said at all," Walt said, "no logic, no cause and effect. A name is a random thing. What's in one? as a better man once said. Yet when I uttered that connection, it suddenly became a thing of power. Did you hear that? Suddenly, your souls, your very lifelines, knit themselves together across the vortex of history. Just the mere utterance of those two syllables have created the linkage. That, Zack, is where magic comes from, I'm convinced of that."

Behind the church, there was a graveyard; every morning at sunup I come to take the sunrise, and they brung Kaczmarczyk out too, and laid him out on the dewy grass. Walt would meet me there and he would speak his poetry, which was writ in a notebook. It wasn't nothing like what he had to read in Mrs. Miller's schoolhouse though. None of them flowers and maidens skipping through the fields. Nothing foreign about it neither. It was America speaking to me, America herself. And not the America I had been walking through, the America that warred against itself, but America, a single, great, compassionate spirit.

I heard that the ancients believed that every creek, tree, mountain . . . every city, every country had its genius, the spirit that
lent it life, and why, Walt's voice was the genius of America.

A damn shame nobody seemed to know it but this no-good
prairie boy.

We spoke of many things, and yes, we sinned. But it didn't
seem like much of a sin to me, and the way Walt explained it, it
was something as natural as them creeks, trees, mountains of
America. So I stopped worrying myself about it, and I gave myself to the old man, as free and openhearted as if I was giving
myself to God. It didn't seem like an evil thing, to slip behind the
gravestones, before the dawn. I guess it sounds mighty blasphemous to you, ma'am, and you a preacher's wife, but there's a lot
more to the world than what preachers talk about. . . .

Between the Reverend Jones back home and the Reverend
Grainger in the wilderness, I thought I'd seen preachers aplenty,
from one end of saintliness to the other.

But about two weeks after I woke up in that hospital, sitting
out on the grass like we always done, though, I heard some of
my fellow wounded talking about yet another preacher.

"From way down south," said a boy named Tyler Tyler, who
had no arms left, and had to be fed by one of us. "It's a kid our
age, and his paw, 'scaped north across the river, and they're
preaching and healing the sick."

"Some people just can't never be healed," said Morgan, from
Connecticut, who had a leg gone.

"But Evelyn, the Negress who cleans my wounds every Sunday, she says that this preacher's even been known to raise the
dead," said Tyler Tyler, in between bites of beef jerky that I held
out to him in my hand. Tyler Tyler lost one arm on the way to
Andersonville, and another on the way out. While he was *in* Andersonville, he lost almost everything else too, body and soul. He
was thin as a skeleton. What did he hope to find? "He's got a
tent set up outside Bethesda. It's just half a day away." He rolled

a piece of jerky around in his mouth, savoring the taste. Sometimes there wasn't no one to feed him for a day or so. We all got problems of our own, we don't think sometimes.

"You ain't aiming to grow new arms, I hope," I said. "Morgan's right, even if it sounds cruel."

"I know there ain't no cure for what I got," said Tyler Tyler, "but what about when a man just lies there, and he might as well be dead?" And with his chin he pointed at Kaz, who hadn't moved, but lay on top of the horse blanket, in the grass, staring straight ahead.

But it was Walt who said, "Remember, Zack, what I told you about words? How we weave them into fabric of such tensile strength that it can become the fabric of the cosmos? Remember, Zack, even in the Gospels, God and a Word are equated. . . ."

"Are you saying there might be something to this talk of resurrection?" I said.

But Walt merely smiled, and looked at me with them deep eyes, and I thought I could see the beginning of a new poem surface in his head, like a dolphin breaching the sea.

2

It wasn't no church like I ever seen before. Me and Tyler Tyler and Walt, we took Kaz over there in a makeshift mule-drawn litter. There is an island in the river, west of Georgetown, and if you want to be truthful about it, that island is in Virginia, and so was, so to speak, on enemy turf; but it weren't nothing but trees, and reachable by only by a ferry worked by a ruddy-faced old man who, seeing us approach, and our uniforms, began croaking out "The Battle Hymn of the Republic" in a wheezy, tuneless voice.

"You'll be coming for the meeting, I reckon," he said to us, looking us over, and collecting one penny from each of us for our journey. "That's there and back," he added, "a penny there and back. Folks comes here with their pockets full, and goes home penniless, so I get the half-cent, each direction, right before you gets on."

When we reached the dock, the ferryman pointed vaguely in the direction of the woods. Me and Walt and Tyler and the mule with its travois, we just followed the only pathway, and pretty soon we were surrounded by a mass of cottonwoods. We just followed that path a bit further and reached a clearing where a tent was set up. There was a line of people standing patiently, not speaking a word. There was soldiers here and there—rebs and yankees together, and nary a one of them glaring down another, or picking a fight; it was a kind of neutral ground, this clearing, and we knew that here, in this little space, the war was suspended.

Walt said, "Look, Zack. In this small circle, all men still are brothers. Would that the world were so."

"He's charmed them into silence," I said. "But that don't mean he can raise the dead."

"I'm hungry," said Tyler fretfully, and I fed him a piece of jerky and gave him a swallow of my canteen. He kept peering at that tent, and I know he was hoping against hope for a thing that couldn't be. And that was a miracle in itself; for I had heard that Andersonville killed all hope in a man, and that those who came out of there alive lost all their humanness, and were for evermore little more than animals.

Kaczmarczyk did not stir. We found places in the line, which inched slowly forward. Someone had lit a fire, and a woman was playing on a dulcimer, and singing an old folk song that went:

> *Tis the gift to be simple,*
> *Tis the gift to be free.*

But from within that tent came a sound of drumming; and it wasn't the dry, rhythmic drumming of a drummer boy, but a chaotic pounding; it had somewhat of a sound of Africa to it, at least to my way of thinking. From the other side of the tent, another line was exiting; these were solemn-faced people, who looked like they had had a thorough soaking in scripture, and I knew well how preachers could be with their constant harping on damnation and sinfulness; but there was a quiet pride in the way they held their heads up. No cripples dancing around waving their crutches and screaming hallelujah. No blind men protesting that they could suddenly see, yet colliding into trees and tripping over stones. I had seen such meetings before, but this was different.

The line moved very slowly, and it come upon midafternoon before we approached within a yard or two of the tent flap, and could more readily hear what was happening. The drumming was louder yet, and I could see its source now; for the tent was dimly lit by candlelight, and there was a dozen or so darkies, big burly ones, banging away at these drums, and flailing at hollow logs, and they was bare-ass naked, the lot of them, save for a strip of bright white loincloth that made their nakedness even more noticeable, sitting at the tent flap and kicking up a ruckus and blocking the view.

"Magnificent creatures!" Walt cried. "The sheen of sweat on sable skin in the flickering candlelight . . . I will not soon forget it. . . ."

"But," said Tyler Tyler, "what's a passel of nekkid niggers doing in a house of God?" And he looked more and more nervous; I, who expected nothing, wasn't really bothered by it.

"That," said Walt, "is the most magnificent thing of all."

"But Walt," said Tyler, "it just ain't civilized."

"Who's to say," said Walt, "that we have a monopoly on civilization? Did not Africa produce the pyramids?"

Well, Walt believed in the brotherhood of man, and he really meant it too, blacks and Chinamen and all—I never saw a man less compromising than he.

I noticed then that behind that smell of candles and incense was another stench, rank, like a cat in heat. And now and then I heard some animal growling. Like a lion or a tiger. Not that I'd ever heard one before, but it's what I imagined it to be.

Well, the drumming continued and we moved closer and closer to the entrance, and by now it was creeping up to sundown and Tyler had to be fed again. And the truth is, I was impatient to leave, except that I was so entranced by Walt's entrancement; this whole affair, silly though it was to someone who had seen every side of religion and knew its trickeries, had a kind of magic for him; and I couldn't begrudge him his little pleasures. Having endured his little talks about the power in the word, and the godliness in the word—knowing from his own curious, rhymeless verses that he could call upon a rhythm in English that was as primeval as this barbarous drumming—I also found that I loved them eccentricities of his, and I come to miss them whenever he tried to act more normal-like.

Right at the doorway, though, I looked back at Kaz, who was lying on the travois, and I thought, there really ain't no hope for him; and I bent down and slapped his cheek a little, and I was pretty sure he wasn't even breathing.

"Tyler," I said, "I think we're too late."

"No," Tyler said, "he ain't dead yet. Sometimes we're too quick to say dead. It's laziness, that's what it is. A man gets shot, you toss him on the heap of corpses, you don't even care if he's still twitching—"

I knew then that Tyler was reliving something that happened to him. By insisting on dragging Kaczmarczyk out here, he was maybe trying to pay back fate for making him what he was. I wondered if Tyler ever thought it would be better for them to have left him there to die. Did he ever, in that Andersonville hellhole, dream himself back into the heap of corpses? Was it some kind of guilt that made him want to save Kaczmarczyk so much?

"Listen," I said, "twitching is one thing, but Kaz ain't even breathing."

"We come this far already," Tyler said. And looked away.

I looked to Walt to be on my side, but I knowed he would want to see what was in the tent, regardless of what happened to Kaz or Tyler or, if I were honest about it, me even; he was a man who had to know things, had to touch, feel, smell—had to fuck things, sometimes, just because they were there.

"He's *dead,* friends," I said.

"Stating the obvious," said Tyler, "don't make it true."

And Walt just put his arms around me, and whispered in my ear, "Bear with him, camerado; he suffers for us all."

At length we crossed the threshold and were within the tent itself. It took some time for my eyes to adjust to the dimness. There was maybe a thousand candles in that space, set up in glass jars—enough candles to out-popery the pope. There was incense, too, incense everywhere; from censers, from broken pots, from old cigar boxes, incense smoking up everything; that's one reason we hadn't been able to see much from the outside.

The floor of the tent was them expensive Persian rugs that I'd seen get looted away from many a Southern mansion. Squatting on that floor was maybe a hundred people, and they were a sickly lot; some had an arm or a leg off, some had a pox or a leprosy or a strange swelling, and some was coughing up blood. And—this was very strange to me—there was a lot of darkies in that tent, many of them wearing nothing but their own bare skins, and they was rocking back and forth to the crazy rhythms of the drums, and waving their arms in the air, and rolling their eyes.

At this sight, Tyler got frightened, I think. He said, "We could go home if you wanted to, Zack," to me, and to Walt, more urgently, "and maybe out of respect for Mr. Whitman's years, we should let him rest."

But Walt was rocking right along with them drums, and seemed to keep time with them; he actually seemed to understand their rhythms. And pretty soon he starts a-dancing up a

storm, prancing and cavorting right along with the niggers. And
he was not a young man, you understand, ma'am, so I became
worried he might fall into a faint, and none of us had smelling
salts handy.

But who, then, was the preacher, or rather the two preachers, father and son, that they were talking about in the hospital?
All we could see were the sick and the frenzied dancing darkies,
who went among the sick now, making mystical passes about
their heads, leaping over them that was too weak to sit, somer-
saulting and cartwheeling amongst them. Then, when my eyes
grew even more used to the dimness, I saw at last into the center of the tent. There was a crude circle drawn, in a white chalky
powder, and inside the circle was painted, in a jittery hand, in
white paint, a four-sided symbol that seemed to shriek out
"Hoodoo, hoodoo" to all who looked on it. I can't even describe that symbol, ma'am, except to say that it seemed to have
animals in it, and geometrical shapes, and wiggly lines like a great
curving river.

I did see a man at a pulpit—a man old before his time, all
bony and hollow-eyed, reading of a Bible, but I didn't see nobody pay him no mind. He was muttering and carrying on, and
now and then I caught something he said, which was, "Listen to
me, my dearly beloved brethren, for I have stood in the circle of
hell itself; I've surely looked the dragon darkness in the eye, and
I've seen the emptiness in the heart of God's grandest creation.
Listen to me, my brethren, listen to me. A kingdom is at hand,
but it is not the kingdom you thinks it is." There was something
unfamiliar about his words; I had heard a thousand sermons,
and the words was all alike, yet there was something about the
way he ordered them . . . I wondered whether our Lord had any
place amid this spectacle.

No one looked at him. Instead, they were staring at the center of that circle, and quite unmindful of all them darkies leaping up and down around him, there sat a boy no older than me,

a mite younger even. There was a leopard sleeping at his feet. So that was where the smell come from, and the roaring I'd heard earlier.

He was a simple blond and blue-eyed boy, like thousands I had seen fighting alongside me, like thousands I had seen killed, for by the time I joined the army our men, and even more so theirs, was mostly boys. He looked like he could have sat next to me at Mrs. Miller's schoolhouse, only no schoolboy could have sat so still for quite so long. He was quite still, quite impassive, quite contorted into his uncomfortable cross-legged position. Only his eyes was moving, back and forth, like the pendulum of a grandfather clock. I half expected him to go "cuckoo-cuckoo" at any moment.

Which, shortly, he suddenly done.

It was when we brung Kaz all the way into the tent and laid him at his feet. The boy looked at him all lying there, and suddenly he goes berserk. Foams at the mouth, flings his arms about, rolls his eyes up in their sockets so they're white, like ghost eyes. And then the boy starts to sing, in a harsh, big voice that seems to come from all around us, and what he's singing ain't in English. Here's how it sounded, best as I can recall it:

> *Koulèv, koulèv O—*
> *Koulèv, koulèv O—*

And then he started to rip off his own shirt, and threw it into the throng. And then he leapt up in the air and begun to whirl, so fast I couldn't hardly see him, he was like a tornado. And the dancing colored, they all formed a circle around him and they was like spokes of a wheel, drawing power from this strange white boy. Presently he tosses off all that he's wearing, and he's as naked as they are, and no look of shame in his face; he's jumping and bending and twisting himself into knots and all the time his eyes are white and glistening.

And meanwhile the old man keeps on muttering, and I thought, well, maybe there's somewhat in what he says that can explain all this. So I listen to him with half an ear, through the pounding which is ever louder now, forcing my pulse to pound in the same senseless rhythm.

But this is what the preacher was saying: "There's a mighty serpent, my brothers and sisters, and we're all of us a-wrapped up in his golden coils, for he is the sun, and the giver of life, and his name is called Jehovah by some, but today I will teach you a new name: Damballah Wedo!"

I ain't never heard no teaching like that from the Bible, no ma'am. The only serpent in the Bible was a bad serpent.

Well, as these words come from the old man's lips, the young boy begun hissing, and bending his arms like he was a serpent himself, and writhing and snapping his head back and forward like it was on hinges, and twisting his head back and forth so fast I could swear it like to twisted all the way round like a corkscrew. And then the darkies all started to chant,

> *Koulèv, koulèv O—*
> *Koulèv, koulèv O—*

and to writhe along with the young boy, and copy all his gestures, and it was madness, I tell you, but the boy began to dance through the company of the sick and the dying, and now and then he leant down to touch someone and that someone jerked suddenly upright and stared about himself as though in a dream, and I don't know if he was healing the sick or driving them mad, but there was some kind of power here, like that animal magnetism that the circus mesmerists use.

Now the drumming began to tug on me like I was a puppet and the pounding was a string. I fought it. I said to myself, I won't be no savage from the jungle, I won't be no ape-man. But you know, Walt was different. He just give in to it. I could see him making little movements, wiggling his hips, waving an arm, holding in himself as best he can but knowing that he was caught in the rapture of this forest music.

"Don't, Walt," I said, and I had to admit there was a twinge of jealousy too, for the boy was lean and shiny and his hair rustled like treetops in autumn, and I knew Walt had a weakness for a comely boy; he wasn't like me, sinning from expediency, from affection, from an urgent need, no, no, to him the sinning was a celebration of himself; he truly felt no shame, no outrage against natural law, not even a trace of guilt. And I could see by now, knowing Walt as I did, this dancing boy, possessed by a spirit-serpent, stirred Walt's loins as well as his soul. And yes, I was jealous when I stayed Walt's arm, but he wouldn't have none of it, no, ma'am, he wanted to grasp that serpent in both arms and drink the spirit of it and suck it deep into his body, the same thing he had done with me, only I am flesh and blood, and this was a thing you couldn't touch. Oh, God, I felt it, though, felt the coils of the snake all sharp and shimmering, felt the lash of its tail on me like a lead-tipped bullwhip, felt the flick of its tongue on my face, my hands, yes, even my private parts, which strained against my drawers like they'd been kissed by the paintedest whore of Babylon. But I resisted. Not Walt. Pretty soon I could almost see that snake . . . maybe a tendril of smoke from the incense, maybe a lariat of flame lassoing the air. I could see Walt in its clutches. I saw him moving in spasms, pulled up, forced down by the power of that snake. "It's Satan!" I screamed, and Walt only turned to me and said, "Satan's just a word, boy, just a word," and then when I tried to say, "But Walt, you said yourself words was all powerful, that they're the source of magic," he laughed and said, "Contradiction's what holds the universe in place, son, didn't you know that?" and then he broke free of my grasp and pretty soon he was up there, dancing right alongside that pretty boy, and even Tyler Tyler was in the grip of a kind of frenzy, cause he kick up his heels some, even though he couldn't wave his arms, but his stumps quivered and his head jerked back and forth and he started babbling, just like them speaking-in-tongues folks and them revival meetings, and soon I was thinking, Shit, Lord, but I'm the onliest one not dancing, and I can feel the rippling of the force, and the heart-beat of the world, but my own heart is a stone, cold, dead, un-reachable. And I begin to cry.

And I don't mean just a little tear here and there, neither. I mean I was bawling like a baby, hadn't bawled this hard since my paw whupped me for stealing a jar of molasses when I was seven years old.

Because of my tears, I could not see much of what happened next. It seemed that the candle flames were smears of light, and the streaks of incense smoke was burning clouds that roiled through the half dark, and it seemed that the serpent coiled and coiled and coiled and squoze so tight I couldn't barely breathe, and then it seemed next that I saw my friends, and all them col-oreds, and all that congregation, all dancing naked in the flames, but it wasn't no witches' sabbath nor no bacchanal of the demons of infernal, it was a stately thing, slow, solemn, a little sad, to a timeless music.

Oh, yes, and through it all, that leopard slept. Oh, now and then it roared, or clawed at the air, but as if in a dream.

And it seemed next that the preacher's boy put out his hand and from that hand came serpents of flame, and they leap across to where dying Kaczmarczyk lay, and lo and behold, they licked his eyelids and his eyelids opened up and you never did see such a look of surprise in a man's face. And he stuttered and stuttered and I guess he was about to say something. And then he did. But I didn't understand it. It was in one of them European lan-guages, I guess, unless he was speaking in tongues too. At first it was a mere mumbling, but then, like a dam that first cracks a little and a little more and then come suddenly bursting all at once, he's shrieking out loud and clear; I don't what he's saying, it sounds something like, *"Dee schlung, dee schlung."* What the hell kind of a language was that? I didn't care. Kaz was coming to life. And me, standing there, resisting the serpent, me the one who'd gone right out and said, "He's dead."

Stating the obvious don't make it true.

"God Almighty, Kaczmarczyk," I cried out. "You ain't dead at all."

"Who said I vas dead?" he said to me. And his eyes accused me. Red eyes, they was, like they was illumined by the flames of hell. And I was afraid. I wanted to run. The battles we fought, the deaths we'd seen, all that was in them eyes of his.

"I did," I said. "I'm sorry."

And Kaczmarczyk rose from the travois, and he too began the dance, and they all danced until they were exhausted, excepting me; of all of them, I was the one too scared to dance. So all I did was stare at the sleeping leopard, who never did open its eyes, which was good, because I would have been afraid to look into them.

But after, the ferryman having retired for the night, we remained on the island, sleeping under the trees.

3

Come morning, it all seemed like another dream. We woke at sunup, and I saw that Walt was already boiling up a can of coffee, and Kaz, wide awake and seemingly sound, was feeding Tyler Tyler a small piece of hardtack.

There was no tent, and no dancing darkies, and no old man preaching about a great coiled serpent.

"Was I dreaming?" I said, and sat up, leaning against a tree trunk. Not far away I could hear the river rushing, and I knew that Washington was but a half day's journey away.

Walt said, "No, Zacko; they folded up the tents, and most of the visitors have departed."

"They never even took up a collection," said Tyler, and that was, to tell the truth, the strangest thing of all, for I never heard of no religions that didn't have both God and Mammon.

Presently, I saw the man who had been preaching on the other side of the clearing; he was watching two darkies load bundles onto a wagon.

"Are they going back down south?" I said.

"No," said Walt. "I hear they're going to try their luck up north . . . they claim to be following some great circle of the universe."

"And Kaz?"

"He ain't spoken much," Tyler said, "but he's alive all right."

Kaczmarczyk turned to me. I could still see the perdition in his eyes. I looked away. Kaz said, "You don't believe I'm back, do you?"

And I said, "Zack . . . Kaz . . . Zack . . . Kaz . . ." mulling over that accident of sonic palindrome, as Walt would have called it, and wondering if by his coming back he was now sending me toward the land of death.

"He's alive all right," Tyler said yet again. Why did he keep saying that over and over? Was it because he knew that I might have turned back if it hadn't been for him speaking up? Or was it because he, like me, did not quite believe in this living, breathing Kaczmarczyk?

It was then that that young boy approached us. I mean, the boy who had been dancing naked in the incense mist. The one I guess I'd felt jealous of. Nothing untoward about him now. He was duded up in a black velvet suit—he could have been going to a gambling house, or to his own funeral. And behind him walked that leopard, tame as a puppy.

"Morning to you," he said. "I'm Jimmy Lee Cox, the preacher's son." He came right up to us, turned and told the leopard to go wait beneath the shade of an oak tree, which it sure enough did, and then bent down to look at Kaz, who was sitting with a cup of coffee by the fire. "You're the one that was touched, last night," he said.

Kaz said, "Touched," and he looked away, "but not healed."

"No," said the boy. "When the fire touched you, you was already past the brink; there was someone kept you from falling in; it warn't I."

"Nor I," I said. "I was the one kept saying, No, no, let him be, he's dead. I think he's mad at me about that."

Jimmy Lee looked at me, looked right into me, don't ask me how; he could read me like a book, though I was willing to wager he couldn't read books. "Can I ask you for a cup of that coffee?" he asked. "Where I come from, we grind up a little burnt-up chickory, and boil it up with river water that's soiled with dead men's flesh, and we strain it best we can, and we drinks it, and we says to ourselves, Lord, here's a powerful fine cup of coffee. I sure do crave the real item betimes."

Walt poured him some from the can. And sat down next to us. He was bewitched by that boy, I think.

"You are not Christians," Walt said.

"Never said we were," said the boy.

"But the tent—the occasional quotes from the Bible—"

"When my daddy still lived amongst us," said Jimmy Lee Cox, "he were a itinerant preacher, but he warn't book-learnt or nothing; he only preached to the colored; so you see, what Bible learning we have comes from the air around us, not from no books."

"What do you mean," said Walt, "while your daddy still lived amongst you? Didn't we see your father, in the corner, orating about the great serpent?"

"He likes to come back," said Jimmy Lee, "for the big services; it makes him feel alive again. Lord, but that coffee sure is tasty."

He didn't speak for a while. You'd think that we'd given him a bag of gold, that's how much the coffee seemed to mean to him. I shared my cup with Tyler, and I saw that he was deathly afraid. He was glaring at the big cat, which sat afar off. But I thought to myself, Why, if that leopard wasn't tame, I guess he wouldn't be allowed to walk about in a tent full of mad dancers; or he'd go crazy too.

Well, at length, finishing his cup of coffee, the boy did turn to Tyler, and he said, "Are you ready?"

Tyler said, "Give me a moment."

Now what did that mean?

"A moment," said Jimmy Lee, "but when it happens, you're gone have to go willing, so make your peace with yourself best you can."

Tyler sank down on his knees. "God, God," he said. "I don't have no arms, I reckon I can't even pray."

Jimmy Lee grasped him by the shoulders and said, "Now listen. The serpent done given you a taste of what you asked for. But the rest of it waits for what you promised."

"I know," said Tyler.

And I said, "Tyler Tyler, what kind of satanic bargain have you gone and made?"

Tyler said, "I was meant to die before Andersonville. What I lived through then, what I'm living through now—it's a living hell anyway. I might as well trade it in for someone else."

"What are you talking about?" I said. "Life ain't a game with poker chips."

Jimmy Lee said, "But life is a ocean, and oceans have tides. And when a thing comes up upon one shore, another thing from a farther shore falls into the depths."

"That sounds so Biblical," said Walt, "yet I've never read it in the Bible."

"Different folks," said Jimmy Lee, "got different Bibles; now ain't that a fact."

Walt laughed out loud. I think he got the idea for a poem from that, somehow.

"Come on, already," said Tyler. "I've had enough of this; just set me free."

"Freedom," said the boy softly. "Freedom, Freedom." But

he wasn't just saying the word. He was calling out to the leopard.

And then Tyler Tyler walked out into the clearing and the leopard ripped out his throat, and he fell, and the leopard circled him three times and did such a roar as you might have heard it even above the sounds of the battlefield. And then the leopard . . . I guess you could say the leopard melted . . . into the trees, the grass, the wind.

And me and Walt run over to look at Tyler, and this is what we saw: another boy, a year or two older'n me, but a whole boy, his arms crossed over his chest, over his heart, like you see in them photographs from Egypt, with the ancient mummies and all. And Tyler was smiling, even though I never had seen him smile when he was still alive. And there was no wound in his throat, no battle scars anywhere, in fact; he was the boy his mother knew when she sent him out to do battle, like my own mother did, with a kiss and a loaf of bread and a passel of hope and fear.

And when we come back to the fire, there was Kaz, standing up, lanky and fit, ripping the bandages away from that part of his face that had been shot open; and he had two eyes, though one was swollen a bit, and two ears, though one was shredded a little, and two of everything that was supposed to be two; he was not restored to perfection, as Tyler was, but he had life, which Tyler didn't, no more, even though he looked so peacefullike, you might of thought he were just sleeping.

"Kaz," I said—

And saw that the hellfire was gone from his eyes.

"Oh, Zacko," he said. "The places I been, the tings I seen—"

And he embraced me, warmly, like a brother, which was strange to me, for though I knew he cared much for me, he was not a man who liked to touch people.

Kaczmarczyk said, "Let's get on that damn ferry," he said, "before I forget I'm alive." He looked at Jimmy Lee Cox, and back at me, and I could see he was afraid of that boy, and I would be too, I guess.

But the boy was deep in conversation with Walt, and when Walt takes a shine to a boy it's hard to get him loose—some of my camerados might say, with a lewd nudge of the ribs, "with a crowbar"—but I never made such jokes about my friend, and I didn't like it when when one of the soldiers would, say, let the man play with his cocker one evening, and call him a filthy sodomite the next; I just ain't built for hypocrisy. Walt had a power; he made you feel like you was king of the world; when he talked to you, you *were* the world; nothing about you failed to interest him. Yes. Ma'am, I did so love him.

I held back my annoyance at the boy for distracting Walt, and I sat down beside them. Kaz stood afar off, afraid, still. And I asked the boy the many questions that burned in me, and some he answered, and others he just allowed to hang in the air while he sipped at a fresh tin cannister of coffee, and others still he answered in riddles.

"Jimmy Lee," I said, "is your father dead or alive?"

"Though I walk through the valley of the shadow of death," he said, "I will fear no evil."

I looked at Walt.

"He's telling us," said Walt, "that his father walks a shadowland, that he doesn't truly know which side of the border he's on."

"Are you a Christian?" I said.

"I am the resurrection and the life," said he, "and whosoever believeth in me shall not perish, but have life everlasting."

Walt said, "He means that his church is a church of rebirth, and what Christ says about resurrection has meaning for him too."

"But do you worship the true God? I mean, the Father, Son, and Holy Ghost, and all that talk that the preachers spew forth on Sundays?"

"What is truth?" said Jimmy Lee Cox, which was, I reckon,

what Pontius Pilate once said to our Lord, before he strung Him up on a tree and did Him to death.

"Is Freedom the name of your leopard?"

"No."

"But when you called him, you cried out, 'Freedom, Freedom, Freedom.' "

"She ain't my leopard," said Jimmy Lee Cox.

"Where is she now?"

"In Africa."

Suddenly, Jimmy Lee began laughing heartily, and he said, "Why, Zacko, we can play at these games all day and all night, and won't none of us be the wiser but one jot or tittle."

"I just want to understand what happened—why it happened—how it happened."

"Why, your friend Tyler was craving for death, that's all, and your other friend, Kaczmarczyk, why he was longing to come back from the other side. They don't notice a soul here, a soul there; they ain't really counting that closely. That's how all magic happens, you know . . . in the cracks, where the pieces of the real world don't quite join up . . . you think the rabbit's really in the hat? Brother, it ain't."

"And that's all that raising the dead is?" said Walt. "A magic parlor trick?"

"No," said Jimmy Lee. "But to tell you all that it is, I have to tell you how the power come to me, and why I wander the earth with my pa, trying to seal up the cracks in the wounded land."

"Tell us," I said. "We can wait for the next ferry."

And thus it was that Jimmy Lee Cox began telling us his story, the strangest of all the stories I ever heard in all the time since I left home to become a soldier. It was a story about love, death, and rebirth, like all the stories I had been hearing, from Kaczmarczyk, from your late husband, and all the rest; but Jimmy Lee's came somehow with a more personal pain than the others'. And so it was that I come to understand Walt's fascination with the boy, and to realize it wasn't just some fancy for his gold-streaked hair or his clear eyes, for what was inside that bright and beautiful body was dark and terrible.

And because of Jimmy Lee's story, ma'am, I will never sleep alone, not ever again.

They go! They go! I know that they go,
but I know not where they go.

—Walt Whitman

A Runaway in
Raleigh

1863

11

JIMMY LEE COX MEETS AN UNUSUAL OLD MAN

1

One day (Jimmy Lee began telling us as we sat around that fire) there'll be historians who can name all the battles and number the dead. They'll study the tactics of the generals and they'll see it all clear as crystal, like they was watching with the eyes of the angels.

But it warn't like that for me. I can't for the life of me put a name to one blame battle we fought. I had no time to number the dead nor could I see them clearly through the haze of red that swam before my eyes. And when the gore-drenched mist settled into dew, when the dead became visible in their stinking, wormy multitudes, I still could not tell one from another; it was a very sea of torsos, heads, and twisted limbs; the dead was wrapped around one another so close and intimate they was like lovers; didn't matter no more iffen they was ours or theirs.

I do not recollect what made me stay behind. Could be it was losing my last shinplaster on the cockroach races. Could have been the coffee which warn't real coffee at all but parched acorns roasted with bacon fat and ground up with a touch of chicory. Could be it was that my shoes was so wore out from marching that every step I took was like walking acrosst a field of brimstone.

More likely it was just because I was a running away kind of a boy. Running was in my blood. My pa and me, we done our share of running, and I reckon that even after I done run away from *him* and gone to war, the running fever was still inside of me and couldn't be let go.

And then, after I lagged behind, I knowed that if I went back they'd shoot me dead, and if they shot me why then I'd go straight on to the everlasting fire, because we was fighting to protect the laws of God. I just warn't ready for hell yet, not after a mere fourteen years on this mortal earth.

That's why I was tarrying amongst the dead, and that's how I come to meet that old darkie that used to work down at the Anderson place.

The sun was about setting and the place was right rank, because the carrion had had the whole day to bloat up and rot and to call out for the birds and the worms and the flies. But it felt good to walk on dead people because they was softer on my wounded feet. The bodies stretched acrosst a shallow creek and all the way up to the edge of a wood. I didn't know where I was nor where I was going. There warn't much light remaining and I wanted to get somewhere, anywhere, before nightfall. It was getting cold. I took a jacket off of one dead man and a pair of new boots from another but I couldn't get the boots on past them open sores.

You might think it a sin to steal from the dead, but the dead don't have no use for gold and silver. There was scant daylight left for me to rifle through their pockets looking for coins. Warn't much in the way of money on that battlefield. It's usually only us poor folks which gets killed in battle.

It was slippery work wading through the corpses, keeping an eye for something shiny amongst the ripped-up torsos and the sightless heads and the coiling guts. I was near choking to death from the reek of it, and the coat I stole warn't much proof against the cold. I was hungry and I had no notion of where to find provender. And the mist was coming back, and I thought to myself, I'll just take myself a few more coppers and then I'll cross over into the wood and build me a shelter and mayhap a fire. Won't nobody see me, thin as a sapling, quiet as a shadow.

So I started to wade over the creek, which warn't no trouble because there was plenty of bodies to use as stepping stones. I was halfway acrosst when I spotted the old nigger under a cottonwood tree, in a circle which was clear of carrion. He had a little fire going and something a-roasting over it. I could hear the crackling above the buzz of the flies and I could smell the cooking fat somewhere behind the stench of putrefying men.

I moved nearer to where he sat. I was blame near fainting by then and ready to kill a body for my supper. He was squatting with his arms around his knees and he was a-rocking back and forth and I thought I could hear him crooning some song to himself, like a lullaby, in a language more kin to French than nigger talk. Odd thing was, I had heard the song before. Mayhap my momma done sung it to me onc't, for she was born out Louisiana way. The more I listened the less I was fixing to kill the old man.

He was old all right. As I crept closer I seen he warn't no threat to me. I still couldn't see his face, because he was turned away from me and looking straight into the setting sun. But I could see he was withered and white-haired and black as the coming night, and seemed like he couldn't even hear me approaching, for he never pricked up his ears though I stood nary a yard or two behind his back, in the shadow of the cottonwood.

That was when he said to me, never looking back, "Why, *bonjour,* Marse Jimmy Lee; I never did think I'd look upon you face again."

And then he turned, and I knew him by the black patch over his right eye.

Lord, it was strange to see him there, in the middle of the valley of the dead. It had been ten years since my pa and me gone up to the Anderson place. Warn't never any call to go back, since it burned to the ground a week after, and old man Anderson died, and his slaves was all sold.

"How did you know it was me?" I asked him. "I was but four years old last time you laid eyes on me."

"Your daddy still a itinerant preacher, Marse Jimmy Lee?" he says.

"I reckon," said I, for I warn't about ready to tell him the truth yet. "I ain't with my pa no more."

"You was always a running away sort of a boy," he said, and offered me a piece of what he was roasting.

"What is it?"

"I don't reckon I ought to tell you."

"I've had possum before. I've had field rat. I'm no stranger to strange flesh." I took a bite of the meat and it was right tasty. But I hadn't had solid food for two days and soon I was a-heaving all over the nearest corpse.

He went back to his crooning song, and I remembered then that I had heard it last from his own lips, that day Pa shot Momma in the back because she wanted to go with the Choctaw farmer. I can't say I blamed her because leastways the man was a landowner and had four slaves besides. Pa let her pack her bags and walk halfway acrosst the bridge afore he blew her to kingdom come. Then he took my hand and set me up on his horse and took me to the Anderson place, and when I started to squall he slapped me in the face until it were purple and black, saying, between his blows, "She don't deserve your tears. She is a woman taken in adultery; such a woman should be stoned to death, according to the scriptures; a bullet were too good for her. I have exercised my rights according to the law, and iffen I hear one more sob out of you I shall take a hickory to you, for he who spareth the rod loveth not his child." And he drained a flask of bug juice and burped. I did not hear the name of Mary Cox from his lips again for ten long years.

Pa was not a ordained minister but plantation folks reckoned him book-learned enough to preach to their darkies, which is what he done every Sunday, a different estate each week, then luncheon with the master and mistress of the house or sometimes, if they was particular about eating with white trash, then in the kitchen amongst the house niggers. The niggers called him the Reverend Cox, but to the white folks he was just Cox, or Bug-juice Cox, or Blame-Fuckster Cox, or wretched, pitiable Cox, so low that his wife done left him for a Injun.

At the Anderson place he preached in a barn, and he took for his subject adultery; and as there was no one to notice, I stole away to a field and sat me down in a thicket of sugar cane and hollered and carried on like the end of the world was nigh, and me just four years old.

Then it was that I heard the selfsame song I was hearing now, and I looked up and saw this ancient nigger with a patch over one eye, and he says to me, "Oh, honey, it be a terrible thing to be without a mother." I remember the smell of him, a pungent smell like fresh crushed herbs. "I still remembers the day my *maman* was took from me. Oh, do not grieve alone, white child."

"How'd you come to lose that eye?"

"It the price of knowledge, honey," he said softly.

Choking back my sobs, a mite embarrassed because someone had seen me in my loneliness, I said to him, "You shouldn't be here. You should be in that barn listening to my father's preaching, lessen you want to get yourself a whupping."

He smiled sadly and said, "They done given up on whupping old Joseph."

I said, "Is your momma dead too, Joseph?"

"Yes. She be dead, oh, nigh on sixty year now. She died in the revolution."

"Oh, come," I said, "even I know that the revolution was almost a hundred years ago, and I know you ain't that old, because a white man's time is threescore years and ten, and a nigger's time is shorter still." Now I wasn't comprehending anything I was saying; this was all things I heard my pa say, over and over again, in his sermons.

"Oh," said old Joseph, "I ain't talking about the white man's revolution, but the colored folks' revolt which happened on a island name of Haiti. The French, they tortured my *maman,* but she wouldn't betray her friends, so they killed her and sold me to a slaver, and the ship set sail one day before independence; so sixty years after my kinfolk was set free, I's still in bondage in a foreign country."

I knew that niggers was always full of stories about magic and distant countries, and they couldn't always see truth from fantasy; my daddy told me that truth is a hard, solid thing to us white folks, as easy to grasp as a stone or a horseshoe, but to them it was slippery, it was like a phantom. That was why I didn't take exception to the old man's lies. I just sat there quietly, listening to the music of his voice, and it soothed me and seemed like it helped to salve the pain I was feeling, for pretty soon when I thought of Momma lying on the bridge choking on her own blood, I felt I could remember the things I loved about her too, like the way she called my name, the way her nipples tasted on my lips, for she had lost my newborn sister and she was bursting with milk and she would sometimes let me suckle, for all that I was four years old.

And then I was crying again but this time they was healing tears.

Then old Joseph, he said, "You listen to me, Marse Jimmy Lee. I ain't always gone be with you when you needs to open up your heart." Now this surprised me because I didn't recollect telling him none of what was going through my mind. "I's gone give you a gift," he said, and he pulls out a bottle from his sleeve, a vial, only an inch high, and in that bottle was a doll that was woven out of cornstalks. It were cunningly wrought, for the head of the doll was bigger than the neck of the bottle, and it must have taken somebody many hours to make, and somebody with keen eyesight at that. "Now this be a problem doll. It can listen to you when no man will listen. It a powerful magic from the island where I was born."

He held it out to me and it made me smile, for I had often-times been told that darkies are simple people and believe in all kinds of magic. I clutched it in my hands but mayhap he saw the disbelief in my face, for he said to me with the utmost gravity, "Do not mock this magic, white child. Among the colored peo-ple which still fears the old gods, they calls me a *houngan,* a man of power."

"The old gods?" I said.

"Shangó," he said, and he done a curious sort of a genu-flecting hop when he said the name, "Obatala, Ogun, Babalu Ayé . . ."

The names churned round and round in my head as I stared into his good eye. I don't recollect what followed next or how my pa found me. But everything else I remembered just as though the ten years that followed, the years of wandering, pa's worsening cruelty and drunkenness, hadn't never even hap-pened.

It was as though I had circled back to that same place and time. Only instead of the burning sunlight of that summer's day there was the gathering cold and the night. Instead of the tall cane sticky with syrup, we was keeping company with the slain. And I warn't a child no more, although I warn't a man yet, nei-ther.

"The *poupée* I give you," old Joseph said as I sat myself down beside him, "does you still got it?"

"My pa found it the next day. He said he didn't want no

hoodoo devil dolls in his house. He done smashed it and
throwed it in the fire, and then he done wore me out with his
hickory."

"And you a soldier now."

"I run away."

"Lordy, honey, you a sight to see. Old Joseph don't got no
more dolls for you now. Old Joseph got no time for he be making dolls. There be a monstrous magic abroad now in this universe. This magic it the onliest reason old Joseph still living in
this world. Old Joseph hears the magic summoning him. Old
Joseph he stay behind to hear what the magic it have to tell
him."

Like a fool, I thought him simple when I heard him speak of
magic. It made me smile. It was the first time I had smiled in
many months. I smiled to keep from crying, for weeping ill becomes a man of fourteen years who has carried his rifle into battle to defend his country.

"You poor lost child," said Joseph, "you should be a-waking
up mornings to the song of the larks, not the whistle of miniés
nor the thunder of cannon. You at the end of the road now,
ain't nowhere left for you to go; that's why us has been called
here to this valley of the shadow of death. It was written from the
moment we met, Marse Jimmy Lee. Ten years I wandered alone
in the wilderness. Now the darker angels has sent you to me."

"I don't know what you mean."

"Be not afraid," he said, "for I bring you glad tidings of great
joy." I marveled that he knew the words of the evangelist, for this
was the man who would not go hear my father's preaching.

He nibbled at the charred meat. For a moment I entertained
the suspicion that it were human flesh. But it smelled good. I ate
my fill and drank from the bloody stream and fell asleep beside
the fire to the lilt of the old man's lullaby.

2

I had not told old Joseph all the truth. It warn't only the need to run that forced me from my father's house. Pa was a hard man and a drinking man and a man which had visions, and in those visions he saw other worlds.

He was unmerciful to me, and oftentimes he would set to whipping the demons out of me, but everything he did to me was in keeping with holy scripture, which tells a father that love ain't always a sweet thing, but can also come with bitterness and blows.

I had visions too, but they warn't heavenly the way his was. I would not wear my shoes. I played with the nigger children of the town, shaming him. I ran wild and I never went to no school. But I could read some, for that my pa set me to studying the scriptures whenever he could tie me down.

This is how I come to join the regiment:

We was living in a shack in back of the Jackson place, right next to the nigger burial plot. Young Master Jackson had all his darkies assembled in the graveyard to hear a special sermon from my pa, because the rumors of the 'mancipation proclamation was rife amongst the slaves. There was maybe thirty or forty of them, and a scattering of pickaninnies underfoot, sitting on the grass, leaning against the wooden markers.

I was sitting in the shack, minding a kettle of stew. Through the open window I could hear my pa preaching. "Now don't you darkies pay this emancipation proclamation no mind," came his voice, ringing and resonant. "It is an evil trickery. They are trying to fool you innocent souls into running away and joining up with those butchers who come down to rape and pillage our land, and they hold out freedom as a reward for treachery. But the true reward is death, for if a nigger is captured in the uniform of a yankee it has been decreed by our government that he shall be shot without trial. No, this is no road to freedom! There is only one way there for those born into bondage, and that is through the blood of our savior Jesus Christ, and your freedom is not for this world, but for the next, for is it not written, 'In my father's house there are many mansions?' There is a mansion for you, and you, and you, and you, iffen you will obey your master in this life and accept the yoke of lowliness and the lash of repentance; for is it not written, 'By his stripes we are healed' and 'Blessed are the meek'? It's not for the colored people, freedom in this world. But the wicked, compassionless yankees would prey on your simplicity. They would let you mistake the kingdom of heaven for a rebellious kingdom on earth. 'To everything there is a season.' Yes, there will be mansions for you all. Mansions with white stone columns and porticoes sheltered from the sun. The place of healing is beyond the valley of the shadow of death. . . ."

My pa could talk mighty proper when he had a mind to, and he had a chapter and verse for everything. I didn't pay no heed to his words, though, because there is different chapters and verses for niggers, and when they are quoted for white folks they do not always mean the same thing. No, I was busy stirring the stew and hiding the whisky, for pa had always had a powerful thirst after he was done preaching, and with the quenching of thirst came violence.

After the preaching the darkies all starts singing with a passion. They done sung "All God's Chillun Got Wings" and "Swing Low, Sweet Chariot." Pa didn't stay for the singing but come into the shack calling for his food. It warn't ready so he throwed a few pots and pans around, with me scurrying out of the way to avoid being knocked about, and then he finally found where I had hidden the bottle and he lumbered into the inner room to drink.

Presently the stew bubbled up and I ladled out some in a tin cup and took it to the room. This was the room me and him slept in, on a straw pallet on the floor, a bare room with nothing but a chest of drawers, a chair with one leg missing, and a hunting rifle. He kept his hickories there too, for to chastise me with.

I should have knocked, because Pa warn't expecting me.

He was sitting in the chair with his britches about his ankles. He didn't see me. He was holding in one hand a locket which had a picture of Momma. In the other hand he was holding his bony cocker, and he was strenuously indulging in the vice of Onan.

I was right horrified when I saw this. I was full of shame to see my father unclothed, for was that not the shame of the sons of Noah? And I was angered, because in my mind's eye I seen my momma go down on that bridge, fold up and topple over, something I hadn't thought on for nigh on ten year. I stood there blushing scarlet and full of fury and grieving for my dead mother, and then I heard him a-murmuring, "Oh, sweet Jehovah, Oh, sweet Lord, I see you, I see the company of the heavenly host, I see you, my sweet Mary, standing on a cloud with your arms stretched out to me, naked as Eve in the Garden of Eden. Oh, oh, oh, I'm a-looking on the face of the Almighty and a-listening to the song of the angels."

Something broke inside me all at once when I heard him talk that way about Momma. Warn't it enough that she was dead, withouten him blasphemously lusting after her departed soul? I dropped the tin of stew and he saw me and I could see the rage burning in his eyes, and I tried to force myself to obey the fifth commandment, but words just came pouring out of me. "Shame on you, Pa, pounding your cocker for a woman you done gunned down in cold blood. Don't you think I don't remember the way you kilt her, shot her in the back whilst she were crossing that bridge, and the Choctaw watching on t'other side in his top hat and morning dress, with his four slaves behind him, waiting to take her home."

My pa was silent for a few moments, and the room was filled with the caterwauling of the niggers from the graveyard. We stood there staring each other down. Then he grabbed me by the scruff of the neck and dragged me over to the chair, lurching and stumbling because he hadn't even bothered to pull his britches back up, and I could smell the liquor on him; and he murmured, "You are right; I have sinned; I have sinned; but it is for the son to take on the sins of the world; the paschal lamb; you, Jimmy Lee; oh, God, but you do resemble her; you do remind me of her; oh, it is a heavy burden for you, my son, to take on the sins of the world, but I know that you do it for love," and suchlike, and he reached for the hickory and stripped the shirt off of my back and began to lay to with a will, all the while crying out, "Oh, Mary, oh, my Mary, I am so sorry that you left me . . . oh, my son, you shall bear thirty-nine stripes on your back in memory of our savior . . . oh, you shall redeem me . . ." and the hickory sang and I cried out, not so much from the pain, for that my back was become like leather from long abuse, and warn't much feeling left in it. I gritted my teeth and try to bear it like I borne it so many times before, but this time it was not to be borne, and when the thirty-ninth stripe was inflicted I tore myself loose from the chair and I screamed, "You ain't hurting me no more, because I ain't no paschal lamb and your sins is *your* sins, not mine," and I pushed him aside with all my strength.

"God, God," he says in a whisper, "I see God." And he rolls his eyes heavenward, excepting that heaven were a leaky roof made from a few planks left over from the slaves' quarters.

Then I took the rifle from the wall and pounded him in the head with the stock, three, four, five, six times until he done slumped onto the straw.

Oh, I was raging and afeared, and I run away right then and there, without even making sure iffen he was kilt or not. I run right through them darkies, who was a-singing and a-carrying on to wake the very dead; they did not see a scrawny boy, small for his age, slip through them and out toward the woods.

I run and run with three dimes in my pocket and a sheaf of

shinplasters that I stole from the chest of drawers, I run and I don't even recollect iffen I put out the fire on the stove.

And that was how I come to be with the regiment, tramping through blood and mud and shitting my bowels away with the flux each day; and that was how I come to be sleeping next to old Joseph, the hoodoo doctor, who become another father to me.

12

WHEREIN MRS. GRAINGER MAKES MANY HITHERTO UNDISCOVERED CONNECTIONS BETWEEN THE VARIOUS EVENTS OF HER LIFE

1

Stories within stories within stories! And always, it took another story to explain the one that preceded it.

There I was, with Zachary Brown, and once more the tea was getting cold; and more and more the sense of dislocation was seizing me.

But the more confusing it all became, the more I was impelled to find out more. It was clear that the late Mr. Grainger had been far more than just a distracted husband tilting at lost causes and ebony-skinned women; he had been involved with something darker.

Once more, the sun had long since set. Phoebe had not returned, and neither had Mr. Whitman, the mad poet. I was alone in the house with a young man. Young enough to be my son, perhaps, but in my entire life I had never allowed myself to appear thus compromised.

Appear? I thought. To whom, this appearance, to whom could it possibly matter whether I be compromised or no?

It occurred to me that this *whom* I was fretting so much over was none other than myself. I feared to be compromised because, from a part of me that I had long thought dead, I could hear a young girl cry out in anguish and in longing, "Love me, for I desperately need to be loved."

And I feared that he could see it in my eyes.

And I feared, like all who had been brought up in a Christian household, I feared that the thought was already the act, and perdition the reward. I feared, because such a fear had been whipped into me as a child, in spite of the fact that I was coming to believe that such fear was groundless, and that the afterlife was far more complex than a mere heaven or hell.

And then Zachary Brown asked me a presumptuous, though quite innocent question: "Widow Grainger, I don't have a place to spend the night. Mrs. Whitman will wonder about me coming up to her stoop in the middle of the night without Walt, and I was thinking, although you've been so kind to me already, a stranger and all, I—"

But what happened next was most unexpected. The boy began to weep, most piteously, like a child. "Oh, God," he cried out. "That poor poor Mr. Lincoln, and I don't even know if what he died for will ever really come to pass—"

The more he wept, the more I saw that this was no hypocritical grief for a man he had not even known; he was weeping for a whole lot else: his lost friends, perhaps, Tyler and Rodney and—Drew, I think his name was—he was weeping because he would never recover his own innocence; and I, I, I, whose womb had produced only the dead, what did I know of how to comfort a child? For a child was what he was, though he had been in battle and slain grown men and been wounded like a man.

And I reflected, If he is merely a child then these other

feelings that seem to be welling up out of myself should be kept to myself; they are unworthy; I must comfort him as a mother comforts a crying child. And so, awkwardly, I placed my arms around him.

But his response was to embrace me with such intensity that I was taken aback; I prayed he did not notice I had recoiled a little, for I did not want him to think I found him somehow repugnant; then I found myself returning the embrace. It brought to mind my moment of weakness in front of poor Mr. Lincoln, throwing myself into Mr. Whitman's embrace like some common harlot, only to discover that he was of a different proclivity altogether.

Now Zachary was putting his arms about me once more, and I was wiping away his tears with a little lace handkerchief I carried in my bosom. He seized my hand and kissed it. A shudder went through my body, for I could tell that this young man had all the ardor for a woman that his masculine lover lacked. My hand must have been trembling, for he grasped it in both of his own and before I could catch my breath his mouth descended upon mine, and—whether from horror or desire I care not to recall—I did not resist, nor did I struggle when I apprehended the moist impression of his tongue against my seldom-kissed, chapped lips.

"Oh, Mrs. Grainger," he said. "You're so soft and so friendly and so, so motherly to me, and—"

Somehow—I had thought I was seated in the fauteuil, beside the tea things—we had managed to progress to the divan. And there it was that the young man hurled himself upon my person and reached into my petticoats, and I, stunned by the impropriety yet thrilled beyond imagining at his proximity, his comeliness, even the unfamiliar smell of manliness that clung to every inch of his coarse skin, I was carried away by the tide of his passion, heedless even of the cracking of my whalebone corset and the profanation of my womanhood. And when he actually began to tease at my nether lips with his fingertips, and gently to caress the surface of my *mons veneris,* I was almost fainting with the unfamiliar ecstasy of it.

"Zachary, Zachary—" I whispered.

"Oh, ma'am," he said hoarsely. "I'm so sorry, I don't mean to, but I just can't seem to stop myself, I need you so bad, ma'am, oh, please don't think I don't respect you, ma'am, but I'm in such need of a woman, and I do care for you. . . ."

The heat of the bare flesh of his hand upon my private parts burst through me like a wave of animal magnetism. My own husband had never dared—had never thought to—and yet, with the maid Phoebe, must he not have scaled these selfsame heights?

"You need not stop, Zack," I said. "Perhaps I have become no better than a common whore, but—"

"Oh, no, Mrs. Grainger," he said, and stopped my protestations with a deliciously invasive kiss. "How can you say that about yourself? Why, Mrs. Grainger, you're a fine woman—"

"But I'm old—and I'm withered—"

"You're strong. And you're loving."

And all the while, he was placing my hand all over his anatomy, daring me to probe, to feel. To my astonishment, I found myself undoing his fly buttons, and actually having the audacity to touch, taste, smell such fruit as had not been mine even when it had not been forbidden to me—for my husband and I had coupled only in the most respectable fashion, fully clothed save for the unfastening of a few small hooks.

His hands began to rove beneath the confines of my stays now, as he unfastened my corset and caressed my very bosom, which swelled and stiffened with the thrill of it. Suddenly I found myself unable to bridle my tongue and I gave vent to noisy, unseemly cries. Thank God the walls were thick! Oh, I screamed, I clawed at him, and relentless, he crushed me to him; oh, we were like the trees and the wind!

But then, as the storm subsided, I heard a growl.

I froze. Listened again.

"Mrs. Grainger—" The youth was shirtless in the evening light—oh, but he was firm and hard, not like my husband at all. He made as though to embrace me once again, and then there came that sound—

"Listen! Listen!" I said.

Where was it coming from? It was close by. In the house. The cry of some animal.

"Sweet Jesus," said Zack. "I know that cry."

2

"What do you mean?" I said. "How can you know it?" Then came another sound. A slow, deep rumbling with a hint of purr.

And I too knew the sound, though I had not heard it before, knew it from the stories I had heard at first- and second- and thirdhand, the stories of Zack and my husband and the slave woman Eleuthera.

It was a leopard.

"Eleuthera?" I whispered. "But that was just one of my husband's stories. . . ."

An angry shriek now, followed by a sibilant snarl.

"Here? But why?" said Zack. "In your husband's story, she killed a man in bed beside him—"

I put my hand across my exposed bosom, and my other hand covered my nether parts. I was suddenly conscious that I had sinned, and sinned mightily, that I had not only profaned the memory of my husband but actually come to the verge of giving myself up completely to someone almost young enough to be my son. What astonished me the most is how little guilt I seemed to feel. Indeed, it was almost liberating. . . .

But now I had no time for guilt or shame. An animal was loose in the house. We had to destroy it.

"Is there a gun handy?" Zack asked.

Hastily buttoning myself back up as best I could, I ransacked the bureau drawer, knowing full well that—

There. A derringer. I had never fired it, but I knew that it was loaded.

"That ain't gonna be much use against—" Zack said.

The roar came once again, and this time it shook the house. This was no natural animal, but a beast sprung from our own dark terrors.

"Upstairs," I said.

We hastened. On the landing, in an old trunk, I found another gun, a fifteen-year-old Dragoon Colt, and I told Zack to scrounge in the chest for ammunition.

"If it's the leopard I think it is," Zack said, "maybe it don't mean no harm—"

It roared again. I was terrified, but I forced myself to be calm. "And maybe it does," I said. I was determined to face this thing and dispose of it. It had an unreal quality to me—or rather a half-real quality, like my own nightmares.

And like my nightmares, it needed to be overcome.

"Let's get rid of that monster," I said.

"You sure are feisty, ma'am," Zack said, with admiration and perhaps even a little apprehension.

"I'm not one of those plantation mistresses, who lie back to be raped and slaughtered," I said. "Something happened just now . . . between you and me . . . and I know now that I must stand up and exorcise every one of those ghosts from my past, or I shall never truly live."

"I knowed you was a strong woman, Mrs. Grainger," Zack said.

"I think you'd better call me Paula now," I said. "It's a little late for formality."

We fairly stampeded up those stairs. Again and again that roaring came, and again and again I felt my heart freeze and my blood race, but choler displaced my fear. Witchcraft and adultery and sodomy in my own house—and now lions and tigers and goodness knows what else! And myself—at the ripe and matronly age of thirty-five—suddenly feeling myself a woman for the first time!—oh! My blood raced indeed, but there was an exhilaration mingled with that dread.

Up another flight. We didn't speak anymore. We listened. The sound came from ever higher up. As though we were being lured—summoned.

Up past the master bedroom. Now up toward the dinginess of the garret. A strange odor emanated from Phoebe's door, which was ajar. A feral odor, a stench of rutting . . . the sourness of cat and the ripeness of the jungle.

The roar came from within.

"I'll go first," Zack said.

He braced the Colt against his shoulder and shoved against the door. Fired. Fired again. I heard the ricochet. Glass smashed. On the bed, a trail of blood that led to the window.

I ran there.

Out on the rooftop terrace, in the twilight, running, a shadow—

"Come on," I said.

"But ma'am," Zack said. "I think we scared her off—"

"No," I said. "I'm going to face this creature down."

I took him by the hand and led him through the landing door onto that terrace. The bottle tree tinkled in its planter. There was the flagpole with its bizarre escutcheon.

I listened. Nothing. The wind. The sun had already set. Across the alley, where my rooftop almost touched the corner house's, a corpulent woman was hanging her laundry by the lamplight. Bedsheets and long johns billowed, as did Mrs. O'Donnell's skirts.

"Evening to yer, Mrs. Grainger," she called out.

"Evening, Mrs. O'Donnell," I said nervously.

I must have looked a sight, with my clothing in disarray, brandishing a derringer, and a dashing young man, his shirt half-

buttoned, pointing a Colt this way and that. I tried to remain po-
lite. When all is in chaos, one's manners are all one has left.

"Do you think it'll rain?" I asked her. Zack must have
thought me mad; it's sometimes hard for Americans to understand our English addiction to little civilities.

"Wouldn't be hanging me clothes up if I thought that," said
my neighbor. "Though there's a strange kind of rumbling about
the terraces . . . thunder, perhaps."

I heard it. It was not thunder. In the gathering darkness, it
was the distinctive cry of a wild animal.

"Mrs. O'Donnell!" I shouted. I could see the leopard now,
not two feet away from her, a shadow behind a great white bed-
sheet.

"For God's sake, woman, run!" I screamed.

Mrs. O'Donnell smiled at me. She took a clothespin from her
mouth and reached up to hang up a pair of children's drawers.

The leopard emerged.

Threw itself upon that Irishwoman. She did not even have
time to cry out.

I could not look at first, but then, my fascination warring
with my rising gorge, compelled myself. The woman thrashed
about only for a few moments, as the leopard wrapped itself
around her and ripped at her chest. I fired my derringer, but to
no avail. I only blew a hole in the lady's gore-spattered laundry.

The embrace of beast and woman was a grotesque parody of
what I had been doing only moments before. Mrs. O'Donnell
moaned. Why, I thought, the woman has children, she has
mouths to feed.

An insensate anger burst out in me. "Come," I said. Grimly
I marched over to the edge of the roof, and, heedless of danger,
leapt over to the other side.

The leopard looked up, saw me, moved away. Further. Toward the next rooftop. Obviously it had only attacked the
woman to provoke me. It wanted *me*. It needed to communicate
with me somehow.

And I needed to kill the leopard. Or at least, I needed to kill the monster that was surging up out of my own dark mind.

Zack followed. "Ma'am," he said, "the lady's alive; she's only badly mauled."

"Zack," I said, "go downstairs, run to Sixth Avenue and take the horse trolley to Dr. Tappan's—try to get him to come—my husband was a friend of his." I ripped off the lower portion of my skirts and handed the cloth to him. "A makeshift bandage. Hurry. She's bleeding."

"What about you, Paula?"

"I'm going to stay here. I'll take your Colt; are there any more bullets?"

He handed me the gun and I did not wait for an answer. He might have tried to stop me. I had to go on. I felt somehow invulnerable. Could a few moments of illicit carnal passion have loosed the fetters of my mind this much? I could not tell.

Where had the leopard gone? I caught her scent in the air. I crossed Mrs. O'Donnell's terrace. The next block was easy to negotiate; the terraces were all connected. And now, suddenly, the rooftops were awash with light, for the clouds shifted and the moon was abruptly revealed. A pistol in each hand, I gingerly stepped over the little brick divider. There was another roar . . . more distant. I followed. The next rooftop was a foul affair, with rubbish blowing about, and broken bottles, and a festering malodor that seemed to emanate from piles of indeterminate objects. In the biggest heap of rubbish, an old hobo was sleeping, surrounded by empty bottles. At his feet was an overpainted young girl who could have been a practitioner of only one profession.

I had not known I lived so close to such human degradation. I walked past these people . . . and there were others, too. The scent of the predator was almost—not quite—overwhelmed by that of human offal and sour wine, and the sickening fragrance of opium.

Why, this was hell! And I had seen the poverty-stricken areas of town—my husband had ministered mostly to the needy—and this rooftop was as nightmarish as any of them.

A baby cried. He was wrapped in newspaper, being rocked back and forth in the arms of what looked like a ten-year-old girl.

The leopard!

She was wandering freely among these living dead. The poor, the malnourished, the indigent gave it little more than a passing glance. She turned, glared at me, roared again. Its eyes were brighter than the stars. I followed. Another rooftop. I clung to a drainpipe as I made my way across. What an evening! Me, the minister's wife, suddenly become a primeval apewoman, tracking a beast of prey in the savage jungles of Manhattan!

"Where are you taking me?" I screamed. Somewhere below, a horsecar trotted past; bells jingled; a hawker advertised meat pies.

The leopard leapt again. This time, I was sure I could not follow. The gap between the houses was too wide . . . although, if I stood upon a rickety wooden ledge, I could surely almost hop across to the other side. . . .

No. The leopard turned away from me and now I saw what the leopard saw . . . what I had already seen once before, but only in a dream . . . I saw my servant, Phoebe, dancing naked in the moonlight.

The roof she danced on was bare, save for a few chimney pots which rose from the cement like baroque buttes or rock formations; one belched smoke, and in that smoke my servant danced, keeping rhythm with her own feet and by shaking a tambourine. She whirled; with hands that imitated the leopard she clawed the air; she sank to the ground and mimicked the stealthy tread; she howled and roared and hissed.

The leopard stared intently at my maid. Then she began to circle Phoebe. Her haunches rippled. She bared her teeth and I thought that she would attack Phoebe. But no. Slowly, Phoebe became aware of the leopard's presence. And she began to gesture to her, stretch out her arms to it, sway back and forth; and presently the leopard, with a shattering roar, hurled herself at her, but not to kill; eerily, the leopard too began to dance.

The tambourine taps accelerated. The leopard jumped over Phoebe as she knelt, staring at the moon, shaking the tambourine. Feverishly Phoebe somersaulted now, cartwheeled over the leopard as she pawed the ground, embraced the leopard. And as I watched this bestial pas de deux, a rainbow of emotions invaded my mind. The demon curiosity of course. And there was a strange beauty to it all. But the anger overcame it all. It conquered all reason—for should I not have been quivering in terror, and fleeing back to my home? Instead, I wanted to kill them all—the phantoms, the confusions, the dark discoveries I had made about my husband—I wanted to make them all go away.

The leopard dancing reached a climax. I could hardly tell which was the Negress, and which the leopard. I no longer cared. I scrambled across where the eaves almost touched, stalked over to the dancers until I was right in their midst, then fired point-blank into the whir that I thought was the leopard.

And then there was only one.

Phoebe stood there in the moonlight, facing me. She was no longer naked. She wore a leopardskin cloak, and she was crowned with a helmet of grass, and she held the tambourine in one hand, and I could see that the tambourine was bleeding, dripping gore all over the paving of the terrace. She looked at me gravely and said, "Well, now, Mrs. Grainger, you know many thing you did not know before."

"The leopard . . . your mother?"

"Eleuthera."

"But did she not die? In my husband's story, she refused to live—"

"Yes," said Phoebe. I noticed that she no longer hid behind the impenetrable patois she had previously affected. "My mother does not live as you or I understand it."

"And where is she now? Did I wound her?"

"She cannot be wounded anymore." Phoebe laughed. "She is in me. But sometimes, when times are dark, she likes to come back and to dance with me; dancing in the moonlight, Mrs. Paula, restores the soul." And she wrapped the leopardskin tighter around herself. "Mrs. Paula, I am not your servant. I never have been. Your husband and I are bound together in the eyes of Mawu-Lissa, and I am a true and honorable second wife. I bound him to me by rites of blood. We even jumped over a broomstick together, so that we would be man and wife in the slave way as well as the free. That I swept the floor and washed your clothes is only my duty as a second wife. That I was your husband's favorite is only natural in a second wife. It is you, Paula, who never understood your place in the scheme of things—"

"But that is so—so African!" I said.

"Why," Phoebe said, "so it is. And so am I."

Together we walked back to my rooftop. Phoebe sprang easily across the chasms between the terraces, then leaned over to help me across. It was obviously something she was used to. Now that I looked at her with new eyes I saw that she had always had something of the leopard about her. How had I missed it before? Even at her most submissive she had been like a household cat, always confident of her superior place in the hierarchy of the cosmos.

3

And now Mrs. O'Donnell was lying in my parlor, being attended to by our family physician. Again, midnight was approaching; again the lamps were lit and the tea kettle boiling; and again I sat down with Zachary Brown in my salon, attended to by my maid, once more in a seemly black-and-white uniform, who curtseyed and poured daintily and played the part of the well-trained Negress with cynical skill.

"How is she?" I asked, when Dr. Tappan strode into the room.

"Well, she is delirious," he said. "I have stitched up the opening in her chest, which is bloody, but not lethal; I have given her laudanum; and she moans, and cries out, and speaks of wild animals on the roof."

"Why, doctor—" Zack began, but I shushed him with a finger.

"We didn't see what happened," I said. "I went up to look at the moonlight. I think I saw a struggle."

"Ah, a struggle," said Dr. Tappan. "But by now the miscreant may be long gone—"

"I shot him," I said, "with my late husband's Dragoon Colt."

By now the house was teeming with ragamuffins, for Mrs. O'Donnell had quite a brood, and all clamored to be fed as well as crying and carrying on about their mother's misfortune. Mr. O'Donnell was, of course, at war, like every other able-bodied, red-blooded Irishman from New York. Once her wounds had been treated, Dr. Tappan had the boys move her next door, and I went out into the hall to see that all was well. But as they left, Phoebe bent down to whisper something in Mrs. O'Donnell's ear.

"More witchery!" I exclaimed, but Dr. Tappan only smiled.

"No harm in it, Mrs. Grainger," he said. "This is the nineteenth century; let's not let our little superstitions muddle our lives."

But as the door closed behind them I heard one of Mrs. O'Donnell's children say, "Jesus, Mary, and Joseph! The bleeding's gone and stopped!"

And Phoebe, at the door, was grinning. She reminded me of something, someone I'd encountered recently . . . oh yes. The Cheshire Cat. I had read the Reverend Dodgson's best-selling bit of nonsense only a month ago; someone had sent me a brand-new copy from England, claiming that its fanciful rantings were really profound philosophies disguised as children's stories. I knew by now, however, that my real existence far out-Aliced Alice's.

"Phoebe," I said, "I understand that things are irrevocably changed between us all. But you must give me the time to come to grips with it all."

She only smiled, and then, in a blur, dashed up the stairs. Again, a cat. Or was she perhaps a leopard cub?

I went back to the salon, where Zack still sat.

"You must be so tired," I said.

"I am," he said, "but there's so much more to tell, as well."

"In that case—" I said.

"I know what you're thinking, ma'am," he said, "and I have to tell you, I'm afraid to sleep alone myself. After all we seen today."

"But—"

"Oh, ma'am, you know I'll respect your person, and I won't take no liberties, no more than you'll permit."

"All right, then," I said. I felt more trepidation now than I had felt during any of my nightmares, during that entire encounter with the leopard on the roof. Nevertheless, it seemed only moments before we were alone together in the master bedroom. It was the first time that I had ever admitted a man into that sanctum since my husband's death.

But Zack walked right in, and began removing his clothes, tossing them every which way right there under the light of two kerosene lamps and the moonlight which still streamed in through the drawn curtains. He was like a boy. His mind was untrammeled by this room's oppressive past. His skin was white and red in patches, and still smooth, still childish.

He stood there, shirtless and in his drawers, and smiled, and I thought, Why, this is no tawdry encounter between a frustrated widow and a thoughtless youth who only wants to sow his oats over any field in sight; this boy is far far more than that. He was, in the best of senses, an angel, for that word, as my husband was always at pains to point out to me, is Greek for *messenger*.

Suddenly I began to weep.

"Ma'am," Zack said, "if I come upon you too sudden like, it's only because I'm a rough and unschooled boy; don't be too harsh with me."

Why was I weeping? Was it only now that I understood that Aloysius was truly, irretrievably dead? In that case, Zack was truly the messenger of death, and of new life, releasing me from my self-imposed imprisonment.

Gently, he unbuttoned my sacque of sable satin, undid the black sash about my waist. Gently he unlaced my corset. "Don't cry, Paula," he said. Yet I could not stop. I think it was regret more than anything. My life was half over, and unbegun. He touched me as a sculptor touches an uncarved block of marble, delicately feeling for the form concealed within. He put over my naked body one of those sheer dressing gowns that he saw draped over a vanity chair, and he carried me to my nuptual bed, the bed which covered a slaughtered chicken and a pagan fetish.

I did not cease weeping all this time. So he demurred from forcing himself on me. I said, "No, Zack, I don't mean to forbid your touch—"

But he smiled sadly in the moonlight and said, "I'll tell you a story, instead, until you fall asleep."

"What story?" I said.

I rested my head against his chest, and he said, "I was telling you about Jimmy Lee Cox and his strange odyssey through blighted Dixie . . . but the strangest thing of all is how the stories seem to mirror what we're living through in the flesh . . . for I was just reaching the point where Jimmy and the old nigger met the leopard woman, the one you know as Eleuthera. . . ."

13

OLD JOSEPH RAISES THE DEAD, AND ENCOUNTERS ELEUTHERA

1

I did not confess to old Joseph or even to myself that I had done my father in. Mayhap he was still alive. I tried not to think on him. My old life was dead. Surely I could not go back to the Jackson place, nor the army, nor any other place from which I run. There was just me and the old nigger now, scavengers, carrion birds, eaters of the dead. There I was, with Zachary Brown, and once more the tea was getting cold; and more and more the sense of dislocation was seizing me.

Yes, and sure it was human flesh old Joseph fed me that night, and again that morning. He showed me the manner of taking it, for there was certain corpses that cried out to be let be, whilst others craved to be consumed. We followed the army a safe distance, and when they moved on we took possession of the slain. He could always sniff out where a battle was going to be. He never carried nothing with him excepting a human skull, painted black, that was full of herbs, the same herbs that he always smelled of.

Oh, it was God's country we done passed through, hills, forests, meadows, creeks, and all this beauty marred by the handiwork of men. Old Joseph showed me not to drink from the bloodied streams but to lick the dew from flower petals and cupped leaves of a morning. As his trust of me grew, he became more bold. We went into encampments and sat amongst the soldiers, and they never seen us, not once.

"We is invisible," old Joseph told me.

And then it struck me, for we stood in broad daylight beside a willow tree, and on the other side of the brook was mayhap fifty tents and behind them a dense wood. The air was moist and thick. I could see members of my old company, with their skull faces too small for their gray coats, barely able to lift their bayonets off the ground, and they was sitting there huddled together waiting for gruel, but there I was, nourished by the dead, my flesh starting to fill out and the redness back in my cheeks; it struck me that they couldn't see me even though I was a-jumping up and down on the other side of the stream; and I said to old Joseph, "I don't think we are invisible. I think . . . oh, old Joseph, I think we have been dead ever since the day we met."

Old Joseph laughed; it were a dry laugh, like the wind stirring the leaves in autumn; and he said, "You ain't dead yet, honey; feel the flesh on them bones, no, your *beau-père*, he nurturing you back to life."

"Then why don't they see us? Even when we walk amongst them?"

"Because I has cast a cloak of darkness about us. We be wearing the face of a dark god over our own."

"I don't trust God. Whenever my pa seen God, he hurt me."

Smiling, he said, "You daddy warn't a true preacher, honey;

he just a *houngan macoute,* a man which *use* the name of God to adorn hisself."

And taking my hand he led me across that branch and we was right amongst the soldiers, and still they did not see me. We helped ourselves to hardtack and coffee right out of the kettle. In the distance I heard the screams of a man whose leg they was fixing to hack off. Around us men lay moaning. There is a sick-sweet body smell that starving men give off when they are burning up their last shreds of flesh to fuel their final days. That's how I knew they was near death. They was shivering with cold, even though it were broad daylight. Lord, many of them was just children, and some still younger than myself. I knew that the war was lost, or soon would be. I had no country, and no father save for a darkie witch doctor from Haiti.

There come a bugle call and a few men looked up, though most of them just goes on laying in their misery. Old Joseph and I saw soldiers come into the camp. They had a passel of niggers with them, niggers in blue uniforms, all chained up in a long row behind a wagon that was piled high with confiscated arms. They was as starved and miserable as our own men. They stared ahead as they trudged out of the wood and into the clearing. There was one or two white men with them two, officers I reckoned.

A pause, and the bugle sounded again. Then a captain come out of a tent and addressed the captives. He said, in a lugubrious voice, as though he were weary of making this announcement: "According to the orders given me by the congress of the Confederate States of America, all Negroes apprehended while in the uniform of the North are not to be considered prisoners of war, but shall be returned instantly to a condition of slavery or shot. Any white officer arrested while in command of such Negroes shall be considered to be inciting rebellion and also shot." He turned and went back into his tent, and the convoy moved onward, past the camp, upstream, toward another part of the woods.

"Oba kosó!" the old man whispered. "They gone kill them."

"Let's go away," I said.

"No," said old Joseph. "I feels the wind of the gods blowing down upon me. I feels the breath of the loa. I is standing on the coils of Koulèv, the earth-serpent. Oh, no, Marse Jimmy Lee, I don't be going nowhere, but you free to come and go as you pleases of course, being white."

"You know that ain't so," I said. "I'm less free than you. And I know if I leave you I will leave the shelter of your invisibility spell." For that I gazed right into the eyes of the prisoners, and tasted their rancid breath, and smelled the pus of their wounds, and seen no sign of recognition. There was something to his magic, though that I was sure it come of the dark places, and not of God.

So I followed him alongside the creek as the captives were led into the wood, followed them uphill a ways until we reached the edge of a shallow gully, and there was already niggers there, digging to make it deeper, and I seen what was going to happen and I didn't want to look, because this warn't a battle, this were butchery pure and simple.

Our soldiers didn't mock the prisoners and didn't call them no names. They were too tired and too hungry. The blacks and the whites, they didn't show no passion in their faces. They just wanted it to end. Our men done lined the niggers and their officers up all along the edge of the ditch, and searched through their pockets for any coins or crumbs, and they stripped them of their clothes and their dignity, and they turned them so they faced the gully and they done shot them in the back, one by one, until the pit was filled; then the Southerners turned and filed back to the camp. Oh, God! As the first shots rung out it put me in mind of my mother Mary, halfway across the bridge, with her old life behind her and her new life ahead of her, dead on her face, and the bloodstain spreading from her back on to the lace and calico.

And old Joseph said, "Honey, I seen what I must do. And it a dark journey that I must take, and maybe you don't be strong enough to come with me. But I hates to journey alone. Old Joseph afraid too, betimes, spite of his 'leventy-leven years upon this earth. I calls the powers to witness, *ni ayé àti ni òrun*."

"What does that mean, old Joseph?"

"In heaven as it is in earth."

I saw the way his eye glowed and I was powerful afraid. He had become more than a shrunken old man. Seemed like he drew the sun's light into his face and shone brighter than the summer sky. He set his cauldron-skull down on the ground and said, again and again, *"Koulèv, Koulèv-O! Damballah Wedo, Papa! Koulèv, Koulèv-O! Damballah Wedo, Papa!"*

And then he says, in a raspy voice, "Watch out, Marse Jimmy Lee, the god gone come down and mount my body now . . . stand clear less you wants to swept away by the breath of the serpent!" And he mutters to hisself, "Oh, *dieux puissants,* why you axing me to make biggest magic, me a old magician without no *poudre* and no herbs? Oh, take this cup from me, take, take this bitter poison from he lips, for old Joseph he don't study life and death no more."

And his old body started to shake, and he ripped off his patch and threw it onto the mud, and I looked into the empty eye socket and saw an inner eye, blood-red and shiny as a ruby. And he sank down on his knees in front of the pit of dead men and he went on a-mumbling and a-rocking, back and forth, back and forth, and seemed like he was a-speaking in tongues. And his good eye rolled right up into its socket.

"Why, old Joseph," I says to him, "what are you fixing to do?"

But he paid me no mind. He just went on a-shimmying and a-shaking, and presently he rose up from where he was and started to dance a curious hopping sort of dance, and with every hop he cried, *"Shangó! Shangó!"* in a voice that was steadily losing its human qualities. And soon his voice was rolling like thunder, and presently it *was* the thunder, for the sky was lowering and lightning was lancing the cloud peaks.

Oh, the sky became dark. The cauldron seethed and glowed, though he hadn't even touched it. I knew he were sure possessed. The dark angels he done told me of, they was speaking to him out of the mouth of hell.

I reckoned I was not long for this world, for the old man was a-hollering at the top of his lungs and we warn't far from the encampment; but no one came looking for us. Mayhap they was huddled in their tents hiding from the thunder. Presently it began to rain. It pelted us and soaked us, that rain; it were a hot rain, scalding to my skin. And when the lightning flashed I looked into the pit and I thought I saw something moving. Mayhap it were just the rushing waters, throwing the corpses one against t'other. I crept closer to the edge of the gully. I didn't heed old Joseph's warning. I peered over the edge and in the next flash of lightning I saw them a-writhing and a-shaking their arms and legs, and their necks a-craning this way and that, and I thought to myself, old Joseph he is raising the dead.

Old Joseph just went on screaming out those African words and leaping up and waving his arms. The rain battered my body and I was near fainting from it, for the water flooded my nostrils and drenched my lungs and when I gasped for air I swallowed more and more water. I don't know how the old man kept on dancing; in the lightning flashes I saw him, dark and lithe, and the sluicing rain made him glisten and made his chest and arms to look like the scales of a great black serpent; I looked on him and breathed in the burning water, and the pit of dead niggers quook as iffen the very earth were opening up, and there come a blue light from the mass grave, so blinding that I could see no more; and so, at last, I passed out from the terror of it.

2

When I done opened my eyes the rain was just a memory, the sun was rising, the forest was silent and shrouded in mist. And I thought to myself, I have been dreaming, and I am still beside the creek where the dead bodies lay, and I never did see no old Joseph out of my past; but then I saw him frying up a bit of salt pork he done salvaged from the camp. Warn't no morning bugle calls, and I reckon the company done up and gone in the middle of the night, soon as the storm subsided.

Old Joseph, the patch was over his eye again, and he was singing to hisself, that song I heard as a child. And when he saw me stir, he said, "Marse Jimmy Lee, you awake now."

"What is that song?" I asked him.

"It called 'Au Claire de la Lune,' honey, by the light of the moon."

I sat up. "Joseph?"

"What, Marse Jimmy Lee?"

"Last night I had the strangest dream . . . more like a vision. I dreamed you were possessed, and you pranced about and waved your arms and sang songs in a African language, and you raised up nigger soldiers from the grave."

"Life is a dream, honey," he says. "We calls them *les zombis*. It from a Kikongo word *nzambi* that mean a dead man that walk the earth."

The fog began to clear a little and I saw their feet. Black feet, still shackled, still covered with chafing sores. We was surrounded by them. And as the sunlight began to dissipate the mist, I could see their faces; it was them which had been kilt and buried in the pit; I knew some of their faces. For though they stirred, they moved, they looked about them, there were no fire in their eyes, and didn't have no breath in their nostrils. Mayhap they wasn't dead, but they wasn't alive, neither.

They stood there, looming over us. Each one with a wound clean through him. Each one smelling of old Joseph's herbs. They was naked, though some found old rags and was wrapping them around their loins, and they was silent, you know, silent as the grave.

"The magic still in me," old Joseph said, "even without the *coup poudre*."

I reckon I have never been more scared than I was then. My skin was crawling and my blood was racing. I think I like to died of fright.

"I never thought that old magic still in me," said Joseph again. There was wonderment in his voice. No fear. The dead men surrounded us, waiting; seemed like they had no mind of their own.

"Oh, Joseph, what are we going to do?"

"Don't know, white child. I's still in the dark. The vision don't come as clear to me no more; old Joseph he old, he old."

He fed me and gave me genuine coffee to drink, for the slain yankees had carried some with them. I rose and went over to the pit, and it were sure enough empty save for the two white officers. "Why didn't you raise them too?" I said.

"Warn't no sense in it, Marse Jimmy Lee; for white folks there is a heaven and a hell; there ain't no middle ground; best to forget them."

So we threw dirt over them and we marched on, and the column of undead darkies followed us. I could not name the places that we passed, but old Joseph knew where he was going. It was toward the rising sun so I guessed it was southeast. Raleigh was to our back, though; I reckon we were heading to South Carolina, or maybe Georgia. But it all looked the same to a boy who had never seen much of the world afore this.

And presently Old Joseph led us into a wood, and we walked the livelong day in a quiet place that had never seen war. We walked until the blisters on our feet hardened over, and I felt no more pain. The forest was cool and the darkness was like my mother Mary, holding me in her arms when that I was a baby. In the forest, birds was singing, and the streams run deep and clear and free of putrefaction. I slaked my thirst and even my soul felt clean.

"What forest is this?" I said to Old Joseph as we sat by that creek and shared us a fish.

"You ask too many questions," said he, "and sometimes the questions you ask, they hard to answer."

"Are you lost?"

"No," said Joseph, "we found."

I once was lost, I thought, but now am found. . . .

Were this salvation then, to camp out in the open next to a sorcerer who knew how to bend the laws of God and Man? Oh, but I knew not. Like as the hart panteth for the water-brooks, so longeth my soul for thee, O God, thought I, remembering my pa, remembering his way of getting close to the Lord.

The dead did not eat, nor drink, of that forest's bounty.

And when we emerged from that wood, we were in a new clean road; war seemed not to have touched this place either. Indeed, we saw not a soul, secessionist or yankee, and every house we passed was deserted. It was many days before we saw another human.

3

At nightfall we rested. We found a farmhouse. There warn't no people and the animals was all took away, but I found a ham a-hanging in the larder, and I feasted. In the night I slept in a real bed. Old Joseph sat out on the porch. The *zombis* did not sleep. They stood in a ring outside the house and they swayed softly to the sound of Joseph's singing; as I looked out of the smashed window I could see them in the moonlight, and there was still no fire in their eyes; and I recollected that they hadn't partaken of no victuals. What was it like to be a *zombi*? Iffen that the eyes are the windows of the soul, then surely there warn't no souls inside those fleshy shells.

We found plenty of gold in the abandoned house. They done hid it in a well, which was surrounded by dead yankees; I reckon they done poisoned it so that the Northerners wouldn't be able to drink their water. But poison means naught to the dead.

We walked yet further the next day. We looked for another farm to spend the night, but the first few which we saw showed signs of habitation, and we didn't want to rouse no suspicion. I guess we were back in the realm that the war had visited, for when I spied upon people in their houses, they looked hungry and sad, and sometimes they sat in their windows staring out at a great grave emptiness, and I wondered iffen they was alive or dead, knowing now that the line between life and death was not as sharply drawn as I had onc't believed.

I suppose, at a pinch, if any patrollers come down the road, I could have said the niggers was all mine, but that were hard to believe, even though I done dandied myself up from a chest of drawers in the last farmhouse, and I pilfered for myself a jacket of fine black silk which was too large in the shoulders, and a goodly horse, too, though I dared not ride him, for I think I smelt of the dead. Oh, I was a sight. We took the narrowest roads, and though I stood at the head, holding the horse's reins, it were Old Joseph that told me which way to turn; and I was thankful for that, for I was as lost as a boy can be, and I knew not even what state we were in, but that I was far from home.

Behind us was that line of niggers.

Presently, I was so damn tired that I said, "Old Joseph, we have to rest, even iffen it's just by the side of the road."

And he said, "Patience, Marse Jimmy Lee. We almost there."

"Where?" I said.

"Where we goin'," he said. And the stars were coming out. And I was bone tired. The dead, I reckon, weren't. They just kept on walking. I hadn't figured out yet as how a dead man could feel.

Every couple of miles, Joseph stopped and took a deep breath of the air around us. "Are you sniffing out someone?" I asked him.

"Yes, honey, I is," he said.

"What, old Joseph?"

"The vision," he said. "It clearer now. It clearer."

And finally he waved his arms and the column come to a stop, the rear corpses colliding with the middle ones, like dominoes. "Look, Marse Jimmy Lee," he said. "Peer through them mulberry bushes alongside the road."

I did. I saw an old decrepit house much like the others that we had passed by. In the front was a old woman rocking in a chair, a-knitting and a-singing to herself, too soft for me to hear the words; and a lantern lay at her feet. And I heard a sobbing child.

"Is this where we're stopping the night?" I asked him.

"I reckon," said Joseph.

So, solemnly, we trooped through that gate, which swung open to receive us, then broke off its hinges and crashed into the mud. The house seemed close from the road, but the stone pathway wound and twisted, and now I heard the singing right close in my ear, and now it seemed afar off, like a angel. The path was made of flat, jagged stones overgrown with weeds. And all along the way there was dead people. There was a laborer with a hoe, a-leaning up against a peach tree, shot through the heart. He was dead a long time, I reckon, because the skull was showing through the drying flesh. There was a baby cut in two, sitting atop a wagon wheel. There was a woman sliced to the bone from bayonet cuts, splayed on the branches of another peach tree, and from this tree hung hundreds of bottles, tinkling in the evil-smelling breeze.

"How," I raged, "can they be so cruel? To their own kind, even?"

Joseph laughed, a dry bitter laugh. "And when your friends done slaughtered the nigger soldiers, it were not they own kind? Do not speak of this kind and that kind, Marse Jimmy Lee. You gots a soul, and you soul the same color like mine."

"But Joseph," I said, "you raised up the dead black soldiers, and left the white to rot."

"I told you," he said, "they warn't no sense in it."

There was a young boy a-hanging from the next peach tree, strung up with his own belt it looked like. He was younger than me, I reckon. Dark-haired, and eyes like emeralds, watery and green. His bare chest thin, like he hadn't eaten in a week before he come to his untimely end; a pair of nankeen trousers on him, much too wide, that drooped down from his hips, and was cut off at the knees. And now come the strange part: his left foot was all chawed off, as if a bear had been at him.

Now Old Joseph, he peered might long and hard at that boy's foot, pinching his fingers together to gauge the size of them fang marks, and sniffing after the bony remnant of the heel.

And he said to me, "Yes," he said, "this the house we stopping at tonight."

And our eerie procession went up the path until we reached the veranda where that woman was singing; and this is the song she sang, and it was a chilling song, for that she sat there, knitting, with two dead women at her feet, young, alike as peas:

> *Run, ladies, run,*
> *Or else we're gonna getcha,*
> *Run, ladies, run,*
> *You'll never get away.*

The two ladies at the woman's feet was dressed all in white, like they was getting ready for church, or maybe even fixing to get hitched, for they had veils over their faces, and little corsages in their hands, and they lay one acrosst t'other, their arms around each other's shoulders. But each had a wound in the chest, a gaping hole, a crack in the ribcage, and no heart where the heart should be.

I marveled on it. But old Joseph seemed to think that sight as natural as any we'd seen already.

And here's what the woman done sung next:

I've got a girl lives over the hill,
If she don't kiss me, her sister will;
And if her sister won't be had,
She's a mother back home who ain't half bad.

And I knew then that she was gone crazy, that the yankees been through this place and ravished every one of them daughters, and her too, and maybe even her son, and that it had made her mad.

"That's a yankee song," I said. "Excepting that, I don't think they sing 'kiss'; I think it's another word they like to use."

"There be songs the Southerners sing," said Joseph, "which say the same thing."

The woman kept singing that song, over and over; and then I noticed something about her knitting; what she knitted with one gesture, she unraveled with another; and so the scarf she was fixing to make wasn't never gone get made. She were frozen inside of a few moments of time, reliving them again and again and again.

"Ma'am," I said, and I doffed the slouch hat that I done stole from the last plantation, "I do hope I can avail myself of your hospitality." For every established Southern home has guest quarters, with their own private entrance, to be used by any which might stray that way. "And mayhap you can borrow us a barn, for my darkies to doss down in."

The lady paused in midnote. I guess I woke her from her reverie, or shattered the spell that had kept her stuck in that span of time, for she looked of a sudden as though she were regaining consciousness. She gazed at me for the longest time. She did not, of course, really notice my niggers, standing and swaying in a long line all the way down that gravel path. "Why," she said at last, "it is such a pleasure to have company at last. I craves company, I surely do. And a fine young gentleman, too, with a rich retinue of bondsmen!"

I bowed.

"Yet," she said, "alas, I regret that my two daughters are already spoke for. Ah, 'tis a pity, 'tis a pity!"

"Are these your daughters, ma'am?"

"Ah yes," she said—she never ceased from knitting and unknitting all the while—"Biddy and Lolly; such a pity that someone has stolen their hearts."

A chill took hold of me. For I think she could no longer tell the reality from the image; it was all one to her.

"Who done it?" I asked her.

"Why," she said, "two gentlemen from the North, both Johnson by name, an elder and a younger."

"The enemy," I said.

"Come now," she said. "All this talk of enemies; surely you don't believe it, sir; brother against brother, father against son; that is abomination, and I won't hear such nonsense in my house. Are we not all, by the grace of God, white?"

"And you, ma'am," I said, "you too?"

"Well, the Johnson brothers did deign to flirt with the old woman, and we did dance a jig or two, yes, these old legs can still caper, you know! But I am, alas, not pure and virginal; the angel did not see fit to take me. But I still have hope."

"Angel?" I said.

"Oh, oh, oh, oh, didn't I tell you?" she said. "Why, after the wedding feast, a mighty angel come down to carry my babies to paradise."

"An angel?"

"Bright as the sun, an angel with a hundred eyes," said she, "and oh, oh, oh, I craves to foller that angel into the sky, but God tells me I must tarry a while yet. Oh, sir, are you that angel? For the ministers of God take many forms."

"I ain't no angel," I said, "although I done preached the word of God once in a while, when my pa was too drunk to open the good book to the right page. Not that the right page mattered; I can scarcely read or write. My name's Jimmy Lee Cox, ma'am, and right honored to make your acquaintance."

"And I, Mr. Cox, am Mrs. David Arthur Knight, Senior; though you may call me Valerie; for since I am widowed, I've a fancy to be a Miss again."

"Miss Valerie," I said.

I looked on her which claimed to have spoke with angels. She was a woman with wild, gray hair and eyes that darted back and forth, and she wore a skirt of calico over crinoline, fashionable but tattered; and stuck in that unkempt hair was an amber pin. People who have seen the supernatural, I know, are changed from within. And that is why I surely believed that Miss Valerie had seen *something*—perhaps not a angel of the Lord, but of the other kind.

"Miss Valerie," said Joseph, whom she suddenly seemed to notice for the first time, "that angel that you seen; perchance he took another shape . . . for angels can come to us in many shapes. Tell me the truth, Miss Valerie . . . did that angel she look to you like a gigantic spotted cat . . . a leopard?"

And then I knew what them bite marks were that I seen on the hung boy's foot. And I wondered whether a leopard could take the heart clean out of a body, and leave the rest.

"Leopard? Leopard?" And Miss Valerie was a-cackling and a-carrying on, and presently she was weeping, too, and she said, "We have no leopards here, boy. My son, David Junior, they say was kilt by one of them critters; but that was in another country—Virginia, I do believe—where mayhap such beasts may live. I told him not to stay at the house of that Ebenezer Judd, for that he was a gambler and a wicked man; they say that a wild animal killed my son, but I think it was old Judd himself . . . the man never liked to lose at gambling, I hear tell. Leopards galore up there, though, and dragons, and unicorns, and all manner of fabulous beast. At least, that's what Junior always told me in his letters. They were not spots, I say, upon that angel's hide, they were its hundred eyes, for seeing all the good and evil in your heart."

Joseph called me aside a moment, and he whispered, "Tell

the old woman you gone call the angel back for her; tell her the heavens gone ope up, and she gone see the glory and the majesty of God on high."

"What?" I said. "But I can't do that."

"Tell her," old Joseph said, "you knows a spell that gone summon him back down, out of the bosom of God the Father."

"But I don't know nothing like that!" I said.

"Tell her," he said. "You know she ain't gone listen to me."

"Miss Valerie," I said, "what iffen I could bring that angel back to you? What iffen I could summon him back out of the mists?"

"Oh, oh," she said, "oh, don't I wish it! Don't I wish he could have come for me too, that we might all be sitting at God's right hand together, Biddy and Lolly and me! Why, I would die happy."

"Well, ma'am," I said, "I have a power."

"You do, my boy? I knew that iffen I was to sit here on this porch for long enough, there would come a savior. It's all in the patience, Mr. Jimmy Lee Cox. Oh, I was tempted to make an end of it; I came to the end of my scarf, you see, and I had naught else to do; then I get the idea to reap with the one hand what I sown with t'other, if you catch my drift; so I've been waiting longer than I thought I had the strength to wait. My daughters are pretty, aren't they?"

"They surely are, ma'am," I said.

The dead Misses Knight shifted a little; with decomposition, with the writhing of the maggots within, they had acquired some semblance of animation, for one stretched out her arm, and t'other fell onto the first daughter's bosom, for all the world like the tenderest dear sisters.

"Well," said Valerie. "It grows late, but you must have a little nightcap before you go to the guest room, and I will have Clytaemnestra show you the stables where you can put away your darkies for the night." And she reached down at her ankles to pull up a little bell, which she rung with all her might.

The front door creaked open and there was a mammy standing there, with her hands on her hips and a bandanna on her head, like I'd seen in a hundred houses of the wealthy. She looked at me, and then looked at old Joseph—and you never did see such terror in a nigger's eyes. And she begun shouting at him in some African tongue.

To which he only responded, with a curious kind of sweetness, *"Mo lá àlá,"* which, he said, turning to me, means, "I dreamed." But what he dreamed, he did not tell her nor me. The slave quieted down a little, and fetched me a glass of bug juice, which I drunk, solemnly, slowly, smiling at the old lady.

"Now," she said, "you must tell me when. When, oh, when will I expect to receive the messenger of the Lord?"

I looked at Old Joseph, who made a gesture as if to say, Say what you will, and so I responded, "Tonight."

"Do you want provender for your slaves?" she said.

"No, ma'am," I said. "They've ate already."

"Why then, sir, good night, and weave your magic well, and I pray that we may meet in paradise."

So saying, the woman set down her knitting and placed her palms together in a prayerful gesture; and so she remained, oblivious to our conversation, for some time, and so she remained still as we walked away to the side of the porch, where the guest quarters was to be found.

But when we reached the door, and I was sure we was out of earshot, I said to Joseph: "What means all this? Why are we staying here? And what is this leopard you keeping talking about?"

"That leopard," said Joseph, "she my wife."

14

THE LITTLE GOOD ANGELS

1

"Your wife?" said I to my ancient companion. "But that's crazy. A man which mates with a leopard?"

"You know, *monchè*," he said, "that God he take many forms, and that He everywhere. And the angels too. Why not in the form of a beast?"

"But surely angels don't mate with men," I said. "They are the purest and chastest of God's creatures. Why, they ain't even made of the dust, as Adam and Eve were, but formed entire from the ether that is God's breath; leastways, that's what my pa told me."

"You did not read you Bible all the way through, honey," said Joseph. "There was the angels who came down to breed with the sons of men . . . in the time afore that Flood."

I had not read the Bible at all, though I knew by rote every chapter and verse which Pa oftentimes quoted; I could not tell iffen the old man was toying with me, knowing full well of my ignorance. I went inside the guest room, and he stayed outside the screen door, knowing his place.

"Joseph," I said, "what is a *zombi*? And how is a *zombi* made?" For he had told me but little, though he had shown me much. I knew it for a African word, a word of terror and power, but I didn't know what it was that made the dead walk.

"A body," said Joseph, "has two souls. One the Great Soul that go to the bosom of God. We calls him *gros bon ange.* But there another soul too. A little soul, a double . . . the Little Good Angel, *ti bon ange,* who hover over the lifeless body for a span, not knowing that the body dust already, and dust to dust; because your *beau-père* a powerful *houngan,* he can see the *ti bon ange* still clinging to the empty flesh, and he can grasp that *ti bon ange* and keep it from ascending to the land beyond; and so that dust he walk again, not knowing that he dead."

"The Little Good Angels . . . the two dead girls on the porch . . . you see their Little Good Angels?"

"I surely do, Marse Jimmy Lee," said old Joseph.

I thought on this. I heard onc't that the ancient Egyptians believed that a body had two souls, called *ka* and *ba.* But I never thought nothing of that fact, since I heard it from a carnival Egyptian who owned a tent where you could see a real live mummy for a penny, and for a nickel you could touch her cunny, which I done, though pa whupped me after, not for doing what I done, but for wasting five cents that could have gone to a dozen Havana cigars.

"Mayhap all Africans have two souls," I said, "but I know a white boy like me couldn't handle more than one at best."

Old Joseph laughed. "Why not two souls? You got two eyes, don't you? Two arms, two ears, two lips?"

"There's a thing I got but one of," I said, laughing. "And it's surely my best part." And that was a thing I'd heard my pa say once, when he was talking about the ladies.

"Rest awhile, Marse Jimmy Lee," said old Joseph at last, "and later, around midnight, you will see what you will see; but iffen you don't got the heart to see, then sleep and dream; ain't nobody gone fault you that you done look away."

The room was comfortable; there were fresh water in the basin, and a pitcher of lemonade, and a sliced ham set out beside the bed for to sup on. And a clean, pressed nightshirt lay upon the bed. I ate and drank and sank into a deep slumber; but when I awoke, it was still dark, and I knew that I would have to look on old Joseph's latest magicking.

2

It was a bright night. Not quite a full moon, but the whole sky were lit up, not just by the moon and stars but something else, too, a soft glow that spread upward from the earth, mayhap from this very house. And it was warm, warmer I think than the season. I walked from that room clad only in the nightshirt, out onto the porch, where the chiggers hummed and the skeeters sang, and the lady of the house were still a-rocking back and forth, back and forth, but this time Clytaemnestra, the mammy, was fanning her, and driving away the bugs from sheer ugliness.

"Have you come to summon me that angel?" said Valerie Knight, looking up at the clear bright sky. "Oh, but I am glad you did."

"Reckon so, ma'am," I said.

"And will that angel be coming?"

"Don't rightly know," I said, "for you can't hurry 'em."

"I remember," she said, "an ancient Greek fable . . . of an aged couple with peculiar names, somewhat like Phyleemon and Bauxis, living in a cottage, simple shepherds. Like me and my daughters, ordinary folks, a little bit saved away for a rainy day, maybe, and a dozen slaves, but nobody fancy. Mrs. Beaumont, our schoolteacher, told us this tale, though she said, of course, it were written by them that had not yet heard the blessed name of Our Lord, and so are condemned to perdition for getting themselves born in the wrong century; nevertheless, she told us, she did, that the ancients still had good things to teach us, morals and manners and such. Well, Phy and Bo, these ancient Greeks, who should come a-walking into their simple abode one day but Jupiter, King of the Gods, and Mercury, his messenger, disguised as plain old peasants. They gone all through the country, and not a soul would take them in, for there's warn't a drop of Christian charity among them. Not that Christian charity had been invented yet, but we may stretch the tale a little bit to fit our situation. So at length the gods came to the poorest house in the land, and the old folks, Phy and Bo, why they took them in, and gave them to eat and drink . . . gave of the last food and drink they had in the cottage, and bade them rest in the finest bed of the house, which was but a pallet of straw, whilst they themselves slept the night on the earthen floor. Well, in the morning, the gods told them who they really were; and they told Phy and Bo how blest they were to have offered hospitality to the gods . . . and they offered them any boon in the world; but Phy and Bo just said, 'We don't ask for nothing at all, just happy to have been doing our duty.' But when the gods pressed them, they said, 'We pray that we may die as we lived, always together, always loving.' And then, when the time come for them to die, why, the gods granted their request, and turned them into one great twin-trunked tree, rooted to the land, but pointing up to heaven. 'Twas a Roman poet who penned that story . . . for we are not without refinement here in the hinterlands, you know, sir, there be some that still know their Greek and Latin. It's a fine tale of love, and fidelity, and the need to be a gracious host, do you not think?"

"Why," I said, "it's a lovely story, ma'am."

"And that is why our door is always open to any stranger that comes by," said Mrs. Knight, "and that is why the Johnsons came to wed my daughters, for we have all, does not the evangelist say, entertained angels unawares . . . and that is why you come to me tonight . . . oh, sir, it has been hard. Do you understand how hard? I have a little book that tells me how to make our meager provisions into something that harks back to more genteel times; do you wish to hear?

"To one small bowl of crackers, that have been soaked until no hard parts remain, add one teaspoonful of tartaric acid, sweeten to your taste, add some butter, and a very little nutmeg . . . there's your apple pie sans apples, sir, for there was some warn't quite so kindly as the Johnsons, and they took away the apples as well as our ladies' virtue. . . ."

Well, the lady was mad, to be sure, but there were a kind of crazed logic to her ravings, and it was easy for me to fall into that way of thinking, where one things calls to mind another, and pretty soon every blame object and thought and idea in the whole universe seems all linked up to every other, like pearls in a necklace, like laborers in a chain gang, and so I started to improvise along with her, "Yes, the apple, ma'am, the apple that started us all on that big old journey from sin to redemption—"

"The apple that was meant for the fairest; sir, do you know that story?"

"All's fair in love and war," I said, for I once heard a captain say that after dumping his woman for a richer.

"War, war, war!" cried Mrs. Knight. "To make artificial oysters, take young green corn, grate it in a dish, to one pint of this add one egg, well beaten, a small tea cup of flour, two or three tablespoonfuls of butter, some salt and pepper, mix 'em all together; a tablespoonful of the batter will make the size of an oyster; fry 'em light brown, and when done butter them. Cream if it can be procured is better."

I could see that the lady was lost to the world. What was I to do? I left her, with her putrefying daughters embracing at her feet, and walked down the pathway a ways, thinking to clear my mind.

The dead niggers had been standing watch around the house, swaying now and then. But I didn't see hide nor hair of 'em. But as I entered the thicket of peach trees, I became aware that they was present all right. Sometimes I could hear a sound like dry twigs crunching. Betimes came a slurping, gurgling sound. I didn't want to think what it could be, but I saw soon enough. For the hanged boy was missing from the tree, and when I turned a corner I saw him lying in the gravel, and one of the *zombis* was pulling out his gut, unwinding it with care, as you might unwind a ball of yarn; another *zombi* was kneeling over the boy's head, hitting it over and over with a stone; I heard the skull crack, then saw the undead darkie reach into that skull to dislodge small handfuls of brain; these he devoured; not with relish, but in a lethargic way, staring dully ahead the while. The chawed foot was now completely off. A third *zombi* was nibbling on it beneath an overhanging branch. Oh, but the smell of it all was rank, yet leavened a little by the sweet fragrance of ripening peaches.

None of them made any move to touch me. Perhaps they only partook of their fellow dead; perhaps the old man had woven a protective spell around me. I did not wait to find out, but walked hurriedly on. But at the next bend in the pathway I saw more ghoulishness. The laborer with the hoe now lay in twenty or thirty pieces, arranged on the ground in a grotesque version of the holy cross of Our Lord, excepting that the head stared up from where the private parts should be, and a dead man was a-chewing on his tongue. The baby that I'd seen split in two before was now put back together, but turned backward on itself so that its head stared in the same direction as its hindparts. Oh, Lord, I was sick from the sight of such deformity, and sicker still from the sounds, for the dead men spoke not while they sucked and slurped and swallowed. What a feast of the damned it was! Hurriedly, I walked on further, toward the barn where the *zombis* was supposed to be bedded down; but at the barn door I saw old Joseph, a-sitting with folded palms, and his eyes closed as though looking on the face of God. But I was too skeert to wait on his awakening. I shook him by the shoulders and cried, "Joseph, Joseph, the dead are eating the dead!"

He smiled and did not open his eye. "Why do it matter, honey?" he said. "They all dead, one way or t'other; they don't feel nothing. But I, I, you *beau-père*, I feel. I feel my woman, she coming down from that luminous sky."

"Your wife? The leopard?"

"Quiet yourself, *monchè*, and listen."

Then he did get up, and he took a sack of cornmeal that he had maybe got out of that barn, and worried a hole in it; and he started to walk up and down the grass, weaving a pattern with the cornmeal; and this is what it looked like:

"What are you drawing?" I asked him.

"Be still," he said. "This a *vévé*, a picture of the holy essence of Legba. Do not ask too much."

"But Joseph—"

"I done told you, listen, listen with you ears, not speak with you mouth!" he cried, and I shrunk back, for he was never stern to me, and I suddenly saw in him a flash of my dead pa.

Here, far from the sight of the cannibal dead, I could still hear the sound of them. At first it might seem just the buzzing of the insects or the call of the frogs, all blent into the sigh of the wind and the rustle of the peach trees, but Lord, behind those sounds of nature were the unnatural ones. I listened harder now, though, and I perceived a yet deeper layer of sound in this night. It were a slow, continuous throbbing . . . like the palpitating of a great heart . . . though it were faint, mayhap even below the threshold of what a body could truly hear, yet if I listened long and hard enough it become the greatest sound of all, a sound that shook me to the marrer, that bubbled through my racing blood and made with shivery all over. It were a sound like the purr of a cat, only big, like that cat had become as huge as the world itself . . . and I knew what the sound was . . . it was the leopard that was spoke of before . . . no circus cat, but a creature wove out of ancient dreams . . . oh, Lord, but I was afraid.

But Old Joseph said, "Be not afraid, Old Joseph sweet child, to you she be gentle as a kitten."

"But where is she? I hear—I can't help hearing—but I don't see nothing."

"Then look up at the stars," said Joseph, "look up at the country of dreaming."

And I gaze up beyond the moon. And I see stars, number-less stars. But then, certain stars among them stars, they didn't sit still up there in the sky, but they were moving . . . and I saw that behind the stars was the shape of a great cat, blacker than the night, its thigh muscles all a-rippling as it dashed among the constellations . . . and it was coming down to earth . . . and as it moved down towards us, it was losing its transparency, it was sucking up more and more of the nature of earth and dust, our mortal nature . . . and finally, when it reached the earth, it was all solid, walking warily towards us. Oh, it were a beauteous thing, this leopard, for in its eyes still shone the luster of them stars, and on its skin still glistened the silver sheen of the moon, and its spots was surely like them hundred eyes that Mrs. Knight done spoke of.

And Joseph whispered, "Freedom, Freedom."

"Freedom?" I asked him.

"That be the leopard name," said he, and his eye too sparkled, with the same starlight that shone from the leopard's eyes, and he spread out his arms and walked toward the creature, fearless as the fightingest regiment in the army; and the leopard came loping toward him, and then, when the two of them stepped onto the *vévé* which Joseph had drawn, when they touched, they merged, in a way, and he became a little like a leopard, and she like a beautiful black woman, old, but not a old nag all broken down like you see on farms, but a tall, coal-black, proud-featured woman such as came from Africa and never got her spirit broke on the auction block. She was right fair, iffen you can call a dark thing fair.

So they embraced, man and beast, and sure it were an act of love.

But then come the part that was full of pain.

For when the man and beast separated, they were no longer Old Joseph and his leopard mistress, standing there upon that mystic symbol that was drawn in the grass; for first come a different leopard, bigger, with a patch of fur where one eye should have been, and with silver hairs mixed in with the tawny; and then the woman that I spoke of, the willow-woman carved from a ebony branch, standing together; and I saw that between the two of them there was but a single man-essence and a single leopard-essence, which they could swap back and forth as easy as they was hats or greatcoats.

"Jimmy Lee," said the woman—she did not call me Massa, which was strange to me, even though I hadn't never owned no darkies myself—"Me Leuthera, and that a ancient word she mean Freedom; Leuthera come all the way from a far country, cross the seven seas and continents; me speak to you from the land of the dead."

"Where is old Joseph?" I cried out. "Where is my *beau-père*?" And I begun to weep full sore, for that I was afeared old Joseph would abandon me here, in the wilderness, which wouldn't be a surprise to me, since everybody I ever loved done leave me, one way or t'other.

"Oh, don't you fret, little honey-chile," said Eleuthera. "Me tell you, your stepdaddy come back to you soon. But first us'ns got to go a-soul-stealing."

She pulled from her bosom—she wore a flowing robe, dyed in brilliant colors, and her hair was plaited and wove like a mass of snakes, indeed when I looked a little more close, her hair *was* sometimes snakes—a kind of rattle, which was a calabash wrapped round with the skeleton of snake, and she begun to shake it. The three of us walked toward the house, where the woman and her dead daughters was still awaiting us.

3

"Oh, Lord," said Mrs. Knight, and it was sad to see her poking her two daughters in the cheeks and shoulders and trying to waken them from their dead slumber. "Oh, look, Biddy, look, Lolly, the company of heaven have arrived. Oh, Lordy, Lordy, hallelujah, our-father-which-art-in-heaven, peace-on-earth-goodwill-towards-men." And her voice became shrill as the excitement told hold of her. "Oh, Lordy, Lordy, Lordy, here comes the angel with a hundred eyes."

"Mrs. Knight," said I, "here is old Joseph, come for to carry you home."

And Eleuthera said to me, so softly that the others could not hear, "Behold, chile, now you gone see them *ti bon anges* dancing."

And she started to shake the rattle, which made a sound like this: *a-SSON! a-SSON! a-SSON!* And now, in the distance, other music began. Tinkling. Plucking. Moaning. Sighing. She lifted the rattle high and the snake bones moistened in the moonlight; it seemed like they was weeping. Where was the other music coming from?

I turned to see the band come up the pathway from the peach orchard. *Zombi* after *zombi*, marching in shuffling unison, and each one held a grisly instrument in his hands. One blew on a whistle that were a human arm bone. Another twanged a harp whose strings was a man's intestines. A third, a fourth, a fifth, banged bones together, a sixth drummed out a solemn beat on a human skull . . . I knew it was the skull of the man whose brains was being ate before . . . but now the cavity was closed up with a stretched-out flap of skin, and the dead man was using a forearm for a drumstick. And others of the *zombis* was singing, if you could call it that, for they oped their mouths and a dry, wheezing, empty melody come squeezing out of them, as from a broke accordion or a ruptured bagpipe. And the music made by this orchestra of the damned filled the night air, and the cries of the night animals and the buzz of insects all mixed in with it together, and it become a surging, tuneless harmony that made my hair all stand on end, yet I could no more shut it out from my mind than you can shut out the roar of the wind, for it invades your very bones.

"Look now," Eleuthera whispered, "here come the Little Good Angels."

I approached the stoop. "Oh, but you sure are a fine figure of a young man, Mr. Cox," said Mrs. Knight. "You are as refreshing to look at, I declare, as a cool glass of water; and you know, a few leaves of sheep mint, held in the mouth, or chewed, just before water, will seemingly impart a degree of coolness to the draft. . . ."

"You can forget all that now, Mrs. Knight. All them receipts for making do in hard times, well, you ain't gone need them no more, where you're going; for there, the water is always cool, and the oysters always fresh, and there's always real apples in the apple pie; you have my word on it."

"Oh, but they are good receipts," she said, "and I worked so hard to gather them, and to make sure that my family had provender, even when there was none to be had."

"I'm certain of it, ma'am."

She smiled. "I've been good, ha'n't I? I never beat my slaves but once or twice."

"You sure have, ma'am," I said, and the tears was gathering at the corners of my eyes.

"Then take my daughters, and take me, and let us rise to paradise in a blaze of glory, all together."

Biddy and Lolly lay there, just as dead as ever. But as the music got louder, I saw a stirring inside of them. Maybe it was just the worms, catching the rhythm, writhing to the drumbeat. Maybe not. For presently, there issued, from the cavities that onc't held their hearts, a rosy pearly light that issued in a tight beam over the wooden steps. The light broke up into little strands that swum in the air afore our faces, and then the strands knitted themselves into the shape of two young ladies; ghostly, to be sure, for you could see right through them to the peeling paint on the doorposts, but flaxen-haired and right handsome. And they was attired in purest virgin white, raiments of satin warped from the air and woofed with light. And their eyes just dazzled me, for they was lit by that selfsame starlight that burned in the eyes of the leopard, and the eyes of the Ethiop woman out of the sky.

And the rattle sang, *a-SSON, a-SSON, a-SSON.*

And the Little Good Angels danced a gentle, dainty minuet. They did not smile, but their eyes did. They danced and danced. And Mrs. Knight watched them, with the tears streaming down her cheeks. For as they danced, and as Eleuthera swayed and shook that rattle, the leopard that was my *beau-père* loped up the steps and, piece by piece, devoured their bodies, swallowing them up into himself until they were no more; there was not even a bloodstain.

When the girls saw that their bodies were consumed, they turned and each one of them took one of their mother's hands, and they begun to tug at her whilst she sobbed; and as the music done swelled up, they yanked her soul free, and there was a third creature of light between them, and she too was clothed in the luminous raiment of the gods.

And the three of the rose up into the sky, and were lost among the clouds.

The music went on awhile. At long last it subsided, and the rhythms became unrhythmic, and the whine of the flutes petered out, and the woman and the leopard walked back toward the barn, and they stood in the midst of that magical symbol, and embraced, tenderly, for a time. I blinked away my tears. For a moment there warn't two of them no more, but a single shaft of searing light. Then that too faded, and along with it all the light that had brightened the sky, and I knew it was truly night.

And I remained alone with old Joseph in the gathering darkness. Even the *vévé* was no more, for the cornmeal done blew away in the wind.

"Not many," he said at last, "can see Mawu-Lissa, the man-woman who done made the universe."

"Old Joseph," I said softly, "who are you?"

"No one," he said, "no one, Marse Jimmy Lee; just a old slave, *monché*, just a old slave."

15

WHEREIN MR. WHITMAN MUSES ABOUT THE NATURE OF THE COSMOS

1

"At that point," said Zack, "Jimmy Lee paused in his narration. He was overcome with weeping. I can't say as I was too surprised at that. It was as tragic a tale as I had ever heard in all of my short life; tragic and beautiful at the same time."

We had lain there half the night already, myself in Zachary Brown's tender and sheltering arms, on a bed which once my maidservant and my husband had profaned together. I don't know whether I really stayed awake through all of what Zack told me; I know that at some point, his tale grew to such a verisimilitude that I must have been hearing him as I dreamt, and dreaming up the images to go with it; I was sure I had lived through that horrific incantation, and the orchestra of the living dead, and the girls' souls dancing on their way to paradise, and the old man and the old woman switching their souls and bodies every which way, and that poor young boy, the preacher's son, whose speech was a strange cross between the grammatical solecisms of the hillbilly and the ornate splendor of the King James Bible. It all seemed real to me, and not at all a fantasy, though quite fantastical.

I wanted to return to the twilit world of Zack's narration. For though it was horrific, it had a kind of clarity, a precisely layered structure, like those dolls they manufacture in Russia, one inside the other, easier to comprehend than my confused and bitter reality.

And, so, though I knew that Zack was tired, I said, "Oh, go on . . . it's soothing to hear you speak."

"Well," said Zack, "then I'll tell you about what Walt said, and what Kaczmarczyk said, when Jimmy Lee Cox reached that point in his story and could no longer go on. Thing is, Walt had a knack of taking stories apart and putting them back together in new ways, and forcing you to see new things inside of them; and he had a lot to say about it all."

"Why yes," I said, "I would like to know what the poet saw in all this."

"Well, it was evening again, and Walt got up—for a moment I thought he was going to board the ferry, though the last ferry had left, again, without us—but after a time I rose to follow him. I found him walking up and down the riverbank, waving his arms in the air and shouting. So I got real close, to see if I could catch what he was saying. It was all a heap of nonsense, I thought: waves and oceans and storms and tempests and suchlike. He was talking to the river, and the woods across the river, and to the soul of the Commonwealth of Virginia, and the setting sun. At length, though, he saw me, and halted.

" 'Why, Walt,' I asked him, 'what was all that about?'

" 'A poem,' he said. 'And a great mystery.'

" 'A mystery?'

" 'Nothing, nothing, nothing, nothing, nothing will ever get in those history books, nothing at all. We are doomed. History is a serpent devouring its tail, and the tales that we tell are air, are so much empty air.' "

2

"There is," said Walt, **"a** truth that underlies all the tales we've heard, from the story of the leopard woman who ruled over an Egyptian kingdom to the tale of a sorcerer who brought a woman back from the dead in the thrust and throes of his carnal passion; oh yes," said Walt, as we sat around that fire, Kaczmarczyk feeling the firmness of his new body, I observing, and Jimmy Lee weeping from his memories of *zombis* among the cotton fields, sharing stale biscuits and good coffee. "Yes," said Walt, "the truth that we're learning is that we're all kin, and tightlier knit together than ever we dreamed possible, whether we're black or white or red or purple or blue; we're not kin because we're all children of God, or any such specious preacher's reason, but because men are men.

"Oh, the splendor and the horror that is man! Oh, the spectacle and the misery that he creates around him! As I have listened to these tales unfold, I see now that all our myths and dreams and fantasies have but a single source. No, camerado, don't you laugh.

"There is a man without an eye, who wanders the earth; a wise man with mystic powers. And once, in the barren snowy wastelands of the Germanic north, there was too one without an eye, wandering the earth, one who had given up one eye as the price of knowledge. They called him Odin, or Wotan, or Woden, and he it is who gives his name to Wednesday, and they called him King of the Gods.

"To the frozen country of the north came a southerly people, with great armies, different gods, conquering, magnificent warriors, with their banners, swords, helmets, caparisoned horses, plumed and shiny helmets, swords of hard steel, and generals named Caesar; they met with the northerners, and conquered many of them, and they said that the gods of the conquered were the same as their gods after all, and they gave each one of them the name of a god of their own; and Odin they named Mercury.

"Why, Zacko, Odin and Mercury? You've heard the ancient tales, and you think you know this Mercury—fleet-footed, youthful, sandal-winged, messenger of the gods, here, there, and everywhere, more puckish than godlike; so the stories have him.

"But before Mercury there was Hermes, a god of the ancient Greeks, who had become suck'd into Mercury just as Mercury was being suck'd into Odin; and within the Hermes that was like Mercury, swift-footed, golden-winged, there was a more antique Hermes still, a grave old man who held the keys to ancient knowledge; a Hermes who came at the moment of death, to lead you to the halls of judgment, and this brings us by a circuitous route to Egyptian Anubis, jackal-headed, black as any Negro, the fetcher of souls, and thence, by a still more southerly route, to this Legba, this messenger of death, this impregnator of leopard women, this keeper of men's souls, this darker angel.

"And they are all angels, Zacko, whatever name we give them, because *angel* is merely a Greek word for *messenger.*

"You see, we can play the same game with all the personages of these stories, Zack. We see that behind each one is another more ancient, and behind that one yet ancienter, and within that another most ancient, and so on so forth till the dawn of time.

"Yet, camerado, we stand here on the territory of this Columbia, braves of brave new worlds. This is the country to whom the poet Donne compares his naked mistress—'Oh my America my newfound land'—Oh the bright shiny newness of America! Oh the polish'd sheen of newfound Freedoms! Where is the hidden ancient truth behind these bright untarnished modern truths? I tell you it's in these stories!"

I looked around and saw that Kaczmarczyk had follered us to

the bank. And he was standing there, listening with rapt attention, to Walt's ranting monologue—for my white-maned friend had gotten himself all puffed up and red, and was breathing hard from waving his arms about so much.

3

He spoke with a passion—he always spoke with a passion when he chose to speak at all—and his passion made us passionate, even though we didn't understand the man half as much as he thought we did. That was Walt, though; he assumed every man was his equal, even coloreds. He spoke of four or five mythologies, while I had a hard time even with one; he connected all the dots of history, even where no one ever meant them to be connected; yep, that was Walt all right.

The only one who seemed to understand somewhat of the things he said was Kaczmarczyk. I don't know why. I guess coming back from the dead had sharpened his wits. Then, you can't always think a man dull because he don't talk the way you do.

And then again, with half his face blown off and all, maybe he too had traded one eye for knowledge, like Old Joseph, or that Odin feller. Because while Walt was carrying on about all that "everything in the whole world is connected" line of reasoning, and me not really paying much attention because I was thinking he'd rave himself into a frenzy and fall into the river, Kaz seemed just absorbed by the whole thing. He nodded at all the points Walt made, and he seemed even to have heard of them ancient gods and goddesses.

"Didn't you have a story to tell, too, Kaz?" I asked him. Because, the last time I'd been with him when he was conscious, he'd been telling me that demented version of Sleeping Beauty, and I wondered if Walt would find that that story, too, was part of everything connecting with everything else.

"A story! A story!" Kaz exclaimed. "Alvays a story! Don't

you vant to know vhere I've been, the sights I've seen, the devils I've danced vith?"

"So you *were* dead," I said.

Walt said, "And which angel did you see . . . how formed, how shaped? Was the angel of death closer in appearance to this Legba, or perhaps jackal-like, like Anubis, or was it the more conventional Christian apparition of a handsome man with wings?"

Well, Kaz clammed up after that. He didn't want to talk about it at all. And that I could well understand. I knew what it was like to drift between life and death.

Slowly we walked back to the campfire. Jimmy Lee hadn't moved a muscle. He was still sitting by the flames, his can of coffee in his hand. Must of grown cold by now.

After a while he suddenly got up, said, "I'll be back," and started off across the clearing. "Got to see to Pa," I heard him say, before he went out of earshot. I wanted to follow him at first, but Kaz touched me lightly on the shoulder and made me sit down again.

"If it's stories you vant," said Kaczmarczyk, "I got a story to finish, Zacko."

"Yes," I said, "you do."

We sat down to listen, and Kaz stared off into space for the longest time before he started to speak again; and I have to tell you, the tale that he told wasn't the tale that I expected, no ma'am, not at all.

4

If you tink (Kaczmarczyk told us) that that sorcerer Nathaniel and his sleeping beauty lived happily ever after, then you been listening to too many goddamn fairy tales. For yah, the princess avoke to a sensual joy, and yah, the sorcerer anointed her with his seed, and they loved each other and so on so forth; and that vould be the end of the story, but it vasn't vat happened at all.

A man can love and love and love, even love his vay back up out of the grave, but different it becomes vhen they're finally together. And so it vas vith the sorcerer and the princess. At first their love was a perfect harmony, and out of this harmony came a kind of life force which radiated outward from the tower at the heart of the kingdom, and seeped into the ground vhere the citizens lay buried for so long; their very bones, vhited by time, it penetrated, and it drew them forth from the grave. And so they lived again, the people of that fair kingdom, and they laughed, and they vept, and they made love, and all the tings that ordinary people do. But no matter how much they pretended, they vere still dead, you see.

That's vat I vanted you to understand.

They vere dead.

And vat means this dead? Did they have no souls? Vere their bodies merely dancing and swaying to the enchantment of a magic flute, namely the love that emanated from the palace of the princess? I know not. Only, I know that tings vere not the same.

For example, the princess and the sorcerer never made love. Oh, they coupled, but it vas like one machine touching another. And like their new king and queen, the people coupled, but it vas an empty coupling, and no new children vere born, and no one ever died. In short, it vas a country of perfect bliss, and perfect harmony, and perfect love; it vas a country of the dead.

For a thousand years they lived this way. The tides came in, the tides vent out; the sun rose and set; by day the rivers flowed to the sea, but by night they siphoned backward, up to their source; the vheels spun, but the vehicle never moved forvards.

But time stands not still forever.

Vat is life but dust and vint? In the deserts at the outer reaches of the country, the deserts that protected the land from barbarian invasion and imperial conquest, there vas plenty dust and vint. The dust blew this vay and dad. The dust vas chaos, perpetual chaos. But as the centuries vent by, the vint played with the dust, and breathed into it, and slowly, slowly, slowly, built a pattern into vat vas the chaos, and the pattern vas life; and the life grew, century to century, from tiny forms to great forms, until the vint and the dust blended in a virling storm, a great leviathan, and at the heart of the storm vas a living heart, and the storm had a soul; and the storm swept over that desert and into the kingdom vhere ruled Nathaniel and his consort, the princess who came back from the dead.

Human in shape became the virling dust, and vhere it stormed, the trees vere pulled up by the roots, and people and animals fled. But vhere the storm touched them, the people were sucked up, and changed back into the dust vence they had come, and became one with the great storm, and the storm grew more and more powerful, and one by one the villages were subsumed into it, and the storm moved ever nearer, nearer to the capital vhere Nathaniel and the princess held court. And vhen the vord come to the palace, that a great storm out of the desert vas swallowing up all vat lived within the kingdom, Nathaniel's heart grew heavy, and he vas sore afraid.

"Princess," he said, "the time together, vhich ve so dearly bought, now needs must end; that is the vay of tings, for life is not life unless it contain the seeds of its own destruction."

"But," said the princess, "I never even got to bear your children. I never even got to love you as a woman loves a man. I perished in the moment of becoming, and vhen I came back to life I discovered that the becoming vas never destined to come; life you call this?"

But the dust vas battering at the valls of the city, and the populace was in a panic, and they beat down the palace gates, crying, "O sorcerer, O great sorcerer, save us from the devouring dust."

They streamed into the courtyard and shouted up at the vindow of the highest tower, the place vhere the sorcerer had avoken the princess from her sleep of death. They broke down the portals and pulled down the great statues of the deceased king and queen, and they set fire to all that vas not stone, and around the tower the timbers of the great dining hall vere alight, and soon all the palace vas ablaze, excepting that tower that rose up from its heart, for that tower had noting about it that vas vood, or cloth, or perishable matter; its builder had made it to last ten thousand years, and dreamed it vould be the last ting to remain on this earth, vhen life itself vas passed avay, and all consumed by the dust. So, round about that tower, all vas flames, and even the crowds vat had set the conflagration vere being burnt up, one by one, vith shrieks of despair vat were horrible to hear. And still that living leviathan of dust was blowing in circles around the palace valls, and still the princess and the sorcerer sat in the high tower.

At length said the princess, "My people are dying; I must go say farevell."

She stood in the vindow and vatched as her people writhed in a terrible agony, still crying out her name vith their dying breath. She stood as the dusty vint raged, and she vept bitterly, because she could not save her people.

Nathaniel said, "I have lived nine hundred and ninety-nine lives, but now I am impotent for the first time. My love for you sustained me through my last death, brought me back to you, gave me the final strength to pull you from the grave, gave me the power to make this whole kingdom come to a kind of life . . . but oh, my princess, oh, my passion, this life has been only a dream. And less than a dream, for a dead man does not dream, and a dead man's dream is only a dream of a dream of a dream."

And the princess replied, "Is this city then a dream? This tower? This palpitating heart? This virginity inviolate?"

Nathaniel said, "I know not."

Then climbed the princess to the ledge beyond her vindow, and then came the living dust, darkening out the flames, and then flung the princess her arms vide, for the dust storm contained the life vhich the sorcerer's limbs did not; and then cried Nathaniel out, "Oh my princess, oh my love, my life, do not desert me for the desert vint, do not abandon me to the tall stones, do not immure me in this flame-girt tomb, for I have loved the love that loves beyond the grave, and braved the dead earth to embrace that love."

But the princess knew that the vint was life, and the sorcerer death.

And she embraced the dust of life, the dust from vhich the vorld vas molded, and the vint embraced her, and she closed her eyes, and leapt.

Then crumbled the sorcerer to dust.

Then tumbled the tower of stone, and crushed all that remained of Nathaniel, and grount his bones to powder.

And all that remained of that magic kingdom was the dream that was less than a dream, the dead man's dream, the dream vithin a dream vithin a dream.

But vat of the princess?

She drifted. She floated in the vint's dark embrace. She vas not dead and not alive. It vas this vint, you see, vat finally made love to her. It seeped into her soul. In the last moments of her dream-existence, she came to life at last, and fulfilled her vomanhood; and then, at last, that dusty monster devoured vat vas left of her soul, and she became the eye of the storm, and one with the earth and sky.

Vat means this tale? That ve should not vake the dead? That ve should not love so much, for fear that that love should destroy all, kingdoms, people, souls? Or that ve even now live in a dream, a dream that vould not even be dreamed if there vere not someplace in the vorld a love vat reaches out from the dark places, a love vat challenges eternity itself?

I don't know. I knew little before. And now I know even less than I did before. Maybe I shouldn't have come back.

And maybe I am yet dreaming.

5

The story got me to thinking. Was this the same ending Kaz would have told, if Jimmy Lee Cox had not called him back from the dark country? Would he have told a tale of a man and woman living happily ever after, like the way I heard that story on my mother's knee? Was Kaczmarczyk trying to send us a message from the land beyond? Lord, I sure wish I knew.

All I know is that I became curious after a time, and I went to find Jimmy Lee, because I wanted to know what happened next in his *zombis'* journey across the South; and I wanted to know what he had meant when he said he needed to go take care of his pa; and truth to tell, Walt had dozed off in the middle of Kaz's narration, or at least was sitting with his eyes closed, not minding nobody, the way old people get sometimes, and Kaczmarczyk seemed not to want to talk anymore. In fact, he was taking care of Tyler Tyler now, wrapping a blanket around his body, which hadn't begun to harden yet, and looked like he was just sleeping there on the grass, with his hands across his chest, hugging himself, like. Tyler Tyler had long hair, dark brown around the roots, pale at the tips; his hair was in his eyes now; God, he looked young.

So I went across the clearing—it gave me a queasy feeling when I walked over the spot where the leopard had tore out my friend's throat. Night was come, now, and the frogs was croaking and the crickets chirping. A fire glowed on the other side of the clearing, and there was a wagon, and a couple of mules hitched to it, and an Appaloosa tethered to a tree. The wagon wasn't exactly one of your Conestogas; the side of it was painted white, and all covered with them symbols. I guessed they must be what Jimmy Lee called *vévé*, them magical signs that the darkies used in Africa. The canvas was dyed black, but now it glowed, maybe from a kerosene lamp inside.

I heard a thud or somewhat, coming from inside. I got myself up closer and listened. I could hear Jimmy Lee talking, saying things like, "C'mon, Pa, you need your strength, just a little bit more's all c'mon, Pa," and suchlike. So I clomb up and listened a little harder. I seen human shapes moving around, shadows on the canvas.

Well, I heard gurgling sounds . . . and I remembered Jimmy Lee telling us about the corpses eating the corpses somewhere in the heart of Carolina or Georgia or some such country . . . and I shuddered, and I started to get goosebumps, almost hopped back down and run back to our campfire. I was scared shitless, if you'll pardon the expression, and it ain't like me to turn yeller over a few shadows and noises.

But then I heard the boy's voice, "Come on in," he said. "I ain't hiding nothing no more."

And he thrust aside the flap and I saw him and his dad. His father had doffed his preacher's garb and was sitting in front of the lamp with nothing on but his drawers, and he was, well, you might say emaciated, with every one of them chest bones showing through skin that was pale as milk, and shiny. And his mouth was all over blood, and he was chewing on a bone that still had raw flesh hanging from it.

The bone came from a colored man who lay half-eaten on the boards, naked and dead; his arms and legs was already cut off. "He's more likely to eat," said Jimmy Lee, "iffen the body they come from died whole; here's a patient come to be healed, which the gods didn't choose to heal. Come in, Zacko, he ain't gone hurt you, and you can share these biscuits, and a piece of salt pork that I saved."

I crawled in through the flap and it closed, and I was in the lions' den, and I knew somehow that the Lord God wasn't going to get me out of this one; it was up to me. I knelt down right next to Jimmy Lee, and that corpse was mighty rank, and I worried myself about the piece of salt pork, too, thinking where it might have come from. But when I saw Jimmy Lee devour it with relish, I allowed as how it might be just what it seemed to be; and when he sliced off a piece with a rusty knife, I ate it greedily, for meat was not entirely easy to come by at times.

"As I say," said Jimmy Lee, "my pa don't like the cast-off scraps of the living. I got these at one of them hospitals," and he whisked aside a cloth to reveal a jumbled pile of severed arms and legs, "for five cents apiece; but like as not, some of their owners is still walking around, and that makes my pa unhappy."

"Why would it matter to him?" I said.

"Well, you know, he's a sort of a halfway creature hisself, and powerful sensitive to the feelings of other halfway creatures, and he surely knows iffen they be dead or alive."

"Good pork," I said.

"Well, so was your coffee," he said.

It took me some moments to grow accustomed to the smell—the stinking raw human flesh, blended with the odor of sizzling bacon, and everywhere the dank, damp musty smell of unwashed clothes and human waste. The sights I never grew used to. Every time I looked around, the shifting of the candle flames brought some new thing to light—the pustulent ooze from a fingernail, the slick surface of an intestine as it curled, snakelike, along the moldy boards . . . oh, I was sickened by it all. But I was curious, too. Remember, I had already harrowed hell. I had seen mountains of corpses. You might think all this sickening, but I had seen more grander spectacles of horror than could have fit inside of one small wagon.

I wanted to know more.

Paula, you understand. You and I are a lot more like each other than you think. We both got this thing where, if there's a door, a chest, a drawer that's locked, we just got to know what's inside of it, don't matter if we kill ourselves trying. So there was things I just plumb had to know, and I flat out asked that boy. "Tyler Tyler," I said. "You knew him before, didn't you?"

"Why," said Jimmy Lee, "what makes you think that?"

I said, "You was just so quick to come to an understanding;

it was like you had, I don't know, arranged this meeting, a long long time ago."

"Iffen a year is a long long time," said Jimmy Lee Cox, "then you are right, Zacko."

So Jimmy Lee told me about his first meeting with Tyler Tyler, and much much more besides, and about how Tyler went from a whole man to no man at all, and back again.

16

THE ONE-EYED PROPHER MEETS THE ONE-ARMED MAN

1

After that day and night (said Jimmy Lee Cox), after that night of pain and horror and love and death, we marched on south, I guess.

We walked and walked and walked and did not speak, for the things I had seen weighed heavy on my heart, and I knew now that the world I thought I knew was wrong in so many partick-lers that it were best for me to start anew, build a new world from all them broke pieces in my mind. Oh Lord, but that mind of mine was a chaos and a void, just a-crying out for a voice to say, "Let there be light." We walked and walked. And sometimes the leopard came with us, and sometimes she did not; and some-times, when she was not with us, I fancied I saw her walking amidst the night sky, her taut and sinewy shape making a ripple in the field of stars. And then betimes she walked alongside us, an old, proud woman, erect and haughty, a woman who was never a slave, no matter how they chained and whupped her.

And we walked on; and the passel of walking dead became a company, for wherever we went we found niggers that had been kilt, not just the ones in yankee uniform but sometimes a woman lying dead in a ditch, or a young buck chained to a tree that was just abandoned and let starve to death when his masters fled from the enemy, and one time we found seven high-yaller children dead in a cage, with gunshot wounds to their heads; for they was frenzied times, and men were driven to acts not thought upon in times of peace. It was amongst the dead children that I found another cornstalk *poupée* like the one old Joseph gave me ten years before, a-sitting in a vial in the clenched fist of a dead little girl; after we done wakened them, she held it out to me, and I thought there were a glimmer in her eye, but mayhap it were only my imagination.

"Get up and walk," old Joseph said. And they walked.

And I said over and over to him, "Old Joseph, where are we going?"

And he said, "Towards freedom."

"But freedom is in the North, ain't it?"

"Freedom in the heart, honey."

We marched. For many days we didn't see no white folks at all. We saw burned hulks of farms, and stray dogs hunting in packs. We passed other great battlefields, and them that was worth reviving, that still had enough flesh on them to be able to march, old Joseph raised up. He was growing in power. It got so he would just wave his hands, and say one or two words, and the dead man would climb right out of the ground. And I took to repeating the words to myself, soundlessly at first, just moving my lips; then softly, then—for when he were a-concentrating on his magic, he couldn't see nothing of the world—I would shout out those words along with him, I would wrap my tongue around them twisted and barbarian sounds, and I would tell myself 'twas I which raised them, I which reached into the abyss and drawed them out.

And sometimes, of an evening, when I thought that old Joseph warn't looking, I practiced drawing them *vévé* signs in the dirt with a twig, but whenever I heard him a-coming by, I brushed the earth back over them, or covered them with dry leaves. I think he knew, though. Indeed, I think he meant for me to learn his art, for that he had no son to teach, no heir to carry on.

Nights, afore going to sleep, I whispered my troubles to my *poupée,* and sure enough, felt that burden lighten up a little.

Still we encountered no sign of human life. The summer sun streamed down on us by day and seemed like I sweat blood. It warn't at all certain to me that we was still alive and on this earth, for the land was a wasteland, spite of the verdant meadows and the mountains blanketed with purple flowers, spite of the rich-smelling earth and the warm rain. Sometimes I think that the country we was wandering in was an illusion, a false Eden. Or that we was somehow half in, half out of the world.

Though I didn't know where the road was leading, yet I was happy. I trusted old Joseph, and I didn't have no one else left in the world. The only times I become sad was thinking on my pa and momma's death, and wondering iffen my pa was with God now, for he said he done seen the face of God before I smashed his head. Sometimes I dreamed about coming home to see him well again. I dreamed about embracing my father, and telling him what I had never heard him tell me; I dreamed of forgiveness, and reconciliation, and love.

But they was only dreams. I knew that I had kilt him.

On the seventh day we come onc't more into the sight of men.

2

And this is how it happened.

We come down from the hills, and we was crossing a level plain; there was fields a-bursting with unpicked cotton, and mansions a-smoldering in the sun. We walked ahead, old Joseph and me, and this time Eleuthera was with us, bounding over the fields. Behind us, the niggers follered, out in the open; I reckon we'd gotten cocky, for there was no one to catch us no more; all the armed men was in the war, or dead.

But towards nightfall I heard a familiar sound. A pack of dogs, yammering in the distance, just beyond a clump of cottonwoods on the bank of a creek. "Listen," I said.

"Nigger dogs," said old Joseph.

He turned and spoke a few words in an African tongue, and lo! our darkies bent themselves over and rolled themselves up, and seemed to blend in with the rocks and the grass; it were a trick of the light, surely, and if you looked real careful-like, they was all still there, but you had to rub your eyes a couple of times to know they were human beings.

You yankees probably never even heard a pack of nigger dogs, but they are the frighteningest creatures on earth, and they'll chase a runaway all day long until they tree that nigger, or wear him out so he falls to the ground and they can gnaw at his vitals and rend his flesh. Even from far away the yelping and the clamoring sounds like death, and you can smell fear on the wind.

Behind the dogs rides the pattyrollers, twirling their rifles and whooping and cussing, fixing for to flay that runaway alive, or leastways chop off one foot so he won't run no more. But there warn't no pattyrollers here. Instead, behind the dogs, there came just one man on a horse.

"I'm going to look," I said.

"Why you risk yourself over one runaway?" said Joseph. "Better to wait until they kills him; then I can work my magic."

"What use is your magic," I said, "if the dogs tear him to shreds?"

"At least let old Joseph make you invisible," he said, "like them others." And he waved his hands over me, and drew a sign in the air, and this time I knew the sign for a symbol of Legba, the messenger of the gods. And this time I felt that invisibility seep into me, as if invisibility was a gas or a breath of air you could just suck in and hold inside yourself, and stay invisible until you breathed it back out.

"Will you come with me?" I said, for I believed that if I allowed my fear to show, mayhap the spell would wear off and there I would be, getting myself tore up by a pack of nigger dogs, and dead before the bounty hunter could call them off.

"I won't be far behind," old Joseph said.

"But I can't just walk right up to them alone," said I.

"Call to the leopard," said Joseph. "Mayhap she come with you."

So to the sky I whispered, "Freedom, Freedom, Freedom."

Instantly, I felt the leopard's breath; I couldn't see her, but I trusted that she was beside me; and I ran toward the cottonwoods, trusting the leopard's strength and speed to take me.

When I got there, out of breath, I saw that the dogs had treed someone, and there was a couple runners with the dogs, with rifles, though they was thin and too wore out to run that fast; and the man on the horse was a old man, round and bald, with a colonel's uniform, and a sword half out of its scabbard.

"I want him down from there!" cried the colonel. "I want those dogs to tear him to bits, by God!"

What kind of runaway could provoke such anger? I thought. A slave, in the end, is but a slave, and can ever be replaced. Why would a white man make such a fuss? But when I got closer I saw that it warn't no darkie in that cottonwood. I saw a flurry of blond hair, a flash of white skin. I got closer to that tree trunk. There was twenty or more of them dogs, and they was howling up a storm, and a-frothing at the mouth, and snarling, and barking. They was black dogs, big and fierce, hounds of hell you might say. But I figure they couldn't see nor smell me, for I squeezed right through them without a one of them noticing, and soon I was a-shimmying up that tree. "Freedom," I called out softly, and I could feel the leopard's breath hard by me, making my neck hairs prickle.

Halfway up, I looked over the plain and saw old Joseph slowly making his way towards us; he was walking slow, but steady, as though he hadn't a care in the world; behind him, iffen I squinted, I could see the army of the dead, but mostly they was difficult to make out on account of the magic.

I clomb up to the branch where the white boy was sitting, shivering, half naked to be sure; and he only had one arm. With that one arm he was a-rubbing his chest all over, back and forth, and I guess he was in a cold sweat, because in truth it was a hot day, and the air choking on its own moisture. He looked up and down and all about, because the branch was a-shaking and I was invisible and so was the were-leopard. He was so skeert, he was 'bout ready to shit his britches, and the dogs was leaping up and snapping at him and just missing his feet, and a-clawing at the bark, and oh, their howling was bloodthirsty enough to terrify a dead man.

Well, anon I crept right up to him, and mayhap he felt my breath too, or something, because he began a-moaning something fierce, and crying out, "Oh, come and get me, I know you've come to take me from here, I'll die up here in this tree sooner than hop down and be ripped limb from limb by them hounds. . . ."

I took a hold of him by the shoulders. He like to jumped out of his skin, but I tried to relax my invisibility to he could leastways see *something*, a shadow, a moving object in the corner of his eye.

"Believe me," I said, "I ain't no angel of death."

"Then why the hell can't I see you?" says he. "Things unseen are spirits—if not angels why then demons."

"I don't understand these things any better'n you do," I said, "but you got to believe I'm your friend, and I wish you well."

"Why should I trust you? I can't even see you. You're just a sort of voice inside my head, and I'm only hearing you because, look, I'm close to death." He talked like a yankee. What was he doing here, alone, far from the rest of his kind?

Well, that blame colonel, he rode right up to the trunk, and he screamed, "Tyler Tyler, git on down from here so I can kill you quick; lessen you want to be all day and all night a-dying."

"Tyler Tyler?" I said. "That ain't your ordinary kind of name."

"My family name is Taylor," he said, "but the kids I growed up with always called me Tyler Tyler, and it stuck, 'cause I enlisted along with my four cousins—now they're all dead. Me too, soon enough."

"Who the hell are you talking to?" cried the colonel.

"No one," Tyler shouted back.

"You're talking to someone up there—I see something else moving on that branch, I don't know what," said the colonel.

"Didn't you know?" said Tyler. "I'm addled in the head. Might as well just shoot me now, while you have me up a tree."

The colonel fired off a few rounds, but he warn't aiming to kill, just to make Tyler uncomfortable. "I'll have you down from there," he said at last. He rode off and left his runners to watch the tree; they stood with their rifles pointed up at Tyler, but they didn't aim to kill him neither; they was yankees just like him. Prisoners of war, I reckoned. The dogs just went on yapping at the tree and old Joseph was loping up to the river by now, so maybe he had some magic up his sleeve. And on the branch above us sat the leopard, purring so loud it made the whole tree tremble.

Well, presently the colonel come riding back, and this time he has a girl with him, a beautiful girl I would say, and almost white, mayhap one of them New Orleans octoroons, with long, dark hair and bright eyes, and just a hint of colored about the lips and nose.

He dismounted. He drug that girl off the horse and yanked her head up by the hair, and she started to cry out, "Tyler Tyler, Tyler Tyler—" and the colonel said, "No prisoner of war's gone play Romeo and Juliet with one of my house servants, do you hear? You done spoilt my property, you have. It's worthless now, and I might as well dispose of it."

I said, "What's the matter with him? So what if you toyed around with his house nigger? A slave is still a slave."

"She's his daughter," said Tyler Tyler.

"You disappoint me, Tyler," said the colonel. "Didn't I give you extra rations while your fellow yankees starved to death? I paid good money for your labor, and I expect a good return for it. Paid as much for you as the two-armed boys I leased, because you could read and write."

The dogs just went on yapping; and the bone-thin yankees raised up their rifles as best they could; though that they looked less lively than the dead, which is a thing I should know, for I live surrounded by them.

"You are going to regret the polluting of my precious goods," the colonel went on, "or my name ain't Griffin Bledsoe."

"No, masta," the girl said softly. "You let him be, masta, I be good to you, do all the thing you allus like the mos'. Don't let him die a nigger death."

"So you do love him," said Colonel Bledsoe, and he laid into her with the butt of his rifle a few licks, but she didn't struggle none, just lay there wide-eyed and still. She didn't answer him neither.

"Don't hurt her!" Tyler shouted.

But Bledsoe picked her up—it was easy, she were a slight, slender thing—and carried her to the next tree, and he set her on his horse, and, calling for a rope from one of his men, made a neat noose, and put it around her neck, and tossed it up over the overhead branch, and tied it tight, and all the while he sung, in a clear high tenor, a song in a foreign tongue.

"You come on down from that tree," he said, "or by God, I'll hang the wench, even if she *is* with child."

"Masta, masta, don't kill me," said the girl—I could barely hear her, for she was ever soft-spoken—"he never laid a hand on me . . . the child you say he planted in my womb, that ain't no child of his. . . ."

"You're lying to save his life," said the colonel. "Who else's could it be?"

"It *your* child, masta," she said.

Even the yankees were surprised at this, and looked away from their target, and from the colonel to the girl and back again, and sure enough I could see it plain as day, that what was ugly in his face was refined and beautiful in hers, and yet there was no doubt of a family resemblence.

The girl looked up at Tyler on the tree. I know that she saw me, for them which stands close to the edge of the river can see past the illusions wrought by magicians. And I know that she saw the leopard too, for fear flecked her eyes, but there was also hope in them. And she smiled, and it was the kind of smile that stories turn on, the kind of smile that changes lives; she smiled and she whispered Tyler Tyler's name, so softly that we only heard it by some trick of the breeze; but when he heard it it made him crazy with rage and desire.

Colonel Bledsoe kicked that horse and the horse run off to-wards the open field. And Tyler screamed. And he done cast his-self down into that mass of writhing dogs. Between him and his woman was just a ocean of frothing jaws, of drool that glistened on white fangs, of beady bloodshot eyes. Afore he could get too far, them hounds had divven in on him, and was a-rending of his flesh. It were too horrible to be borne. And so I dove down after him, and I fought off the dogs, and the leopard sprang out of the tree and right away bit one of the dogs to death, just cracked its back wide open with one great crunching of the jaws.

And there was Tyler, in the mud, dragging his skeleton of a body toward the other tree by his one good hand, and there was that high-yaller maiden a-thrashing and a-kicking in the air, and Lord, it were a sight to see.

I was hollering and kicking at the dogs, and then I turned and saw how Tyler had reached the trunk of the tree, and was thrusting himself up it so he could shore up the girl's legs and stop her from choking to death; then Colonel Bledsoe pulled a whistle out of his pocket and blew a ear-splitting squeal out of it, and the dogs all turned, all at once, like they was parts of some vast machine, and descended on Tyler, and one bit down on his hand and another on his wrist and soon they was a-pulling on that arm and like to pulled it right off his shoulder, and pretty soon Bledsoe was bearing down on him with a cavalry officer's saber raised up high like he was fixing to slice that arm all the way off; and Tyler shouted, "Take my arm, damn you, colonel, but spare Amelia's life—"

"I will have both," said the colonel, but at that moment I saw—

Joseph, standing upon the leopard's back—nay, wearing that leopard around his shoulders, *fused* with that leopard somehow, and his demeanor so fierce and forbidding it would have struck terror into the very devil—

And he raises his arm and grabs hold of the girl's legs so she won't be jerking back and forth no more, and turns and stares that colonel dead in he eye and says, "Griffin, Griffin, how soon you forget—"

"Joseph!" he cries out. Oh, Zacko, 'twas a cry of pity and perdition. I knew then that Joseph was known to this man, and that our coming together here was no accident, but rather the will of whatever dark god it was that now ruled over our lives.

"Yes, Griffin," Old Joseph said—and though he spoke not above a whisper, yet his voice was like unto thunder—"You always knowed I was a-coming back; and here I is."

"You walked away . . . over the cold gray sea," said Colonel Bledsoe.

"Yes, Griffin. And now I done returned, I stride to you acrosst the brilliant sky."

"You didn't have to come."

"No, I did not," said old Joseph. "But I heard your voice over the burning plain; you done called to old Joseph; it were you which brung me here, which made me for to break my journey in this valley of dry bones; for you see me as the angel which fetches men's souls, and you know that your time is come. But for this boy, there be another season."

"No!" screams that Colonel Bledsoe, and he brings the saber slashing down on Tyler Tyler's shoulder and—

The leopard leaps up and rips into his throat and—

I looked up.

There was no young girl a-hanging on that tree; instead, it were old Joseph himself, but not himself; he was bigger than life, and his feet rested on the leopard's back, and his arms was stretching out to embrace us all, like we was all his children, his beloved—

And I saw the dogs tear Tyler's one remaining arm out of its socket, and run off with it into the densest thicket, and the blood come streaming out of him whilst he screamed out "Amelia, Amelia!"

Where was that girl? I saw her slumped down at the base of the tree trunk, half shielding her eyes, half staring with horror at the spurting stump of her lover's arm.

And old Joseph just glared down from that tree, his good eye more fiery than the sun, and a great light come pouring from his upturned palms, a light so white, so dazzling that my eyes burned, and like to wore out my eyes from weeping. A fire come bursting from his lips and wove itself about his face and burnt a halo in the empty air above him; and when I looked up into the sky above the trees I could have sworn I saw a company of heaven, and a host of angels, though they was dark-faced angels, and I heard a music that stirred the very clouds and the music itself was light. And this was what they sung:

> *Oba kòso*
> *Onibanté owó jinwinnin*

And though I didn't understand them words, I suddenly remembered that I done heard them onc't before; for whenever old Joseph spoke about a African god he called Shangó, he would say them words, with a curious hopping as he uttered them.

Shangó was a African king who hung hisself, yet did not die, and become a god; that's what old Joseph told me onc't. So he was the king of death and resurrection, like our Jesus in a way, a-hanging on a tree that men might live. And what Old Joseph was doing was what his god done, what our Lord done for us on the cross; or mayhap it were blasphemy, but I saw that it was all one.

And then I seen, painted in light above the old man's halo, the *vévé* of the messenger of the gods. And I knowed that the leopard named Freedom come to take the soul of that colonel, though I knew not where she would take him, whether paradise or the everlasting fire, or whether there were some third place that was knowed by neither God nor Satan.

"Don't look no more," Tyler was gasping. Suddenly, I realized, he could see me; I warn't invisible no more. And he knew something I didn't know. "For God's sake, friend, for God's sake, Amelia, close your eyes to the light—"

I reckon I done closed my eyes just in time; for even with them closed, there come over me such a intense and shattering wave of heat and terror that I was sure I would be consumed. The fire rolled over us. I waited as the dark angels sang their refrain again and again.

> *Oba kòso*
> *Onibanté owó jinwinnin*

With my eyes closed I saw another picture altogether, and suddenly I found I could understand the words . . . and this is the image that passed before me: black women, naked as the day God made them, hopping up and down, and black men wearing the skins of leopards, pounding on drums of human skin, and others in fantastical masks of beadwork that looked like the faces of outlandish birds and mythical beasts, in bright colors of red, blue, green; the women jumping up and down on an earthen pavement, and their slender breasts slapping against their slick skin, and this was what they sang:

> *The king he don't hang*
> *Cause he blessed with a million cowrie shells.*

What the hell did that mean? All I knowed is that the vision was supposed to explain what was happening in the here and now. The song was high and sweet, and the drums low and bitter. The rhythm of it dug deep into my mind and I let my spirit go and I found myself dancing amongst those darkies, singing out the words, and feeling my own bones rattle with the pounding of the drums . . . I don't know how long the vision lasted, but I knew that something awful was happening in the world outside . . . and so I danced and I danced, and I tried to forget the flames that danced around me, I danced away what seemed to be a night and a day and a second night; and finally I awoke, still curled up beneath the cottonwood like a newborn babe, but the plain was a different place completely.

3

We sat in a circle of snow that stretched from the creek all the way to the distant hills. The cottonwoods was burnt; they had no more leaves, and their branches was blackened from the burning. No man was hanging from that tree no more; stead of a-hanging, my *beau-père* was seated on a mighty trunk that had fallen and been carved out by the lightning of his hands, and now it was like unto a throne; old Joseph sat in it, every inch a king, as 'twere he had been doing it all his life. And he wore about his shoulders a massive cloak of leopard skin, and the head of the leopard was a crown over his head; and this is what I knew from that: iffen he and the leopard were wholly or part mortal, combined there warn't nothing human about them a-tall. Sadly he shook his head and pointed to the creek. I sat up and turned my head.

In the stream stood Amelia Bledsoe. Her hair was wild and her arms outstretched and she whirled about, and run this way and that, and her eyes was white and cold, for that the blast had made her blind. And where was Tyler? Buried in the snow, staring up at the sky, with a smear of blood where his shoulder onc't was. And he cried out in a voice of anguish, "Amelia, Amelia, why did you look? Didn't you know that the glory of the gods will burn right through those eyes of yours, and taint your mind forever? Oh, Amelia, if you were going to look, why didn't you tell me so I would have looked too, and we could be together in our madness and our blindness?"

And Amelia sang:

> *There was a flower in the field,*
> *Pluck me, pluck me, cast me away.*

And she began to laugh, and she ripped at the flowered white calico she wore and rent her bare breasts, which bled into the clear water; and then she laughed again and cried out, "I baptize thee in the name of the seven white devils," and "Toil! And spin! And weave! And rut!" and many other sayings which done stood at the very boundary between sanctity and blasphemy.

Old Joseph shook his head, and I seen a single tear form at the corner of his good eye. He was full of compassion for these creatures which had survived the scene, but there warn't nothing he could do to save them from themselves; and I know it saddened him.

I went over to where Tyler was laying, picked up a handful of that snow, rubbed it between my fingers; thing is, it warn't cold to the touch at all, and it were dry as dust.

Here and there in the snow was the skull of a dog, or a human thighbone. So I figured this warn't snow at all; it was the ground-up bones of the dogs and the men and mayhap that Colonel Bledsoe, all those who had been struck down by that burning light that old Joseph done summoned from the heavens.

Tyler looked up at me, and he said, "I wish I was dead." He sat up—he warn't much older than me, but at that moment he seemed a thousand years old, and I could see that he was racked with pain, that he bore more pain than a human being should bear—and he said, "Oh, Lord, how am I going to eat? How can I embrace the woman I love? How can I hold Amelia in my arms? How can I even pray?"

And old Joseph said, "Tyler Tyler, you should have had a care for what you axed for. You should have knowed everything come with he own price which you must pay."

Amelia splashed us with water and when the water touched the powdered bones, the water fizzled, and smoke rose up from the earth. She cupped more water in her hands and run up from the stream, and she sprinkled the water over Tyler's bleeding shoulder, and right away the wound begun to sear itself shut.

Amelia whirled and danced and her dance reminded me of the vision I had when the fire come down from the sky; I think she had had that vision too, only she hadn't closed her eyes to the searing flame, and it had driven her mad. I followed her as she danced. She sang in that selfsame African tongue of my vision, but I had lost the understanding of it. I called her name once, but she did not reply; mayhap she had become deaf as well as blind. Lord, I do not know what scene she gazed upon with her sightless eyes, but I think that Tyler envied her, because she no longer had to see the world.

Tyler was sitting up now. The wound was healing up clean. I reckon the water of the stream had some strange magic power. He stared at the girl which he done give his arm up for, and quietly he wept to himself, and would not be consoled, though I put my arm around him and tried to comfort him a little.

"Who are you?" I asked him. "What did we come here for?"

"I'll tell you," Tyler said, and all at onc't we found ourselves inside of another story.

*Till the bridge you will need be
form'd, till the ductile anchor hold,
Till the gossamer thread you fling
catch somewhere, O my soul.*

—Walt Whitman

A SORCERESS IN
SANTO DOMINGO

1804

17

TYLER TYLER IS HIRED BY COLONEL BLEDSOE, AND FALLS IN LOVE

1

Andersonville was hell (said Tyler Tyler), but Colonel Bledsoe's place was worser yet. Except that I met Amelia there, and she became my life.

When I was taken to Andersonville, I'd already lost the right arm; there wasn't anything special about that, just a cannon blast. I lay in a makeshift hospital tent with fifty other wounded men, and our company retreated, and the secesh overran the camp, and took all the wounded men prisoner. Except the ones they shot. They were the ones too weak to be moved, or the ones too filthy from the flux to be deemed worth moving. And after a time they brought us to Andersonville, which is in Americus, not far from where we are now.

I come from Baltimore, and I can read and write well enough, and carry a tune as well; and before my arm got hacked away I played the fiddle some, and the dulcimer a bit. Before the war, I worked for my father in the music engraving business, learning to etch all the little symbols for the plates to print out songs for bands and churches all over Maryland. He died of a pox, though, and we needed money; I joined the army and sent that thirteen dollars a month direct to my mother and sister, and I escaped fighting for two years because one of the generals liked my good round hand, and kept me as a clerk, copying letters and sending fair copies to Washington to be filed. Well, Jimmy Lee, he died, and they sent me south on the very next train, and in three months I was at Andersonville.

At Andersonville they sometimes forgot to feed us. They shot us if we strayed too near the walls. They shot us if we got sick. They packed us together so we didn't hardly have room to breathe, and sometimes they shot us for breathing, and sometimes, when we weren't breathing anymore, they shot us just for the hell of it.

They buried us in mass graves, and they kept shooting us, day in, day out. The ones that survived grew thin. The skin just hung on our bones like laundry on a clothesline. The first few weeks I thought of my mother and sister, and I wondered if they were told I was dead, or whether they were still getting the thirteen dollars a month; but soon I wasn't thinking about them anymore, only about how I might steal a small wormy potato from another inmate, or how I was going to avoid getting shot, or sometimes dreaming of it, hoping to be shot, to lie beneath the earth and not be hungry no more. It was hell all right.

Once in a while, they sold us like slaves, or rented us out to dig trenches, making sure we were all chained together so we couldn't escape; the ones that got rented out were glad of it, because sometimes it meant an extra bowl of gruel, or a little piece of meat. It didn't happen to me but once, though; who'd want to hire a laborer with only one arm? But then, one day, I saw Amelia Bledsoe.

The colonel came riding into camp, and they started driving us out of the huts and making us stand in long lines in the sun, and now and then shooting at some of us when we straggled; we stood there, ragged and miserable, one or two of us collapsing from the heat after a while, and the colonel dismounted and peered at us, and now and then picked one of us out. There was a horsecart by the gate, and the ones he picked out were led away in irons. I knew I wouldn't be picked, so I wasn't paying much attention. But then, all of a sudden, a woman climbed down from beside the driver's seat, and she ran up to the colonel, and she tapped him on the shoulder, real familiarly, which was strange to me, because though she was very pale of face she was clearly colored.

"Masta," she said, "don't you forgit now, you needs a clerk."

He turned to her. He didn't censure her for her rudeness, though she was obviously his slave, but said in a kindly voice, "Of course, Amelia. Stupid of me to forget." Then, to nobody in particular, he said, "Reading and writing—who can do those things?"

Before I knew it, I had answered, "I can, sir." Maybe it was because the girl was beautiful, or because of the way she looked at me—not like a caged animal, but like a person who, in some other world, some other circumstance, might have been her friend.

"But you don't even have a right arm, boy," said the colonel.

"Well, sir, I'm ambidextrous."

At which he went into such a gale of laughing and spluttering that even I smiled a little, which is how come I got picked. They chained me up right in the front of that cart, next to where the colored lady sat. The driver was a powerful Negro with scars upon his face, and a black uniform, like the driver of a hearse. She spoke softly to the driver in a language I didn't quite understand, except that it was almost French, which I studied a bit in school: *"Alé, alé legliz-la,"* she said, and he responded, *"Wi, machè."*

I made bold to speak to her—why not? For all her airs, she was just a slave, wasn't she?—and I said, "Where are they taking us?"

"To build a church," she said.

"A church?"

"Slaves burnt it down," she said, "and run away north."

"Quiet!" a guard shouted, for we were watched over by two well-fed secesh, with guns pointed in our direction, as the horse-cart moved slowly down the pitted road toward our destination. I found myself staring at the woman, and not noticing anything else we passed.

She wore a simple calico dress, white with pretty blue flowers, and there was also a hint of blue in her dark eyes.

"What you staring at, soldier?" she said after a while. The sun beat down on us, and the sweat was beading on her brow a little, and running down her cheek; for a moment I fancied they were tears.

"At you," I said.

"What, never seen no octoroon before?" she said.

"What is that?"

"One-eighth part darkie," she said, "and the rest of me white as snow; and yet that one-eighth tincture she enough to keep me all eight parts a slave."

"But you are beautiful," I said.

"And so," she said, "are you, you one-armed angel."

"You think so?"

"Well," she said, "you a mite thin, but we take care of that soon enough. I tell my daddy take good care of you."

"Who is your daddy?" I asked her. "The driver of this wagon, with his impressive-looking frock coat?"

To that, she just gave the slyest, slightest little smile, and said, "Oh no," she said, "that Hercules, one of the house niggers."

"Is your daddy an important slave then?" I said. I didn't

know anything about these people's hierarchies, but I knew that there were different degrees of status in the slave world. "Maybe the head butler? Or some kind of overseer?" I knew that on some plantations blacks were set up as overlords above others of their own kind; surely this led to much ill-feeling.

Again that strange little smile, and she replied, "Some things don't need to be talked about."

So all I did was look at her, after that, all the way into the town.

2

The work was easy enough. I had to keep records of the rebuilding: so much lumber, so much plaster, so many barrels of nails. The other men had it real hard. They worked alongside slaves, were kept in irons, were whipped if they lagged, the same as if they'd been bought straight from the auction block. The whipping was done in a strangely bureaucratic way: there was a man in town who was the official slave-whipper, who went by the name of Cordwainer Claggart; he also owned a pharmacy, and sold, among other things, an unguent that supposedly salved the pain of his own whippings. When a man was to be whipped, I had to make out a chit that showed the offense, and the number of stripes, and it went up to be signed by the colonel; then the victim was delivered up to the slave-whipper at dawn, to be returned that evening. I understood that with the shortage, the vast numbers of runaways, some citizens had taken to purchasing labor from the prisoner-of-war camp in Americus—all against regulations, of course, but there was no one to object. Out of consideration for these men's whiteness, Mr. Claggart did not rub salt and pepper into their wounds after their whippings, so they were often well enough to work the next morning, though others died from it, being unused to such ill treatment.

This colonel to whom I now belonged was retired, and he now devoted his life to what he considered to be good works; the rebuilding of this church was only one of many projects.

Griffin Bledsoe had a house in town, and they let me sleep in the coal scuttle, and fed me well enough; and pretty soon I came to realize that the pretty young girl Amelia was a real power in the household, for no one ever dared contradict her. I also learned that the house slaves spoke amongst themselves a kind of French, which they called *kréyol,* and even the colonel was somewhat conversant in their speech, though not entirely fluent.

I had lied; I'm not really ambidextrous, and my left-handed writing was atrocious, but they let me keep on working there; I think it was because Amelia interceded for me, and because, to tell the truth, they pitied me.

By the week's end I had come to love Amelia, and she me.

It happened by very quick stages. Before she retired for the night, she would bring me a glass of milk, and a couple of buttermilk biscuits from the kitchen. They handcuffed me to the stove each night. I never could get comfortable. So she took to letting me lie with my head on her lap, and it was the first soft thing I had felt since I left Baltimore. And she would stroke my brow for a time, till, thinking me fast asleep, she slipped away.

The second night, she stayed a little longer, and, weeping, I think, though my eyes were closed and I could not see her, she talked to me in a gentle whisper, "Allus wanted a sweet white angel, allus wanted someone like you; even one-armed, you gots all the arms I ever needed."

I gripped her wrist then, hard, and almost said something back. I didn't think of the mother and sister, didn't think of Baltimore, the salt wind in the harbor, the tall cramped gray brick houses, row upon row, the smell of the engravers' acid in the back room of my father's house, which the bank took away from us; somehow I could only think of her. She obsessed me. I thought of no one else, and I lived for the sight of her.

And on the third day I was allowed to take my meal in the

dining room, though I was seated at another table, and my an-kles were put in irons for the duration of the meal; and I was al-lowed to listen to the discussion, though not to speak unless I was spoken to. But if a look can be a conversation, and a glance a kiss, and a smile an act of love, then Amelia and I sinned a dozen times over the soup, and twice as much during the main course.

That night she kissed me many a time, but I could not hold her in my one-armed embrace, because of the handcuffs. And nothing happened that was less innocent than those kisses, though I know I wanted more, and think that she did too.

And yet we did not speak much to each other. In silence, much was said. But just before she left, I tried to tell her how much she meant to me. I said, "Amelia, darling, in another time, another world, perhaps we might have—"

"Don't speak of such things," she said. "I must go now. To another man."

"The colonel? But isn't that a sin, I mean to say, isn't he your—"

"Nigger ain't human being," she said. "No crime to violate one of us. No sodomy, no rape, no incest. We ain't human being. Don't you ever understand that, yankee boy?"

"No," I said. "I don't understand that. I'll never understand that."

"What? You a abolitionist then?"

"How should I know? I'm not a politician."

"You think Amelia should be free?"

"I never thought about things like that before," I said.

"Nor I neither," she said, and kissed me, and slipped away upstairs, to the man who was her lover, her father.

The fourth evening, there were many people to dinner, Southern aristocrats I suppose, in their white suits, and their ladies, fanning themselves and looking askance at Amelia, who sat at the hostess's end of the table, playing the mistress of the house. There was a glazed ham, and biscuits, and chicken-fried steak, and green beans boiled with hunks of salt pork. I hadn't seen such a meal in a long time, and I felt for the other laborers from the prison camp, who were kept in irons in the basement of the church, and fed on the same mealy rations.

Wine, too. I had heard that there was a shortage of everything in the South because they were losing the war; but you couldn't have guessed that in this house, not at all, Jimmy Lee. I couldn't eat that much. Andersonville made me so thin that I knew I'd have vomited my guts out if I tried to eat like a normal man.

I didn't pay much attention to the conversation. Not at first. But then, one of the ladies made some remark about a lady of color. "Really, colonel," she said, "I love my slaves as much as if they were my verra own children; but I sure wouldn't have them to sup at table."

"And why not?" said the colonel. "Am I not a generous man? Do I not suffer even the yankee to eat the crumb which falleth from my table?"

The dinner guests turned to me, sitting at the side table, trying awkwardly to eat with my left hand, and they laughed at me, and applauded the colonel's clever quotation from the scriptures, and I raged and fumed inside, but there wasn't nothing I could do except sit there and take it. I felt less than a man. Oh, I felt ashamed. I wanted to die. Wasn't the first time in this godforsaken war that I wanted to die, but this time I'm sure I meant it.

Amelia got up from the table and went to my side. She said, "Don't be cruel to him, masta. He seen enough bad times."

The colonel purpled with anger. But he didn't say nothing; he just turned to his guests, ordered Hercules to pour more wine, and clapped his hands for the maid to bring on dessert, which was one of those flaming puddings.

Nobody spoke much for a little while. I think that, even though they were dressed in their best, and keeping up the pretenses of gentility, they were probably all of them pretty hard up, and some of them might not have had a decent meal in a day or three; for they were wolfing down that pudding as if they hadn't seen one before.

I myself could only swallow a bite or two. I thought they would soon start to mock me again, but instead the old colonel began to tell war stories, which were like all war stories—so many killed, so many rescued from certain death, so many cannon and corpses and cavalry charges. By now I had heard plenty of such stories, and they were no different for being told in the accents of Georgia.

But after a while, I guess the guests tired of hearing those tales, and a lady—the same one that had made the disdainful remark about Amelia's presence at the table—said, "Colonel, why don't you tell us some romantic story of your childhood? We know you traveled far abroad in your youth—the Caribbean islands, England, France, even further afield. In fact, it's said you acquired some of your, well, quaint little ways on your journeys abroad."

She eyed the octoroon girl once more, and Amelia scowled at her, then turned to me and gave me a longing look, which I am sure the colonel noticed, for he squinted hard at her, and me, and then stared into the fireplace, and gulped down an entire glass of wine.

"I'll tell y'all," he said, "about magicians and madmen, about coffee-colored beauties, about hurricanes and tempests, and revolutions and atrocities, and an island where niggers run free and white men fear to tread—a place called by some Santo Domingo, by others Saint-Domingue, by others still Haiti, the earthly inferno."

"Heavens, colonel!" said the lady who had requested the tale. "That beggars the imagination."

"Indeed it does," said Colonel Bledsoe. "Yet bear with me. I shall make it all seem real to you, ma'am, as iffen you all were living through it, as I did."

18

WHEREIN YOUNG GRIFFIN BLEDSOE COMES TO SANTO DOMINGO

1

Some called my father a pirate, but he himself preferred the name of merchant. At the turn of the century, he had interests in the islands, and often sailed to Port-au-Prince, which was in the French sector of an island name of Santo Domingo, a country which thrived on the sweetness of sugar, which it extracted from the earth by the hellish bitterness of slavery. The Indians from which the Spanish stole this country called it Haiti. But when I was there, I never did see any Indians, by God. Indians don't make good slaves, the Spanish say; some say they died of heartbreak and despair, and others that it was measles and influenza; but no matter how it happened, their bones have long since been ground into that rich soil, along with the bones and the blood and the sweat of a million darkies that came after them.

In Port-au-Prince, my father was something of a princeling himself. For in the year 1803, when I was a twelve-year-old boy, a bloody civil war had been going on in Santo Domingo for many years, and—in a strange reversal of the natural order of God—the blacks had actually conquered much of the island, and murdered their masters, under the leadership of a cunning, mis-shapen little dwarf named Toussaint L'Ouverture, black as the ace of spades, and black-hearted, too, I reckon. Now, L'Ouver-ture was in a prison in the Alps, I heard tell, but the war was still raging, for Napoleon was determined to bring Santo Domingo back under French domination. That country was in a turbulent chaos, friends. But money being always the lifeblood of the world, the sugar trade continued with nary a quiver, and foreign merchants such as my father were taking over from the slain Frenchman which had so mistreated their darkies as to engineer their own destruction.

Frenchmen were fleeing the island in droves; and so were its mulattoes, quadroons, and octoroons. Haiti had the curiousest sort of hierarchy, where the degree of whiteness of a darkie dic-tated his place in the order; in the mind of the lowliest, the lighter-skinned niggers were as despised as the whites, and the high-yaller most detested of all, for they were often more cruel to their dark-skinned cousins than the masters themselves. Thus it was that there were many who needed a middleman—either to smuggle possessions out of the country, or sometimes to smug-gle themselves; for the country was a sinking ship. My father was making a fortune from this country's misery, though I was too young to understand the source of my family's good living.

My natural mother having died of consumption shortly after I was born, I traveled everywhere with my father, and my edu-cation, until my thirteenth year, was a random thing, with tutors sometimes, or oftentimes stacks of books without the benefit of guidance. Yet somehow I managed to learn the basic arts of reading, writing, and mathematics. Later my father was to decide I needed a far harsher species of schooling, but I will speak on that later.

My father had never participated in the slave trade himself; but one of his ships, the *Persuasion,* had once been outfitted as a slaver. For that reason, I as a boy was not permitted to descend into its lower depths; there were rumors of hauntings, specters in the night, clanking of ghostly chains within the hold, moaning and screeching from the futtocks. Yet when we were docked in the harbor, and my daddy hard at work going over his accounts with the various bankers and such, I found time to explore the environs of Port-au-Prince, oftentimes in the company of a black lad the same age as meself, a lad named Jozéf, who despite the duskiness of his complexion had received a number of privileges, for his mother was the concubine of an influential mulatto named Jacques Leclerc, my father's host—a man who, horrifying though it may seem to you and me, friends, held large holdings in sugar and plantains and who possessed a fair passel of slaves of his own. Such was Haiti—slaves owning slaves, blacks lording it over whites—so complete a perversion of the natural way of the world laid down in the scriptures, that it won't a-tall surprising the country was going to hell in a handbasket, iffen y'all pardon my language, ladies.

This Jozéf, you know, had a sister of fourteen named Améli, who was as pale as her brother was black. One night—I slept beneath a mosquito net in Leclerc's little guest house, Jozéf on the veranda—the lad woke me up in the middle of the night, and drug me out to the balcony.

"Look down there, Griffin, *monchè,*" he said, "Beautiful, ripe, non?"

"Ki koté?" I said, which in their barbarous Negro French means "Where?" And where he pointed I saw Améli in the moonlight—and she was indeed what you might call ripe; she was standing, quite shameless, under a copse of mango trees,

splashing herself with water from a rainwater jar that was almost as tall as she was.

I was not entirely unacquainted with the female form, you understand; my mammy was still in the habit of dandling me between her titties. My father caught me bouncing up and down on Mammy's breasts once, both of us completely nekkid; I thought I would merit a taste of his hickory, but he merely laughed and said 'twas a good thing for a boy to study the feminine anatomy, and a Negress was built much the same as a white woman, for all they'll try to tell you different. But Mammy's endowments were capacious things, not dainty and delicate like these, just as sweet and juicy as the mangoes a-hanging off of the trees around her.

Oh, ma'am, don't you start complaining about the profanity of my sentiments. A woman is a beautiful thing, and I won't have you lovely ladies denying it—you are partaking of my hospitality, and furthermore, you have requested this story, and I'll tell it any way I damn well please, if you'll pardon, again, my French.

Ah, yes, the French! Améli was French and Ethiop, melded into one—ravishing, unplucked—and I was twelve-year-old boy just a-gaping at her plenitudinous charms. It was with profound regret that I watched her pull a shapeless garment, which they call a caftan, over her body and bind up her tresses in a white bandanna.

"Why was she bathing in the middle of the night?" I asked Jozéf.

"Don't know," he said. "You want to find out?"

Well, ladies, I was ripe for adventure, the world was my oyster, and I won't used to anyone thwarting me; so, in a strange country, with an impertinent young nigger, I found myself slipping out of our guest house and into the bustling streets of Port-au-Prince . . . on the trail of that high-yaller girl, and as keen on her traces as the sharpest nigger hound in this county.

The girl darted from doorway to doorway, and so did we.

These were dangerous times—people were being knifed in the dark, and white folks cut to pieces whilst they slept—but I reckon I was leading a charmed life, for all I saw was her, though we ran through a throng that was fleeing some soldiers and saw a man atop a pyre in an empty market square, screaming as he burned, and no one to even watch the spectacle. I was not in the least bit frightened now; y'all have to understand that I was so young and foolish that I never dreamed I might be in danger of dying. It was one big adventure, shadowing a beautiful young girl down the alleys of the doomed city; when I think of it now, I blanch to recall the danger.

An alley . . . a wounded legionnaire crawling beside a heap of rotting plantains, doubtless to die. A company with bayonets trotting by the roadside. Women in white robes with baskets on their heads, singing in their barbarous *kréyol*. Oh, this was a beautiful island even though the air stunk of the dying, for behind the reek of rotting corpses was always the fragrance oozing from the night-blooming flowers, and though the streets were littered with dung there was another odor too, the sweetness of putrefying fruit. And alongside the blood and mud there were always flowers blooming in wildest profusion. And Jozéf's sister was by no means the least of these flowers.

This ravishing Améli, why she led us straight down to the harbor, where as it happened, the *Persuasion* was at anchor; and to our amazement—even though two burly men with cutlasses and muskets stood guard—scampered right past them and up the gangplank, almost as though she were invisible.

"Well," I said, for I was becoming a mite scared, and don't mind admitting it, "maybe we'd best be getting home."

"Oh, it nothing," Jozéf said, "only invisibility spell. Come." He knelt down and picked up a handful of dust from the side of the street, spit on it, and mumbled something. Before I could murmur "witchcraft," he had marked my forehead with a smear of dirt.

"What the hell is that?" I said.

"Disappearing mud," he said. And here's the strangest thing—he applied a little to his own forehead, and, well, he didn't exactly vanish in a puff of smoke, but all of a sudden he became difficult to see. Trickery of the light, mayhap? The moon? The shadows of the ships? It was a mystery all right. I held up my hand to my face and you know, the moonlight shone right through it—it was still there, but I had to squint, or look askance, to catch sight of it.

"Is this voodoo?" I said. I was excited now, for the blacks of Haiti were well known then as now for practicing the black arts, and they did it better than any other race on earth. "I don't want any voodoo," I said. "I don't want to go to hell."

Whereupon my dark companion began a-laughing, loud enough to wake the dead and surely to arouse the suspicions of the guards; but they said nothing.

"Hell," he said, "is where you make hell."

I took him at his word. Why not? We were only children, were we not? For children there is no heaven or hell, nor really any past or future—there is only now. And so, following my friend's lead, I slipped past those watchmen and boarded my father's ship. Desolate, and devoid of the crew, the scurrying cabin boys, the strutting midshipmen, and the porters grunting and groaning under their sacks of sugar, and most of all of the imperious presence of my father, the ship was an alien territory to me.

But where had Améli gone? I saw no one. There was only the moon, the hot moist wind, the familiar creaking and settling of a ship at port, an occasional rat scurrying past. I do not know why, but there was also a sense of dread; it gnawed at my gut; it caused my fists to clench and unclench of their own accord. Perhaps it was merely fear of the hiding I'd get if I were caught. At any rate, my heart was pounding furiously, and I quite forgot that we had come here fixing to spy on an attractive girl.

"Griffin!" said Jozéf. "You shaking."

"It's nothing," I said, affecting a confidence I surely did not feel. "My heart is a-pounding, that's all; there's a chill, I think."

He laughed again. "A chill! This island hotter than your hell, *monché*," he said, "but that not your heart, Griffin, that the pounding of voodoo drums."

And sure enough, when I listened more carefully, I realized that the drumming was coming from the bowels of the *Persuasion* herself.

"Come," said Jozéf.

"I'm not allowed down there," I said.

"Ha! You *pays-blancs* people all cowards."

"That we ain't!" I said shrilly.

"Come, then."

I followed. We descended. My sense of dread was mounting, but with it there was also curiosity. Lower and lower, down narrow, squeaky steps, feeling our way because there was nary any light; now and then a moonbeam penetrated some crack in the boards, but as we reached the old slave decks, the gloom became total.

"Me born in a place like this," said Jozéf.

He took my hand. Placed it against a hard board, made me feel my way to the next level . . . couldn't have been more than two and a half feet.

"They stack us up," he said, "lie down, all together, flat . . . no room to sit up, hundreds upon hundreds. Oh, the stench! Some chained too far from the shit buckets, they just foul themselves in the night. I pray to Pè L'éténél, never send me forth in a place like this again."

"But you say you were *born* in a place like this . . . you'd be too young to remember. . . ."

"The heart she 'member everything, Griffin, don't you forget."

The drums were louder now.

"Come," said Jozéf.

I followed in the dark. He knew his way around the slave deck. I could not see, but his hand gripped mine, and I huddled right behind him; he smelled of sweat and mangoes.

We made our way down the aisle. I heard the clank of chains. Surely it was in my mind. Toward the bow there was a slit of light. Mayhap the door to a storeroom. We approached it. The drums were louder now, and I could also hear singing. The singing was almost like the spirituals the darkies sing on our plantations here in Georgia, but wilder, and accompanied by laughing and clapping of hands and pounding of feet, too; as the sound grew, it was hard for me to imagine it all came from one little storeroom.

But all of a sudden the door was flung open. I suddenly saw the cavernous hollowed-out hell that was the slave deck of my father's ship. I saw the timbers caked with blood and ordure. Saw the posts, some still adorned with cuffs and leg-irons. I glimpsed this horrid inferno but for a moment, and then I was pushed into the storeroom and the door slammed shut behind me.

Within—the chamber was no more than fifteen feet square— were dancers, drummers, chanters, all festooned with feathers, the women half-naked, the men almost altogether so, and children, too, butt-naked, running in and out amongst the dancers, giggling, chattering. There were human skulls along the walls, and on the skulls were black candles, giving off a sooty light. I was the only white person. I broke out in a cold sweat. I knew that a civil war had raged here for many years. I knew that the children of white plantation owners had been split open, roasted, eaten. In horror I turned to Jozéf and said, "Get me out of here, save me!" but he only laughed, and pointed to his sister, who was flinging herself up and down in the middle of the room, her tight body slick with sweat, and her pale nipples enticing me, like eyes set in the dusky shimmer of her body; I swear to you that Améli was the most beautiful creature on earth. Another woman, wrapped in a crimson caftan, glided past us, undulating her hips and bending her elbows at impossible angles. One who looked just like her—they could have been sisters, except for the second one's massive girth—danced behind her, echoing her every movement, but she wore garments of green, and when she spun, her hair whipped about her shoulders like a black wave.

The drums beat faster and faster and, well, these two women, their eyes rolled up into their sockets and they began shaking in a kind of religious ecstasy—you've seen it, of a Sunday, in your own darkies, I'm sure—and they began to moan, and utter long strings of gibberish in deep, mannish voices.

"Who are they? What's happening?" I said to Jozéf.

"That woman she my *maman*, Zétwal, and her cousin, Marie Laveau," he said. "They *mambo*—high priestesses. Tomorrow Marie she fly away to America, cause the revolution. My family stay here in freedom, 'cause the French they soon surrender."

I shuddered. I knew that the male voodoo practitioners were called *houngan*, and the female *mambo*. I knew now that my companion Jozéf was more than he seemed. I knew that the beautiful girl who fascinated me—I did not yet know that this thing was called lust—was also a victim of these dark practices. "Jozéf," I said, "we have to get out of here and tell my father. You know it's against the law to practice black magic on the island."

"What magic white," he said, "what magic black? This a old religion, religion belong my father father and my father father father. Is not magic, when white man *houngan* change the wine to blood of your god? You insult our gods?"

"No," I said, for whatever was in my heart, I knew I was outnumbered. "But why are they doing this dance aboard my father's ship?"

"This ship," he said, "he have a curse upon him."

"A curse?" Again, my mind was trapped between the twin poles of terror and fascination. For I was a merchant's son, and I loved nothing more than yarns about pirates, and curses, and sunken gold, and haunted ships; such tales were only one step beyond the world I knew.

"Yes," my companion said darkly, "yes, a curse."

"What is the dancing for?"

"They dance the French away, on a cursed ship over the sea."

"Dancing'll get rid of the French?"

"Why not?"

Yet as I watched, I sure as hell believed that a roomful of writhing Negresses could send Napoleon's army all the way back to France. I knew that thousands were already dead from yellow fever and exotic tropical diseases. I knew that the heat just drove all the fight out of them. And the heavy uniforms didn't help. Now why wouldn't this magic work on them, when the island itself had already worn them to tatters? That's why I shut my mouth after that, and watched the dancers.

"The *loa* are riding them," said Jozéf. "The gods have entered their bodies."

They became ever more frenzied, and one of them took a goblet, and shattered it, and leapt up and down on the shards of broken glass, and another began rolling about in it, while the cousins, the high priestesses, shrieked out their mumbo jumbo at the top of their lungs.

Well, with absolute abruptness, the whole performance came to a stop. The women, which seemed possessed before, returned to normal. The two high priestesses, Jozéf's mother and aunt, became quite still, almost like statues.

The fat one, Zétwal, saw me suddenly, and cried out, *"Ki sa-a ye? Ki ti blan-nan?"*

"Li frè mwen," said Jozéf.

Marie Laveau, the thin one, regarded me with a strange mixture of disgust and awe, and spoke to us in good clear English, "No white boy is your brother, my nephew. Remember that." Then she crooked her finger, calling me to her: which was the only time, then or since, that I have felt impelled to obey the command of a nigger.

"Tell me your name," she said, and stroked my hair, and made me think for the briefest of moments that I had found my mother, long departed to the other side; what a strange notion that was, what a feeling to have about a half-savage creature—but I was young.

"Griffin," I said.

"A fierce name," said Marie Laveau, "for such a *ti poupée*."

"We're staying in the guest house at Monsieur Leclerc's," I said.

"We have told Jozéf not to consort with white children," said Marie, "because a time is coming when the world will be torn asunder, and we must choose sides."

"It don't bother me iffen he's a slave," I said, "for he's my only friend on this savage island."

"I am not talking about whether it worries *you*," said Marie. "It is Jozéf who concerns me."

And that was a strange thing to me, that a black woman would be concerned about a black child above me. Didn't my own mammy scream at her own pickaninnies if they but touched a hair of my head, and whup them savagely if they hurt me, then turn to coddle me between the massive titties which had suckled me so many times even when I was four and five years old and felt lonesome for their warmth? Well, I just couldn't understand this Marie woman.

Well, she smiled, and said, "We are fleeing this madness soon; tomorrow we will take ship for New Orleans; but my dear cousin, she is, how you say, intimidated by America. *Pa mwen.* I will be a queen in New Orleans, even as I am here."

"Are you really a queen?" I said. "But where is your retinue? Your palace? Your crown jewels? Your country?"

She smiled even wider, and said only, "Don't you read your own holy book, child? 'My kingdom is not of this earth.' "

I felt a hand in each hand and I was yanked from that room, and the door slammed shut once more, so that I was suddenly in that dank and ghastly corridor down the middle of the slave deck. I felt as iffen I had suddenly been blinded, or else that all I had seen in that storeroom were a dream of sorts; I remember a poem like that which I read once, "La Belle Dame sans Merci," the knight, the ravishing woman, the grotto, the elves, the nightmares, the awakening, the desolation.

2

Well, the very next night, something very different happened; as I lay sleeping beneath my mosquito net, I woke from a dream of sweetness and flowers, and I found another dream hovering above my face—it was Améli. She was wearing nothing but a white cloth wrapped about her hips; her breasts were shapely, her areolas of extraordinary width, her pert little nipples—oh, enough of your tittering, ladies, I know your minds are as filthy as any man's, if you would but allow your darkest thoughts expression. Besides, I have not even said anything of her face, which was as fine as a Dresden doll, and just shy of white, save for a single dark blemish below her left eye, which made her look strangely vulnerable, as iffen a jealous lover had just fetched her a smart blow in the face.

"What the hell are you doing here?" I said softly.

She only laughed, and said, *"Ti frè, ti frè,"* which means in their tongue "little brother."

Then suddenly her hand darted between my legs. I felt something cold sneak under my nightshirt, felt a chill tickling in that little space between one's . . . well, ladies, we need not perhaps be *that* specific, though I know you are positively salivating to hear these juicy details, the better to gossip and complain at church next Sunday . . . I looked up to see her giggling in the light of a lone red candle. With a start, my little peter hardened like a rock, and she cried out in delight: *"Oh! Ou kapab!"*

Which means, I am told, "Thou canst."

Well, you can imagine the emotions that I felt, for worldly though I seemed to those I encountered, I was yet a bookish kind of boy. I was hot and cold all over, and flushed with embarrassment and excitement. Before I knew it, she had bent down over me, and my lips were in proximate propinquity with those divine areolas. Lord, I felt greater than myself, and I would surely have seized the opportunity right then and there had I known what opportunity to seize.

Instead, my father burst into the room.

Améli screamed. He tore at the mosquito net and grabbed her by the shoulder, and thrust her onto the freshly waxed floor, which shimmered in the moonlight from the window. My father then turned to me. He had a little riding quirt in his hand, and I was certain he was going to lay to right then and there. Instead, he gave Améli a light touching-up on the buttocks, not enough to break the skin; she squealed, half, I suspect, in delight; and when next he looked on me his countenance was positively jovial.

"Didn't realize you were quite ready, eh, Griff!" he said. And he clapped me on the shoulder—which hurt, for he was a big man—and went on, "But you mustn't fiddle with your father's belongings. She's not for you. I'll find you something, me boy. His father's son, eh! Well done, lad."

He found me something the very next evening, for when I was done playing with Jozéf—kicking a ball around the garden after supper—I found a grown woman waiting for me in my bed. It was, to my amazement, the generously endowed Zét-wal—mother of the girl who had last night called me her *ti frè*. Zétwal held out her arms to me, and said, "Me gift to you from you papa," and in a few moments she began teaching me all the rudiments of the congress between the sexes.

Well, we need not dwell on that, though I'm sure you ladies would love to learn a thing or two—for let me tell you that backward as their race may be in most respects, the Negress is by far the more passionate than the Caucasian female when it comes to the *ars amatoris*. I daresay it's the heat of their native clime that drives them to such heights of clinging, clawing, clambering, and caterwauling. I had not known the uses to which my little peter could be put, but that night I learnt three or four of them.

After a few hours, she left me, and as I drifted off I was starting to hope that my father's sojourn on this forsaken island might be extended for a time. For to tell the truth, I had not really had a companion before, and Józef filled my days with games and running about and fresh air; and now it seemed that the night, too, might prove pleasurable.

But all was to change the next morning.

3

It was at the breakfast table, which, that morning, was well populated—my father and some business associates, the mulatto Leclerc, our host, wearing a cloth-of-gold waistcoat and a wig a foot high; and next to him my companion of the night before, who now and then looked on me, and giggled a little, but otherwise showed no sign of having cavorted in my bed. Then again, was she not the mistress of Leclerc, and also his slave? There was, among these people, an endless confusion about rank and propriety; as I have said before, it was their downfall.

Well, we were about halfway through this breakfast, an inconsequential meal, part stolidly European, with *jambon,* sardines, toast, poached eggs, kippers, and the like, and part exotic, with fried plantains, mangoes, and strange soups with unconventional sea creatures staring up at us; well then, there came a pounding at the gate, and a whole detachment of gendarmes came trooping into the *salle à manger,* demanding the arrest of Zétwal.

"What means this outrage?" Leclerc protested. "On what charge?"

"Treason," said one of the officers.

At which Zétwal let out an earsplitting scream, and her lover

Leclerc rose to his feet and said, "We had an agreement. Trade to be sacred. No one, Frenchman or black, to interfere with the goings-on in this house!"

"Don't protest, Jacques." Zétwal managed to calm down. "Is Marie they want, and me never betray her."

"Even if you don't," said the officer, "you are a practitioner of magic, and that's forbidden under the island code."

"Then," Zétwal said softly, "you will kill me whatever me say, and so better me say nothing."

"Sorceress!" the officer screamed, and they began to slap her in the face, repeatedly and without mercy. "Mistress of *zombis*!"

There was a commotion as her two children came running out of the kitchen and struggled with the soldiers; when it was clear it was useless, Améli set to wailing, and it was a cry of heartbreak and of horror.

"She not a sorceress!" Jozéf shouted. "She holy woman—blessed by the gods—vessel of Legba—"

"You dance naked in the night—you wake the dead—" the officer said.

Leclerc said softly, "What you do is wrong, and will be revisited upon you, and your children's children. Why do you think you are losing this war? The island does not belong to *Pè L'éténél*, the white man's god, but to the *dieux puissants* that came with the slaves from Africa."

The officer stopped beating Zétwal. "Don't curse us," he said softly. "We're only doing our job." He turned smartly on his heel and saluted Monsieur Leclerc—first and only time I ever did see a white man saluting a black.

"M'alé," said Zétwal.

Then they dragged her away, and it was the last I ever saw of her.

The next days saw a flurry of activity. I didn't much understand what was happening. My father and Leclerc spent a lot of time huddled over documents and maps. The seamen in my father's employ were busy, too; no longer did they spend their days in the tavern, but were at the mansion every dawn to hear my father's instructions. I knew that a lot of money must be involved. I wondered if Leclerc was fixing to flee the country, or whether he was going to try to purchase Zétwal's freedom. Jozéf played hard all day long. No doubt he didn't want to think on all that was going on. I didn't think too much that it was his mother in the prison, and doubtless being whupped and tortured to reveal whatever she knew; I had always been taught that blacks do not really come in families, but can be disposed of in whatever groups are most convenient for their masters. It didn't occur to me that it might pain him, that his mother had been awarded to me one evening as a plaything. I was often angry at him. He didn't look me in the eye as much, and he hardly ever called me *monchè*, or *frè mwen,* anymore, but always *mèt*—master.

So one evening, when we sneaked out after supper to watch a midnight execution, I told him I was still his brother, and he shook his head slowly and sadly.

As he did so the blade of the guillotine fell on the neck of the hapless criminal—a traitor, though I didn't know to who—and the onlookers all gasped, and the head flew into the basket and a band began to play—I saw that he won't watching the beheading at all, but only me, staring at me with a terrible sort of mournfulness, as though it were me who ought to be pitied, and he were some dark-skinned prince of an ancient kingdom.

"Me wish," he said.

And without ado, he began to weep, bitterly and inconsolably.

19

WHEREIN MRS. GRAINGER BECOMES MORE ACQUAINTED WITH HER ANIMAL NATURE

1

Zack was fast asleep—and who would not be, after trying to unravel the many strands of his narrative? For now there were many voices clamoring to tell their stories. Not only Zack, but Jimmy Lee Cox, that preacher's boy, wandering through the blighted South in the company of that one-eyed witch doctor.

It was a few hours before dawn, when I usually rise. I left the young man sleeping, and crept down stairs in my dressing gown, with only a candle for company. I was thinking to myself that a cup of tea would do much to assuage the contortions my mind was going through.

I rarely enter the kitchen, which is basically Phoebe's domain, but I did not want to ring for her at this hour. Last week

I should have done so without thinking anything of it, but now that we had become a little more equal, I demurred.

But there was a lantern on in the kitchen, and hot coals in the stove, and Phoebe was there at the kitchen table, furiously chopping herbs and pounding them up in a mortar that was made from a human skull. There is usually a pretty lace cloth over the kitchen table, but tonight it was covered up by the leopardskin.

Here I was, in the latter half of the nineteenth century, the age of the greatest scientific advancement since the dawn of man, and a witch was brewing spells in my mundane little kitchen. I set the candle down. Phoebe acknowledged my entrance, but did not stop what she was doing.

I didn't say anything for a while. I ran my fingers over that leopard's fur, marveling both at its softness and its toughness. The skin was marred and pitted in a dozen places. This was not an animal who had lived in the sheltered confines of some zoological garden; this creature came from the jungle. I could tell.

Presently, Phoebe said, "You be wanting some tea, Paula?"

"Yes," I said, "thank you."

She set a kettle on the stove and fanned the coals, and went back to her magicking. How could she keep it all straight? Now and then she'd close her eyes and rock back and forth and murmur a phrase or two in that Yoruba language; then she would calmly walk over to the cupboard, get out a tin of tea, and measure it into the pot, fetch the strainer, take the milk and the sugar from the larder, set it all neatly in place, then go back to her chanting. . . .

The kettle boiled. I did not want to waken her from some demonic trance, so I went to pour the hot water myself, but before I reached the stove she was already there and pouring, as though she had arrived by some kind of instantaneous motion—if one had to coin a word for it, it might be *teleportation*, from the Greek and Latin.

She poured, I stirred and sipped; she returned to her labors. I watched for a while, and, when she seemed to be taking a break from it all, I asked her what it was all about.

"Oh, Paula," she said, "me trying to bring peace to this sad home at last."

"Peace?" I said. "Using human skulls, and goodness knows what else?"

"Paula smell the fumes now. Breathe in the sacred communion of Mawu-Lissa. God is a man and a woman. When a man cleave to a woman, they god. So it written in the stones of the earth. So it written in the stars of the sky."

She poured the contents of the skull-mortar into a saucepan, and brought it to a boil. Sure enough, a delicate smoke filled the kitchen. It had a touch of mint and a touch of cinnamon, but also something darker, something bloody. "What's in it?" I asked her.

"Best Paula not think on it," Phoebe said.

"Animal sacrifice? I know you people have animal sacrifice."

She laughed. "You should be grateful your house not filled with rats and mice and cockroaches, and you never have to buy no cat."

I suppose I should have been appalled at the revelation that my maidservant was boiling rats and mice in my very kitchen. But . . . I don't know . . . something in the air . . . perhaps those fumes . . . made me see only the humor of it. I burst out laughing.

"So what ingredient is stilling my terrible inner anguish? I suppose it's the rat's blood that's keeping me from shrieking out in terror?" I said.

"No ma'am, that the hemp."

I began giggling uncontrollably. "Hemp?" I said. "I'm inhaling ropes and jackets?"

She, too, seemed to see a strange humor in this, and collapsed in a fit of shrill, evil-witch-like cackling.

"Maybe me not bring back us husband, Paula," said Phoebe,

"but leastways you got youself a pretty young'un. Now you don't keep him all to youself, you hear!"

"How can I share what I don't own?" I said.

"Nobody ever own nothing, Paula, except they hands, they feet, they heart, they soul."

"What about the gift you seem to have, the ability to turn into a leopard? Is that something you can own?"

"Of course not. It come from the gods."

"So"—I took a really deep breath now, and my whole being was aglow with a wondrous sense of warmth and well-being, and I felt brave and able to do anything—"does that mean that *I* can be a leopard too?"

Abruptly, she ceased her laughter and looked at me with her large, mournful eyes, and when she next spoke, it was no longer in the accents of the plantation: "Paula," she said, "are you asking in jest, or in all seriousness?"

"What do you think?" I shrieked, astonishing myself that I was capable of such fishwifery. "I'm surrounded by magicians, am I not? My husband turned a pickaninny into an Oxford-accent-spouting proper young lady—you change yourself into a she-cat at the drop of a hat—Mr. Whitman weaves the common tongue into discordant symphonies of meaning—even young Zacko has managed to transform me from a well-brought-up matron into a prurient libertine—well, well, my heavens, woman, why shouldn't *I* have a touch of magic?"

"You want me to share the beast-power with you."

"Yes."

"We will truly be sisters then, you and I. Not mistress and servant. Though to the world it were best we continue to appear so."

"Yes! yes! yes!"

"Strip," she commanded.

"What? In front of you?"

"No time for niceties," she said. "Disrobe immediately, Paula."

I shed my dressing gown and folded it. Then I slipped out of my nightdress, and carefully folded that too, and topped the pile with my Chantilly nightcap. Phoebe, too, divested herself of her maid's uniform. We stood there for a moment, the black and the white; in my nudity—despite the warmth of the stove, there was a draught from the windowsill—I began to have second thoughts.

"Dismiss them," said Phoebe, reading my mind.

She then did something which I had previously thought of as a kind of parlor trick done by stage magicians: she seized the leopardskin by its two hindpaws, and yanked it from the kitchen table, leaving the skull, the canisters of ingredients, the teapot, and my ever-so-English cup of char, all utterly untouched.

"Hunch down," she said, and she knelt beside me and threw the leopardskin over us both—

2

And straightaway we hit the pavement running.

Running!

In the gray gloom that prefigures dawn—running!

Oh! The strangeness of it! The exhilaration! My nose down close to the hard ground, my paws banging against cement, the taut musculature tensing and untensing in my hind legs, the welter of smells—the dried leaves, the spoor of old prey, the rancid butter in a discarded sandwich, the keen reek of absinthe from an alleyway.

"Sister!" the leopard who was Phoebe calls to me in the roar of the night wind. "Sister, rejoice! We are the night itself."

She runs beside me. I am the spotted, she is the black. Black, black. "The black panther is the rarest of the leopard family, dwelling only in the densest forest." Where had I learned that from? Oh, black. We are no longer thinking like humans, who must travel down time in a one-way stream, who always have the past behind them and the future ahead . . . no. We are the night. We are the present. We run in perfect tandem, our paws pounding the paving stones in time with our hearts, in time with the spinning world. Sixth Avenue is unlit; Broadway is dark. We run.

We run. We are in full communion with each other.

We run. We are sisters in the flesh and soul.

We run. The world stretches out, becomes elastic, and behind the filth of the streets we can sense the pungent purity of the jungle. We smell the spoor of a million New Yorkers and know they are mere prey. We chase the wind. We chase our own tails. We spook the horses as the trainmen hitch them to the trolleys, readying them for the first predawn downtown commute. We run. Everything is new, and bright, and full of vibrant color, for I have never been able to see so clearly in the dark, to hear so keenly, to smell so sharply. I can hear the ball bearings sliding in those trolleys, I can hear the patter of the rats in the sewers, I can smell the curlicues of tobacco smoke and the sweat of the stevedores, all the way from the dock, a mile away . . . oh, yes, we run.

And finally, in a back alley, aromatic with discarded fish, we stop running for a little while. Fog rises from the sewer; the smell is not foul to me but strangely enticing. Cats lie amid piles of yesterday's news, fattened from rats and pigeons, replete. We pause. We regard each other.

Leopard is strong. Leopard is beautiful. Leopard lacks the weakness of cogent thought. Leopard feels. Leopard does.

We claw at one another, playful, purring. My black companion lets out a roar that shakes the canisters of rotting fruit. I paw at her face. It is an electric touch. She paws me. A jolt of animal magnetism makes me arch up. A tart perfume of arousal sprays the air. It's emanating from the black cat's hinder parts. Oh, it stirs me. Heat races through my blood. I'm burning up. I spring onto my dark companion. It is more than play. We throw our front paws around each other, rub our nether orifices, lick the sour wine of lust. This is not love as humans know it. It's love and rage and communion and aggression all rolled up into one. Humans cannot know it. Their instincts are dulled by their capacity of thought. In the darkness is the perfect joy. In the darkness is truth. Only the darker angels are the true angels.

Leopard is strong. Leopard is beautiful. Leopard is eternal. Leopard is now.

Yes! Sluice leopard's cunny with your abrading tongue! Scratch her skin with your embracing claws! Yes! Fuck me! Fuck me! As a human I cannot even think these thoughts, but tonight I find freedom!

Leopard is the light! Leopard is the leap! Leopard is love!

Fuck fuck the passion fuck the ultimate joy fuck fuck eternity fuck life fuck death fuck fuck

Then, suddenly, humanity.

Two naked women in a tawdry alley, wrapped in a single leopardskin. A few shafts of dawn light, leaking over the heaps of refuse; an old warehouse wall covered with outdated abolitionist broadsides. It was over.

Why? Oh, a terrible grief wracked my whole being, and I let out so heartrending a moan that, were there anyone there to listen, it must surely have convinced him that the world were ending.

"The sadness," Phoebe said gently, and stroked my cheek. "You never get used to it. When you seen that rage, that joy, that dark dark truth, you don' ever want come back to the man world. Me understand that, sister, me understand."

My practical human side soon started to gnaw at my consciousness. "How are we going to get home?" I cried. "Why, I don't even know where we are."

"Be not afraid," said Phoebe. "What us done is magic. And magic have a way to work hisself out. Be patient. Still your heart. Look, me think help already on the way."

She sniffed the air. So did I, though not with the keen sense I had had before. "Coffee?" I said. "And . . . and salt."

"Come."

We helped each other up, and, still wrapped up together in that skin, waddled toward the warehouse like an improbable pair of Siamese twins.

And then we saw him, seated on an old cigar crate, staring out to sea, for we had reached the docks. The ancient white-maned poet in his serge coat, sipping from a can of coffee and writing in a little notebook.

"Psst!" I said. "Mr. Whitman!"

He turned and saw us, peering over piles of junk.

"Why," he said, "Mrs. Grainger . . . and . . . Phoebe, is it not? And you've been out riding the night wind. As have I."

"What you must think of us!" I began, but he shushed me with a broad smile and an easy laugh.

"My opinion of you lovely ladies," he said, "would not change whether I saw you completely as God made you, or clothed in the shapelessest potato sacks, or the finest Paris fashions—I speak only to the woman within. Would you care for coffee? If you wouldn't mind drinking from the same canister as a filthy old man."

I took the proffered cup. He took off his overcoat and handed it to me, looking discreetly at the ground while I put it on.

"I haven't another," he said to Phoebe, "but on the other hand, my dear, you have the gift of invisibility."

He was right. She was nowhere to be seen.

"And now," said Mr. Whitman, "we must catch the horse trolley back to Washington Square."

And when we arrived home, Zacko was already helping himself to toast, and setting coffee on the stove, and he proceeded to tell us more about Jimmy Lee Cox, and Tyler Tyler, who was telling us the sad tale of the colonel and the Haitian revolution.

20

GRIFFIN BLEDSOE LEARNS A PAINFUL LESSON

1

Colonel Bledsoe continued his narration, even though many of the ladies were drifting off; I, Tyler Tyler, remained awake, not necessarily because of the fascination of his tale, but because Amelia was still making eyes at me, and I knew that his tale had much to do with her, or with some ancestress at least. The thought hadn't escaped me, that this colonel had thought nothing of the prospect of bedding a mother and a daughter, and that his latest mistress must be a descendant of Zétwal and Améli—and perhaps therefore of an unthinkable degree of consanguinity to the colonel himself. But I was an indentured slave in all but name. I was hardly one to criticize, I suppose.

I listened, and the colonel's tale turned sadder, and I almost sympathized with him, in a way. . . .

2

A few days passed (said the colonel) and then I was pulled out of bed in the middle of the night. It was my father.

"We're leaving," he said.

I rubbed my eyes. My clothes were being stuffed into a trunk by maidservants.

"Leaving?" I said.

"We are returning to Georgia," said my father. "I've managed to get all sides involved to grant us letters of safe passage, but we must be gone by dawn."

"Monsieur Leclerc—"

"Fled," he said. "And we are left with all his worldly goods, to be disposed of by auction once we reach civilization. We'll transfer the money to his bankers in Europe. Oh, why am I bothering to tell you all this? Get out of bed, boy!"

"My clothes—"

"Oh, don't worry about clothes. If you dawdle, we're done for."

Suddenly I realized that the room was strangely bright, and I sprang up and ran to the veranda. I could see that then that the main house was on fire, and that men with torches and muskets were running amok, throwing chairs out of the windows, setting tables ablaze in the courtyard.

"What about Jozéf?" I cried, panicking that I might lose my friend. "And Améli? And Zétwal?"

"She's dead . . . gutted, impaled, quartered, incinerated. Don't think of her. Just be happy that she told them nothing."

"She protected Marie Laveau?"

"I don't know anything about that," said my father. "All I know is that she did not betray us. Our assets, our documents, the whereabouts of our bank accounts—she knew all those things, and she died to protect them. Admirable creature. But you must hurry!"

I raced down the stairs. An ox-drawn cart held most of our

belongings. In the courtyard, slaves were being rounded up. Yokes were being placed around their necks.

"Father—" I said.

"All of Leclerc's property," said my father, "is to be auctioned off by us. Don't look; it'll only upset you." And I was indeed perturbed, for two gendarmes were herding the slaves into the yokes, and a third was wielding a whip, and a fourth was methodically branding each one as he was locked into his fetters, and the odor of charring flesh suffused the whole courtyard; I was nigh vomiting.

Suddenly I saw Jozéf and Améli. Sleepy, naked, they were being lashed out of the guest house by a uniformed soldier, who was shouting at them, *"Vite, vite!"* and really making them hop to it. Lord, they were a sight! There was a passel of pickaninnies in a separate cart—these did not have the neck yokes, but were only trussed up a little, their arms being tied behind them and a pole thrust through the rope, so that they could be lifted up two at a time, for better balance. The soldier was driving my two friends toward the wagon full of young 'uns.

"Father!" I shouted. "They're putting Zétwal's children with the slaves!"

"They *are* slaves, son," said my father. "But you're right, they shouldn't be kept with the baser merchandise." He shouted at the officer to release them, and they came running to us, bawling their eyes out. Améli huddled with her arms around her breasts, though she had shown them to me proudly many a time; now, it seemed, she felt shame for the first time, like Eve after eating of the apple. Jozéf was all over welts. He must have resisted. He looked poorly. I'd never seen anyone lay a hand on him, not even a smart box o' the ear.

My father nodded, and they climbed in amongst our baggage, and we were off into the night.

To be sure, all hell had broke loose in Port-au-Prince that night. Our little convoy clattered through streets of mayhem. The night sky was about bursting with the light from burning

houses. Everywhere I saw white people spitted on sticks, decapitated, lying in pools of blood, or burned into bubbling lumps of
flesh. Blood ran over the cobblestones. Somewhere a mob was
howling, and the thunder of their feet made the very street
shake. With a couple of French soldiers to guard us, with a white
flag before us, we hurried as best we could, through alleys, avoiding the avenues. The slaves, as it dawned on them that they were
not to participate in the *révolisyon,* that they were never to be
free, become more and more agitated, and shook their chains
and battered against their yokes and hollered and carried on, so
they constantly had to be whipped into silence; and as we neared
the harbor they set up such a cry of *"Liberté, liberté!"* that was
piteous to hear, for they were unmercifully lashed up the gangplank into the *Persuasion,* whilst behind them Port-au-Prince
went up in flames. Jozéf and Améli were weeping too, though
whether for their dead mother, their dying city, or their lost
childhood, I couldn't rightly say. Yes, ladies, it was a heart-
breaking sight. And we didn't cast off a moment too soon, for
the crowd came surging into the port just as we did, and began
having at us with rocks, and firebrands, and even the occasional
musket.

Captain Tucker, who commanded the ship, came out to
greet my father. "We're as ready as can be, Sir Andrew," he said,
"given the circumstances."

Though my father had supported the revolution, and considered himself a thorough citizen of the state of Georgia, he
never quite managed to relinquish his knighthood; he never used
it on American soil, being a wholehearted supporter of the
American constitution, but was quite insistent upon it as soon as
we sailed into foreign waters. Indeed, he had flogged a cabin boy
once for calling him Mr. Bledsoe.

Hearing himself called by this familiar title, he felt himself
fully in his element. "Captain," he said, "have the slaves stowed;
let these peasants have a taste of the cannon; and let's get our
arses back to civilization!"

Tucker barked out a few commands, and the slaves were hustled belowdecks. When I saw that they were forcing Józéf and Améli down there too, I cried out, "No!" and rushed to retrieve them as the ship began to rock from the firing of our cannon into the mass of fulminating darkies in the port, who scattered at the first explosion.

"Mwen pa esklav!" Améli cried, and rushed to my father, throwing her arms about him, sobbing. *"Pa esklav, pa esklav!"*

"Non, non, choucoun mwen," my father said, calling her by the name of some native bird. "You will not be a slave." But he didn't look her in the eye, or me. And he called to one of the midshipmen, to have the two black children sent to our own quarters.

What use, I pondered, was their mother's sorcery, if it couldn't keep them from being shipped away, if it couldn't stave off her own death? Mayhap there had been a deeper reason behind their savage dancing, but I couldn't figure it out.

In my cabin, I went back to sleep, with Józéf on a pallet at my feet. The ship's movement soon lulled me back into my state of dreaming, and in my dreams I saw dusky women, dancing, possessed by strange gods, and I thought of sweet Améli, stifling and suffocating beneath the hulk of my grunting father.

3

At first the changes were few. My companion and I scampered about on deck during the day, lay abed talking of inconsequential things by night. We knew little of what was going on, and lived only from moment to moment. The salt meat and stale wine didn't bother us any, and the only painful time was the hour of exercise the slaves were afforded each day.

Leclerc's holdings had been vast, but there weren't enough slaves to make a whole shipload; most of our cargo was sugar. The slaves were stowed in the lowest deck, where once my friend and I had gone exploring in the dark, where we had discovered the voodoo ceremony. I won't allowed down there, naturally, and so the only time we saw them was during that hour.

It was a different type of dancing altogether. The slaves were brought up into the sunlight, which hurt their eyes, and they were made to jig up and down to the beat of a drum and an Irish tune on a fiddle. Iffen one didn't caper high enough, why then the quartermaster stood by to trounce him with his cat. Though the melody was spritely and the beat lively, you saw nary a smile in those faces, ladies; they danced frowning, weeping, some of them, with their shoulders hunched, hugging themselves. Most of them spoke but little English, only the barbarous French patois of Santo Domingo, but they were made to sing good English hymns, like "Rock of Ages," for to exercise their lungs. I caught some of them murmuring other lyrics to the songs, though . . . words like *Damballah Wedo* . . . and *oba kòso*.

I didn't speak of such things to anyone. I knew that the slaves would be whipped if anyone thought they were practicing witchery. I watched the slave dancing one or two days, and thereafter stayed away; but Józéf, he watched it every single day without fail, peering out at the deck through a little knot in my cabin wall. When the dancing was through, the slaves were cleaned off with buckets of vinegar; it reeked for hours afterward.

One evening, though, at supper, everything changed.

Captain Tucker and my father were deep in conversation, having dismissed all the other ship's officers; I knew that my father was about to lose his temper at Tucker, which he did not want to do in public lest authority be lost. Curiosity caused me to lag behind; I sat in a corner, a child, unnoticed, watching the contest of wills between a captain and the man who hired him.

"How could you possibly have been so incompetent?" my father shouted, as soon as the last officer had left.

"We left in a hurry, Sir Andrew," said Tucker. "We had no way of knowing that you'd bring human cargo as well as—"

"Should have been prepared," he said. "How many days' water?"

"Seven."

"And how many weeks to—"

"Two, sir. But we could put in to Havana for supplies—"

"The question, then, is economic: whether the expense of two or three days wasted in Havana is financially commensurate with the profit to be gained from slightly larger cargo—"

"What alternative is there, Sir Andrew?"

"Sit down, captain. I must needs teach you a lesson about the art of the hard decision."

Gulping, the captain took a seat.

"First," my father said, "how many fewer men must we have, that we may arrive at our destination without having to put in for fresh water? Calculate, man—and throw in an allowance for bad weather, becalming, and what have you."

The captain took quill and ink and began figuring sums in a spidery hand. "Sir, ideally we should lose about ten men."

"Well!" said my father. "And is our cargo not fully insured by Lloyd's against such calamitous occurrences as a captain's singular ineptitude? Need I say more?"

"You mean to—dispose of some of our cargo?"

"Yes, of course. The sickly ones first, naturally."

"And how are we to execute—if I may call it that—such a disposition?"

"Why, I don't know, man! Toss them overboard, I suppose. You're the captain, not I. But if we end up losing money on this trip, I'll have your hide. And send the bursar up; we'll need to fill out the insurance forms."

Well, the captain seemed none too happy when he left, and my father even less so. But in the morning, the grim consequences of what I witnessed were all too clear. All the slaves were being brought up on deck, even the ones too ill to move. They were muttering darkly, knowing that some dreadful fate awaited, for it was hours before the obligatory dancing. I and

Jozéf watched as the captain walked among the rows of sullen creatures, pointing now and then to one who seemed particularly disease-ridden, whose chains would be struck off. The chosen ones were led to a makeshift pen on the starboard side. They had no idea what was to happen, but they had an inkling it would be bad. Some could not even stand; they lay there dully, staring at the morning sun.

When the captain reckoned he had selected enough, he ordered the rest of the slaves sent back below. A French padre who was traveling with us read a few perfunctory lines from the Bible, and then they hove the niggers over the side, one by one.

Some did not complain, but others struggled to live. I couldn't look away, I was so transfixed by the horror of that spectacle. I saw an old man who everyone thought had no life left in him at all just get up and charge his captors and butt a man in the stomach so as to knock him down, and then another seaman just slashed at him with a rusty cutlass and took his arm clear off and sent it flying into the ocean . . . and that's when me and Jozéf came running out for a closer look, and that's when we saw the sharks, homing in on the bloody trail left by that severed limb, and finding sweet pickings all around us. It was terrible to behold those sharks, ladies; they thrashed, they worried the niggers as they desperately tried to cling to the side of the ship; it was what seafarers call a feeding frenzy.

I felt my gorge rise. I couldn't look anymore. I sprinted over to the larboard side and puked into the sea.

Then, all at once, from belowdecks, we heard the darkies' voices rise in chorus, and the words were all that African mumbo jumbo. Now and then a solo voice, and then the others in response; it was haunting and beautiful. But presently my father came stalking out of his cabin, and he cried in a passion, "Somebody silence those savages!" and then I heard the cat sing out a few times, and the song ceased.

He looked at me a moment. He saw my discomfiture. and patted me lightly on the shoulder. "Don't worry, son," he said.

"It's good that you see these things. You must appreciate the source of our family's wealth." Then he turned to Jozéf, and with a certain sadness, beckoned to one of the waiting seamen. "Stow this one below, too," he said. Before I realized what was happening, Jozéf was in irons and being carried below.

"Father—" I said.

"It's just as well, Griff, eh," he said. "You have to distinguish between a human being and a piece of merchandise. I know it's painful, but it's a lesson you must learn to survive in this world. We're going to have to make up the shortfall; the insurance payment will not entirely balance the books; and we cannot afford to keep these for ourselves; they are part of the estate of Leclerc, and must go to auction. So steel yourself."

"And what about the girl, then?" I said. "Are you going to chain her up down there, too? After what you and she did? I know what that is. You sent her mother to teach me. Will you take away my friend, and keep your plaything?"

His eyes narrowed. I had never seen him so angered at me. I shrank back, fully believing he would slap me. But he straightened up, and said, in a softly menacing voice, "Boy, don't presume to challenge me."

And he called the seaman back, and told him to seek out Améli, and to shackle her in the slave deck with the others.

4

The shame of it! My friend, languishing in the darkness, chained to a post, unable even to sit up, while I had the run of the ship, and feasted daily on such treats as salt pork and stale biscuits—ambrosia itself to one who only had a handful of cornmeal and a cup of foul water every day! Oh, ladies, I was angry. I knew my father was right, but at night I dreamt of all the games we'd played, of the time we'd followed Améli all the way to this very ship, of Améli bare-breasted in the moonlight, of Jozéf and me laughing together all night long at some childish joke. I was beside myself with rage. Some days I wouldn't even eat, and I know that my father knew why, and I knew we could afford the price of a couple of slaves . . . children at that . . . a hundred dollars on the market . . . but he and I were of a piece, stubborner'n mules, and I knew he'd never go back on a command once given.

I told you before that I was forbidden on pain of a severe whipping from ever going down into the hold. But one night that anger just built up in me so much that I couldn't hold it in anymore. I guess what happened next had to happen. And so it did. And I am what I am today, for better or worse, because of it.

It was, as I recall, my thirteenth birthday. All night long I had slept fitfully, plagued by nightmares. It was Zétwal who haunted my dreams. I would see her wrapping her arms around me, holding my face against her soft breasts, nuzzling against my shoulder, and then, when I looked up, there she was, hanging from a gibbet, her face ripped apart by crows, her lips torn away to reveal smashed teeth, her tongue ripped out by the roots, the branding marks still burning on her cheeks . . . and before I could scream, she clasped her hand over my mouth and whispered, "Do not speak, *monchè*, or you betray us all, oh, do not speak, *ti poupée mwen*. I still love you from beyond the grave. But you must not speak."

In this dream . . . if it was a dream . . . I was still in my cabin, with the candle still flickering by my bed, and the sea still heaving and whispering, and the slaves still moaning in the hold, and the whales still crying in the distance . . . yet she was there, in the cabin, amongst all that was familiar. She smelled of rottenness. Though I heard they had hacked her to pieces, yet her pieces were still all there, stitched together with wire and thread. Blood streamed from the gashes in her body, and her eyes were white, like the time I'd seen her in the throes of possession, ridden by some savage god. Flies buzzed about her wounds. A maggot crawled in and out of the holes in her face. Yet I still loved her. I still longed for her embrace. It is difficult for you to imagine that, ladies, I know, but she was the one who had taught me how to love a woman.

"Come, Griffin," said this apparition. "I take you now."

"Where?" I said.

"To hell," came the response.

She gripped my hand in her great, cold fist, and pulled me from the bed. I don't know iffen it were a dream, for the cold seared me and yet I did not wake. I took the candle from the nightstand. Held it right up to her face. It could not be illusion. The mistiness of dream was lacking. The worms, the dribbles of blood, the squeak of the wires that held her arms and legs to her body, all had a ghastly realness to them. This time, I was truly afraid. I shivered and shivered and only the firm grip of that frosty hand kept me from turning to jelly.

Still clutching me, the chill still burning into my very marrow, she led me from my chamber clad only in my nightshirt. On deck, all was at peace. A tropic breeze blew. Watchmen dozed. The moon was but a crescent. But there were thousands upon thousands of stars, and the ship had an unearthly glow, for the sails entrapped the starlight and cast it over the deck like a pale halo.

We reached the padlocked entrance to the hold.

"I think I'll go back to sleep now, Zétwal," I said. "We can't get down there anyway."

"Doors and locks not stop me, *mèt* Griffin. Me dead."

"If you're dead, Zétwal," I said, "what in tarnation are you doing here? Shouldn't the dead stay dead?"

"No true in Santo Domingo. Me come because me love you, *mèt,* and because me sent for you."

"Who sent for me?"

"You see soon."

She pointed to the padlock with her foot. It dissolved into thin air. And so did the wooden hatch.

We descended. Down the narrow stairs. Down, down. The stench of human ordure became intolerable. I started to retch. She squeezed my hand tighter and the hold caused the vomit to lie hard in my throat.

"It no so bad, white boy," she said. "Get used to it soon."

Down a long corridor lined with sacks of sugar and coffee beans and other rare delicacies. The odor of coffee and human waste blended into a sickly mélange, ladies, which I am sure would make y'all faint dead away.

Down more stairs now. And then we were there. Not the cavernous emptiness I had seen before—now the place seemed cramped and crammed. It was pitch dark. I only saw a little at a time, within the radius of light of a single candle flame. Each slave was connected to his neighbor by a length of chain, and those chains hung on rings to wooden posts at intervals. The slaves were packed on those wooden boards, some lying in pools of their own excrement, for the pails were beyond the reach of some, and others were too weak to reach them.

Strangest thing was, my friends, though I was passing through this corridor lined with misery in the company of a walking corpse, none seemed to see or care, though many were awake, and some stared dully at me, their eyes devoid of life.

Then I saw Józéf and his sister, chained up right next to him, for they had not even bothered to segregate the sexes, penning them all together like animals.

Jozéf was tossing and turning in his sleep, and moaning, "*Maman, maman,*" in a piteous small voice.

"Jozéf," I whispered, "it's me."

"*Maman, maman,*" he cried. And then he opened his eyes and saw me. But he didn't seem to see his mother. "*Mèt Griffin,*" he said. "You see how they punish me for me say you *frè mwen.*"

"No, Jozéf," I said. "That won't why they took you out of the world upstairs. It was all insurance, and mathematics, and logistics, and things we children can't grasp."

"Grasp one thing only," he said. "Black is black and white is white."

"No," I said. "We *are* brothers. I swear it. And one day I will set you free."

"How you do that? You no own *ti Jozéf.*"

"I don't know how," I said. "But I'm going to do it. I swear." Zétwal's hand closed tight around my wrist, and I gritted my teeth from the pain of it. "I swear it by *Pè L'éténél.* I swear by your gods too, if you want."

"No say that. Legba he hear everything."

"I don't care," I said.

But Jozéf only turned over—making the chains clank all the way down the row and tug at the rings—and went back to sleep. I started to slip away, but at that moment Améli awoke. There was no question that she saw her mother, for she smiled.

"You brought my *ti frè* to me," she said, laughing a little. Oh, she was wan, but still beautiful in the soft candlelight; her eyes sparkled; she never did have, then or later, the downcast demeanor of a true bondsman.

"Améli," I said, "don't you see how they've tortured her, how they've cut her to pieces?"

"Me see her as she was," she said, "because me no carry guilt."

"How do you see her?"

"Me see her in the starlight. Me see her shining like the night me not can see no more. Her name, you know, mean Star . . . *zétwal . . . les étoiles.*"

"But why couldn't Jozéf—"

"He need to give up something of himself first. To enter the spirit world and come back alive, must leave something behind—perhaps a limb, perhaps an eye—"

"And you, Améli? What did you leave behind?"

"My innocence," she said, and she looked away from me, past me, wistfully, at a past I could not imagine.

For a time she communed with her mother's ghost in silence; I could see that they were speaking without words, without gestures, and I felt lost and alone. But after a time it seemed that they were saying their good-byes. The circle of ice about my wrist was dissipating. I turned to see Zétwal dissolving into the flickering light, becoming one with the malodorous gloom that surrounded me.

Then Améli seized me with both her wrists and pulled me down to her level with a surprising firmness. "I must give you a *ti kado*," she said, "for today you are a man, no?"

And she blew out the candle, and set it down somewhere in the darkness.

My thirteenth birthday had passed unnoticed. Not even my father had remarked upon it. But Améli rewarded my new manhood in full measure. The lessons I learn from Zétwal weren't but a prelude to what Améli showed me. Oh, I was contented that night, ladies! My little peter delved new caverns of pleasure . . . you might say that it grew from a snake to a dragon that night . . . oh, you cannot imagine it . . . in that hell-pit of tormented souls, in that reeking hole of shit and misery, oh, there was such an ecstasy to be had! Oh, ladies, ladies! Oh, you young yankee sitting at t'other table, with your lustful eye on Améli's granddaughter, three times my blood—oh, y'all know nothing of such ecstasy, and never will! I owned her utterly, body, heart, and soul. Oh, we moved the ship over the waters, we made the world go round. That, ladies, was what men call love, though my preacher might name it lust.

I sank into that plenitude of darkness, and I was sucked under the waves, and sunken; and so I lay there all the night, in my first peaceful slumber since we left Port-au-Prince.

5

They pulled me off of her, and drug me up to my father, who was in the officer's mess, eating his breakfast with the captain and the quartermaster, who was telling my father, "My keys was stole, Sir Andrew; stole from my side as I slept."

"It isn't true!" I shouted. "It was Zétwal . . . she came to me in a dream . . . unlatched it with some magical power—"

The two officers laughed, but my father slapped me so hard in the face that I nigh passed out from the loss of breath.

"Listen to me, Griffin," he said. "This has gone on long enough. They have corrupted your very soul with their outlandish superstitions." He surveyed me with an overwhelming sadness; he had often whupped me in anger, five or six strokes with a battered hickory, which I never minded much, for whippings are part of being a boy; but I understood not at all this new, aggrieved demeanor which my father affected, save that it must bode ill. I can tell you, I was shaking all the way down to my toes.

"Now, listen, Griff," said my father, "I want you to understand that you're all I've got, and that since your mother's death I have lived but to ensure that you have the very best of everything. But there are times when the child must be hurt in order that he become the better man. And the lesson you must learn today may be the bitterest lesson of your life, but learn it you must."

"Father," I said, beginning to panic, "I'm sorry I went down into the slave deck. I didn't mean to. I had a nightmare and . . . something impelled me. . . ."

"Silence!" my father shouted. "You are white, Griffin. They are black. You are a human being and they are chattel. If you long to be with them, to associate with them, then you shall know what it is like to *be* one of them. Quartermaster, please put him down for thirty-nine lashes."

"Very good, Sir Andrew," he said.

"Sir," said the captain, "with regard to the boy's extreme youth, and delicate condition—"

"I trust and pray, sir, that you will never be forced to discipline your own child with such severity."

"But Father—I'll die!" I squealed. "I didn't do anything that bad. I just went adventuring in the middle of the night, is all. I did nothing—I harmed no merchandise—"

"That's not what I am told," said my father.

It was at that moment, knowing I could not escape my doom in any case, that rage emboldened me, and I screamed right to his face, "It's nothing to do with white and black, is it, Father? It's jealousy pure and simple—because I did with the girl what you did—because I'm a man too now, and *kapab!*"

My father would not look at me as they took me away. He did not witness the punishment, which was the most awful experience of all my days, nor did he speak to me while I lay, near death, ministered to only by the two children of Zétwal, who miraculously *were* brought up out of the inferno below in order to tend to me.

And when we finally put in at Baltimore, which was where the auction of Leclerc's assets was to be held, I learnt that Jozéf and Améli were not to be sold after all; they were to be our house servants; my father had apportioned them to himself as part of his commission for the disposition of Leclerc's property. And on the way to Georgia, I learnt as well that Améli was with child . . . with the mother of Amelia which you see here tonight; and the girl would be named, after her *granmè,* Estelle, which is the proper French for Zétwal.

I never forgot—though everyone else did—that had the children hidden a little more carefully that night they burned down Leclerc's mansion, that they would no longer be slaves. For the French surrendered shortly after our departure, and the territory became the Republic of Haiti, the first free black country of our times.

Think about this, ladies, when you rail about the evils of the yankees. They too are human beings. If they were not, my friends, they could not hurt our feelings. They could burn down our houses and destroy our manhood, but they could not touch our souls . . . as, ladies, they most frequently have.

21

FROM AMERICUS TO BALTIMORE

1

All the while that that colonel was speaking (Tyler Tyler continued), he was eyeing me with a look of curiosity and displeasure. He knows, I thought, he knows, and he means to kill me for sure, because he thinks I have already laid hands on this creature of his, his daughter, his daughter's daughter—oh, to think of it, how he had been breeding his own lovers as though they were mere dogs, and whitening them up with each succeeding generation. Oh, but the man was evil, even though he was at heart a pitiable creature too.

That night, she came to me again. I told her, "Don't come back. It's too dangerous. The old man knows."

But all she said was, "I love you."

"Leave!" I said.

"The old man ain't no man. At night he don't touch me no more. He powerful afraid. He dream about a old man with one eye, come to fetch him to the land of the dead."

"Who?" I said. "Jozéf?"

She nodded. I remembered that in the colonel's story he had said that the reason his friend could not see his own dead mother was that he had not yet given something up—a limb—an eye. There must be a lot more to that story, I thought. If I stayed here many more nights, I'd probably know everything.

"It's too dangerous," I said. "You really have to go—you must."

Reluctantly, with many a tear, she departed.

This is what happened the next day, Jimmy Lee, and this is why you find me here today, armless in the wilderness, with a madwoman for my companion.

In the morning, sitting in my little bureau by the church that was being rebuilt, watching my companions slaving away, an errand boy came to me with stack of papers to initial—so many yards of concrete, so many bricks, so many cords of wood. There was also a whipping chit.

I did not like to look at those; I would generally just initial them and hand-throw them in the box, for they passed through my hands only as a convenience to Colonel Bledsoe, who was trying to create a single filing system for his entire household.

This one, though, I could not help but look on, for it read:

> To Cordwainer Claggart, Esq., proprietor of the city punishment house:
> Amelia Bledsoe, thirty-nine Lashes
> For Insubordination, at the Colonel's earnest and urgent Exhortation.

"What have they done to her?" I shouted, and the errand boy looked at me in confusion, and stammered, "Why, sah, she at the whipping post already."

I left the church right then and there. They didn't have me chained up like the others. I was a man with but one arm, wasn't I? What could I do? I stormed out onto the street. I ran to the whipping house, which was hard by, no more than two block away. I damn near broke the door down with my good fist, pounding, and when Claggart let me in, I could see her tied up to that bloodstained post, and a few stripes on her already.

"Oh, come to get a closer look?" he said. "I know there's many that likes to see their lovers whipped; excites them, it does."

"Cut her loose, Claggart. She ain't done nothing wrong. We never did nothing."

"Oh, is that a fact? But you are mighty anxious, ain't you, to defend whatever nothing it was you done, sir! Ain't that a fact."

"Come on, man, let her go, just say you did it and let her go."

"I am an honest man, yankee," said Cordwainer Claggart, "and to tell the truth, it don't much matter if she be guilty or innocent; a master's whim is all what matters; these are slaves, man, not human beings; you Northerners never seem to grasp that—three-fifths of a man is all a slave is, and that's just for the sake of the census."

"Go back to work, Tyler," said Amelia. "Ain't nothing to be done nohow. In a year or two we gone be free, even the masta says so, we losing this war, we just needs to suffer just a few short years—"

"Silence!" Cordwainer Claggart brought his whip down with a resounding crack, and a welt ran clear across Amelia's back. "That may very well be true, mistress, but until they rams that 'mancipation business down our throats, and puts me out of a job, I may as well do what they pays me for. Hell, when the war's done, I'm moving west . . . got plans, I has, mighty big plans . . . I'll bottle up some inefficacious nostrum, and sell it to them civilization-starved Westerners for a dollar a bottle . . . I'll start up a church, mayhap, and collect a fortune from tithing id-

iots hoping for a pew in paradise . . . oh, yes, Cordwainer Claggart's gone manage all right . . . away from this dead-end job of
whupping niggers day in, day out, with a lily-white prentice lad
now and again to lighten up my load. . . ." He laughed at his
pun, whipping furiously the while.

I couldn't stand his chattering anymore. I may have been
puny and unfed, and I may only have had one arm, but I was
pretty damn enraged, and the sight of Amelia, naked and helpless, stirred my affections as well as my pity. I looked around for
a weapon, saw nothing to hand, so I simply rushed at the man
and sent him sprawling, more from surprise than anything else,
I imagined; he hit his head against a wall; I cut Amelia down with
a pocketknife I found stuck to Claggart's belt, and told her to
follow me.

"Don't be silly, Tyler! Where to?"

"There's horses tethered outside. I'll steal one. We'll escape.
The Northern lines can't be that far."

"Oh, you impossible, Tyler! Don't you know what you done
a hanging offense? A whipping just a whipping. They won't gone
kill me or nothing. A slave worth *money,* Tyler—a yankee they
can hang."

"I love you," I said.

She began to weep as I found her clothes and handed them
back to her. "Ain't no man ever said that to me afore," she said.

"Then come," I said, and took her hand in my good hand,
and we hastened from the place, and I did steal a horse, but a
mile away from the town we started to hear the nigger hounds,
and what happened but Amelia pushed me off that horse, and
turned around and started back toward the town.

"What the hell are you doing that for?"

"Them dogs they trained to sniff out niggers," she said. "If
I go back, mayhap you get lucky . . . go free."

I struggled to my feet. "No!" I shouted. But she was already
galloping to meet the hounds. She had spoke so eloquently
of her monetary worth, and my own worthlessness, but now

she was riding off to die, so she could save my worthless life.

I limped towards what I hoped was north. The rest, Jimmy Lee, you know.

2

Tyler Tyler didn't speak for a while (Jimmy Lee continued) but just lay there in the snow that was really the crushed bones of the dead. And Amelia just went on sightlessly dancing and tunelessly singing about plucked flowers.

It were a tragic sight to see, Zacko, and I did not know how a man so crushed by circumstance could ever be truly comforted.

"Oh, Tyler Tyler," said I, "what help is there for you? How can I bring you succor, when there is no remedy for such pain?"

"Kill me," said Tyler Tyler.

But how could I bring myself to do such a thing? He warn't no wounded horse that I could just shoot him in the head, and think no more upon it excepting that I'd put a poor creature out of its misery.

"We could take you with us," I said.

"And where are you going?" he said. "Surely not north. Further and further into the arms of the enemy. I have the blood of a colonel on my hands . . . that's how they'll see it. Better you kill me, Jimmy Lee, for I've nothing to live for now. Amelia's happy in her madness. She don't need me. She don't need eyes to see."

"What then?" I said. "We can't just leave you here, not after heaven and earth moved themselves for you."

And Amelia sang:

> *The fields turn white*
> *With death's delight;*
> *The fields run red*
> *With flowers of spite.*

I turned to Old Joseph . . . hard to imagine him as little Jozéf, the Haitian pickaninny, brother to a white boy . . . seeing him now, in his leopard raiment, resplendent against the tree trunk. "Help me, *beau-père*," I said, "for the man won't let himself be helped."

"Then, honey, how can we help him?" said Old Joseph. "Ask, and ye shall receive, saith the gospel; but it don't say nothing bout what happen iffen a man don't ask. Best to forget him," he added, and I recollected that that's what he said, too, about the slain white boys which lain amongst the darkies, which he done neglected to resurrect.

For the first time, I felt angry with old Joseph, and ashamed, too. If he could open up the heaven and the earth, why couldn't he rescue the love of Tyler and Amelia? I shouted at him, "Why, Joseph, you're just as hateful as white folks are."

"Oh, no, *monchè*," he said, "but I know that to take away a man choice is like to kill that man; so I will not say him, come, or go."

So saying, he turned from us, and started walking, I know not where exactly; mayhap toward the rising sun.

And Amelia sang:

> *Roses are red,*
> *Violets are blue,*
> *He fucked my mammy*
> *He'll fuck me too.*

"Listen to her!" I cried after Old Joseph, but he was moving rapidly out of earshot. And one by one the *zombis* was fixing to follow, shambling acrosst the stream, a regular army of the dark.

I went to Tyler and tried to rouse him from where he was, half sitting up against a tree. "You got to move on," I said. "You got to have friends, you can't just lay yourself down to die, not after all you've been through."

"You heard the old man, didn't you?" he said. "It's my choice to lay down and die. Give me that dignity at least."

Amelia was already following the *zombis,* weaving in and out of them, using their bodies to gauge her step. And last came Eleuthera, who I guess had been hiding somewhere, leopard-fashion, blending in with the trees. But Tyler wouldn't budge, spite that his wounds were healed enough.

Still furious, I ran up to Old Joseph, marching at the head of his column of the living dead.

"Why can't you order one of them dead folks to pick him up on their shoulder and carry him with us?"

"Cause he have to ax to be carried."

"Why can't we wait for him to change his mind?"

"Cause he already dead, Marse Jimmy Lee; mark my word, honey, just because a man moving and walking don't mean he living; you of all folks should know that."

"You called down the wrath of heaven for him! You blew that colonel and his minions to pieces! Shouldn't you at least try to save him?" Getting right red in the face, I finally cried out, "Why, Joseph, you're no better than my real father was. You abandon a body to die, and you just moves on."

At that, he became impatient with me at last. He turned. Stamped his foot. All at once the *zombis* ceased their shambling and Amelia her singing.

"Put you ear to the ground," he said to me. Not a request, but a peremptory command.

I crouched down. I obeyed.

I heard nothing at first. But then, as in a dream, there came a distant and insistent rat-tat-tat, and above it the whistle of a fife, so faint that it might have been the wind itself; but the tune was "Battle Hymn of the Republic." "The yankees," I said softly.

Now I could distinguish the tread of their feet . . . like faraway thunder in a clear summer sky . . . *boom, boom, boom.* "You knew they was coming," I said. "Why, old Joseph, you knew he was gone get rescued, didn't you?"

He answered not a word.

"You knew all this time," I said, "yet you mumbled on about choice and human dignity, and all the while you knew!" And I embraced the old man, and kissed him on the cheek. For my belief in his powers was such, I thought he might have summoned the yankee host down from the North himself, to pull this lost sheep from perdition.

Finally he said to me, "Choice, honey, is ever an illusion."

And we moved on.

3

Jimmy Lee Cox told me all these things (Zack said to us over our morning coffee) even as we sat in that covered wagon, watching his reanimated father chowing down on human entrails. As always, he spoke in a plain, unemotional voice; and that gave his tale a quality of truth, you see; it was plain there was nothing to exaggerate.

"So in the end," said Jimmy Lee, "death came to Tyler after all, and he died whole."

"Are you still angry that he had to die?"

"I reckon. But there warn't nothing I could have done."

Which was true enough, I guess. But there were still things I burned to know. What happened to Amelia? And where was old Joseph now? And how was it he come to lose his eye? Jimmy Lee didn't have all the answers. And Tyler sure wasn't talking no more.

I said, "Where will you go now?"

Jimmy Lee said, "I don't know. The gods don't tell me much. Mayhap I'll become a carnival sideshow . . . waking the dead alongside the giant rat and the imperishable mummy . . . I reckon I'll head out west, though. Where everything's still new. Where a body can start fresh."

4

Tyler Tyler!

When I walked back on over to the others, Kaczmarczyk and Walt had wrapped him in a makeshift shroud cut from an old piece of canvas they found fluttering in the wind.

And at dawn there came a strange sight indeed. It was Walt who saw it first, because he was in the habit of, as he called it, "striding Byronically" along any convenient shore.

I heard him calling, and come running out of the tent. Kaz was there before me, though. We sat on three boulders and watched it bobbing up and down in the river.

"Is it some kind of crate?" I said.

"Vy no," said Kaz, "that tink is a full-fledged coffin if ever I saw one."

And indeed it was: a casket floating on the river, like a piece of driftwood. Well, it was almost within our grasp—maybe ten feet out—and Walt just rolled up his trouser bottoms and stalked out into the muck to pull it in.

"Something for Tyler Tyler," he called out, "thrown up by the river of time." And he drug it to the bank.

The coffin was empty. Guess it might have held someone once, but whoever ever it held was long since washed away; it was all clean inside, bleached by the sun and the water. We took it back to where we had our fire, and where Tyler was still laying. It was an antique thing, and on the lid was sculpted a beautiful angel, with spread wings, its hands in prayer, looking up out at the world. And at the angel's feet was a skeleton, and the angel was crushing its head beneath its heel; and a serpent crawled out of one eye of the skull; the angel's eyes were blank. So I run my fingers over the old wood, and it felt good, solid, ancient.

"Don't see much vork like this no more," said Kaczmarczyk, "except maybe in the old country."

So we put Tyler in the coffin and we closed the lid, and we each of us, in our own way, said a prayer.

"Where will he go now?" I asked.

"To Baltimore," said Walt, "where he was born; I'll write his mother, and we'll go up on the train. And perhaps, Zacko, we'll stop by the grave of Edgar Allan Poe."

"Who's that," I said, "a friend of yours?"

Walt only smiled, and gave me a quick hug, and told me that he loved me.

Close on its wave soothes the wave behind,
And again another behind
embracing and lapping, every one close,
But my love soothes not me, not me.

—Walt Whitman

A Chorister
in Cambridge

1811

22

MRS. GRAINGER RECEIVES A MISSIVE FROM HER LATE HUSBAND

1

"Baltimore!" cried Phoebe. "And Edgar Allan Poe! Why then, Paula, it time to do what our husband told me to do."

"And what is that?" I asked her.

"He said me know when the right time come," she responded, and abruptly left the salon where we had all been taking coffee.

"Heavens," I said. "It never gets easier to understand Phoebe, no matter how many new facts I discover about her."

"Odd," said Mr. Whitman. "The mention of Edgar Allan Poe seemed almost to be a magic word, an 'open sesame' as it were. Perhaps your husband had a special affinity for that macabre gentleman?"

"I think they may have corresponded once or twice," I said. "Twenty years ago or more."

I heard Phoebe's footsteps, and when she reentered the salon she was carrying a wooden box. It was covered in some kind of lacquer, and painted in black with those signs which I now knew were called *vévé*. She handed me the box and said, "Mr. Grainger say give you this, when you ready."

I looked at the box, unable to decide whether to open it in front of all these people; after all, though it seemed we had lived through lifetimes together, I had known the poet and his friend for only a couple of days.

"We'll respect your privacy, Mrs. Grainger," said Mr. Whitman, and he and Zack walked over to the divan beneath the window. I wondered whether Mr. Whitman had already divined that my relationship with his friend was no longer as innocent as before. I was sure that Phoebe knew everything that was in the box, for she evinced no curiosity. At any rate, there I was on the fauteuil, undoing the clasp, and my friends were at varying locations, all studiously avoiding my gaze. It was an almost comical moment. I felt exquisitely embarrassed for a moment, for I had not even changed out of the serge greatcoat which was the only thing that covered my nudity; on our return to the house, however, I had found Phoebe in her black-and-white maid's uniform, and the kitchen spotless, without a hint of black magic.

Be that as it may, I opened the box.

I realized then that Phoebe must have been completely aware of its contents, for I recognized one of the objects therein right away; it was the notebook I had found in the ottoman beneath her bed, with the lists of African words and drawings of those divine sigils called *vévé*. I leafed through it briefly, understanding little more than before. There, too, was the letter from President Lincoln.

"I've seen these things," I said.

"Look farther, Paula," said Phoebe. "I was in the middle of gathering them all together for you, that day you rifled through the papers in the chest. Now they are all in order. You should start with the letter that's sealed up, in the fat brown envelope."

I pulled that out. The wax seal was unbroken. It was addressed thus:

To my Darling Wife Paula,
    from Aloysius Grainger, her much-tormented husband:
    With the earnest wish that she will not read these words
    until I am long gone.
    Phoebe shall name the time and place.

My husband's handwriting was generally neat, and very small, but this was crudely written, and in haste, in a hand that seemed to have been trembling. Quickly, I broke the seal. There tumbled out several documents; the first, in my husband's hand, was a letter of some five or six pages, more tidily written than the address; it was clearly something he had labored over.

With trepidation, I began to read.

2

Dearest, the letter began, By the time you read this, I shall undoubtedly have been in my grave for at least a year or two. It is well. I would not want you to come to my words so torn by grief at my passing as to be unable to appreciate all that I have witnessed and experienced. You must rest assured, my dear, that I love and cherish you above all things. I know that there have been times when it did not seem so; but I have ever been a diffident man, trying to overcome my social inadequacies by the performance of acts which I perceived to be noble, or humane, or for a just and righteous cause.

Causes, causes, causes! My dearest Paula, you know me well as a follower of lost causes; you have indulged me, overindulged, if the truth were told—and still you do not know the half of it. The abolitionism—perhaps the only one of the causes not wholly lost—you helped me with tremendously. The debunking of mesmerism, Darwinism, and other pseudosciences turned out less successfully, but we certainly had fun, didn't we, my dear? But there were causes and obsessions I never told you about, my dear, because I felt you would have been disturbed by them.

One such cause was the resurrection of the body.

I hope that doesn't shock you too much, my dear. But I have told Phoebe she must not hand you these epistles until you are already reasonably forearmed; and I have always suspected that you did not adhere as strictly to the precepts of our Christian faith as you might have our acquaintances believe; like me, my dear, you have always really been agnostic.

Does it astonish you when I say this? Did you think, perhaps, that you were only paying lip service to the scriptures for my sake, because I am an ordained minister, and it would not do for a minister's wife to show any vestiges of doubt? But, my dear, this is the nineteenth century; he who adheres to the gospels as though we still dwelt in the Dark Ages is a fool.

Let me say again, then, that I have always been obsessed with resurrection. You know that we have lost several children. In ancient times we might have thought your womb cursed, and asked for some kind of ritual cleansing; but my first thoughts were scientific ones; I had, after all, read *Frankenstein*—what educated person has not?

When our first son did not live past a month, I was maddened with grief. I wanted to see him live again. I would surely have given my soul for such a thing.

I held that dead child in my arms, and Frankensteinian visions swarmed through my mind; oh, God, I admit that I tried to raise him from the dead, using the techniques of Volta and Galvani, but of course, to no effect; science, it seemed, availed naught in the war against death. Yes, dear, when you took to your bed with grief, in the week before the funeral, your husband was trying to become the modern Prometheus.

I was so disconsolate that—oh, I am ashamed to admit it—I could not bring myself to consummate the act of love with you, for my desire wilted even as it began—and I began to seek the quick relief of other women. Only occasionally, that is, and when I simply could not control myself any longer. But that is when it began, my dearest.

Then we moved to America, and I thought to start afresh. That nightmarish week was hidden in the dark recesses of my private memory, and I swore never to tell you what transpired. In Connecticut, you were with child again, and never had I been so happy. But that child, too, died—after barely half a year. You took to your bed once more, and I . . . I descended from the Apollonian heights of science to the slough of superstition . . . I, like so many before and since, tried the notorious Indian burial ground two miles north of Branford, of which many have written . . . which was rumored to be able to revive the dead. Whilst you wept yourself to sleep, I was trying to revivify the dead, sleeping with ghosts on the cold cursed ground of the ancient ones. There, too, I was disappointed, and in my despair I threw myself with increasing fervor into the causes I espoused, hoping thereby to forget. Charities, benevolent foundations, taking up collections for the indigent helped me forget my sorrow for a time.

But my fascination with death and resurrection did not abate. Nor was I alone in it. There were many who had not only an interest in, but some real knowledge of these arts; one such was a certain Mr. Poe, with whom I corresponded briefly, in 1849, the last year of his life. Mr. Poe had himself been carrying extensive correspondence on this subject since the death of his wife.

It was then that I decided to study the wisdom of the ancients on these matters, and to read every tome of lore I could lay my hands on . . . and it was then that I discovered, in a scholarly treatise about the black arts in the Caribbean islands, that the *houngan,* or witch doctors, of Santo Domingo were in the habit of resuscitating the dead, whom they referred to as *zombi.*

Here are certain letters from Mr. Poe, and a document he claims to have rescued from a fireplace in London while he was in school there. Read them first, my dear, and then I will tell you what has transpired since then, and why it is that, by the time you receive this missive, I will almost certainly be cold in my grave, unless, unless—

3

There followed a sheaf of missives in another hand, and a bundle of manuscript pages tied up with string, the edges of which were charred and impossible to read.

I proceeded first to the epistles, which were mostly short, except for the last, which ran to several foolscap pages.

My dear Aloysius (the first read),

Have attempted the use of the African sigils without much result. I do not think they will admit me to the morgue again; they already think me an obsessed, impossibly morbid person who will not let well enough alone.

But ah, I loved her so! How can I be blamed for wanting her returned from the land beyond? Though she is now a triumph of the embalmer's loathsome art, her face a luminous mask of wax and formalin, her flesh is yet cold. I will essay another one of these rituals, but I do not think they will let me alone with her again. The undertaker leers when he sees me come to ask to spend a moment with my beloved Virginia; I think he suspects some unspeakable perversion. And—it is strange that I am confessing this to one whom I hardly know, yet for some reason I find myself trusting you.

We must have another evening at the coffeehouse soon.

With respect and affection,

Your servant

Edgar

Fordham, New York

There was another letter from Mr. Poe.

My dear Aloysius (it read),

Your support, during these most turbulent months of my life, has been most welcome. It is good to find someone with whom to compare notes, someone who does not find the thing we are attempting so hopelessly theoclastic, so appallingly unnatural, as to brand us instantly instruments of Satan.

Tonight's experiment must be my last, as my beloved Virginia is soon to be inhumed in the world below. Oh, could you but dream what I have dreamt, Aloysius! You would have cause never to sleep again, or to swill quantities of laudanum and liquor till you descend into a dreamless stupor. I will attempt to say all the words you suggested to me, and do my best with the pronunciation, which does not rest easy upon my Richmond-London-Baltimore tongue! I hope that some slip of enunciation does not cause me to conjure up the wrong dark god!

With my best wishes,

Edgar

Fordham, New York

There was a third letter, in the selfsame handwriting, but scrawled in haste, with many scratchings-out and words obliterated by inkblots. . . .

My dear, dear Aloysius,

I fear that I shall not be writing to you much longer. Tonight my beloved waked for a brief moment. Do you think me mad? Can I prove without a single witness, without the possibility of ever repeating the experiment, that the dead can open their eyes, can think, can feel, can love? Can they, indeed, still feel the torments that they felt in life, the wasting, the coughing-up of blood, the gradual dissolution of being that is consumption? Can horror hound a person beyond the grave itself? Can a still, solemn, ethereal beauty conceal an agony of diabolical origins?

Oh, God, I *am* mad! Tell me I am mad! It were better to be mad than to believe that what I have seen is real. . . .

Let me tell you what happened. You are a man of God; you have the strength to understand, perhaps forgive.

I arrived at the undertaker's at midnight. His boy let me in, and I observed that he, too, would not look at me, and suppressed a supercilious smirk when I asked for another moment alone with my Virginia. Why, even the apprentices thought there was something faintly obscene about my nightly visitation with my beloved!

At length, however, he led me to the little chamber where Virginia lay; the undertaker had finally completed his attentions, and Virginia rested in a simple casket of ebony—black being the only appropriate color for a casket—in an attitude of prayer. Every trace of the consumption that had ravaged her seemed to have been lifted from her lifeless form. Oh, she was beautiful! Oh, how I loathed myself that I had not been a model of uxoriousness in my ten-year marriage, that I had driven myself to drink from time to time, and not paid her the attention she deserved . . . oh, how I tormented myself as I sat there gazing into her perfect face!

But I knew I did not have much time. I had a small vial of the *coup poudre,* which, it was claimed, had been mixed in New Orleans by the Queen of Voodoo herself, Marie Laveau. I had the ritual words, culled from my conversations with you and from another document, which one day I shall show you. I had all the African sigils I had been able to collect, from you and from other sources. I could not wait any longer; I had to attempt reanimation.

I sprinkled the *coup poudre* on my beloved. It was a plain, white, ashlike substance—rumor had it that it was manufactured from the dried liver of the puffer fish—and I laid the cloth I had prepared, inscribed with several *vévé,* upon her face. Then I proceeded with the recitation.

I called upon *Damballah Wedo,* the great *koulèv,* or serpent, whose tail the savages believe circumscribes the entire universe. I called upon Legba, messenger of the gods. I called the names of many a darker angel; called upon them again and again until I was sure my howling must bring the apprentices running in to have me hauled away to some lunatic asylum.

At length, I fell upon the body in a passion, for Virginia lay unmoving in spite of all my efforts. I threw my arms about her cold cold limbs. I kissed her stony lips. She had no warmth, and so I made my own; my body awoke to a desperate and disturbing ardor. I tore at the ribbons that laced her bodice. I shook her. I flailed away inside that coffin, weeping yet aroused, pulling my own small serpent loose from my fly buttons, loosening my collar stud, gasping for air—

It was at that moment, Aloysius, that I fancied I felt some response from within her chill flesh. Methought her fingers kneaded a little at the small of my back.

Methought her tongue, blackened and befouled by the unguents of preservation, pried loose those icy lips and flicked at the corners of my own. Methought her eyelids fluttered. Horrified and yet stirred to a passion beyond even horror, I spent my lust in a sticky ooze upon the black satin of her funeral dress.

Appalled at my incontinence, I lifted myself off her corpse. I was panting. She slumped back into the casket . . . I stared . . . for that which I thought I had merely imagined seemed suddenly to be actually happening . . . the twitching of her fingertips . . . the eyelids fibrillating . . . the lips pursing up, as though on the verge of speech . . . and then it was . . . oh, God above! Virginia opened her eyes.

"Ohhhh . . ." she moaned.

Then it was that I fell on my knees and beseeched her forgiveness for all the wrongs I had done her. I confessed my womanizing and my alcoholic binges. I swore that I would henceforth live only for her . . . if she would only return. . . .

And she spoke to me, in a still, small voice suffused with the intensest of suffering: "Edgar, Edgar, leave me be. . . ."

"Virginia," I cried out, "tell me at least that you are well . . . that you dwell in paradisial bliss . . . that you are free of the anguish that your consumption brought you . . . that you know peace. . . ."

"No!" she gasped. "The pain!" She let out a scream of intolerable torment, which seared my very soul, and then grew still; but yet her eyes remained open, accusing, taunting, and I dared not close them, dared not even touch her, knowing the abominable act I had just committed upon her person. . . .

I ran out of the chapel. The apprentice was in the reception room, playing dice with another . . . bringing to mind the soldiers who gambled over our Crucified Lord's raiment.

I stared at them, wild-eyed.

"What did you hear?" I shouted.

"Why, Mr. Poe," said the boy, "what should we have heard?" And the boys giggled together, and poked one another in the ribs. The fools! They had reduced my moment of truth to some obscene assignation! Perhaps they had mistaken my lover's hideous scream for some paroxysm of necrophiliac lust!

But what if . . .

What if indeed I had imagined it all? What if my grief has driven me mad, and I'm living an illusion? Yet to believe I'm trapped in an ecstasy of mourning is better than the alternative, which is to think that yes, there is a consciousness that lives within the putrefying flesh . . . that when she is put into the cold ground, there will remain some part of her that screams forever. . . .

Oh, Aloysius, my friend, what have I done?

I beg you, come to the coffeehouse again next week, so that you can give me a few words of solace. It is a pity I no longer live on Broadway, so that we could meet and speak at a moment's notice. . . .

Your very aggrieved friend,

Edgar

There was a final document in the hand of Mr. Poe. This one, in fact, seemed earlier; my husband had not arranged the letters in chronological order, but by some system of gradual revelation, I supposed, so that I would come to the truth in stages, and not be too shocked all at once.

Dear Reverend Grainger (commenced this final epistle),

You asked me at our first meeting how I came to be interested in the whole question of resurrection, and I told you it was a story scarcely to be believed, so bizarre and synchronicitous were its coincidences. I have often been accused of lying—alack, some of those occasions have been not entirely untrue, for I did claim to have fought in the Hellenic War of Independence, but that was obviously a sort of fiction, designed to show my affinity with Byron, whose works I admired greatly as a youth—and I will not take it amiss if you do not believe my tale. Nevertheless, I do have a document that will, I hope, prove its veracity to you.

As you know, my parents died when I was but three years old, and I was adopted by Mr. Allan of Richmond, Virginia, where I was raised mostly by Nancy, my adoptive father's maidservant. Because I barely knew my real parents, and in gratitude for the Allans' many kindnesses, I now always preface my real surname with Mr. Allan's. In 1815, we moved for a time to England because of my father's business. I was enrolled in a London boarding school, one of the best of its kind, though full of the petty cruelties common to such institutions; as an Englishman yourself, I'm sure you're all too familiar with that sort of thing—the floggings, faggings, and the like. As those places go, it was not, I suppose, that bad; but you do not need an exegesis of the British school system here. Suffice it to say that it was in London that I first became utterly entranced by the works of Lord Byron, and devoured every volume of his poetry I could badger my beleaguered father into buying for me. I was only seven years old, and of a malleable and impressionable character; precocious in reading, yet innocent of almost all else in life.

My father invested in a great variety of businesses over the years we spent in London. But his interests frequently foundered, sometimes because of poor judgment, sometimes because of ill luck. Nevertheless, in 1820, Mr. Allan decided that he might now be interested in putting some money into the publishing industry, and he befriended a certain Mr. Murray, Lord Byron's publisher.

I was awed to accompany my father to a dinner at Mr. Murray's residence in Mayfair; more impressed yet that such luminaries as Lady Byron, Tom Moore, and Augusta Leigh were present, though the great poet I so much admired was somewhere in Italy, or Greece, or some such romantic place—as I longed to be myself. London is a dreary town, even more so than Baltimore.

The dinner itself was astonishing—for I sat open-mouthed, not eating a thing, as everyone chattered on about "George this, George that," and to hear this divinity referred as simply "George" simply boggled the mind. There was much talk, too, of the Shelleys, and of *Frankenstein,* which I had only just read; much ominous rumbling about things "man was not meant to know," and the like; and then the conversation turned to "George's" memoirs, which Tom Moore had been entrusted with, and which he was about to turn over to John Murray for publication.

After dinner came the coffee in the smoking room— and, in a daringly modern twist, a couple of the ladies actually braved the men's holy of holies, and puffed away on the communal hookah, as well as becoming inebriated on port! As a child, I was perhaps the only sober person left in that smoking room after an hour or two. My father had passed out on the divan, after agreeing to a small investment of three hundred pounds. The talk was no longer about Byron, so I contented myself by looking at the books that lined the shelves—many a quaint and curious volume of forgotten lore, indeed! For Mr. Murray had many occult tomes, and grimoires, and odd little chapbooks, and there was much to occupy my mind.

At length I became aware that there was an argument going on.

"Absolutely not, Mr. Murray!" Lady Byron was shouting. "This book will drag us all through the mud. Imagine if the truth were known about George's little fling with his half-sister?"

"That's not the point at all," said the half-sister herself. "It's these nasty little escapades with Cambridge choirboys that worry me. Well, everyone knows such things go on, of course, but heavens, he actually talks about sticking, well, his *cocker,* into a—"

"Oh!" Lady Byron squealed.

Mr. Moore said, "Well, can't you just lock it up somewhere? Posterity and all that, what. I mean, parts of it are ravishingly written—"

"I suppose you're referring to the section where he compares the relative sizes of my and Mrs. Shelley's quims?" said Augusta Leigh, causing everyone who was not dead drunk to gape at such language from a lady's lips.

"Not only that," said Lady Byron, "but some of it's sheer rubbish—for example, the scene where the little Negro slave brings back some dirty little boy from the grave—"

I pricked up my ears at this. Though they all seemed dismissive, that little nugget seemed to me so delicious, so frighteningly piquant, that I longed to hear more, as schoolboys do who terrify each other with ghost stories long into the night.

They didn't speak of it more, but they did become steadily more intoxicated, and at length Mr. Murray said, "Why then, if you ladies absolutely insist, I shall do it! Here I go! Thousands of pounds go up in smoke, for the chimney sweep to enjoy!"

I crept up on the fireplace and peered out from be-

hind the sofa—they had quite forgotten my existence—
and saw Mr. Brown pull out, from a velvet ottoman, an
enormous pile of papers, scribbled in a large, self-
important hand. I saw the title page and almost cried out
in amazement, for it was the memoirs of Lord Byron,
written whilst on the continent and entrusted to his
friend Mr. Moore for safekeeping.

"This is most imprudent," said Mr. Murray. "I should
really lock this thing up, and wait until all of you are
quite, quite dead—*then* make my fortune!"

He threw a sheaf of the papers into the fire.

"Fortune!" said Lady Byron. "Haven't you made
enough money from that Mary Wollstonecraft's vulgar
little gothic?"

"Nay, before you change your mind—" said Augusta
Leigh, and seized another handful of the papers, and
tossed that too.

Soon all of them were burning the priceless manuscript, laughing as they did so.

Presently, a cuckoo clock sang out the hour.

"Heavens!" said Mr. Murray. "We have dawdled too
long—we must join the ladies."

At which the two ladies who had elected to smoke
with the men collapsed in gales of laughter. Everyone
trooped out, except my father, dead to the world, and
myself, a child, ignored and invisible.

I wasted no time. I ran to that fireplace and pulled out
what papers I could—a tiny remnant of the burning mass.
I lifted a corner of the Persian carpet and beat the pages
repeatedly to put out the flames, then stuffed them into
my sailor suit.

Aloysius—may I be so bold as to call you that?—those
pages were to plant within my psyche the seeds of my interest in the undead. I cared not a fig about Lord Byron's
incestuous amours, or his flirtations with sodomy; but

the pages I managed to rescue from the flames contained another story, one that is, I believe, not entirely irrelevant to your own preoccupations.

I send them to you herewith. Do keep them for a while. To be honest, my home feels haunted by their presence . . . what with Virginia coughing up blood in the bedchamber next to the study where I have been penning these most morbid verses.

Perhaps these papers will add some details to the material you yourself have been collecting on the *zombi* of the Caribbean African.

I remain, my newfound friend and fellow student of the occult,

Your obedient servant,

Edgar Allan Poe

3

I was so absorbed in this series of epistles that I did not notice the passing of time. But when I next looked up, I saw that my companions were looking anxiously at me; so I passed what I had read so far to Mr. Whitman.

There followed another note from my late husband—a single paragraph, which said: "My dear, if you would care to look through those selfsame pages from Lord Byron's hand, you will, I think, acquire a perfect understanding of how all this touches our lives . . . and then I will be able to explain to you why it is, my dearest, that everything you have suspected about our maid Phoebe has been but a sham, and why I must do the things I must now do: why I must die now."

With the greatest sense of dread imaginable, I undid the bundle of burnt papers and began to read.

23

WHEREIN JOSEPH DISCOVERS HIS TRUE CALLING

1

Thyrza . . . Thyrza . . . Thyrza (this manuscript began, and thereafter were numerous lacunae, and parts that seemed sketchily composed, as if they were intended to be filled out later . . . and then of course there were the sections entirely missing because the page was charred through) . . . Thyrza, Thyrza. Thyrza . . . in a perfect world, O Thyrza, I would not have had to disguise your

Thyrza and

*   *   *

John Edleston, a chorister here at Trinity, sixteen, voice as yet unbroken though; yet assuredly no gelding, since I

and then there was the American. His father was English, but had become a citizen of Georgia during the American revolution; I think it was a purely financial decision, for he was able to save a fair penny on taxes that way. He was perhaps seventeen years old when he came up to Trinity; saw him supping at the High Table, and the most curious thing was, he had a Negro servant with him, in a charming blue satin suit, with a quaintly antiquated wig. An ostentatiously wealthy fellow, this Griffin Bledsoe; and seeing that I was some four thousand pounds in debt that Michaelmas, I resolved to make his acquaintance. At the very least I was sure I could get him to buy me a few rounds of ale; colonials are easily awed by an honest-to-goodness lord, especially when one tells them that they really don't have to refer to one as one's lordship—"Byron" will generally suffice—or even Gordon, at a pinch.

Not this Bledsoe chap, though. He was, if anything, lordlier than the genuine article. Nevertheless, after I accosted him outside the hall, and suggested he come to my rooms for a glass of port, he seemed pleased enough; and he brought his servant with him. He was a little ill at ease. He needed a friend, and I was only too happy to become that friend—at least for a period sufficient to divest him of a few hundred pound. I needed a new suit; I had worn the same clothes for almost two months. My spirits rose when he knocked at my door and I saw that his servant was carrying an entire cask of port, purchased, doubtless, from that little establishment next to St. Edmund's.

Perhaps Bledsoe had heard rumors of the debauchery that went on in my rooms—this was in reality something of a myth which I had carefully nurtured by allowing myself to be discovered, apparently asleep, by the bedder, on occasional mornings, in what appeared to be compromising positions with a bear, a choirboy, a skeleton from the medical faculty, a sheep, and the like; these were, I hasten to add, mere trickeries I used to enhance my legendary status, and to conceal the actual debaucheries that went on, about which people knew nothing.

The bedder in our wing of the quad rarely entered my rooms at all anymore, to be honest; I had frightened her once or twice too often. Because of this, my apartments at Trinity College were perhaps the untidiest in all of Cambridge.

In any case, Thyrza had been staying in my rooms for the week, so it seemed a golden opportunity to show this provincial youth, and his overdressed slave, a taste of decadence.

I had Thyrza fling open the door in full regalia—lace dressing gown, little beauty spot daubed onto the left cheek, lips painted crimson as any whore's—and shriek out a greeting in tones of seduction that left little to the imagination. "Oh, George, it's that *delightful* American and his petit-nègre! Oh, how utterly charming."

"Welcome, Bledsoe," I said, indicating the divan with a languid wave, "and I should very much like you to meet my paramour, Thyrza."

"Enchanted, madam," said Bledsoe, and proceeded to kiss Thyrza's hand.

"Enter, my dears! Oh, good heavens, I do so adore a little black boy," Thyrza squealed, really enjoying our little game.

That little black boy immediately burst out laughing. "Why, Marse Griffin," he said, "that a boy inside of that dress."

Thyrza frowned. "I had thought I was a little more convincing than that," he said in his eerily ageless voice.

The boy said, "Oh, you convincing all right, sah; you has that gift; I think you a disciple of Mawu-Lissa, the sacred manwoman she done made the universe."

Well! If I had set out to intrigue and mystify, the tables had certainly turned. This was a fascinating couple, and I soon learnt a great deal more about them, in between heavy bouts of port and opium. In fact, Thyrza, who had entered the bedroom and presently reappeared as John, was decidedly listless at no longer being the center of attention.

The Negro had a very interesting way of talking—not exactly the "nigger talk" much overused in those jungle romances you can buy for a penny, but—despite the barbarities of his gram-matical constructions—a speech with rules of its own, and plenty of learned, Latinate words, not to mention a smattering of French. Nor did he behave much like a slave, but participated quite freely in our conversation.

Griffin Bledsoe was an ugly fellow, but he had a history worth some attention. His father had sent him to Cambridge in order to tame his wildness, and to let him imbibe a little of Eu-ropean culture. If half of what he told me was the truth, he had had an exotic childhood indeed—sugar plantations on Santo Domingo, cotton fields in Georgia—and his father was a verita-ble king, with slaves, ships, and endless money at his disposal. I was beginning to think my latest accrual of debts might at last have found some possibility of relief.

It transpired that Bledsoe and I shared the same classics tutor, and would therefore be seeing each other fairly frequently, even though I made a habit to appear before the various directors of study as rarely as possible, for to do so belied my reputation for dissolution, dissipation, and romantic melancholy.

"Why, to tell you the truth, Lord Byron," he said—

"Oh, call me George," said I. Noblesse oblige and all that. He didn't seem that flattered, though. Well, people are a lot less formal in the provinces, so he might not have realized quite what a privilege I was bestowing him.

"As I was saying," he went on, "the real reason I've been ex-iled here for a time is that my father caught me, well, a-fiddling with the merchandise once too often."

"Ah, the dusky maidens," I said.

"Well, there was an unhealthy competition between the two of us, and now he can have them all to himself."

It seemed that—far from viewing his sojourn in England as

a pilgrimage to Parnassus, wherein he could commune firsthand with the mother of his culture—he actually saw his time in Cambridge as a hideous, grey imprisonment, far from the luxury and lascivious excesses of his life at home. I had thought to impress him with my tales, but I found myself instead being drawn to his own; encounters with slave women in mango orchards, the fires of Port-au-Prince in the throes of a black revolt, the frenzied ceremonies of the *houngan* and *mambo,* and yet more fascinating still, the voodoo ritual of the raising of the dead.

It was Joseph, the black servant, who gave us the most lurid details about this practice.

"You see, you Lordship," he told us, "when the elders of a village, or the chief *houngan,* decide that a man is too evil to live in this world, or a woman need to be punished for adultery, they decide this person will become a *zombi.* The man which perform this ceremony called a *houngan macoute*—a magician of darkness. So this *houngan macoute,* he assemble all the ingredients to make a thing he call *coup poudre,* a *zombi* powder. When this powder all mixed up, he place the powder on the threshold of the victim, or he blow it in he eyes, or into a cut in he skin; and in a day or two, that man he fall into a kind of death, and they bury him in the ground. But on the third day, they pull him back out of that ground, and they feed him the juice of a plant he call *concombre zombi,* and the man become the living dead."

You can imagine how my skin crawled to hear such talk—oh, deliciously so!—and as for John, he was so frightened, he curled up into a ball on the divan. Vampires, ghosts, and demon lovers were as naught compared to this black boy's matter-of-fact descriptions of grave robbing and reanimation! Since that time, many have thrilled to the melodrama of Mary Wollstonecraft's silly little book, but I assure you, no frisson evoked by that tome could equal the sincerity and honest believability of this slave's story! And to think that the woman never even acknowledged hearing me speak of it!

But there was one aspect of all this that made me curious above all. Was all this merely supernatural magic, or was there some scientific basis to it all? Powders and potions argued for alchemy . . . yet the secret of life and death itself . . . was there not something metaphysical about that?

"And what," I asked him, "if you had no access to such ingredients. Could a spell still work?"

"Me surely not know that, you Lordship," said he, "but mayhap, a truly powerful *houngan*—"

"I see. Deeper and darker secrets yet."

"To gain knowledge," said the boy, "allus must pay price."

"How positively Faustian!" I said. "We must drink to that!"

We had more port all round, and then

punting down to Granchester for strawberries before we

d found a little swimming hole by a shaded copse, wherein we disported ourselves in much the manner of the ancient Greeks, utterly unashamed of our bodily imperfections, for as Donne said,

> Full nakednesse! All joyes are due to thee

and indeed much laughter, and much comparison of our *phalloi* in their various stages of development, whereupon Griffin made some remark about the stallionlike quality of certain Ne

and died. O, ye immortal principles, ye gods above, and died! so that I

> Thyrza!

in the college chapel, the gothic stone itself oozing a kind of tears, but yes, John could sing tears out of a stone, there was one evening a Palestrina motet which

> that tone, that taught me to rejoice,
> when prone, unlike thee, to ~~repose~~ repine,
> the ~~tune~~ song, celestial from thy voice
> but sweet to me from none but thine

Granchester again; Bledsoe and the slave; Hobhouse gone down for the weekend; of course, no John. John had been buried a week past. Green meadows, a comely waitress to pour tea, daisies and prettily rippling water, the punt tethered to a weeping willow. And, of course, the strawberries.

"Joseph," I said, "can you not do that voodoo thing . . . that *zombi* thing as you call it . . . and bring him back?"

"Lord Byron," Bledsoe said, "you really place too much stock in the superstitious chatterings of a slave. Remind me to give him a thorough hiding tonight."

Joseph popped another strawberry in his mouth. He did not seem the slightest bit chastened by his master's threats. His lips were quite, quite red; sensuous, perhaps, were it not for the pug nose. I confess that John's death had quite unmanned me. I looked for succor in every scruple of hope, no matter how forlorn. Jove! But we were young. John Edleston, I realize now, was merely a pretty, slightly grimy member of the lower classes, with an angelic voice and a few other acrobatic skills which I need not enumerate here, though they will doubtless be familiar to all my fellow Old Harrovians . . . it was not love. Love would not come until my reencounter with my half-sister, Gus . . . but that awaits in another chapter of these secret memoirs.

"You know, Griffin," I said, "it is not idle superstition. You know. You've seen things, man! What you've described to me, I know cannot come merely from imagination. Why, even I could not have—and I am a poet, with a direct spiritual link to all nine muses!"

Bledsoe said, "It's all very well to believe that such things are possible. But that Jozéf here might possess such powers—" He sniggered. "His mother was a sorceress of sorts. But the French cut her in twenty pieces, and she never came back from the dead."

As he said this, he would not look me directly in the eye. I knew he was hiding something. I had, I confess, been analyzing the various tales he had told me, trying to find some inconsistency, some flaw. Then it came to me.

"Sacrifice," I said. "That's it! Everything has its price, does it not?"

"What do you mean?"

"You told me, Griffin, that the reason Joseph was unable to perform magic the way his mother and sister could was that he hadn't yet given anything up . . . a limb, an eye . . . in Améli's case, her innocence. Well, the answer's simple then. I want John Edleston brought back from the dead; Joseph shall bring him to me; he'll give up what needs to be given up."

"I can hardly compel him to rip off a limb, Lord Byron—"

"Whyever not? Is he not a slave? Is he not your property—life, limb, body, soul?"

"Actually," said Bledsoe, "his papers are in my father's name, not mine. And, well, whipping them is one thing, but hacking off an arm, why, would you cut a leg off this table? We wouldn't be enjoying these strawberries on a three-legged table, would we?"

I knew I was making Bledsoe very uncomfortable. I had heard his tale of the slaves being thrown overboard to collect insurance monies; I really didn't think he would balk at cutting off an arm, in principle at least; but he and the slave were more like brothers than master and servant. Still, the loss of Thyrza blinded me utterly to the constraint of reason. I was not yet twenty, and

my littlest whim had been indulged all through my childhood—
for I would exaggerate my limp when I did not get my own way,
which was usually enough to sway most people. I did not learn
selflessness until I was at least twenty-three. I wanted that chorister back! I wanted him to sing again . . . to sing for me alone
perhaps this time . . . to sing and much else besides.

"He will have to do it of his own free will, then," I said.

Joseph spoke up. "Marse Griffin, and you Lordship," said he,
"ain't nothing in the world that can make me give up what I
needs to give up, to learn the secret of life and death; ain't no gift
in the world that sweet enough to make me taste that kind of
sorrow."

I beckoned Griffin to follow me. We strolled over to the
shade of another willow.

"Your friend is dead, George," Griffin said, addressing me familiarly now that we were out of earshot. "I think you should
leave well enough alone."

Limping furiously as I strode hither and thither, I said, "For
God's sake, man—promise him gold! Promise him women!
Promise him his freedom, only make him bring back John Edle-
ston from the dead!"

"His freedom?" said Bledsoe. "But it's not mine to bestow."

"Perhaps not—but *promise* it!—or I'll—I'll write your father
and tell him you've been caught buggering the bedder's
boy—"

"But that's nonsense," said Bledsoe.

"He'll believe me. I am a poet. More to the point, I am a
lord, and from what you've told me of your father, he will have
nothing to do with the egalitarian heresies of his adopted
country."

without a stone to mark the spot,

and freedom was the bribe that

Hail to thee, Eleuthera!

the chapel choir school had not expended much on poor John's burial; this was not like King's or John's, with their ancient, royally charted choir schools, and Evensong attended daily by royalty and bishops and suchlike; indeed, the provost and fellows were often disposed to eliminate this choir school altogether, since it really added nothing to the reputation of the college . . . ergo, a pauper's burial, four miles outside Cambridge.

And perfectly easy to invade that churchyard, by dead of night, for it was a mile's walk from the village, and the vicar was eighty years old, and deaf, and purblind too, I think, though he celebrated communion well enough.

Myself, the American, and the slave, a pair of shovels, and a bag of magical accoutrements; it was easy enough for us to climb the wall and find ourselves amongst the dead. But now that the hour was approaching, and the reality of the blasphemous act we were about to commit was beginning to dawn on me, I admit that I was afraid, though I did my best to conceal it; I do not think the others suspected it. I did not truly believe anything would come of the ritual anyway. What student worth his salt has not crept into college chapel to perform a black mass, or attempted to conjure up the devil for some Faustian bargain? It was just another game, I told myself, and a thrilling, chilling *divertissement* to while away the joyless hours of carnal deprivation.

There was no moon. The only light was from three lanterns, which we hung up on an oak tree above the grave. In my poem, I said there was no stone to mark the spot, and there is a certain license I have taken, for there was a marker, though it were but wood, and it read:

John Edleston, a chorister, aged XVI.

The slave did most of the digging—my lameness saved me much of the manual labor of it—and I was able to stalk about the graveyard, giving full vent to my inner torment, letting the terror of the moment seize me and have its way with me. For as Joseph dug, he sang some African ditty to himself in a cracking, adolescent voice, and the tune twisted and turned in the night air like a tortured nightingale.

Joseph dug swiftly—had he not been promised his freedom?—and the grave was shallow, and the coffin unfinished pine. We soon had that box hauled up out of the ground, and with a crowbar had the lid pried off. And there, in the dim light, was the boy whom I called Thyrza.

Seeing him dead changed everything. I had been trying to leaven my fear with levity, but now my mind was filled with the images of all we had done together—of furtive glances in the college chapel, of assignations in the night, of secret kisses stolen behind the chaplain's back—oh, and that voice! Angels could not have sounded more sublime. In death he was pathetic. Nothing had been done by the way of the embalmer's art, of course—after all, who was there to want to look upon this corpse, who save one love-besotted lord who had never dared give public utterance to his fondness, nor his grief? Oh, I worked myself up into an ecstasy of grief. And meanwhile, the black boy was bestrewing the corpse with strange-smelling herbs, and crying imprecations to his Ethiop gods, and rending the air with animal howls; then, taking a small tambourine from his bag of magician's tricks, he gave it to Bledsoe, saying "Slowly at first, then faster; you shall feel the pace of it, Marse Griffin, and the *loa* he soon be descending upon you and ride you as a man ride a horse."

Bledsoe, unused to it at first, tried a few tentative drum taps; then, growing confident, remembering some witnessed ceremony from Haiti no doubt, beat out a slow, firm rhythm, and Joseph called out in a mighty voice to the great *koulèv* whose tail encircles the welkin, by these savages' mythology:

> *Koulèv, koulèv O!*
> *Damballah Wedo!*

and now he

and with a ghastly shriek

"You promise me freedom, yes or no, Marse Griffin, don't you be lying to me now and

swear it and

for you see, *monchè, ché mèt mwen,* Joseph he must go down into the dark country, and Joseph he must leave something of hisself behind, them are the rules of it

lifted the corpse up in his arms and embraced it in a horrific parody of the act of love and then

and bury me," he said, shutting the lid down upon himself and the dead boy. And abruptly Bledsoe ceased his pounding, and we stood in silence there, gazing at the pine box which now held two boys, black and white, alive and dead.

"No more shamming lameness now!" Bledsoe shouted at last. "Help me to bury them!"

So he had known all along that I

shoveled. Shoveled. Shoveled. And each spadeful of dirt heavier than the last, and still we shoveled, and Bledsoe was weeping the while, and I knew that for all his pretense at indifference he loved that slave; that being was his most precious possession, and because I could see the truth in that love, and how much Bledsoe had given up in order to make him this promise of freedom, I shoveled the harder, not desiring to face the falsity of my own feelings, not wanting him to know how I hated myself for a hypocrite and a whorer of words.

And the last shovelful seemed to weigh as much as the whole world.

But presently it was done. We patted the earth down. No one would be the wiser, for the grave had been freshly dug in any case. We sat there all night long, waiting, I suppose, for the two of them to come bursting forth . . . at length I said, "Man, let us dig your servant out at least—"

But Bledsoe would not; and the grief he felt was for a friend forever lost.

2

At dawn, we walked back to Cambridge, in time to have breakfast in the hall—kippers, sausages, and porridge. Then, after stowing the shovels safely in the gardener's shed, from which we had stolen them the night before, we crossed the great quadrangle and went up the narrow flights of stairs to my rooms.

Joseph was standing in the center of the living room.

The grave clung to his clothes. His hair had gone white. There was dust on his face, his hands; through the holes in his garments, more dust; dust in his hair, dust trailing from his lips; dust, dust, dust.

One of his eyes was gone, ripped out; and from its socket oozed a blend of blood and gall and dust.

"I done come home, Marse Griffin," he said softly.

"Jozéf!" cried Bledsoe. "Are you cold? Do you need a posset? A cup of chocolate?"

"Nothing at all," he said. "It good to see you again, Marse Griffin . . . *frè mwen-an*. It only been a hour or two for you, but for me it were a long long time. I crossed a mighty river and a dark forest. I done spoke to the king of the other world, the one who do not hang, *oba kòso*, Shangó. I lived many lifetimes in that dark place, *monchè*, and I found the lost soul that he lordship was a-looking for. And allus was freedom on my lips."

"You've done well, *monchè*," said Bledsoe.

"I done come home, Marse Griffin," he said, "and I done brung Marse John Edleston back from the country of the dead."

"What?" I cried. "Where?"

"He waiting for you in the bedroom," said the servant. "But first, you got to understand a few things. Me been to a far far place. He done paid a heavy price for the knowledge he bring back. Listen to Joseph words now. When a body come back from the other side, there always a few conditions."

"Yes," I said. "Of course." Strange how all the world's mythologies converge; it proves that man's soul springs from the same place, I suppose. Orpheus was not allowed to gaze on Eurydice . . . I met an Indian once, who told me that they have the same story in India, only it is Eurydice who braves the underworld to bring back Orpheus . . . in India they call her Savitri. A few euphonic changes and they are almost the same name. If I digress, dear reader, it is only my trepidation at what I must next relate. "Tell me, Joseph. But if I may not look on my beloved Thyrza, then I do not know why you should have harrowed hell."

"Give me my freedom," Joseph said to Bledsoe.

But Bledsoe would not look him in the eye, and merely mumbled, "You know, Jozéf, it isn't mine to give you . . . but I will write Father for your papers . . . I'm sure he will permit your emancipation, once he learns what a service you've performed . . . and for an English lord at that. . . ."

"My freedom," said Joseph. Quietly, and without a hint of

menace, his empty eye socket a gaping wound that continually reproached us both, until Bledsoe, unable to look on it any longer, ripped the kerchief from his neck and wrapped it around the boy's head in a makeshift patch.

Was his freedom the only condition? I thought to myself, Well then, I've managed to escape; for that condition is up to Bledsoe, not to me.

Then Joseph seized my wrist, and his grip was hard and cold as steel; he looked me in the eye with his good eye, and in that I methought I could see the sulphurous flames of some infernal place . . . a place, I was as sure then as I am now, to which I am destined one day to travel.

"My Lord," he said, "this is the condition. The king of death, he gave me no conditions. This condition come from Marse John himself. He would not let me take him by the hand and lead him out of the ground, lessen you understands this: henceforth, my Lord, you shall live in truth with him."

"That is an easy condition to satisfy," said I, "for I am, when needs be, an entirely truthful person; a poet must be thus, I think."

"See that it so," said Joseph. "See that it so."

And thus it was that I entered my bedchamber, and found my precious chorister awaiting me, and woke him with a kiss, and spent such a night as I never spent when he was still alive.

3

Time passed; an idyllic time, to tell the truth. May Week was approaching—I did not bother to sit the tripos that year, for to tell the truth I had been to no lectures, and would probably have failed all the exams. I was planning to use my sickliness to obtain the designation of *aegrotat*, so that I could be deemed to have passed the examinations without having to sit them, because of an illness. It had occasionally worked at Harrow, even before I obtained my barony.

I had not, of course, told John, but I was frankly finding his anatomy a bit noisome; perhaps my obsession with cockers had been but a phase of sorts, for I was becoming much excited by cunnies instead, especially that of Irène Pérrier, the college chaplain's French maid.

Bledsoe did well in *his* exams. Got a II:i, he did—what a swot—although he also seemed to have plenty of time to get drunk of an evening.

But eventually it came time for reckoning . . . time to pay the piper, as it were . . . time to make a serious sacrifice in the chess game that is life. And it happened, not surprisingly, on another punting expedition, though we hadn't got nearly as far as Granchester when all hell broke loose. Well. Joseph was doing the actual punting, and the backs were lovely this time of year, the meadows a lush green to our left, the colleges to our right a dreamy, hazy concatenation of spires. Joseph stood there, working the pole with a steady motion, staring ahead, and the river was smooth and babbled prettily, and birds warbled in the trees . . . all in all, one of those days when one doesn't contemplate suicide quite as frequently as usual . . . not a good day for your brooding, Byronic individual . . . Byronic is a word now, isn't it? And all over Europe young men are cultivating my manner of hair, my wild-eyed striding about, even my limp . . . but this day, I was yet to be a household name . . . I was Byronic, I suppose, without even knowing it. And John Edleston, unknowingly, was exacerbating my Byronic malaise by badgering me for some proof of affection. "Why, George," he was saying, "don't you love me anymore?" and such tiresome things. I did not answer. I was, in fact, trying to consider how I would tell John I really didn't want to take him on my grand tour of Europe. But how could I tell him that, when—having conjured him back from the dead—I was in a sense responsible for his very existence? And so I brooded.

Joseph then took it upon himself to be petulant, and he began to demand of his master whether the freedom papers had arrived yet from Georgia.

"Griffin," he said, "I *know* you done heard from your daddy by now."

"I do have a letter from my father," Bledsoe said at last.

Joseph pulled the punt to the river bank. He leapt ashore, and sat there, with his arms folded, beneath one of the many willow trees. Bledsoe pulled out the rumpled letter from his pocket. "I didn't know how I was going to tell you this," he said.

And then he read:

Son,

I have told you time and time again that a slave is chattel. He is an extension of yourself, just as much as a pocket watch, a musket, or an article of clothing. When you put a slave to extraordinary use or service, it is because he is an exceptionally useful or serviceable slave. If your watch did you a great service—stay, stopped a bullet from entering your flesh—would you liberate it? If you did, what purpose would it serve? It is a watch, and must tell time; Jozéf is a slave, and must obey; you cannot just throw away all he is worth. Remember all you went through to keep him! Remember how he would have been sold long since, and the thirty-nine stripes you bore to make him yours!

And that, finally, is the crux of the matter—I was prudent in keeping this valuable property in my own name—for I knew that, having your own way, and believing in some sentimental fashion that this creature is somehow your friend, you might well be foolish enough to grant him emancipation, and thus wantonly discard several hundred dollars of your own net worth.

I pray you, son, do not countenance such a folly again,

for your education and upbringing is an expensive busi-
ness, and we must above all be frugal.
    Your Loving Father,
                Sir Andrew Bledsoe

Listening to the tone of this letter, I began to realize that innocent of financial matters though young Griffin might be, his
father was not, and I should not seriously consider using the lad
as a way to settle my larger debts (though I *had* managed to pry
five or ten sovereigns from him now and then).

But Joseph's countenance was darkening. "You done
promise me," he said.

"I did my best, *monchè*, but my father—"

"You no call me *monchè* no more."

Well, in the midst of all this, my Thyrza, too, decided to become bothersome. "George, George," he was crying, "you must
tell me that you love me."

The scene was almost farcical—a witch doctor demanding
his freedom, a *zombi* screaming to be loved. What an incredible
spectacle to be taking place in this verdant, yet dull, East Anglian
countryside! I could not decide whether to laugh out loud and
break the spell, or sit back and enjoy the spectrum of human
emotions that played out before me—Joseph like a juvenile Spar-
tacus, railing against the world's injustices, my living dead lover
playing for attention when, frankly, my eye had begun to rove
even before his death, were I but honest with myself; and the
troubled Griffin Bledsoe—torn by conflicting loyalties to caste
and comradeship—oh, what a fine Shakespearean comedy we
would have made, were we only allowed to show a bit more carnal intercourse on stage—for John made such a perfect winsome
wench.

So, Thyrza badgered me, and Joseph his master, and I sat
back against the stern of the punt, detached, seeing the irony in
it; until, with one little word, comedy metamorphosed into
tragedy, for John asked me one time too many whether I still

love him, and I said, "Yes," more to quiet him than anything else.

Then everything changed.

A hush fell over that little gathering. John Edleston looked at me. "Good-bye, my dear Lord," he said. A tiny crack appeared in his left cheek, and out crawled a tiny, white worm. He held out his arms to embrace me, and his skin was yellowing, and now more worms were eating their way out of his flesh.

"What I done tell you?" cried Joseph. "He come back from the dark country only iffen you swear to live in truth with him."

"No, John," I said, trying with desperation to correct my error. "No, John, I never loved you; please, understand, you were very entertaining, and you sang so sweetly, and you reminded me a little of Harrow, I suppose, and it was only selfishness that made me insist on bringing you back from the dead—oh, what a mess I've caused—" and much else besides, admitting to this putrefying boy more of my self-loathing than I had ever dared say to anyone before. But I knew it was too late. I knew that this moment was the real reason Thyrza had come back. He had always seen my emotional dishonesty. It was I who needed to learn about what truth really is.

I, the self-styled poet, had mistaken my prosodic facility for some profound metaphysical awareness of the human condition. . . .

"Come back," I said. "I could learn to love; the carnality of it is nothing; I could discover who you really were, nay, are, within that wormy flesh—"

"Farewell," said John Edleston, and he kissed me.

Gods of High Olympus! I shall never forget that dreadful kiss, the taste of maggots on the choirboy's tongue, the fingers cracking about my waist like twigs, the waxy coldness of those lips; for even as the kiss ended, so did John Edleston crumble into dust; the harder I held on, the tighter I tried to hug, the quicker the flesh was pulverized, and the gray dust poured from his sleeves, from his trousers, his collar, his fly; and finally there were only the clothes, the clothes he could not have afforded, the clothes that I went into debt for so that he could dress like a proper dandy and not be an embarrassment to me in public; the clothes lay on the polished wood of the punt, topped with a heap of dust.

I wept real tears.

Then Joseph said to Bledsoe, "Now, Marse Griffin, I must say farewell too."

"What do you mean?" said Bledsoe. "You ain't fixing to run away, surely! The police would bring you back to me."

Joseph said, "I is going away, Marse Griffin, acrosst the cold gray sea; because I has found my true calling. In the dark country, I done learned what kind of a thing I is, and now I know I have a destiny, and a purpose, and a path which I must walk."

Joseph got up from beneath the willow tree. He drew himself tall; taller than I thought possible for such a little fellow. He stood by the edge of the water. His good eye burned with a dazzling white light, purer than sunlight.

Bledsoe said, "What nonsense are you talking, nigger? How can you go across the sea? We're not even close to the sea. And how will you pay for passage? Don't you know that the only way you can ever take ship is chained up in the hold?"

"If I cannot go to the sea, Marse Griffin, then the sea he come to me."

The boy's master was overcome by one of those unthinking rages. He leapt from the punt and, in a fine passion, boxed his ears. I smelled burning flesh. Bledsoe screamed and recoiled. Smoke was pouring from his fists.

"You ever done been branded, Marse Griffin?" said the boy—ever more softly, so we had to strain to listen—"Now you know what it feel like."

Bledsoe plunged his hands into the chill Cam. Steam rose from its depths.

"Now listen to me," Joseph said again. "I been you friend sometime, and you brother, and you chattel. I only ever axed you for one thing in my whole life, and you wouldn't give it me. So I going my own way now. But one day I be back. When I be back, you gone see me riding freedom like she a mighty leopard. All you life long will be torment, till I come back, and when you see me you will know I come to set you free."

Joseph took off his powdered wig, and threw it on the water. The water began to churn. He took off his tailcoat, embroidered in gold thread, and cast it in the stream. Tore at his collar, rent his neckerchief, ripped away at the seams of his trousers, stepped out of his drawers, stood naked in the water like a young black Jesus waiting for John the baptist, waiting for the Paraclete to come fluttering above his head in the form of a pure white dove; and lastly he threw down the patch over his blind eye, and a light streamed forth from the eye socket, a light that outshone the very sun; and he stretched out his hands, and the Cam began to overflow its banks. Where was the water coming from? It rushed upon us both from downstream and from upstream, from the sky and from the land. The water was gray and bitter cold, though the day had been bright and warm, as though its source were the Styx itself, the river that divides the quick from the dead. There came a torrential rain. The punt became un-moored. The spires of King's and Trinity and Caius were plung-ing beneath cascades of dark water.

"Good-bye, dear masta," said Joseph softly, "for I done loved you well."

He kissed his master on the cheek, and turned his back from him, and began walking away across the waves. And Bledsoe clutched his cheek and screamed, for the kiss had burned like the flames of hell.

There was no sight of land. There was no sun. The sea and the sky were gray, all gray, and the wind howled, and the water tasted not like brine, but bitter, like gall, like wormwood.

Joseph walked and walked until we could see him no more. And slowly the vision faded, and we found ourselves once more on the banks of the Cam, in the merry month of May, sitting in the tall grass: two people and a pile of clothes, and punt smashed to smithereens, which doubtless someone would have to pay for.

These lines I wrote, then, are a lie:

> *Well hast though left in life's best bloom*
> > *The cup of woe for me to drain,*
> *If rest alone be in the tomb,*
> > *I would not wish thee here again—*
>
> *But if in worlds more blest than this*
> > *Thy virtues seek a fitter sphere,*
> *Impart some portion of thy bliss,*
> > *To wean me from mine anguish here.*

What falsehood! What pretension! I did not even know what love is, when I wrote about John's death. I had not experienced the glorious heights and ignominious depths of true passion. Gods! But I was callow. I can imagine Mr. Murray reading these words now, and finding it hard to believe that the great Lord Byron might herein evince a single iota of humility; well, Mr. Murray, here is the nugget you have yearned for; I trust you will enjoy it, for rarely comes such another.

The boy, it seems, loved me. That was the sadness of it; I had a little pleasure of him, and mistook that for a far sublimer sentiment. Oh, and he did sing well. Perhaps I should not have changed his sex in that poem of mine; it was cowardly, wasn't it? I didn't have the courage shown by Plato, Theocritus, or Callimachus, or Catullus . . . but those were other times, were they not? I do not say better, only other.

As for the American, and the young Negro mage—

I do not know what became of Bledsoe after May Week. I know he did not bother to collect his degree. I know he reported his servant missing to the Cambridge constabulary, thus allowing his father to realize a small insurance payment.

So that, at least, finished well for him, in a sense.

And the crumbling to dust of my friend? And the rising of the sea? And the bursting of the light from the Negro's sightless eye? Oh, I have had similar experiences since then, but only under the influence of some herb, drug, or mushroom; this remains my only bona fide encounter with the supernatural.

In the end, I was well rid of John, I suppose. Although I'm sorry I told Shelley's mistress the story; she blended it with science and turned a hefty profit, whereas I was unable even to pay off a few drinking debts.

And yet, a part of me remains submerged with poor John Edleston in that illusory gray sea. What part, you ask me, did the choirboy take with him to Hades? Was it my hubris? Perhaps so. But I suspect it might also have been a small piece of my

4

That was the end of the manuscript that purported to be in Lord Byron's hand. One small missive remained; it was, once more, in the hand of my late husband.

Trembling, knowing that now, at last, all the pieces of this arcane puzzle must soon fall into place, I went on reading.

24

AND THUS OUR WAR CAME TO AN END

1

My dearest Paula (the missive began),

You now understand what lies behind that dark obsession of mine. And by the time Phoebe gives you this package of letters and manuscripts, I will probably have been dead at least a year; and you will have been told that I was killed at the front, by some stray enemy bullet perhaps, or while reaching out to help drag some poor wounded soldier back to the encampment; at any rate, you have been told, I died a hero's death.

That could not be further from the truth.

I die, my dear, already damned, predestined for the flames, if what we were taught in Sunday school be true. I am a suicide.

I have already spoken of our first two children, and my desperate attempts to bring them back from the dead. Our third,

Nathaniel, I loved the most of all, though he lived only a few minutes. Oh, Paula, you lay there in a stupor of laudanum and grief; you did not know that I took the baby in my arms, and placed him in a box along with seven mystical herbs, and wrapped the box in a black cloth, and laid it down on a *vévé* I had drawn up on the rooftop of our brownstone; you did not know how I changed and drummed the livelong day, and halfway through the night, hoping for a miracle; you do not understand how, in the moments before dawn, I heard a tapping at the lid of that tiny coffin, and oh, how my heart leapt with hope and momentary joy; you did not see me break open that wooden box and hold that infant, watch him squeeze and unsqueeze his powerful little fist, laugh as he begun to gurgle out his first cry. You were not there in that momentous twilight.

Paula, my delight was but short-lived. The tiny thing seemed preternaturally intelligent; in minutes he was already pulling at my finger, demanding to crawl around on the concrete; and I watched him, prideful and content. That was when he found the dead mouse under the bottle tree. I imagine that Phoebe might have left it there as an offering. But what our beloved child did next was nothing less than obscene. Seizing the tiny corpse by its tail, he ripped it asunder, pulling its guts out, snapping its breastbone, plucking out its heart and squeezing the blood into his mouth; and then he turned to me, and his eyes were perfectly vacuous; if eyes are indeed mirrors of the soul, there was no soul to mirror.

Oh, my darling, I placed the child back in that box, I hammered that box shut, ignored the hammering fists and angry shrieks, sat there waiting for the sounds to weaken and die down to nothing.

That was years ago, before the war began.

There is another war, my dear, and that is a war that will never end; the war between the darkness and the light. Ours is the middle passage; our world is like the slaver ships of old, and we are chained up in the hold, all of us together, black and white, not knowing whence or whither our journey lies. We are all slaves, in the end, because we cannot see our own fate; poetry, and art, and religion too, are all illusion.

Do I, perhaps, sound bitter?

Let me tell you what I've learnt from all these tales, what I failed to exercise in those abortive attempts to bring back our own children. It is that I made no sacrifice. Joseph the bondsman understood that. He gave his eye to gain mastery over life and death; more, really, than his eye, but the eye is a symbol of what he sacrificed, like Odin, hanging on the tree of life, like Jesus, giving up his all on the very tree wherefrom Adam and Eve once plucked forbidden fruit.

Paula, by the time you receive this missive, you will know more than I ever knew. You *will* have the power to bring someone back from the other side. And I know there will be someone who *must* come back, to finish the task of setting mortals free. By the time you use this gift, I will be dead.

My death is a sacrifice.

I pay it happily, now, in advance, knowing that in so doing I am also expiating for all the grief I have brought you, not showing you the truth about myself, not loving you enough, perhaps, taking strange women to my bed. But do not hate Phoebe.

This is the last truth I need tell you, for I know you have believed that I took the Negress as my paramour, that I ceased desiring you, and that I am a heartless adulterer. Well, I did sin, but not with Phoebe. After our third child's death, I did consort with women of ill repute, and presently I suffered from the unsightly chancres of syphilis, and dared not approach you any more, or even try with Phoebe. Oh, Paula, I am ashamed.

But my death will end this shame, and end the war that rages in my breast, now and for ever. Amen.

Tearfully,

Your loving husband,

The Rev. Aloysius Grainger, M.A.

2

Indeed, there was a final page, but that contained a complete listing of the magical formulae of revivification, in the Yoruba, Haitian Creole, and English tongues. I will not repeat it here, lest wanton use be made of it, and the whole world be filled with the living dead.

That was the sum total of my husband's writing to me.

I sat dumbfounded for a time, while Mr. Whitman looked over the papers, nodding now and then; at the end his eyes were full of tears.

"Truly, Mrs. Grainger," he said, "our war must needs come to an end. Even for troubled Jimmy Lee Cox, it did."

"Did it?" I asked him.

"I'll tell you," said Zack, "the last story Jimmy Lee told me, as we said our good-byes, watching the ferry slowly glide to us over the river."

3

The road become wider (Jimmy Lee said) and we was coming into the vicinity of a town. I knew this was a port, maybe Charleston. There warn't no signs to tell us, but Pa and I had been booted out of Charleston once. I remembered the way the wind smelt, wet and tangy. A few miles outside town our road joined up with a wider road that come in a straight line from due north. On the other road, straggling down to meet us, we saw a company of graycoats.

They warn't exactly marching. Some was leaning on each other, some hobbling, and one, a slip of a boy, tapped on the side of a skinless drum. Their clothes was in tatters and most of them didn't have no rifles. They was just old men and boys, for the able-bodied had long since fallen.

They seen us and one of them cried out, "Nigger soldiers!"

They fell into a pathetic semblance of a formation, and them which had rifles aimed them and them which had crutches brandished them at us.

I shouted out, "Let us pass . . . we don't have no quarrel with you." For they were wretched creatures, these remnants of the Southern army, and I was sure that the war was already lost, and they was coming back to what was left of their homes.

But one boy, mayhap their leader, screamed at me, "Nigger lover! Traitor!" I looked in his eyes and saw we were just alike, poor trash fighting a rich man's war, him and me; and I pitied the deluded soul. Because I knew now that there warn't no justice in this war, and that neither side had foughten for God, but only for hisself.

"It's no use!" I shouted at the boy who was so like myself. "These darkies ain't even alive; they're shadows marching to the sea; they ain't got souls to kill."

And old Joseph said, "March on, my children."

And through it all, Amelia danced.

They commenced to fire on us.

This was the terriblest thing which I did witness on that journey. For the nigger soldiers marched and marched, and not a bullet could stop them. The miniés flew and the white boys shrieked out a ghostly echo of a rebel yell, and *les zombis* kept right on coming and coming, and me and old Joseph with them, untouched by the bullets, for his magic still shielded our mortal flesh. The niggers marched. Their faces was ripped asunder and still they marched. Their brains came oozing from their skulls, their guts came writhing from their bellies, and still they marched. They marched until they were too close for bullets. Then the white boys flung themselves at us, and they was ripped to pieces. They was tore limb from limb by dead men which stared with glazed and vacant eyes. It took but a few minutes, this final skirmish of the war. Their yells died in their throats. The *zombis* broke their necks and flung them to the ground. Their strength warn't a human kind of strength. They'd shove their hands into an old man's belly and snap his spine and pull out the intestines like a coil of rope. They'd take a rifle and break the barrel in two.

There was no anger in what the *zombis* done. And they didn't make no noise whilst they was killing. They done it the way you might darn a sock or feed the chickens; it were just something which had to be done.

And through it all, Amelia danced, blind and oblivious to that terrible carnage; for she did not inhabit our world; and sometimes Eleuthera danced with her, round and round, a blur of cat and woman.

And we marched onward, leaving the bodies to rot; it was getting on toward sunset now.

Oh, I was angry. The boys we kilt warn't no strangers from the North; they could have been my brothers. Oh, I screamed in rage at old Joseph; I didn't trust him no more; the happiness had left me.

"Did you hear what he called me?" I shouted. "A traitor to my people. A nigger lover. And it's God's plain truth. If you wanted freedom why didn't you go north into the arms of the yankees? You spoke to me of a big magic, and of the coils of the serpent *Koulèv*, and the wind of the gods, and the voices of darker angels . . . to what end? It were Satan's magic, magic to give the dead an illusion of life, so you could kill more of my people!"

"Be still," he said to me, as the church spires of the port town rose up in the distance. "Your war don't be my war. You think the yankees got theyselfs kilt to set old Joseph free? You think the 'mancipation proclamation was wrote to give the nigger back he soul? I say to you, white child, that a piece of paper don't make men free. The black man in this land he ain't gone be free tomorrow nor in a hundred years nor in a thousand. I didn't bring men back from the outer darkness so they could shine you shoes and wipe you butts. The army I lead, he kingdom don't be of this earth."

"You are mad, old Joseph," I said, and I wept, for he was no longer a father to me.

5

We marched into the town. Children peered from behind empty beer kegs with solemn eyes. Horses reared up and whinnied. Women stared sullenly at us. The yankees had already took the town, and half the houses was smoldering, and we didn't see no grown men. The stars and stripes flew over the ruint courthouse. I reckon folks thought we was just another company of the conquering army.

We reached the harbor. There was one or two sailing ships docked there; rickety ships with tattered sails. The army of dead men stood at attention and old Joseph said to me: "Now I understands why you come with me so far. There a higher purpose to everything, *ni ayé àti ni òrun.*"

I didn't want to stay with him anymore. When I seen the way *les zombis* plowed down my countrymen, I had been moved to a powerful rage, and the rage would not die away. "What higher purpose?" I said. And the salt wind chafed my lips.

"You think, *monchè*," said old Joseph, "that old Joseph done tricked you, he done magicked you with mirrors and smoke; but I never told you we was fighting on the same side. But we come far together, and I wants you to do me one last favor afore we parts for all eternity."

"And what sort of favor would that be, old sorcerer? I thought you could do anything."

"Anything. But not this thing. You see, old Joseph a nigger. Nigger he can't go into no portside bar to offer gold for to buy him a ship."

"You want a ship now? Where are you fixing to go? Back to Santo Domingo, where the white man rules no more? Back to reclaim that freedom that were cheated from you so long ago?"

Old Joseph said, "Mayhap it a kind of Haiti where we go."
He laughed. "Haiti, yes, Haiti! And I gone see my dear *maman*,
though she be cold in her grave sixty year past. Or mayhap it
mother Africa herself we go to. *Oba kòso!*"

And I remembered that he had told me: "My kingdom is not
of this earth." He had used the words of our savior and our
Lord. Oh, the ocean wind were warm, and it howled, and the
torn sails clattered against the masts. The air fair dripped with
moisture. And the niggers stood like statues, all-unseeing. And
before us stood the leopard, and on the leopard's back sat the
blind, mad girl.

"I'll do as you ask," I said, and I took the sack of gold we had
gathered from the poisoned well, and I walked along the harbor
until I found a bar and ship's captain for hire, which was not
hard, for the embargo had starved their business. I took the girl
with me—for she were white enough to pass, especially in a town
like Charleston—and a handsome dude took a fancy to her, and
told her his wife and all his kids had died at the yankees' hands,
and asked her if she would go with him.

Amelia sang:

> *If a flower is for plucking*
> *then a lady is for fucking.*

and she made them all laugh, for the war had lost them all their
sense of what was proper.

"Amelia," I said, "don't talk to these men, come home now."

But suddenly she stopped her dancing, and she ceased her
crazy gestures and weird songs, and she said, so softly that only
I could hear it: "Poor dear Jimmy Lee, I am not, you know,
truly mad; it is the world that is mad; I have found sanity in the
illusion of delusion . . . so, Jimmy Lee, let me be." And she re-
sumed her dance, and presently a piano struck up, and she was
waltzing with that dandy, with her head held high, queen of the
ball, as though the war had ne'er begun, and she had never been

a octoroon. And sure the war was over for her, for it had made her white.

So presently I come back and told old Joseph everything was ready. And the niggers lined up, ready to embark. Night was falling.

But as they prepared themselves to board that ship, I could hold my tongue no more. "Old Joseph," I said, "your kingdom is founded on a lie. You have waked these bodies from the earth, but where are their souls? You may dream of leading these creatures to a mystic land acrosst the sea, and you may dream of freeing them forever from the bonds of servitude, but how can you free what can't be freed? How can you free a rock, a tree, a piece of earth? Dust they were and dust they ever shall be, world without end."

And the *zombi* warriors stood, unmoving and unblinking, and not a breath passed their lips, though that the wind was rising and whipping at our faces.

And old Joseph looked at me long and hard, and I knew that I had said the thing that must be said. He whispered, "Out of the mouths of babes and sucklings hast thou ordained strength, O Lord." He fell down on his knees before me and said, "And all this time I thought that *I* the wise one and you the student! Oh, Marse Jimmy Lee, you done spoke right. There be no life in *les zombis* because I daresn't pay the final price. But now I's *gone* make that sacrifice. Onc't I done gave my eye in exchange for knowledge. But there be *two* trees in Eden, Marse Jimmy Lee; there be the tree of knowledge, and there be the tree of life."

So saying he covered his face with his hands. He plunged his thumb into the socket of his good eye and he plucked it out, screaming to almighty God with the pain of it. His agony was real. His shrieking curdled my blood. It brought back my pa's chastisements and my momma's dying and the tramping of my bare feet on sharp stones and the sight of all my comrades, pierced through by bayonets, cloven by cannon, their limbs ripped off, their bellies torn asunder, their lives gushing hot and young and crimson into the stream. Oh, but I craved to carry his pain, but he were the one that were chosen to bear it, and I was the one which brung him to the understanding of it.

And now his eye were in his hand, a round, white, glistening pearl, and he cries out in a thunderous voice, "If thine eye offend thee, pluck it out!" and he takes blind aim and hurls the eye with all his might into the mighty sea.

I clenched the *ti poupée* in my hand.

Then came lightning, for old Joseph had summoned the power of the serpent *Koulèv*, whose coils were entwined about the earth. Then did he unleash the rain. Then did he turn to me, with the gore gushing from the yawning socket, and cry to me, a good-for-nothing white trash boy which kilt his own father and stole from the dead, "Thou hast redeemed me."

Then, and only then, did I see the *zombis* smile. Then, as the rain softened, as the sky did glow with a cold blue light that didn't come from no sun nor moon, then did hear the laughter of the dead, and the fire of life begin to flicker in their eyes. But they was already trooping up the gangplank, and presently there was only the old man, purblind now, and like to die I thought.

"Farewell," he says to me.

And I said, "No, old Joseph. You are blind now. You need a boy to hold your hand and guide you, to be your eyes against the wild blue sea."

"Not blind," he said. "I *chooses* not to see. I evermore be looking inward, at the glory and the majesty of eternal light."

"But what have I? Where can I go, excepting that I go with you?"

"Honey, you has lived but fourteen of your threescore and ten. It don't be written that you's to follow a old man acrosst the sea to a land that maybe don't even *be* a land save in that old man's dream. Go now. But first you gone kiss your *beau-père* good-bye, for I loves you."

My tears were brine and his were blood. As I kissed his cheek the salt did run together with the crimson. I saw him no more; I did not see the ship set sail from the port; for my eyes was blinded with weeping.

But the leopard remained with me, you see; for freedom's work is never done, I suppose.

6

So I walked and walked and walked, night and day and day and night, until I come back to the Jackson place. The mansion were a cinder, and even the fields was all burnt up, and all the animals was dead. The place was looted good and thorough; warn't one thing of value in the vicinity, not a gold piece nor a silver spoon nor even the rugs that the Jackson done bought from a French merchant, nor even a ham a-hanging in the smokehouse; all was left for dead.

I walked up the low knoll to where the nigger graveyard was and where our shack onc't stood. The wooden markers was all charred, and here and there was a shred of homespun clinging to them; and I thought to myself, mayhap the yankees come down to the Jackson place not an hour after I done run away, whilst the slaves was still a-singing their spirituals. That cloth was surely torn off some of the slave women, for the yankees loved to have their way with darkies. And I thought, mayhap my pa is still laying inside that shack, in the inner room, beside the locket with Mamma's picture, with his hickory in his fist, with his britches down about his ankles.

And so it was I found him.

He warn't rank no more. It had been many months since I run off. Warn't much left of his face that the worms hadn't ate. At his naked loins, the bone poked through the papery hide, and there was a swarm of ants. It was a miracle there was this much left of him, for there was wild dogs roaming the fields.

I set down the *ti poupée* on the chair and got to wondering what I should do. What I wanted most in life were a new beginning. I spoke to that doll, for I knew that old Joseph's spirit was in it somehow, and I said, "I don't know where you come from, and I don't know where you are. But oh, give me the strength to begin onc't more, oh, carry me back from the land of the dead."

Without thinking I started to murmur the words of power, the African words I done mimicked when I watched him raise the dead. I knelt down beside the corpse of my pa and waited for the breath of the serpent. I whispered them words over and over until my mind emptied itself and was filled with the souls of darker angels.

Then came the leopard into that room, and she began a-licking of them bones, as iffen they were wounds that could yet be healed.

I reckon I knelt all night long, or mayhap many nights. But when I opened my eyes again there was flesh on my father's bones, and he was beginning to rouse himself; and his eyes had the fire of life, for that old Joseph had sacrificed his second eye.

"You sure have growed, son," he says softly. "You ain't a sapling no more; you're a mighty tree."

"Yes, Pa," says I.

And the leopard stepped away from him, and disappeared into the shadows. But I knew she would ever remain with us, for her name was Freedom.

"Oh, son, you have carried me back from a terrible dream. In that dream I abandoned you, and I practiced all manner of cruelty upon you, and a dark angel came to you and became your new pa; and you followed him to the edge of the river that divides the quick from the dead."

"Yes, Pa. But I stopped at the riverbank and watched him sail away. And I come back to you."

"Oh, Jimmy Lee, my son, I have seen hell. I have been down into the fire of damnation, and I've felt the loneliness of perdition. And the cruelest torture was being cut off from you, my flesh and blood. Oh, sweet Jesus, Jimmy Lee, it were only that you made me think on her so much, she which I killed, she which I never loved more even as I sent the bullet flying into her back."

And this was strange, for in the old days my pa had only spoke of heaven, and of seeing the face of God, and when he done seen God he would wear me out, calling on His holy name to witness his infamy and my sacrifice. But now he had seen hell and he was full of gentleness. For hell had taught him how to love.

And then he said to me, "My son, I craves your forgiveness."

"Ain't nothing to forgive."

"Why then," he said, "I craves your understanding."

"Ain't nothing to understand," I said.

"Then give me your love," says he, "for you are tall and strong, and I have become old; and it is now for you to be the father, and I the child."

It were time to cross the bridge. It were time to heal the hurting.

"My love you have always had, Pa."

So saying, I embraced him; and thus it was our war came to an end.

7

"Since then," said Jimmy Lee (as Zacko continued to narrate), "we go where the leopard takes us. We have wandered from city to country, and sometimes we set up our tents and preach, and sometimes we wake someone from the dead, but mostly we keeps to ourselves. My pa's bout ready to go back under the ground, but least we got to say we loved each other; it's the most you can ever ask."

We said our good-byes there by the ferry, and never saw Jimmy Lee again, or his pa, though sometimes there've been rumors of a boy preacher who can raise the dead; from as far away, I believe, as Indian Territory, and once, a wounded boy at the hospital told Walt he'd heard a story somewhat like that, and he came all the way from Dakota Territory, near where I grew up.

Then, Paula, there was more good-byes. Kaczmarczyk, who was a whole man now, was listless, and after a while took ship back to the old country; that was after we went to Baltimore to bury Tyler Tyler, and, yes, Walt showed me the resting place of Edgar Allan Poe.

They discharged me from the army, and gave me a bit of money—some of the other men chipped in, too, and I left with more than a hundred bucks—and I took a train all the way back to Nebraska.

I visited more graves. Drew Hammet's grave, I knew, was empty, and so was Rodney's; they was there mostly for show, so that their parents could say proudly, See, see, see, our son died for his country.

The hundred dollars was soon down to a mere ten, and so I come to New York, to seek a new beginning, knowing that Walt lived with his mother in Brooklyn, and I could visit with him for a while; but I don't reckon he'd want me to stay; people might talk.

My war, I guess, just ain't come to an end yet; I'm footloose and don't know where to turn, and I still have dreams sometimes, especially about Rodney; and now and again Drew speaks to me, a head rooted in the ground like the stump of a tree.

Anyhow, I'm here now. I've told you what I know. How I grew from a boy to a man, how I almost died, how I survived the worst war in the world, and only now found out that war ain't over yet.

Why are we here, Paula? Why? The four of us, with all our tales inside of tales, we've been brung here for a reason. There's something the four of us have to do . . . so that we can truly say, like Jimmy Lee did, that our war has come to an end.

Tell us, Paula. It's your place we all come to now, tonight; it started with you deciding to go visit with Mr. Lincoln.

You're the one who knows what we must do.

8

It was then, and only then, that the grand vision came to me, all at once, and all of a piece.

"We're going to see Mr. Lincoln again," I said. "We four: the poet, the sorceress, the motherless child, the childless mother."

"That's it, isn't it?" Walt Whitman said, and oh, you should have seen the fire that sparkled in his ancient eyes. "How often have I sung of the mystery of life, the mystery and enigma of our being, yet never divined I would stand face-to-face with an ultimate truth; through a glass darkly was all I had ever hoped for; but now no more."

"Yes," said Zack. "We've got the book . . . the magic words . . . the secret of life. . . ."

"And the lessons learned through the others' tales," said Mr. Whitman. "Oh, we will see beyond what Poe and Byron saw."

"And the life my husband sacrificed," I said. "Anticipating this moment. Daring damnation." Though it was a sin to think so, I was sure that the fires of perdition had not consumed Aloysius. In the end, he had found his inner nobility.

"When does the train leave?" Mr. Whitman said.

"Tonight," said Zack.

"And where does it go next?" I asked.

"Cleveland, then Chicago," said Zack.

The three of us all turned, expecting Phoebe to chime in; but, as so often before, she was nowhere to be seen. She was, I suppose, invisible again. I had better get used to that. Was she still with us? Or had she already left on the mission which all four of us must perform?

Spread out on the divan, where it had not lain before, was the leopardskin. I picked it up. It tingled. There was magic in the air. In my fingertips. Tonight, all things were possible.

"Now," I said, "crouch down, the both of you, on either side of me. Huddle closely, or else the skin won't cover all three of us. Closer now, closer."

For I had become the mistress of magic—I, a middle-aged, mundane white *mambo,* toying with the strangest, most ancient, blackest of all sorceries . . . I was the vessel of Legba, messenger of the gods . . . I, most ordinary of women, was to become mother earth herself, who cradles the dead in her dark and secret womb.

There was a word in the lexicon my husband had gathered together:

Anaforuana—messenger of death.

Was that who I was? Or was I destined to be the giver of life?

I drew the leopardskin over the three of us, and waited for the spell to take effect.

O my brave soul!
O farther farther sail!
O daring joy, but safe! are they not all the seas of God?
O farther, farther, farther sail!

—Walt Whitman

ANAFORUANA

1865

25

A JOURNEY BY TRAIN

1

Night! O night! O night night night! Night more brilliant than day could ever be, night seen through feline eyes!

Thus speaks the snow leopard in the language of night, a wordless language of cries and purrs punctuated by pungent odors. The snow leopard is the poet; the tawny leopard, frisky, rippling, leaping over the cold concrete, is young, sleek, shiny; I am the third, the female, spotted, quieter, prowling ahead in the alley—for with cats it is always the female who is the huntress—sniffing out danger in the air.

We do not speak of course; we have lost the power of speech; in its stead comes the power of the beast, the resplendence and splendor of our animal selves; the snow leopard exults in it; what was poetry in him now becomes the sheer snap patter pound

pound of paws on paving, more than poetry, goes beyond word to the be and not-be of beasthood. I've felt it already, but for them it is new. But I feel what they're feeling; they pour their feelings out into the wind—animals can do that, by spraying a thousand subtle scents into the air, scents which men, too, could interpret, if they but lived a little closer to their bestial natures. I feel their newness, their awe, and so for me too there is newness and awe redoubled. The divisions between men, self from self, that make men individuals, are softer in the animal kingdom.

We are moving up Broadway now. No one sees us. It is night. When passersby look on us, what they see is so beyond comprehension that they dismiss us as shadows, tricks of the light . . . not a pride of great cats frolicking in the moon.

Oh, the night! The snow leopard rhapsodizes. This night that is electrically charged with scents and sounds! This night where whispers glow more dazzlingly than sunlight!

Sleepers on the townhouse steps, ragamuffins in the road, a lady of the night, fumbling with her feminine cigarette; a robed and bearded Jew, heading uptown, I know not why; a lonely Negro, dancing to and fro; close to the ground, the scent of ground-in horse manure, earthy and oddly sweet.

Afar off yet, steam hangs close to the ground. Metal has a sour tang. We are close to the trains. There it is. Sleek and black. Itself a beast of steel. Steel, steam, and smoke, the somber drapery of red, white, and blue. Guards at the platform . . . Chris Flanagan again, though this time in a much improved uniform, without the bullet holes; many more guards, some with swords, the platform dimly lit with candlelight and kerosene. Strange that they cannot see us creatures of the night!

The locomotive is Number 331. The cowcatcher is scrubbed to an unwonted, satin silveriness.

We curl under the couplers. The guards are relaxed; what danger is this dead man in? They talk, they drink a little, they share their chaws and pipes.

I listen.

"A shame Mrs. Lincoln was too wore out with grief to come," says one man. "A damn shame."

"A widder should see her husband buried," says another. "It ain't right. I hear she's gone plumb out of her mind, though."

"When's General Hooker arriving? Ain't he supposed to be taking over?"

"All this," says the first, "and we're just watching a dead man; as if he's gonna get up and walk away."

"Two dead people," says young Flanagan. "We shouldn't oughter forget the boy."

I ooze out of the shadows a little way. Boy? I ask myself. I had not known they were transporting two corpses.

"The president and his son," says a third guard, "Willie."

"Yeah; they dug Willie Lincoln up, and they're to be interred side by side, in Springfield," says Flanagan.

Side by side. Father and son.

I think of my late husband, clasping his three dead sons to his bosom, burying them one by one. I think of Jimmy Lee Cox, embracing his dead father as he came back from the dead. Mothers and daughters, too: the leopard woman giving birth to my girl Friday, the *mulattresse* in Haiti engendering whiter and whiter versions of herself until one passed through madness into whiteness. I alone in this story am different; my womb was ripped open three times, yet I never truly gathered its fruit; others grieved far more than I; I have never faced my losses, always glanced over them, never admitted to myself that I had been a mother.

I wonder if the others understand.

But only look! Now the platform gates swing open. Now come the dignitaries that will travel on this sorrowful journey. There is no Mrs. Lincoln, but there are generals, officers of state, all clothed in black; there is a minister, and with him, in a touching show of ecumenical accord, a priest as well. But I see no women; I, a beast of shadows, am the only one . . . except . . . who is that dark-skinned creature who has slipped in behind two self-important men, one with bushy muttonchops, the other with a salt-and-pepper mane? How is it they don't see her, when she wears a pure white robe, as a priestess of the great serpent? She stands there, half subsumed in the train's shadow, her hand shading her brow, looking off toward the east . . . toward the sea? . . . toward Africa? Does she know that we are here? She flits in and out of the gathering mourners; she is so bright you can almost see straight through her . . . yes . . . she *is* transparent now, and I realize that it is only my attenuated leopard-senses that have shown her to me; I had constructed the image from an odor lingering the the air, from the rustle of a caftan against the cement, from a whiff of a perfume blended from cinnamon and old dead creatures. In the radiance that haloes her, I see the others more clearly, I can almost read their thoughts, which are as variegated as the men themselves. . . .

> *my wife, my wife, sitting beside the fire*
> > *a naked woman answering the door*
> > > *this president might almost have come to dinner*
> > > > *coffee coffee*
> > *beside the outhouse, listening to the moon*
> > > *spring is not beautiful*

which are little snatches of cogitation, fragments of memories, drifting in the close and sweat-drenched air of the railway station platform.

Cleveland is next

It's time, I think. The snow leopard rouses himself. He has been dreaming of another time and clime, I think, of the dark dank dampness of some furnace forest; he stretches; he lets out a mighty roar but at that moment comes the squeal of a steam-whistle, and the roar and the squeal combine in a dissonant conjunct of beast and machine; now, too, the tawny panther, bursting with masculine energy, springs up from the track. Finally come I, the mother not a mother, and all of us are following the crowd; the crowd thins as the various guests enter their appointed cars, but we know where ours will be—second from the end, the sleeping car from which emanates a stale perfume of putrefaction, too faint for the human olfactory sense to detect, but easy enough for the three of us.

We hop up, one at a time.

The clanking of couplers being checked by hand, the tread of the brakeman stepping from roof to roof, inspecting, tightening here, loosening there; echoes of conversations down metal corridors:

"I'm afraid Mary has taken it hard, I doubt she'll recover . . . but the war will soon grind its way to a close, there's always that to be thankful for. . . ."

The thick black velvet drapes shutting out what meager light there is, except for the slits of moonlight through the clerestory windows. . . .

Shall we transform? Shall we be human again?

No. Better this way. Better to absorb the sounds and scents; later, in tranquillity, we shall pause and make our own sense of them—

More voices. And wafting tobacco smoke, too.

". . . why do we move out at such an ungodly hour?"

"My dear fellow, to flee the crowds that must needs stifle us at every stop; for death has made him a saint, and perfected his life; he will become like a religion, mark you."

Will they see us if we transform, if we go walking amongst them?

Shush . . . I know not . . . smell the air . . . they are supping on *sole meunière* . . . a hint of capers.

Who is speaking? It's hard to say. As I've said before, the peripheries between our persons have become porous somehow.

But Lincoln? Where is Lincoln?

Beyond. Through the swinging mahogany doorway. Hear it

creak as the train starts up. Hear the steam gathering force. Feel the heat seize hold of the railway cars, one by one . . . and then, with an imponderable ponderousness, we move.

But where is Phoebe?

We move. We move.

I crawl behind a leather-bound divan. The snow leopard selects a curtain, the tawny one a black drapery. Day comes slowly; we sleep. It is yet a few days' journey to Ohio.

2

Night! O night! O night night night! Night comes again; the drizzling day diffuses into desultory darkness. The others are still sleeping. I cannot. I am restless. Of course. The female of the species is the huntress. I get up. I wander from car to car. There is no corridor between the cars; each crossing is a chill encounter with the rain. The train clatters, belches fumes, sways as it rounds a bend.

Little to see. Soldiers playing at cards. In the more luxuriously appointed compartments, fat men sit, constipated, self-important, well aware of the momentousness of it all. Where is the humanity of it? Where is the spirit of a man who spoke of charity towards all?

I decide to go where we all mean to go, I mean to look upon Lincoln one more time. So I return, reach the small foyer where my companions lie still sleeping, push open the door, and find myself once more in the selfsame *sanctum sanctorum* with which this tale began. There lie two coffins, side by side, one abnormally long, for a tall man, and one piteously short, for it holds an eleven-year-old boy.

There is far less moonlight than yesterday. A single candle, in its holder, has been placed carelessly on the coffin of the president. The light from the clerestories is mottled and murky.

Someone is weeping in this darkness; a child.

What? Have they gone and waked the dead without me?

But no, this child does not have the aura of the grave. He is ten or eleven years old, and like the other journeyers he is in mourning, a miniature penguin. He is sobbing all alone, and there is nothing I can do . . . he cannot see me, can he? But now he's crying out: "Oh, God, God, God," and I cannot help myself; I reach out; I caress his cheek with a paw. Startled, he stops his crying for a moment. Holds up the candle. His eyes widen.

"Tiger, Tiger, burning bright, in the forests of the night!" he starts to chant. "Who are you? Are you God? I called for God, you know. I wanted him to take me away too. My mother's gone mad. She stayed at home. She's swimming in a private world of laudanum, trying to forget. I wasn't supposed to come, but it *is* my father's funeral. You're not tiger at all, are you? More like a leopard. And you're a girl; I can tell."

People can't see me, I say to him in the language of my kind.

"I'm not people yet," he says, "I'm just a child. My name is Thomas Lincoln; they call me Tad."

Why did you—

"Oh, I just wish I could have said good-bye."

And then he starts to weep again. And again, I cannot help myself; I've never had a child live to be as old as he, yet perhaps I've an instinct for it after all. I throw my forepaws around him—

—and they shimmered in the moonlight and stretched out and I found myself shifting into a woman, still wearing the rumpled garments of the previous day, and I was crying too, almost as though not a moment had elapsed between my weeping in city hall and my weeping on this train; I found myself reliving that moment as vividly as the moment I was living.

"Why," said Tad Lincoln, "you *are* a woman; I hoped for a woman; I just wanted someone to hold me, and mother—"

"Has gone mad," I said softly, thinking of Amelia Bledsoe, waltzing in a Charleston barroom, singing on a Georgia plain.

"Go on," I said to the boy, "go on, Tad, cry, Tad, cry."

"Why," the boy said, "but I know you. I've seen your portrait once, in a locket . . . why, you're the Reverend Grainger's wife. Now I am sure this is a dream, so I won't be afraid at all."

"A dream?" I said.

"I read *Alice in Wonderland* only a few weeks ago, so I know there's things that only children see . . . well, I was sort of hoping it would be you, you know. Mother always loved Willie better, you see. But he never used it against me."

I sat on the floor of the train, cradling the president's son in my arms. I let him babble on. Sometimes the whistle obscured his words. Sometimes the roar of the wheels drowned everything out. But he needed to talk; it did not matter much what he said, I suppose.

"Once we were playing at soldiers, and we set a little rag doll up as guard, and the doll fell asleep! That was strange, because the doll came from an island far away, where the dolls, and the dead, never sleep; the doll's name was Tippy. The Haitian Counsellor's wife gave it to us, and she said his name was *ti poupée,* but we could never say that right."

By now my heart was beginning to pound. Because this child had unwittingly brought us back to the subject at hand, and I knew that soon we would accomplish what we had come here for. And even as he finished speaking, I saw that my fellow travelers were emerging from the shadows. Tad did not seem shocked that an old man and a young man were condensing out of the gloom.

"Are you Mr. Whitman?" he asked. "I've heard about you; you're very scandalous, they say. You I don't know, but I think you're a soldier . . . I'll call you the Unknown Soldier, if you like. Oh, this is a visionary dream! Father would have loved to share it with me!"

But when the doors swung open yet again, he grinned, and wiped away his tears with a sleeve, and cried out, "Phoebe," with such delighted recognition that I knew we were in for one final, perhaps apocalyptic, revelation.

Phoebe was resplendent. She was clothed all in white, but

white alone cannot describe the candid brilliance of her raiment. How hubristic I had been to think that *I* would be the *anaforu-ana*! For Phoebe was the quintessence of a darker angel. Indeed, it was not too much to imagine, somewhere in the hurtling clatter and the roaring steam and the whistling wind, the beating of great wings. She was beautiful. She was a goddess.

"I knew you would come back," said Tad.

"Master Tad," she said, "me missed you very much."

She took him in her arms and kissed him on both cheeks. And I admit it; I was rent by jealousy, because I thought of my barrenness, and my husband's dashed hopes, and how my life was racing to its end, even as this locomotive, rushing towards a graveyard.

"Oh, Thomas," I said, "if you but knew the twists of fate that have brought us all here . . . if you knew how much, in our different ways, we loved your father, even though we knew him not . . . but the world still needs him. The war is not quite over. The slaves are not quite free. The wounds are not healed at all. Oh, Tad, your father cannot rest yet . . . his work, alack, must yet be finished . . . for the sake of America . . . for the sake of mankind."

Oh, I had worked myself up into another passion of emotion, but Phoebe stayed me with a touch on my shoulder, and said, "No, Paula, no. That not why we here."

"But why then these stories within stories? Why then this awful war?"

Walt Whitman said, "All momentous events, Paula . . . all wars, all grand conquests, all subjugations, all human atrocities, all are in the end small tragedies, domestic games of love and death, family affairs. This war was a family quarrel. It was about fathers and sons, about brothers, about the love of friends gone sour; that is why it has been so hurtful, and so catastrophic."

"We ain't here to save the world," said Phoebe, clasping my hand in hers. "We just here because of a promise I made to old Marse Lincoln. Now, friends, lift up the coffin lids, and I will tell you one last story; I tell it both to the living and to the dead, who were there, but mayhap need reminding; listen to Phoebe now, listen, and know I speak the truth."

Walt and Zachary each opened one of the coffins. Mr. Lincoln was as I remembered him, though, in the sputtering candle, even craggier than in the remembrance. Willie Lincoln was much decayed, almost a skeleton, though his suit was as neatly pressed as on the day they buried him. When Tad saw his brother, he let out a most terrible cry, and I thought for certain that someone would come; but no. Perhaps it was true that this was all happening within the territory of dream.

Phoebe spoke. Sometimes she sounded as English as I, and sometimes she spoke in her lilting Negro creole, and sometimes in a language in between. Hers was the shortest of the tales we had heard, yet also the longest, for it stretched from the present all the way to the creation of the world.

26

PHOEBE MAKES A PROMISE

1

In the beginning (said Phoebe) was only a song and a dance. That's all they was. No earth and no sky. Just the song and no one to sing, just the dance and no one to dance. The song and the dance was God. God sing and God dance over the emptiness, and then, all of a sudden, in a moment that was the first moment, because before that moment there was no such thing as a moment, God become two: Mawu-Lissa, man-woman, Phoebe father and mother.

Phoebe father he done make the sky, and Phoebe mother she done make the earth. Between earth and sky there go all the creatures visible and invisible. There go all kind of creature he stay in one place, tree, flower, root, and creature he fly, swim, run, dance, speak, sing.

You already heard bout how Phoebe mother born many times over in the world history. Sometimes in Egypt land, and sometimes in Africa, which the people of Santo Domingo they calls Nan Guinée. Sometimes, when the world dark and troubled, she call on Phoebe father to send he messenger down to her, so Phoebe born again, to bring Phoebe people out of the darkness and into the light.

Phoebe always born on a Friday. Phoebe a name which mean girl-child she born on a Friday. Why a Friday? Friday a day of darkness and death. Look your own Jesus Christ, how he die on a Friday, but the Friday he die the beginning of the great light that shine down on the white folks and give him the mastery over the world we in today, here and now.

Phoebe mother have many names. Today she name Leuthera, a ancient white folks word. Leuthera mean freedom.

Leuthera born among the leopard people in Africa. She come to America land and see she people all in bondage, like Moses in the land of Egypt. So she call on the messenger of the sky, and this time Phoebe father name Joseph, same as the name of the husband of Mary, mother of the white folks God. Joseph come to her out of the sky, and me born into the world on a Friday, to carry my people out of slavery. . . .

But no, Tad, no, I am no Moses. What you see is all you see. I am no sorceress, but sorcery uses me sometimes for its own ends.

I speak the black language and the white language, and when language cannot say what need be said, I speak a language called music, a language that speaks directly to the soul.

Paula, your husband found me as a filthy child, my mother chained in the garden of his Virginian host. I looked into his eyes and saw his deepening sorrow, and I knew he was a good man. He could not know the whole of the great plan, but only one piece at a time; but he was innocent, and his intentions true.

I loved your husband. But I never knew him carnally. That was, in a way, my deception. It was easier for you to understand a physical desire than a seduction of the mind. Toward the end . . . perhaps . . . well, there was a sensual side to our love, but no . . . he always loved you, only he never could express that love, not after the children died, one by one; he kept his love bottled up inside himself, Paula, but oh, he did love you.

I molded myself to Aloysius's vision—the dusky beauty who could change the white men's minds. I already had the gift of music, given to me by the gods; it was easy for me to send my gift flowing into those silly melodies he taught me, those trite words, and use them as a direct conduit to the wellspring of all feeling; and so it was I sang for him, and his friends over at the printing press, and sometimes in his church, and eventually I sang to the soldiers at the front, and for the beleaguered president of the United States.

Inside me is the first song that ever was sung, the song that brought the universe into being. I could not help but make men weep, even though they thought me a mere Negress, lowly and contemptible, fit only, in their mind, for bearing water jugs on my head, or being the quick satiation of their lusts.

And so it was at last your husband brought me to Mr. Lincoln, after a long exchange of letters. His purpose was, I think, to convince the president that there was more to the Negro than some dull-witted beast of burden. It was known that the president was in two minds on the question of emancipation. Perhaps the dark nightingale of freedom (as Aloysius delighted in calling me) could bring our nation's leader over to the side of what was right in the eyes of God.

And so I sang. It was a private dinner. I sang everything from German lieder to Appalachian folk tunes. The Rev. Aloysius Grainger, a few other infamous abolitionists, I believe a senator or two, and Mrs. Lincoln, who was the only one who sat unmoved. Perhaps she viewed me as a sort of performing monkey, parroting my betters without understanding. Perhaps she saw how her husband looked at me, and was afraid he might view me as a woman—unlikely, I think, given that despite his theoretical inclination to believe that all men are created equal, he had not really considered the practical aspects of including the Negro in such an equation.

At any rate, everyone but Mary Lincoln was moved to tears. Mrs. Lincoln, indeed, stormed out after a while, muttering "Nonsense, nonsense," to herself.

(Tad, you was there with us. You was about eight years old, I think.)

Later in the evening, the conversation turned to the subject of raising the dead. The president mentioned a woman named Marie Laveau . . . a free person of color who lived in New Orleans, who claimed never to have aged since the year 1804.

"I have heard," said the president, "that this woman—a sorceress of sorts—raises herself from the dead at regular intervals, rejuvenates herself, and continues on forever; but others say that the present Queen of Voodoo is actually a daughter, impersonating her mother, and that that is the real source of her perpetual youth. . . ."

"Yet another example of African savagery, I'm afraid," said one of the guests. "That is why our worlds will never intersect."

"Naturally, they will not," said the president, "and yet there are times when I dream of just such a possibility. . . ."

There were some cries of "Impossible!" at these words, even from the abolitionists.

Well then, it was little Tad who tugged at his father's sleeve, and said, "She should sing for Willie."

And so it was that I was brought upstairs to Willie's sickbed, and I saw this pale boy, wasting away, waiting at death's door; the room smelled of death already, though the stench was covered up with a sickly fragrance of potpourri and opiates.

So in that room there was just me, and Tad, and Master Lincoln, and the dying boy.

And Willie cried out, "Father, you've brought me an angel."

"No, son," he said, "this is a freedwoman; her name is Phoebe; I thought you might want to hear her sing."

"I already have," Willie said. "A voice came wafting up the stairs. I was afraid, Father, and the voice banished all my terror."

I sat by the little boy's bedside, and I sang to him an old Yoruba song:

b'aiyé tàn e ko má tan 'ràre
(If the world deceives you, at least don't deceive yourself. . . .)

We had no talking drums, so I tapped the rhythm lightly on his bedside table. Willie laughed. Oh, Tad, he was wan; his skin was translucent, like a yellow candle; but he still smiled. I know he was in pain. I sang:

E má sikà l'aiyé nitori à nr'òrun,
a ba de 'bodè e ro ro'jo
(Do not be cruel in the world for in the next we will go to heaven
And at the entrance to that place there will be a reckoning.)

Surely Willie could not understand the words, and yet he understood that the song was about death and what must come after death. He closed his eyes. He held on to my hand, and smiled a little more, and presently he fell into a deep sleep; I do not think he even dreamed, for his eyes were still. And Tad, too, had fallen asleep at the foot of the sickbed, so I was alone in this chamber of death with the one man who had the power to let my people go.

Master Lincoln sat down in a stuffed armchair upholstered in a pattern of eagles. A candelabrum stood by Willie's bed, but one by one the candles were burning out. I saw Master Lincoln through the guttering, sooty flame, and I knew that two great agonies racked him: the agony of his divided country, and the agony of a father who can do nothing to save his son.

He said to me, "I am coming to an inevitable conclusion, Phoebe. Do you know what that must be? Oh, I am as much a slave of history as its master."

"Yes, Master Lincoln," I said. "No need to say what we both know. The light she always follow the dark."

"But I do need to say it. Despite all my misgivings, despite my doubts, I will free the slaves."

My heart soared, because I had accomplished the purpose that brought me down into this world.

"You go on down to Richmond," I told him, "and a thousand Negroes kiss your hand, and kneel to you, and call you father."

"And yet I cannot be father to my own son!" he said. And then he began to weep. "The war drains me, I come here to be with him, and a hundred thousand ghastly dead call out to me from a hundred burnt-out fields; and I find fatherhood slipping away from me. Oh, why am I thus unburdening myself to you . . . a woman I scarcely know, a songstress brought in by some mad abolitionist preacher to show me that there's hope for the Negro race?"

"Because me black, Master Lincoln. Me invisible. Me just like the walls, the furniture." Perhaps I sounded bitter, but we both knew it was the truth.

"Yes, now I see the hypocrisy of it all . . . yet how can I ever escape from it?"

"You do what you can, Master," I said. "It more than enough."

"Are you really a sorceress? Are you really an angel?"

"No. Only a vessel."

"Oh, but I know there's more to you than what you claim. Yes, I have made a secret study of your people's superstitions; they are, perhaps, nothing more than that, and yet I have a lingering feeling. . . ."

"I am what you make of me."

"Then promise me something . . . if you can."

"Yes, Master."

"If the pressures of the world come so greatly to bear upon me that I am unable to say farewell to my own child, I beg you to contrive for such an opportunity, even if it be in another life, or another world."

2

"And that," concluded Phoebe, **"is** what brought us here tonight. Not some grand scheme for the restoration of the world, not some unfinished work that Mr. Lincoln must achieve, for these great works, in the end, achieve themselves, and do not depend on one individual—we are here to help a man and his man-child. Nothing more."

But that did not prevent us from performing the whole ritual. If there is any truth I have learnt from all this, it is that to redeem one man is as great a task as to save the entire world. There, in the cramped compartment, suffused with the odor of decay, where a forlorn child mourned his family, we danced the dance which, I do fervently believe, was the same music with which the world began, the music of creation.

Instead of drums, we had the rapid patter of the train. For chorus we had the wind. For words we had Phoebe, calling out in a tongue more ancient than my own, the tongue of Shakespeare and Milton; perhaps more ancient even than the undeciphered language of the Sphinx and the pharaohs; in counterpoint to the clattering wheels we clapped our hands and shouted out, "*Oba kòso,* The king is not a-hanging."

In the dead of night, the railway carriage was illumined by a warm, sourceless light. We danced. Slowly flesh formed on Willie's bones. We danced. Life twitched on Mr. Lincoln's monumental brow. We danced. Willie's hand began to drum out the beat. Zachary danced with the vigor of youth; Mr. Whitman danced more slowly, savoring each moment; I tried to be stately, but finished with unladylike abandon; and Phoebe danced most savagely of all; when she danced, she pulled thunder and lightning out of the close air. And even Tad danced, laughing with the wonder of it, his tears forgotten.

I was not dancing to bring back anyone from the grave. It was the sheer joy of it. In the end, I know that I was possessed by some great nameless spirit, for I became, for a moment, the entire universe, and held truth itself within my grasp.

When the dance was done, the president and his son sat up in their respective coffins, and stepped down, and embraced one another, and Tad as well; and the president turned to Phoebe, and bowed, and thanked her and all of us, with simple solemnity.

"My dear," he said to my maidservant, flushed and sweating from her frenzy, "you have set me free."

But Phoebe did not respond; for she had vanished again, and this time I knew I would never see her again, not in this life at least; for she had done all that she came to do.

Discreetly, then, one by one, we quit the compartment, the young man, the old poet, and I. What secrets father and sons shared, what wisdom they imparted to young Tad from beyond the grave, we shall never know. But in the morning, the coffins were as before, and the two were as dead as ever; and Thomas Lincoln was asleep on the rug in front of them; and the funeral train was pulling into Cleveland.

EPILOGUE

Why, then, did my husband kill himself? Why, then, was this war fought at all? Why were so many sacrificed, from the highest to the most lowly? Upon whose bloody altar are those millions dedicated? And who, or what, then, is God?

As well to ask why the sun shines, or why the seasons change.

Yes, I held truth within my grasp. But I did not grasp it. I was not the god . . . only the vessel of the god.

Walt Whitman did publish the poem I admired, the one he himself hated so much; he did many other things that one might consider less than honorable—such as printing ecstatic notices about his work under pseudonyms. He did, in the end, acquire a kind of fame, for the British proclaimed him a mad genius, and his following included such luminaries (if such they be) as Bram Stoker.

The war itself ended shortly after the events I have been describing. And yet, I fear, it still goes on.

In 1871, Tad Lincoln followed his brother and father to the grave. Why? Was it some dark truth that they shared with him? Or was it merely the natural incursion of some sickness? I would not presume to speculate.

Mary Lincoln sought refuge in madness; unlike Amelia Bledsoe, she did not find anyone to liberate her.

Mr. Whitman found himself other friends quickly enough; there was no animosity between him and Zack, but I do not believe they shared any more sinful moments; for Zack, it had all been merely something of a phase, I suppose, or a special circumstance, because of the extreme anguish of the war.

Besides, he had got me with child.

Perhaps he should have done the right thing at that point, but I am a middle-aged woman, and he a mere boy; I could not force him into a marriage of convenience or necessity, for I cared for him too deeply, and I knew that he should find a girl close to his own age, perhaps in Nebraska Territory, and till a farm and raise a houseful of children, not be doomed to spend his young manhood caring for an old woman.

I threw away my widow's weeds. I didn't care a fig for the scandal, but I began to long for a place that was not New York, a place without lowering buildings and glowering faces; and so I sold all my possessions, and, with young Zachary in tow, I took the train west, never looking back.

In the town where I live today, they know that I'm a widow, but they don't know Zachary is not my husband's son. They know that I'm wealthy, but they don't know where the money comes from. My money shields me from too much attention, and I have befriended all the right people.

Today my son saw a dead Chinaman on the boardwalk, in front of the general store.

He came running home.

"He was all over blood, Mama," he said. "Some gunman shot him down for looking too long and hard at Miss Percy, over at the saloon. Mama, I poked and prodded at him, but I couldn't get him to move."

"Son," I said, cradling him to my bosom, "he is dead."

That night I tucked him in. I kissed him over and over; he let himself be kissed, thinking no doubt that I was smothering him too much. Sometimes I think that this child is what Aloysius died for; sometimes I think that my womb was cursed, somehow, until my husband broke the spell with his sacrifice; sometimes I am sure such thoughts are silly fancies, for I know that men like to impose their paradigms and patterns upon the unknowable, hoping thereby to know it.

Tonight, my son asked me in all seriousness, "What is dead, Mama?"

I said, "That's when you stop living; you don't move anymore, and you don't breathe, and your soul goes away."

"But mama," he said, "can your soul come back again?"

I hugged him tight, and I said, "I think you're old enough now, so I'll tell you a story . . . but it's a long story, and it will take many nights to tell, and some of it's scary."

"I ain't afraid of *nothing*!" said little Zachary.

"But sometimes," I said, "it's good to be afraid. . . ."

"Tell me then," said little Zachary.

I began. And so all the events came back to life once more, though only in words, and only in remembrance, unable to wreak harm; to speak the hidden thing is to exorcise it, and to sear the quick wound is to heal.

"A dead man in a darkened room . . ."

Los Angeles, Denver, Bangkok: 1991–97

S. P. SOMTOW

Somtow Papinian Sucharitkul, the "Terrifying Thai," was
born in Bangkok of a distinguished aristocratic family (his grandfather's sister was a Queen of Siam, his diplomat father was vice-
president of the United Nations Academy of Human Rights),
and, after growing up in Europe, began his professional life as a
serious, avant-garde composer. But in the late 1970s, he began
producing a succession of science fiction stories, and soon won
the John W. Campbell Award for Best New Writer of 1980–81
and garnered two Hugo Nominations. He went on to write in
almost every conceivable genre, from children's literature (the
award-winning *Forgetting Places*) and fantasy (he has had two
World Fantasy Award Nominations) to historical novels (the
Daedalus Award–winning *The Shattered Horse*) and a semi-
autobiographical memoir, *Jasmine Nights,* which prompted

George Axelrod, screenwriter of *Breakfast at Tiffany's,* to refer to him as the "J. D. Salinger of Siam."

However, it is in the field of horror that Somtow's writings are best known—from the groundbreaking *Vampire Junction*—the first teenage rock star vampire novel—to the bestselling and multiple-award-winning *Moon Dance,* a werewolf novel to end all werewolf novels—and *Darker Angels,* based on a Bram Stoker Award–nominated short story, which remakes the zombie myth as a fable of redemption.

S. P. Somtow has also directed two films, *The Laughing Dead* and *Ill Met by Moonlight,* and has recently returned to music with the much-anticipated ballet *Kaki,* premiered at a Royal Command Performance in Bangkok in 1997.

Somtow keeps in touch with his readers through a news-letter, and can be reached by writing The Valentine Society, his fan club, at 6440 Bellingham Avenue #192, North Hollywood, CA 91606, or through his Web site at: http://www.primenet.com/~somtow.